A River

Edward Wilson served in Vietnam as an officer in the 5th Special Forces. His decorations include the Bronze Star and Army Commendation Medal for Valor. Soon after leaving the army, Wilson became a permanent expatriate. He formally lost US nationality in 1986. Edward Wilson is a British citizen, but has also lived and worked in Germany and France. For the past twenty-six years he has been a teacher in Suffolk. The author enjoys sailing and has a twenty-foot sloop at Orford on the River Ore.

A River in May

Edward Wilson

ARCADIA BOOKS
LONDON

Arcadia Books Ltd
15–16 Nassau Street
London W1W 7AB

First published in Great Britain 2002
Copyright © Edward Wilson 2002

Edward Wilson has asserted his moral right to be identified as the author of this work in accordance with the Copyright, Designs and Patents Act, 1988.

All rights reserved. No part of this publication may be reproduced in any form or by any means without the written permission of the publishers.

A catalogue record for this book is available from the British Library.

ISBN 1–900850–72–9

Designed and typeset in Palatino by Discript, London WC2N 4BN
Printed in the United Kingdom by Bell & Bain Limited, Glasgow

The following quotations are reprinted by permission of their respective publishers:

T. S. Eliot, *The Waste Land*, Faber & Faber Ltd (London, 1940).

Robert Frost, 'The Pasture' from *Come in and other poems*, Jonathan Cape Ltd (London, 1944).

Arcadia Books distributors are as follows:

in the UK and elsewhere in Europe:
Turnaround Publishers Services
Unit 3, Olympia Trading Estate
Coburg Road
London N22 6TZ

in the USA and Canada:
Consortium Book Sales and Distribution, Inc.
1045 Westgate Drive
St Paul, MN 55114–1065

in Australia:
Tower Books
PO Box 213
Brookvale, NSW 2100

in New Zealand:
Addenda
Box 78224
Grey Lynn
Auckland

I want to thank Roger Bloomfield and Eric Bloomfield for stimulating and confirming my memories. I want to give a special thanks to Mary Sandys, my editor, for her sensitivity and advice in shaping and checking the manuscript. I am grateful to my agent, Maggie Hanbury, for keeping faith with me down the years. I want to thank Gary Pulsifer for his appreciation of this novel. Finally, thanks to Daniela de Groote and Richard Bates for grace under pressure.

I also found the following books useful for reference and checking facts: Neil Sheehan, *A Bright Shining Lie* (New York, Random House, Inc., 1988); Ronald J. Glasser, *365 Days* (New York, George Braziller Publishers, 1980); Barbara Cohen, *The Vietnam Guidebook* (Boston, Houghton Miflin Company, 1991); Gareth Porter (ed.), *Vietnam: The Definitive Documentation of Human Decisions*, (New York, Earl M. Coleman Enterprises, Inc. Publishers, 1979).

Real places and real events are described in this book. A few real names are used, but no real people are portrayed. This is a work of fiction.

When I have used titles of rank and official positions, I do not suggest that the persons who held these positions in the past are the same persons portrayed in the novel or that they have spoken, thought or behaved in the way I have imagined.

Edward Wilson
Suffolk, England

In memory of my mother, Agnes Wilson,
who deserved so much more.

Prolog

HO CUC WAS ON HIS WAY BACK from an ambush patrol when he heard the American planes begin their attack. He knew the bunkers of Son Loi were deep and well timbered, but there was something about these bombs that sounded like fracturing bones. Cuc broke into a cold sweat and started to run; the path was overgrown, but he was oblivious of the thorns tearing his skin. When he reached the open paddy bordering the village he could see that the familiar silhouette of bamboo and palm trees was now broken and distorted, as if there had been a great wind.

Ho Cuc sprinted across the paddy dyke, hardly bothering to sidestep the defensive land mines. There was an acrid scent of explosive and burnt earth. He pushed through a tangle of broken palm trees. The first thing he saw, as he emerged on the other side sweating and bleeding, was an outer circle of flattened huts and a line of deep overlapping craters. Trees were burning and the earth itself was steaming.

One of the 750-pound bombs had made a direct hit on the bunker where Ho Cuc's wife and two-year-old daughter were sheltering and, fused to burrow deep, had killed Cuc's family and eighteen other civilians. He flung himself at the earth and began to claw the erupted soil with bare hands, screaming his wife's name like a madman. He found an arm – but when he pulled, it came away attached to nothing. It took three men to drag him away.

Cuc's wife had been seven months pregnant when the bomb blew her apart. The last night that he had slept beside her she had woken him in the middle of the night, taken his hand and placed it on her womb. 'Can you feel the kicking?'

she asked. 'This is such a strong restless baby.' He felt the child thud a secret message against the palm of his hand. Cuc placed his face against his wife's womb so that he could be closer to their baby, and kissed the child through the taut rounded flesh.

One of those who dragged Ho Cuc away from the collapsed bunker was Nguyen Ton, the cadre chief. Ton made Cuc sit on a log under the banana trees and tried to comfort him. Cuc was aware of a voice, but could not make out the actual words – it was like a muffled voice sounding through the walls of a tunnel. He wondered where he was. This was no longer Son Loi: the ripe bananas hanging from the trees had become festering bodies. Overcome by nausea, he turned away and vomited. When it was dark the cadre chief embraced Cuc, told him to sleep and gave him a packet containing dried aromatic cassia bark. 'Chew this,' said Ton. 'It will help.'

Cuc returned to his empty house. He chewed a mouthful of cassia bark; the narcotic juice invaded his weary body, and he fell into deep dreamless sleep. When he woke up it was one in the morning. For the rest of the night he lay awake sweating and groaning; sometimes he sat up and howled the names of his wife and his daughter into the dark.

In the hour before dawn, the village began to stir: voices, cooking noises, people padding on bare feet to the night soil heap to squat and defecate. It all meant nothing to Cuc: nothing connected to nothing. The woven partitions and the bamboo beams above his head were only meaningless patterns. The dawn twilight was a sickly pale nothingness. Later, as the sun dispersed the morning mist and the southern wind dried his tears, Cuc discovered hate – a hate that was blind, undirected and anarchic. Hate would nourish him and he would nourish it. Hate would become his foster child.

Cuc knew that he could not spend another night sleeping

on the rush mat that still bore the musky scent of his dead wife. His home, the life they had lived there, had turned into a gangrenous limb that needed lopping off. He remembered the leaflets dropped by American planes like millions of paper blossoms, which offered bribes to Hoi Chanhs, deserters. Few people even bothered to read them. Cuc himself had no desire to desert his unit, only a need to leave. He couldn't even breathe: the air of Son Loi was poisoned by the death of his own flesh.

The leaflets also offered money for surrendered weapons. Cuc knew this was a stupid idea – anyone approaching an American compound carrying an AK-47 rifle would be shot before he had a chance to shout, 'Chieu hoi! – I surrender!' Nonetheless, he didn't want to walk the twelve miles to An Hoa, the district capital, without a weapon. He remembered a Chinese 9mm automatic pistol in one of the village arms caches – it had belonged to a North Vietnamese major who suffered an attack of recurrent malaria while passing through Son Loi and died. As soon as night fell, Cuc went to the cache and made the pistol his own.

Later that night, when his neighbors were either sound asleep or portering supplies of rice to the NVA division in the mountains, Cuc prepared for departure. He spread out his wife's best blouse to use as a satchel. He laid out a water bottle, a ball of cooked rice and a tin of Russian mackerel; then photographs of his wife and child bound between layers of oilcloth. He slowly picked up a gold hair clip that had been his wife's dowry, closed his eyes and kissed it before tying it to the photograph parcel. Finally, an extra magazine of 9mm cartridges, and he had finished packing. Cuc tied the arms of the blouse together, slung it around his neck and set off into the night.

The first obstacle was the Son Thu Bon. Cuc unmoored one of the flat-bottomed boats which were used for ferrying supplies. The boat had been hidden under a camouflage of freshly cut green vine – it was the job of the village children to renew the camouflage before it wilted. Cuc sculled across the current with a stern oar. There was no moon. The river gorge was so dark that he felt his spine tingle; it was like passing over a black chasm.

When he reached the other side, he moored the boat under an overhanging bank. He knew the next four miles of river valley intimately, knew how to avoid patrols, ambush sites and minefields. But beyond the place where the river hugs the steep slopes of Black Widow Mountain, he knew nothing. The far side of the Black Widow was a foreign country. Cuc had never been more than six miles from Son Loi in his entire life.

Two hours after setting out, Cuc had reached the outskirts of Xuan Hoa, the last village before the mountain. He kept well away from the village by walking along the paddy dykes in the surrounding fields. Despite his detour, a dog started barking from the kitchen garden of the nearest house, and Cuc felt a twitch of fear; he knew that government patrols often spent the night in the village and set ambushes on the adjoining trails. A few seconds after the dog had begun to bark, a parachute flare from the camp at Nui Hoa Den lit up the entire river valley with a ghostly green light. Cuc threw himself prone on the paddy dyke; he squeezed his eyes shut. Nothing happened; the flare sank and expired, womb-safe darkness returned. Cuc waited two minutes, then got up and continued his journey.

Soon he reached the end of the paddy fields and the end of his known world. His next obstacle was Black Widow Mountain itself. The most direct route was a steep cliff path above the river, but this path led straight to a Regional Forces outpost. Even if its defenders were asleep it would be difficult to get round the outpost because of barbed wire and mines.

Cuc chose instead a long detour through the low scrub covered hills on the far side of the mountain. These hills comprised a barren uninhabited landscape so untypical of Vietnam's green lushness that Cuc felt as if he were on another planet. The going was much more difficult in the moonless night than he had expected. There weren't any trails, but this was also a good thing because it lessened the dangers of encountering an ambush or patrol. The vegetation was chest-high thorn and prickly vine. His legs were soon covered with deep scratches and his clothes torn. His progress slowed to less than one kilometer an hour. It wasn't until just before pre-dawn half-light that Cuc found the outermost rice fields of the cultivated valley bottom. The North Vietnamese Army purchased many of their supplies from the large productive farms there.

The village of Que Son and its sprawling Saigon government refugee camp was on his left and the valley of Que Son and its scattered hamlets was on his right. For Ho Cuc, the Que Son was the place of the greatest danger. He knew that the village and the refugee camp were occupied most nights by the Viet Cong, who disappeared into the hills and countryside just before daybreak. He was afraid of running into them, afraid that he might be recognized, and annoyed at himself because he couldn't think of a likely story to explain what he was doing so far from his village and his unit.

He walked rapidly, at times breaking into a run, wanting to be as near as possible to the safety of An Hoa by daybreak. He was lucky: he saw no one and no one saw him. When the sun had burnt away the dawn mist Cuc found himself on a busy road that passed close by the river.

As the day brightened there was a small traffic of peasants carrying produce – live chickens in baskets, dried fish, cured tobacco leaves – to the market at An Hoa. Cuc was impressed by how rich and prosperous everything seemed on this side of Black Widow Mountain. Even the people looked fatter and cleaner.

He squatted on the riverbank near a landing stage to eat his rice and mackerel. Just as he finished, a motorized sampan arrived at the landing and a crowd of prosperous chattering peasants disembarked, laden with bulging baskets of market produce: vegetables, fresh herbs, noisy ducks, even a few piglets. The stout peasants hoisted the baskets on the ends of poles which they balanced across their shoulders, then trudged off towards the town. Cuc caught fragments of gossip – 'Big' Trinh's niece was sleeping with the carpenter – and hopeful talk about prices.

Cuc knew that he wouldn't be safe if he traveled on the road; there were Communist cadres even in the most secure villages. He was sure that his soiled torn clothes and emaciated features would give him away as a Viet Cong deserter. There were no vagrants in the Vietnamese countryside, and beggars in rags were found only in the cities; Cuc feared that one of these plump peasants would report his cropped hair and ragged clothes to a local cadre. He knew that if he were seized and bundled off to a camp in the hills he would be severely punished by his former comrades. A week earlier, he himself would have beaten a deserter without pity – it wasn't anything personal; it was just the way things were.

Determined that nothing would delay him, Cuc left the busy road at the first opportunity and set off across country along paddy dykes and disused trails. He soon arrived at a place where the paddy fields had been abandoned and left to revert to weed and scrub. Two years before there had been battles with American marines. The paddy dykes had been destroyed by the treads of tanks and armored personnel carriers, and the houses torched by the infantry or incinerated by napalm. The hamlets had then been abandoned and the population re-located. The area was now a parched wasteland of thorn and crater inhabited only by ghosts, and the hulks of burned out armor and downed helicopters had already been obliterated by straggly vine.

The sun was high and hot in the late morning sky. Cuc was passing through the most devastated of the deserted hamlets when a voice greeted him from behind, 'Chao anh – Hello, elder brother.' The words, even though an ordinary greeting between strangers, were full of menace. Cuc turned and stared into the blank eyes of a North Vietnamese Army lieutenant. The lieutenant's face was pitted by smallpox and as narrow as an ax blade.

'Chao anh,' said Cuc.

The NVA lieutenant had an automatic pistol in a holster slung over his shoulder, identical to the one that Cuc was wearing concealed under his baggy peasant blouse.

'Do you live near here, Ong?' Ong – uncle – was a term used to show respect for an older or distinguished person. The lieutenant was mocking.

Cuc didn't know how to reply. He wondered what an NVA officer was doing alone in such a wasteland. The officer repeated his question. Cuc remained silent. 'I suppose you need an interpreter, Uncle?' The lieutenant spoke in the harsh guttural tones of Tonkin, the dialect of Hanoi and the North. He asked his question again, but this time he pronounced the words for interpreter – thoung dich vien – not in his own northern dialect, but in an exaggerated imitation of the lilting sing-song speech of the Annamite peasant, with its diphthongs and soft consonants. 'Do you need a "thoouung yich wien", Ong Que Lam – Uncle Dullard?' The lieutenant laughed and placed his hand on Cuc's makeshift satchel. 'What have you got in here, Uncle Que Lam?'

Ho Cuc handed it over and, while the lieutenant had both hands occupied with the parcel, drew his pistol and shot the Hanoi officer in the face. The bullet entered the skull through the left eye. The body was still twitching, so Cuc bent over and shot the lieutenant again in the temple. The twitching stopped. Cuc nudged the corpse with his foot. 'Dog shit.' Then he picked up the feet – the lieutenant was wearing faded green espadrilles – dragged the body off the path and rolled it into a ditch overgrown with prickly vine.

Cuc retrieved his bag and started walking. He still couldn't understand why the lieutenant had been there and what he had wanted. Could they be after him? After walking twenty meters, Cuc turned around. He felt that someone was following him, watching him – but there was nothing, just blinding sun and dry thorn.

Ten minutes later, Ho Cuc came to a large road that carried a good deal of military traffic between the coast and the American base at An Hoa. The convoys were heavily guarded and escorted by helicopter gunships. Cuc was stunned. He had never seen a motor car, not even a motorbike, and here, roaring up the road in a grinding inferno of sound and steel, were a battle tank followed by two armored personnel carriers, a convoy of two-and-a-half ton trucks, and, hovering above it all like deadly wasps, two pencil-thin Cobra gunships. The armor thundered past in the heat haze, the helmeted and goggled crew looking more like giant insects than humans. Cuc shouted 'Chieu hoi – I surrender', but they ignored him. He had never felt so small and insignificant in his life. Each truck had four marines armed with machine-guns and M16s searching the road verges for the likes of Cuc in his previous incarnation, but utterly uninterested in his re-born persona. He shouted 'Chieu hoi' at each passing vehicle and gestured frantically.

Finally, a marine gunnery sergeant acknowledged Cuc's existence and shouted back, 'Hey, gook! Slopehead! Wanna Coke?' The American gave Cuc his first contact with the western world by throwing a half-full can of Coca-Cola at him and hitting him square on the side of the head. Too terrified to dodge it, Cuc at first thought he was bleeding, but it was only the sticky brown Coca-Cola trickling down his neck.

The convoy passed and all was suddenly and strangely still. Cuc squatted in the dust of the road, weeping with exhaustion and humiliation, and lamenting his decision to leave Son Loi. He was on the verge of turning back when a jeep appeared. Cuc waved and shouted – it stopped. An American smiled a flash of perfect teeth and greeted him in fluent Vietnamese. Cuc had just met the senior advisor for Quang Nam.

Over the next few weeks Cuc was interrogated, assessed and made to swear an oath of allegiance. He was 'a good catch' – strong, intelligent, adept at handling weapons and equipment. He was selected for the elite Kit Carson Scout program where the best defectors were trained as scouts to serve with the Americans, just as Apache and Sioux warriors had scouted for the US cavalry in the last century.

Ho Cuc was assigned to an American airborne infantry battalion where his expert knowledge of mines, booby traps and guerrilla tactics saved dozens of GIs from being killed or maimed. His bravery won him an American Bronze Star, and he was shown off as a prize defector whenever VIPs visited the division HQ. On one occasion, Cuc even appeared on US national television with a Republican senator. The senator, attired in flak jacket and helmet for the TV cameras, was a notorious hawk who believed in more bombing including tactical nukes. He also believed that the Vietnamese had to 'stand up for themselves' and picked out Ho Cuc as a prime example of one who was doing just that. The television screens showed the senator with his arm around Cuc, describing him as 'a brave young Vietnamese who had chosen freedom.'

A week later the airborne battalion's luck ran out in a big way. They had been lured into attacking a ridgeline at Dak To. The North Vietnamese allowed them to pass through well-concealed positions before attacking them from behind. The battalion was trapped in a well-planned crossfire and decimated. Ho Cuc was written off as missing, presumed dead.

F RANCIS LOPEZ WOKE an hour before dawn and watched the light creep in through the frayed curtain. He was hung over and wanted to get drunk again: it was the only way to cope with being at his step-parents' home. At first light, Lopez dressed and went down to the jetty. He found raccoon tracks just above the high water mark; they led up the beach to where a lightning-split oak leaned over the bank. Tom, his adoptive father, always kept him informed about the raccoon: she had a den and cubs where the river had eroded a cavern under the tree roots.

Though it was mid-May, it was too early in the morning for dragonflies, but there were whippoorwills calling from the wood, and a hummingbird in the marsh. Lopez thought that *Stormy Petrel* looked low in the water, so he jumped on board to pump the bilges. The tide was full and the river a mirror. A yellow perch hovered near the weed bank and further out, towards the point, a school of alewives rippled the water. He wanted to slip *Stormy Petrel*'s moorings and sail out, away from Rideout's Landing, into the broad bay, past the white clapboard lighthouse on stilts, past the islands and down into Virginia. The rivers and bays, he thought, had always been fresh and wonderful. Nothing ever went wrong out there.

Lopez went back to the house. Tom used to call it 'the tomb': it was too big to heat in winter and always seemed damp and cold. He went into the studio and sat at the big roll-top desk where Tom did the farm accounts. He started to write a farewell letter – but then he stopped and looked at what he'd written. It was so, so stupid; it was fantastically awful – melodramatic 'to be opened only in the event of my death' crap. Unless one does manage to get killed, he thought, letters like this prove pretty fucking embarrassing.

He tore the letter into tiny pieces and instead doodled a cartoon on the blotter of Tom's Hampshire boar holding trotters with a sow and singing:

> Pour voir la vie en rose
> Je n'ai pas besoin de grand' chose...

Lopez knew that Rosie was proud of his being good at French. He drew a picture of a bridge and sketched in the two pigs leaning over the parapet and captioned it:

> Sous le pont Mirabeau coule la Seine
> Et nos amours...

Lopez added a few swans to the river and a spying periscope. It felt good to be doing something stupid. And silly things like that made Rosie happy, showed he wasn't being morbid. He knew that after he was gone, Rosie would date the drawings and put them in her diary for safekeeping. She kept everything.

Rosie Ardagh had gone to a lot of trouble to organize her adopted son's life and education. She had arranged the lycée exchange in Paris, and later his year at the Sorbonne. His fluent French was tangible proof that she had accomplished something, that she had civilized him. Learning Spanish, on the other hand, would have been a sign of regression, of ingratitude even. Rosie had envisioned him becoming some sort of genteel professor or diplomat bouncing back and forth across the Atlantic. And then he had spoiled her silly dream. He had spoiled everything, forever. And Tom and Rosie had forgiven him. And he couldn't bear it. So, unable to live with that terrible forgiveness, he was running away from it, knowing that they would forgive that too.

Lopez stared out the window and tried to make his brain melt into mush. He held his head in his hands: he could feel the soft tick of his carotid pulse. 'They love me so much,' he said to himself. 'They need me.' The day was starting to get warm. In the honeysuckle the bees were going berserk pillaging pollen.

Lopez looked around the studio and remembered why he hated it so much. He and Ianthe used to call it 'the dead brats' room'. The disrespect was a childhood dare thing started by Lopez. But Ianthe's eyes watered and her lip always shook when she called it that, for one of the 'brats' had been her father. All the photographs, the sports trophies, the scrapbooks, the newspaper clippings and the other relics of those lost lives were there. Maybe, he thought, that was why Rosie's paintings were so depressing. She ought to work someplace else. Lopez used to hate being alone with the ghost sons. He could feel their presence, and was even afraid to turn around too quickly lest he should catch one of them smiling and staring at his back. And there was always this dull musty smell: the stale perfume that clings long after the party's over, the scent of wilted funeral flowers.

A photograph of Arthur, in a gilt frame, stood on the baby grand next to a silver salver of dried rose petals. Arthur looked more corpulent and affable than Peter – there was even a hint in his face of something voluptuous and carnal. Rosie never said much about Arthur, even after the secret was out. At least he'd done what pleased him. Maybe that was why the eyes in the photograph looked sleepy – but the mouth beneath the moustache seemed cruel, perhaps sadistic. It was the younger son, Peter, for whom Rosie truly and passionately mourned. There was a photograph of Peter on the writing desk, about to take off from an airfield in Suffolk, giving the thumbs up from the cockpit of his plane. He was a celebrity hero even before he died and his photo had appeared on the cover of a national magazine.

Lopez found Peter's scrapbook in the desk drawer and turned to the final page. The newsprint cutting was yellow and brittle. It was from a local English paper that described the explosion as 'the largest ever to have shaken the British Isles'. Eighty-nine buildings were damaged by the blast, including the church of Holy Trinity, Blythburgh, which had all its windows blown in. Lopez closed the book and put it back. Ianthe had known the contents by heart: when she was young she had read all the articles over and over again so that she could recite them from memory like the Hail Mary or the Apostles' Creed. It had been her only way of connecting to her father, all that was left of him.

Peter had volunteered for a secret operation to attack the sites that were launching V1 rockets at London. Conventional bombing had had no effect on the V1 sites for they were protected by concrete fifty feet thick. The plan involved packing a B-24 Liberator with twelve tons of high explosive. The idea was for Peter and his co-pilot to get the bomber off the ground, point it in the right direction and then parachute out. The pilotless plane would then be flown by remote control until it reached its target. Something, probably an electric fault, had blown them up fifteen minutes into the flight – right over the garden.

The coincidence was so bizarre and so cruel that Lopez wondered if there really was such a thing as a family curse. Ianthe's mother, three months pregnant, had been sitting in her garden enjoying the late afternoon August sun when the father of her child disintegrated to atoms in the sky above her. The casement windows were blown in, and for several seconds afterwards there was a gentle patter of white ash, all that was left of Peter Ardagh. Lopez reckoned that the whole thing – so freakish and gruesome, like someone tipping a loved one's cremation urn over your head – must have deranged Peter's fiancée. When the baby was born she christened her Ianthe – the code name of the very mission that killed the father. The poor woman never did get her marbles back. Instead there was a lot of drink, a lot of men and even more self-loathing. When Ianthe was three her mother walked into the sea at Walberswick with a bottle of gin in her hand – and Tom and Rosie, as usual, picked up the pieces.

Sometimes, when Rosie was a bit drunk, she used to sway back and forth, telling people that Peter had been headed for the White House and would have beaten Kennedy for the Democratic nomination in '60, and would then have 'absolutely clobbered that shit Nixon.' It was at times like this that Lopez had hated Peter. He hated him because he had tried to be like him – tried to replace him – and failed. Later, hate turned to disdain. Then to pity. Peter had been strong, brave and loyal, but his fresh honest face showed nothing of furtiveness and complex duplicity. In the end, Lopez began to feel superior: he was sure that he knew things, was conscious of a world, that neither son had ever imagined. To be fair, he knew that Rosie and Tom had never expected him to replace their sons or to be a 'grateful' child. They let him keep his birth name, Lopez, not wanting to steal that faint fragment of his lost past. Lopez knew the Ardaghs wanted nothing in return – but they didn't know, could never have imagined, that he would take from them the last precious fragment of their own beings, their own blood.

Lopez knew that his adoptive home was beautiful: the mellow eighteenth-century brick, the purple shadows of oak and walnut trees, the river in spring a virginal white corridor of dogwood blossom. But he also knew that the beauty was the corrupt, too-honeyed beauty of a place that lay under a curse. The land was cursed because it had been stolen from one people and then enriched by the slave labor of another. The dead sons were not the only ghosts in the shadows of Rideout's Landing. At one time, this knowledge would have liberated him, saved him. But now he was one of the ghosts himself, part of the blood tragedy.

There was a clunking noise from the corridor as 'Sambo' struck the hour. Sambo was a nineteenth-century clock cast in the shape of a Negro minstrel. The clock face was the base of the banjo, and the minstrel's bulging eyes rolled to their whites during the hourly striking. The clock was an heirloom kept as a joke. One of Ianthe's classmates from Smith had found it offensive – 'Hey, Ianth baby, you have to get rid of that thing. It's so *racist*!' – but it didn't bother Lopez: he loved the clock and as a child had been endlessly fascinated by the rolling eyeballs. For a while the minstrel was his best friend and he used to tell him all his secrets. He remembered that day – the worst day of his life – when he had pleaded silently, 'Oh Sambo, my old pal, please make your hands go backward. Please, Sam, *please*...'

He had learned, too late perhaps, that Tom and Rosie's love was perfect and unconditional – that forgiveness, no matter how much he betrayed them, was always there. Lopez was moved by their love, but knew he couldn't return it. He wondered if he could ever give anyone the sort of love they had given to him. And indeed, he thought, why should he? He had never asked to be translated into their world, to lose the austere pride of a mestizo's poverty. It wasn't *all* his fault.

And he knew that their world was far from ideal – it was decayed and wilted. It was only by returning after so long away that Lopez saw the house as, he imagined, others must see it: the frayed Indian carpet, the rotting curtains, the walls stained with smoke and damp, and the harsh clash of Rosie's abstract expressionist canvases with everything and with each other. Her clock – all their clocks – had stopped ticking a long time ago. Lopez looked at the photographs for one last time: Arthur, Peter – and Ianthe, wearing a plain white blouse, her thick chestnut hair brushing her shoulders, her arms full of books, her first day at college. He gently brushed his fingers over the photo, as if caressing her. 'Now you're a dead brat too.'

Lopez pulled his hand away as if burnt and wiped the tears away. He nearly upset the silver salver of pot-pourri. On impulse he emptied the pot-pourri into the fireplace.

The dried petals had lost their color and scent decades before. He picked up a poker and stirred the dead flies, fragments of moths' wings and brown rose petals into the cold oak ash.

T**HE WEEK BEFORE LOPEZ LEFT** for Vietnam seemed to be permanent night. Now it was the night of departure, an unreal sick-inducing California night. It felt like their removal, their expatriation, was so shameful that it had to be done under cover of darkness. Complete nausea. The officers' club at Travis Air Force Base was the worst example of Hollywood kitsch that Lopez had ever seen: pink flamingos, black vinyl furniture, cocktail swizzle sticks and pilots who looked like Dean Martin. Just as he thought he really was going to be sick, he found another Tequila Sunrise floating in front of him. He looked up and saw Garcia Vargas smiling at him like a nurse handing out medication at Spring Grove. 'Get that inside you, chico.'

'Go 'way, I'm drunk enough already.'

Vargas ignored him and set down the drink.

Earlier in the evening, Lopez and the other officers had been full of bravado. But as departure time approached the mood changed. It was no longer a joke: they really were on their way to Viet-fuckin'-nam. There were eighteen Special Forces lieutenants in the replacement levy. A few months ago, while still in training, they used to joke about the casualty statistics: it hadn't seemed real then. Once, when an instructor had warned them that one in three could expect to die, the class of trainee officers burst into laughter: 'Uno, dos – tough shit, Travis!'; 'Ah mah Gawd, ah doan wanna die!' – and so on. And half the survivors could expect to be crippled.

Most of the instructors at Forts Benning and Bragg had been maimed, often hideously. Lopez wondered if they had been selected for their shock value, to make the young lieutenants 'get real' about war. They flaunted their wounds with the professional pride of self-mutilated medieval beggars. He remembered one especially twisted captain who seemed to get an almost sexual kick from telling them about the wounds and deaths that were waiting for them: penectomy, colostomy, castration, amputations various including full hip disarticulation. The captain's own wound was from a bullet that had entered the top of his wrist and then ploughed the length of his arm, shattering his elbow and blowing a jagged hole through his upper arm the size of a baseball. The bullet had gouged a ridge between his forearm bones so deep you could roll golf balls down it. The arm was a hideous useless thing that stuck out from his body like a coathanger with a claw on the end. He couldn't use it or hold anything with it. Lopez wondered why he didn't have it amputated and replaced with a useful hook. Maybe that would have been too final, too much of a goodbye.

It was going to be awful, obscene. And yet Lopez had volunteered for the whole business: infantry, airborne, Special Forces. He wished that he could explain it to someone. But he couldn't explain it to himself. It was irrational, a drug, a compulsion, an escape. But it was also penance, atonement. And only he knew for what. He finished off the tequila.

Vargas handed him another, and breathed in his ear: 'Hey, chico, you ever been to California before?'

Lopez shook his head.

'My dad used to work in the fields around Soledad as an illegal, before he got some forged papers so he could get a job in the canning factory. That's some shit, isn't it. Him needing papers?'

'Why's that, Garcia?'

'Because California used to be Mexico till the gringos stole it.'

'So what?' said Lopez.

'I'll tell you "so what", my little chico who can't speak ten words of Spanish. If those richies back East hadn't adopted you and the immigration cops were to walk in that door, they'd deport your ass. But don't worry, chico, you got the right papers, so they're going to send you to Vietnam instead. Hey, d'you know the difference between a gringo and an onion?'

'No, Garcia, what *is* the difference between a gringo and an onion?'

'Cutting up a gringo doesn't make you cry.' Vargas laughed so hard he spilt tequila all over his uniform.

'That – is – *bad*,' Lopez sighed.

He closed his eyes. There was a vague memory of incense, candles, a still brown face in an open coffin in a church in Vera Cruz that they said was his mother. So long ago.

It was nearly midnight when they boarded the flight. People formed their own seating groups according to rank and units. A lieutenant sitting behind Lopez was returning to Vietnam after a couple of weeks' compassionate leave. His wife's brother had been killed in the Ia Drang and his parents-in-law had asked him to accompany their son's body back to the States. Lopez wondered why America was a country of ghouls: embalmers, escorted corpses, the high altitude danse macabre over the Pacific. He found such necrophilia weird. A death like Peter Ardagh's – complete obliteration, so clean, so final – was the best way to go. He woke up Vargas and tried to talk to him about it: 'What's the point of embalming all these dead guys and sending them back twelve thousand miles? Why don't they just bury us where we fall? Who the fuck wants to be pickled and slung back through the stratosphere? We're not fucking Egyptian pharaohs.'

Vargas peered at him through sleep-thickened eyelids and grunted, 'Que pasa, chico?' He obviously wasn't listening. Vargas was always a disappointing audience. Lopez tucked him back up in his field jacket. Later there was a film about a teacher, played by Anne Bancroft, working with mentally retarded adults in Boston. It all seemed so gentle, so un-American. Lopez fell asleep when the film was over. When he woke again the plane was making a steep anti-aircraft-fire-avoiding descent into Bien Hoa air base. There had been no sense of passage: the journey hadn't seemed real.

Bien Hoa was the second biggest air base in the Saigon region. When Lopez got to the top of the disembarkation ladder, he could see nothing but tarmac and acres and acres of warehouses and aircraft hangars. It looked like someone had paved over the whole of Vietnam. He made out a fringe of tree line in the distance, but the horizon was so distorted by heat haze that the trees might have been mirages.

After disembarking they were herded past a huge open shed where a hundred or so infantrymen who had survived their duty tour were sprawled among their bags, waiting to board the plane for the trip back. Their uniforms looked bleached and threadbare as if they'd hung on a washing line for a year. The infantrymen themselves seemed dusty and washed out, but the sight of the replacements roused them like a double dose of amphetamine. The newcomers were suddenly subjected to a barrage of obscene gesture and verbal abuse. 'Lookit all that nice new dead meat – You guys're gonna get your cherries blasted – Who you lookin' at, you fucking four-eyed dufus? – Hey, dipshit! I'm talking to you, fuckhead! – Bet your wife's got a nice tight pussy, but it ain't gonna be tight when you get back – What sort of wheelchair you want?'

Lopez and the others were then put on buses with anti-grenade wire mesh over the windows, and shuttled a couple of miles to the transient billets at Long Binh.

During the rest of the day there were tropical uniforms and boots to collect and forms to fill in. One of the forms asked if you wanted your next of kin notified if you were only slightly wounded. Lopez ticked the 'no' box. Later they were given stale sandwiches and sent to a barracks. Lopez lay awake most of the night listening to the creaking of metal bed frames as the other new arrivals turned, also unable to sleep, in the dank and suffocating heat. There was also the distant thunder of eight-inch guns firing pointlessly into the darkness. He got up thirsty in the early hours, but couldn't find any taps without notices warning 'Unpotable: Do not drink'. There were the smells of disinfectant, flatulence and cigarette smoke. There were rumbling bowel sounds and a voice coming from one of the toilet cubicles where an alcoholic sergeant, thinking he was alone, was talking to himself, apparently re-scripting past conversations: 'Found me half a Johnnie's head in a helmet, Lieutenant, all crawling with maggots. I was a combat engineer in Korea when you were still sucking a sugar tit, so who you think you talking to?' This was the side of the army that Lopez hated most. He gave up looking for a drink and went back to his bunk.

The next day Lopez was assigned to the 5th Special Forces Group. Three of the other SF-qualified officers found themselves assigned to line infantry units and were boiling with resentment: they felt like thoroughbreds sent to plough fields with teams of mules. SF officers found it difficult to get on in other units: Lopez knew of one who had been sent to the 5th Mech, and was dead within a month. A rational side of Lopez knew that the whole business was puerile: guns and the other toys of war were emblems of infantile regression; armies were evil playpens full of panzers, oompah music and funny walks. But it was still queerly fascinating. He felt like an impostor who had infiltrated a cult – he wore the vestments, but didn't have to believe.

The flight to the Group HQ at Nha Trang was delayed for a half-hour because of a mortar attack. Lopez hadn't heard any explosions and thought all the fuss was silly. The airfield was so vast that he couldn't imagine a few mortar rounds doing much damage – potholes in a remote corner of the runway perhaps, nothing more. After the All Clear sounded they set off across the sweltering tarmac to their aircraft. They passed a group of forty Viet Cong prisoners squatting in neat little rows, all blindfolded with their hands tied behind their backs, compact and sinewy men who radiated an aura that was arrogant and obstinate. Lopez felt something pulse within himself, a faint but clear whisper of recognition. It was something older and more inexhaustible than the concrete techno-desert, the shrill incessant turbine whine, that whirled all around him.

The truck that picked up Lopez and the other 5th Group replacements made a detour along the Nha Trang esplanade on the way to the HQ. Travis, a languid Texan from an old military family, drawled in a fake English accent, 'Nha Trang rather reminds one of Cannes. Do you not agree, Don Francisco?'

Lopez nodded. There were a lot of French colonial buildings with ornate balconies and gray shutters, and it had that Riviera ambience of elegant seediness and decay. Also like Cannes, it was located on the curve of a mountain-fringed bay. The bay was a bright cobalt blue and rocky islands materialized out of the morning mist like the fantasy scenery of a Disney film. The mainland mountains were less unreal and changed from gray to blue to bright green as the sun climbed, and then back to gray in the evening. Between the gaps in the first rank of mountains were views of steep verdant valleys and the silhouettes of more mountains beyond them, overhung with dark gray smoke from a bombing run.

After they had settled into the transient barracks – bright airy dormitories with views of the mountains – most of the lieutenants went off to the town to find prostitutes. The search parties were led by earlier arrivals who, after all of three days 'in-country', wanted to show off that they knew their way around. Lopez was tempted to go with them, but stretched out on his bunk and tried to get some sleep instead. He hated the idea of prostitution, but was tormented by sexual frustration. He started to think about all the women – not very many – with whom he'd had sex. He tried especially to focus on a rampant Ocean City weekend with a shopworker called Mary-Louise – both of them had only wanted one thing, and there hadn't been any emotional complications. He tried not to think about Ianthe.

He closed his eyes. He always liked being alone in barracks, whitewashed, austere and smelling faintly of disinfectant. He liked the simplicity of a personal space reduced to a green footlocker and a narrow bunk – taut stretched sheets, crisp hospital corners, a coarse wool blanket. If you needed anything else – a desk or a bazooka, a jeep or a tank – they gave it to you.

Travis had also remained behind in the barracks. He put aside his copy of Mungo Park's *Travels in the Interior of Africa* and called over to Lopez, 'Hey, Francis, you awake?'

'I am now.'

'You remember that medical briefing in Bien Hoa? That pinhead quack and his scare tactics about how your dick would rot off if you pleasured yourself with the locals?'

'Yeah.'

'Remember him saying Vietnam was in the throes of a clap epidemic and that Saigon had the second highest VD rate in the world? But he sure didn't say which town was number one, did he? Bet you don't know where that is.'

'Where then?'

'Houston. Don't you forget, Lopez: America's always number one – and Texas, boy, is always number one in America. Our poontang is the most dangerous poontang in the world and we're proud of it.' The other officers had begun to filter back from the brothels. 'Here come the whoremongers,' said Travis. 'They found girls, and are now calculating their chances of having found gonococci and spirochetes as well. La tristesse post-coite.'

All the 5th Group newcomers had to go to Hon Tre Island for the Combat Orientation Course, a final training exercise. The course included a 'live' patrol against a 'real' Viet Cong fishing village on the eastern side of the island. The same two old men were always taken prisoner and then released a few days later. The joke was that the men really were Viet Cong and occasionally took time off from fishing to attach limpet mines to ships anchored in Nha Trang Bay. They were, however, too valuable a training resource to be killed or kept as prisoners. In any case, the newcomers proved more of a risk to each other than did the enemy. A week earlier a new lieutenant embarrassed by diarrhea had left his patrol's night perimeter to do his business. When he came back a nervous colleague shot him dead.

Lopez and the others were billeted in a former hunting lodge, a rambling wooden building with verandas and large airy rooms. The island had once been a game reserve for the last of the Annamite emperors. In the evening, when Lopez relaxed on the veranda with a beer in his hand, he tried to conjure up the shades of the emperors. He could imagine them reminiscing over their brandy about a close call with a tiger in the elephant grass or a tryst with a mistress in the Rue du Faubourg St-Honoré. But that was a different empire. There weren't any more tiger or emperors on this island, just the training camp and the constant whir of a rotating radar dish.

At five each morning they had to double-time up the steep mountain road to the radar station, burdened with combat gear and a rucksack filled with forty pounds of sand. Lopez always got to the summit well ahead of the others. He liked those few moments of being alone in a wilderness. Across the moon-silvered furrows of the bay,

Vietnam lay like a dark recumbent beauty. A few tactically important knolls and hills were ringed with high intensity lamps. In the dawn twilight the rings of illumination looked like pieces of jewelry carelessly discarded across rumpled bedclothes in the passion of the night. She was, he thought, so beautiful, so beautiful.

After completing the Hon Tre course, the replacement levy returned to Nha Trang to get their postings. Someone said that getting your assignment from the Group Adjutant was like going to see St. Peter. When Lopez went into the headquarters building he felt he was descending into a tomb; one moment he was sweating in the blinding glare of the midday sun, and a moment later he was shivering and blind in a windowless corridor. The air-conditioning seemed to reach for his testicles, like a sly scoutmaster, before sliding its hand along his sweat-damp spine. When his pupils finished dilating he could read the tall wall plaques adorned with little brass nameplates commemorating the Fifth Group's 544 dead and missing. Lopez scanned the roll of names, dates and locations – often marked Classified – as he waited his turn to see the adjutant.

The adjutant was a major who had a face as lugubrious as Gregorian chant. His head and arms had been badly scarred by burns. 'You look pretty fit,' he said to Lopez. 'Enjoy your stay on Hon Tre?'

Lopez said it wasn't too bad and tried not to make it too obvious that he was looking at the adjutant's wounds.

'We've had two really bad weeks. I've got to replace fourteen officers and I have all these fucking citations to write up.' He hefted a ragged pile of rough handwritten notes from his in-tray, some looked smeared with either mud or blood. 'I wonder,' he said, 'if a decoration makes the family feel any better?' The adjutant paused and stared into space for a second. 'You all come across this desk, one way or another.'

The adjutant began searching through another pile of paper. Lopez wondered if he'd forgotten he was there. After a minute he broke the silence and asked where he would be going.

The major went over to a wall map and pointed to a place called Nui Hoa Den in the upper left hand corner of the country: it was the second northernmost of the border camps. He then pointed to a place next to the Laotian border. 'It used to be there, at Kham Duc, but that one had to be shut down.' He then handed Lopez two dozen copies of his orders – it was necessary to leave a trail of paper at each stop along the way – and wished him good luck.

As soon as he left the office, Lopez started to feel nauseous; his armpits were soaked with cold sweat. He thought that once he got outside, away from the tomb-chill of the HQ building, it would be better. The sudden blast of sunlight struck like a hammer and blinded him, and the heat haze rising from the parade ground was making the barracks shiver. Lopez wanted the dry midday heat to sweat the sickness out of his pores, but it made him more nauseous still.

Lopez and four others who had been assigned to the northern camps had a long sweaty boring wait on the edge of the runway at Nha Trang airfield. Their flight was two hours late. The aircraft, when it finally arrived, was a Command and Control 'Blackbird': a C-130 camouflaged black and dark green for covert night operations. There were no markings to identify the plane. The newcomers filed up the loading ramp and found the forward section of the cargo hold blocked off by a black curtain stenciled with TOP SECRET KEEP OUT. After the plane took off, Travis tried to lift the curtain and peep underneath. There was a quick movement behind the curtain and a large boot nearly crushed his fingers. Then a hidden voice, 'Do that a-fuckin'-gain and I'll chop your fuckin' hand off.'

Vargas shouted, ironically, 'That's an officer you're talking to.'

The voice replied, long and low, 'No sheee-it!'

Travis whispered, 'Non-commissioned filth,' and everyone else laughed. The incident broke the tension. For the first time the new officers felt like comrades, with a sense of shared pride. It was they, after all, who had been assigned to I Corps, the northern border sector – Khe Sanh, Hue, the DMZ, Lang Vei, Hamburger Hill – 'where the action was'. By the time the plane landed at Da Nang they were all high on bonding and shared adventure. As the pilot taxied to an unloading area Lopez stood up, slung his rifle and donned his beret. He felt almost heroic. The engines shut down and the hydraulics wheezed as the rear ramp lowered into place. He squinted into the sunlight. At first he thought it was a mirage or some trick of the light, but then he realized they were real. Five coffins. The five new arrivals marched off the aircraft, and the five coffins were carried on. Travis said, 'That's just a load of bullshit. They're probably empty. I bet it's just an act they put on to scare the new guys.'

'Yeah, sure,' said Vargas.

The bus waiting to transport them was riddled with bullet holes. Two sergeants, from a covert project known as C and C, were leaning against the bus. The driver, a languid Chinese Nung mercenary with long Mandarin nails and fabulous Fu-Manchu moustaches, was blissfully slumped in the driver's seat until one of the sergeants kicked him awake. There was something odd about the C and C NCOs. Instead of green berets, they were wearing black bowler hats. Then Lopez saw that they weren't real English bowlers, but narrow-brimmed jungle hats that had been dyed black and starched to remove the floppiness.

The headquarters compound was on a strip of beach four miles south of Da Nang. To get there, the bus skirted the shanty towns that fringed the city and went over a girder bridge guarded by a detachment of sleepy-looking Vietnamese soldiers and a team of US Navy divers who had to continually check the bridge abutments for explosives. The black twisted remains of the previous bridge stuck out of the river about a hundred yards away. As the bus crossed the bridge one of the sergeants said, 'Now, Moustachio.' The Nung driver did something with the choke and starter, and the bus responded with an explosive backfire. The Vietnamese guarding the bridge flung themselves to the ground; one guard's helmet clattered into the road. The C and C sergeant rocked with laughter and shouted, 'Fuckin' asshole slopes!' Moustachio hissed liquidly through gold-capped teeth.

Further on, the bus had to stop for a few minutes to allow a column of armored personnel carriers to rumble by in a cloud of dust. On one side of the road was a huge scrapyard, covering acres of land and sealed off from scavengers by chainlink fence, barbed wire and armed guards authorized to shoot on sight, where billions of dollars' worth of blown-up, shot-down and worn-out war equipment was stripped for its scrap value by a private contractor.

On the other side of the road was a depressing group of shanties constructed from discarded ammunition boxes and cardboard ration cartons. The prostitutes who lived in the shanties – 'the RMK girls' – were named after the scrap company that ran the junkyard. One shanty had a sign above the door which said, SUCK 'EM SILLY SALLY. Her next door neighbor had a sign advertising SUCK 'EM SILLY SALLY'S SISTER. Travis was fascinated. 'Do you suppose,' he said, 'they're part of a franchised chain?' Two US marines, one white and one black, were haggling with two of the girls. One of the girls left the group and came over to the bus. She looked up at Travis and said, 'You Special Forces, Trung Uy?'

Travis nodded.

'Special Forces eat pussy.'

Lopez surveyed a wasteland of dust, diesel fumes, tank tracks, barbed wire and acres of scrap iron, and listened to the taunting laughs of beautiful teenagers who sold their bodies to foreign soldiers. He wondered if it had been anything like this when Cortes landed in Mexico – exotic galleons at anchor in the offing, smaller cargo boats carrying supplies and men ashore, sacks and crates piling up on the sand, while the Aztecs stared full of wonder and wrath from the forests.

The commanding officer of the northern camps was a black lieutenant colonel named C.J. Cale who came from a background of abject poverty in rural Mississippi. Behind his back his fellow blacks called him 'home-boy'; among the white officers he was known as Catfish.

As soon as the new officers arrived, they were ushered into Cale's office for an introductory talk. He started off by saying that he had no wife, no family, no friends – and that was the best way to be. 'I see,' he went on, 'that none of you rabbit-hung studs ever been to Vietnam before, so you don't know how horny you can get when you got a permanent hard-on and there ain't no place to stick it 'less you're some kind of pervert that gets turned on by body count hangin' in the wire. But it don't matter, you just do the job you been trained for. Your needs don't matter. Now, some of you little sodomites may have a reg'lar piece of tail back in the so-called world. You may even be married to it. And she probably told you – with tears running down her cheeks, all smearin' her Jezebel make-up and rouge – about how faithful she going to be while you in Vietnam. That is one steamin' load of bullshit. Human nature ain't like that – healthy young tail need it just as much as you do. Jody's probably been around checkin' out the situation already, and it won't be long before Jody's shaftin' her up one side and down the other. That just human nature. But, gentlemen, that sort of thing just don't matter. You just do the job you been trained for and that's it.'

While Cale was speaking, Lopez noticed a copy of a Roadrunner cartoon under the glass cover on his desk. In the colonel's cartoon, however, the coyote had finally turned the tables. His front paws were grasping Roadrunner's neck and his disproportionately huge penis had skewered the bird, almost splitting it in half. The caption read, 'Take that, you bastard.'

'Now it just so happens,' Cale continued, 'that the people you replacing are not doing the jobs which they were trained for. This may be because they got killed or hurt real bad or stepped on their dicks.' The officers had been conditioned to believe that 'stepping on your dick' – being relieved for incompetence – was an even worse fate than death. 'So finally, gentlemen, don't let any of these things – as far as can be prevented – happen to you. Writin' a certain sort of letter makes me feel rotten as hell. Maybe I'm just selfish, but I want you guys to spare me that particular feeling. So be careful.'

Cale ended the talk abruptly, said he was late for a meeting with his Vietnamese counterpart. Lopez wondered if this was an excuse: he thought he could see the tears forming in the corners of Cale's eyes. As they filed out Travis whispered to Lopez, 'Do you think Rastus writes his own scripts?'

'At least he can write, you racist gringo asshole.'

Travis obviously knew he meant it and looked a little speechless. Lopez was usually 'one of the guys' – but sometimes he reacted badly to racist remarks; sometimes there were even fights. Travis took Lopez by the arm. 'I'm not a racist – you ought to know that.'

Lopez smiled. 'You think I give a fuck?'

'Sometimes I think you do.' Travis answered. 'But then again, sometimes I really don't know what's going on with you at all.'

It was still early evening when Lopez heard rumors that one of the new officers was already missing. Earlier he had seen the adjutant running around asking, 'Any of you guys seen Lieutenant Whiteford?' There hadn't been any enemy action, he hadn't been taken prisoner; it was just an accident. Someone later said that they had last seen Whiteford on the beach fooling about in the breakers on an inflatable mattress. The current must have swept him out to sea.

The company commander called in a helicopter equipped with a Xeon spotlight capable of throwing a million candle-power of light for almost a mile. All night long they heard the sound of the search helicopter beating up and down the coast. At first light Lopez and some of the others heard they'd found the body rolling in the surf near Monkey Mountain on the northern end of the peninsula, and ran up the beach in the early dawn to see. 'So stupid,' whispered Travis. 'So fucking *stupid*. He only just got here.' The body was fish-belly white and there were crabs clinging to soft puffy tissue that had already become frayed by their hunger. This was a truth long lost to North America and Europe: that humans are meat.

Later that morning Lopez went swimming, but it didn't feel right – he couldn't help but think that the sea was tainted. The sea near Da Nang wasn't translucent like the sea at Nha Trang; it was brown gray like the Atlantic.

It reminded Lopez of a trip to Cape Hatteras with Tom and Rosie and Ianthe. It had been early May, the weather fresh and crystal clear. He and Ianthe went walking along the dunes and noticed some fishermen gathered around something that had washed up. Lopez thought it was a plastic buoy: it looked round and beige colored with brown blotches. They continued walking, turned around when they got to the new inlet where the ocean had broken through into Pamlico Sound during Hurricane Hazel, and walked back the way they had come.

There were a whole lot more people there, and a North Carolina State Police car stuck in the sand with its wheels screaming and spinning. Lopez remembered one of the police shouting, 'Curtis, you done sank the goddam thing in up to the axle.' He went to help and so did the fishermen and they finally managed to push the big police Pontiac back on to the hard track. Then Lopez saw the ambulance, behind a dune, and got there just in time to see the buoy – it was on a stretcher and strapped in a canvas sack by then – being loaded into the back of it. He asked the driver what had happened. It was a little boy, about eight years old, but no one knew who he was or how he had died.

Lopez came back and told Ianthe. She winced and grabbed his hand. They walked on a good distance, maybe two miles, and didn't say anything. Ianthe was crying. And there was nothing there except clean May morning sun and sand and marram grass dunes and the bright glossy Atlantic. 'Let's swim,' she said. She stripped naked first – she was completely unselfconscious about her body, her innocence knew no prudery. Lopez kept his underpants on and followed her into the ocean: he looked at her hips and realized that she was turning from a waif into a woman. It frightened him. The water was still cold from winter, and much saltier than the tepid Chesapeake. The Atlantic rollers were like houses.

They came out and lay in the dunes to dry. He tried not to look at her body, but noticed that her eyes were shut and she was breathing hard. He left her to catch some grasshoppers in the dunes. When he came back, she was sound asleep. He dropped a grasshopper between her breasts. She still didn't wake. He noticed how the pale green of the grasshopper blended so naturally with the pink and brown of her nipples and breasts. The insect – *une sauterelle*, he translated to himself – drew itself up to spring away. She opened an eye. 'I'm cold,' she said.

'Maybe you should get dressed.'

As they walked back, Ianthe started talking about the dead boy, fantasizing that he had been their son – his and hers. Lopez thought it was sick and perverse, and wanted to tell her to shut up, but knew she wouldn't. She started talking about the funeral, what sort of flowers they would plant on his grave, how they would invite his school friends back to the house to share out his toys, all except his favorite little red fire engine which they would bury with him. Lopez tried to put his hand over her mouth, but she pushed him away and shouted, 'Don't take him away from me.' Later, she wrote a haiku about the boy; Lopez had kept it ever since. He still carried it in his wallet as a talisman – not for luck, but for remembrance:

> *Dream-bright river, May.*
> *Our son rows a wooden boat.*
> *Spring-no-sorrow-time!*

THE NEXT MORNING Lopez left Da Nang on the helicopter that went to Nui Hoa Den twice a week. There was no other way to get there; the land routes were all cut off and there was no place for a fixed wing aircraft to land. The helicopter flew a few miles out to sea before banking south to follow the coast. In the distance, the jagged peaks of an offshore island showed through the morning sea mist. Near the mainland shore were many small round fishing boats bobbing in and out of their drift nets. The beach was continuous white sand and behind the beach were salt pans which stick-like figures under conical hats were scraping with wide rakes. The land behind the salt gatherers was sandy and desolate in some places, but – where the sea had broken through – there were villages on stilts and children tending flocks of ducks.

When the helicopter reached a point where the sea was stained beige by silt flowing from the river mouth, it banked inland and began to follow the course of the river.

A coaster was taking the tide to Hoi An, a busy traffic of sampans scattered like pieces of bark by her wake. Hoi An was the provincial capital and dominated the delta like a Mediterranean fortress town. According to Lopez's briefing folder, the Portuguese landed there in 1535, and made lots of money selling Western weapons and military advice to the Nguyen to help them in their insurrection against the Trinh.

The helicopter had to fly high to avoid anti-aircraft fire, but Lopez could still make out the leafy squares and walled gardens of Hoi An, as well as a pagoda and a white church, and civil servants in white shirts leaving their offices for lunch. The town seemed a perfect self-contained pocket universe – neither East nor West, just itself. Something about it reminded Lopez of Camus's *La Peste*.

After Hoi An, the river became narrow and serpentine as it twisted through the flat coastal strip between the mountains and the sea. The land was a spider-web of paddy fields and hamlets with thatched roofs. Some of the larger villages still had French colonial buildings with bright red roof tiles. Lopez saw a hamlet where the thatch was burning beneath a towering plume of black smoke. It looked almost nuclear because of the way the air currents sucked up the greasy oily smoke into a mushroom cloud. The door gunner shouted into Lopez's ear above the noise of the rotors to say that a Phantom jet had been shot down from there the previous day and both crew killed. A pair of fighter-bombers were exacting retribution: as soon as their bomb racks were empty, another pair would take over and then another, until five o'clock in the afternoon when the officer's club bar began serving half-price drinks for Happy Hour.

The scenes of devastation got worse as they flew further inland. It seemed to Lopez that awful things had happened. The land became a wasteland mangled by tank treads and pockmarked with craters fetid with pus-yellow water. The paddy dykes were broken, the fields abandoned and reverting to scrub, and blackened hulks of burnt out tanks, armored personnel carriers and crashed aircraft littered the valley.

The foothills finally began at An Hoa, the district capital. It was a bleak place: nothing but trench lines, sandbags, watchtowers and bunkers. An Hoa had a Marine battalion and an artillery battery. It was the last outpost before Nui Hoa Den. It was where Lopez's team were supposed to retreat if they got overrun.

After An Hoa the river twisted into the green shadows of the Annamite Mountains and the countryside was beautiful again. The ravage of war was less evident. There were no tank tracks in the mountain jungles and the thick green foliage of the mountains was more resilient to bombing than the fragile farms of the coastal plain.

The pilot climbed to 10,000 feet to get beyond the range of the .51 caliber guns. The altitude made the air cold and Lopez, dressed only in a tropical uniform, was freezing. All the helicopters had been stripped of panels and doors so people could get in and out quickly, and they were as open to the elements as World War One fighter pilots in biplanes.

Three minutes later they were above Nui Hoa Den. From two miles up the camp was an insignificant sand colored scratch on a mountaintop. The helicopter dropped quickly, then banked tightly twice around the camp. Lopez watched the pilot shake his head at the co-pilot: they looked angry. The door gunner shouted in his ear that there was no one on the landing pad to guide them in with a smoke grenade. 'Incon-fucking-siderate,' he said. 'Always the same shit with this place.' After one more circle the pilot shrugged, the co-pilot nodded and they landed anyway.

The engine was shut down and the rotor blades, after a few pirouettes, became still. There was utter silence. It was midday at the end of the dry season and the place was as dead as a stone. The scraped earth was yellow and baked hard by the sun. The only signs of life were two pairs of eyes staring out of the shadow of a bunker entrance like the eyes of desert reptiles hiding from predators underground.

The stasis was finally broken by the noise of a truck banging over the ruts and potholes of the camp. A two-and-a-half-ton truck appeared, driven by a black American stripped to the waist, his body well muscled and gleaming with sweat like a sleek middleweight in the seventh round. The truck ground to a halt by the helicopter pad; the driver jumped down and shook Lopez's hand. 'Lieutenant Lopez, sir, welcome to Nui Hoa Den. I hope you like it here and don't step on your dick like the lieutenant we just got rid of.'

'I'm not going to. Who are you?'

'Sergeant Calvin Jackson, sir, junior weapons NCO.' Jackson then looked around furtively, as if he were about to make a guilty admission. He looked at the ground and whispered, 'Lieutenant Lopez, would you give me a hand, please?'

'Sure, with what?'

'Follow me, sir, and I'll show you.'

He led Lopez around to the back of the truck. There was a large lumpy object covered by a poncho. Jackson drew the pins from the tailgate, let it drop and flicked aside the poncho. 'That's Sergeant First Class Monroe, he's the senior weapons NCO.'

Lopez tried to hold his breath, but it was too late; he'd already breathed in the stench. The body was bloated and distended. The lower lip had split and Monroe's features, originally African, had puffed out into plump oriental roundness like a black Buddha. The dead man's camouflage uniform seemed several sizes too small; the fabric was stretched taut around the swollen flesh like the skin of a cooked sausage.

Lopez hadn't been ready for this. He felt sick. The stench hit him and hit him again – repeat waves of putrefaction. He had a weird flashback. When he was eight, Tom and he had gone to the stockyards in Baltimore with a load of pigs.

It was a hot July. There was something lying on a wagon near the railroad sidings. At first Lopez thought it was a dead pig. Tom went over to see what it was and came back with his handkerchief over his mouth and nose. Lopez wanted to look, but he was quickly and firmly led away. Later, Tom told him it was a dead vagrant who had accidentally set himself on fire in a railroad cattle truck. The body had lain undiscovered for days. At the time Lopez was angry that Tom hadn't let him look: now he knew why.

Lopez became aware that Jackson was still talking to him, explaining that some fishermen had found the body floating down the river shortly before dawn. 'We couldn't fit him in a body bag because of the way his arms and legs are stuck out.' Monroe had the posture of a frog caught in mid-leap.

'What happened?'

'What happened? What do you think happened? He went and got his self killed, sir.'

Lopez put his bag and rifle in the truck, and had begun to help Jackson shift Monroe's body to the helicopter when another American appeared. He wore a black hat, a black T-shirt and long Mexican bandit style moustaches. He nodded at Lopez, said something in Spanish, then jumped on to the bed of the truck and began to take photographs of Monroe's body from various angles and distances.

Jackson said, 'Get the fuck outta here, Mendy. You got enough pictures this morning.'

Mendy said, 'These aren't pictures, they're color slides,' and snapped a half dozen more frames before he was satisfied.

They finally got Monroe's body into the helicopter. The helicopter crew didn't like it; one of the door gunners knelt down and vomited hamburger and beer on to the baked earth.

Then Jackson drove Lopez to the inner perimeter, the camp's American sector. There was a double hedge of concertina barbed wire, bristling antennae, and two machine-gun bunkers facing, not outwards, but – ugly and distrustful – into the heart of the camp itself. As the truck bounced and lurched across the camp, clusters of curious Vietnamese appeared, wearing flip-flop sandals and camouflage uniforms, trying to get a peep at the new lieutenant.

The CO, Captain Redhorn, was standing on top of the command bunker with a pair of binoculars around his neck as they pulled up. Redhorn was a tall rangy man of twenty-six who wore thick glasses and looked like a caged wolf that hadn't been fed for days. Lopez unloaded his gear from the truck. He sniffed his bag to see if it had picked up any taint of Monroe's putrefaction. The camp interpreter, a Montagnard-Vietnamese half-caste with shoulder length hair, was squatting next to Redhorn holding a radio handset. A patter of small arms fire began to drift up from the river valley. As Redhorn gazed through the binoculars towards the action, he spoke to the interpreter. Lopez had heard that sort of voice before: it was that soft honeyed Southern drawl that chills the gut and makes the blood curdle. Those purring diphthong vowels were the unmistakable androgynous voice of Southern Gothic: the soft feminine tones cooed by an Alabama policeman undoing his trousers in a lonely jail or the velvet whispers of a Klansman about to wield the castration blade. 'Tell him, Ly, that he had better bring back hands. And I don't want to see two rights and two lefts.' After Ly had finished translating, Redhorn took the radio and repeated the instructions: 'Je ne veux fucking pas, Trung Uy, deux droites et deux gauches. Biet, Trung Uy, biet?' He eyed Lopez closely and explained, 'You need proof.'

'Proof of what?'

'Body count verification. That's what the hands are for. You can't trust these slopeheads when there are no Americans on the operation. We pay them a bonus for body count out of the non-accountable funds budget and they'll do anything, no matter how stupid, to jack up their score. At first, I used to ask for thumbs. Big mistake. One day the slope commanding Dai Doi 107 handed me a sack half full of thumbs and half full of big toes – like I wouldn't know the difference – wanted me to think he'd wiped out a couple of platoons. They all lie and cheat; it's their way of life. I'll tell you one thing that's fucking certain: these people have no moral scruples whatsoever.'

Redhorn finished his radiotelephone harangue and asked his new lieutenant to follow him into the underground accommodation bunker. Lopez winced when he saw Redhorn's back. Half the flesh was ugly scar tissue – a huge shrapnel wound in the shape of an inverted S, which began at Redhorn's left shoulder blade and ended just above his waist. Two parallel lines of bright pink suture scars, each an inch wide, seamed the curvature of the wound like an anatomical zipper, and gave the impression that the back could be unzipped for further repairs. The surgical plate that been bolted in to replace Redhorn's shoulder blade made the upper half of his back seem taut and unnatural. Lopez suddenly had the impression that Redhorn too might be a corpse, one that had been repaired and sent back from some Satanic underworld forge.

Redhorn led the way down the stairs out of the harsh light of day. Lopez half expected to find Cerberus the three-headed dog, Charon and the River Styx at the bottom. It was suddenly cool, dank and dark. Along either side of the corridor there were cubicles divided by plywood sheets. The officers and team sergeant had their own cells, like monks in a troglodyte monastery. 'Here's yours,' said Redhorn flicking aside a door curtain. There was a pine desk, shelving, hooks for weapons and equipment, and a bed consisting of a thin mattress lying on two strips of perforated steel planking resting on ammunition boxes. Redhorn pointed underneath the bed. 'Get under there if they throw satchel charges into the bunker. It'll protect you against blast and the roof collapsing.'

Lopez dropped his gear on the bed.

'It's nice and cozy down here. Sorry about the bullet holes.' Redhorn pointed to places where the plywood was splintered.

'What happened?'

'One night your late but not lamented predecessor went a little crazy. He came in and found that the rats had broken into a box of chocolate chip cookies that his mommy sent him. He emptied a whole clip from his .45, and missed every single fucking one. He nearly got Sergeant Mendoza though – Mendy was sleeping next door – and certainly made a mess of his mommy's cookies.'

'Are there a lot of rats?'

'Thousands. Place is overrun with them. But we're not permitted to poison them because the Vietnamese eat them when they run out of dog.'

As soon as Redhorn had left Lopez began to unpack. He looked at the subterranean earth of the bunker walls and – for the first time in years – he felt totally happy. There's nothing beyond here, he thought; this is the end. Here is zero. This was where he wanted to be, had to be. He had lost everything of value in his life and it was all his own fault. At first, Lopez had been frightened by the emotional void and had wanted to find something to embrace and put in its place. But he was now learning that it might be better to embrace the void itself.

His first night at Nui Hoa Den, Lopez dreamed of Sergeant Monroe's corpse. He dreamed that Monroe was smiling and winking at him as they carried his bloated body from the truck to the helicopter. He was only pretending to be dead, it was just a clever ruse to get sent home early. Lopez felt relieved. Just as he was about to whisper to Monroe that he promised not to let anyone know what he was up to, he woke up.

The bunker smelled of earth – dank earth. There were the rustle of rats and almost always the cackle of radio noise –

the communications bunker was only a few cubicles away. Lopez knew that it wouldn't be so bad when day came, then he could look out over the valley that was fresh and beautiful.

Nui Hoa Den was built on top of a mountain. The planners had wanted to avoid another Dien Bien Phu or Kham Duc, but they failed to see other problems. The camp was easily cut off and only accessible by helicopter, the monsoon rains washed the sandbag bunkers and barbed wire down the slopes, and the entire camp was often lost inside banks of low lying cloud.

It was most dangerous when the thick mist came at night. Enemy sappers then crept up close and threw grenades into the trenches. The sappers were naked except for loincloths – barbed wire snags on clothing, but not bare flesh – with tourniquet thongs around their upper arms and thighs to help staunch blood loss from the wire cuts, as well as shrapnel and bullet wounds. The job of the lead sappers was to dismantle the mines and the warning devices – in the case of Nui Hoa Den, mostly empty beer cans with pebbles in them – and then cut holes in the wire through which other sappers carrying grenades and satchel charges could follow. Redhorn told Lopez that after an attack at Lang Khe, they found bodies with tattoos on their forearms: 'Born in the North to die in the South'.

Nui Hoa Den was supposed to be defended by three hundred Vietnamese CIDG (Civilian Irregular Defense Group) soldiers, but Lopez had the impression that they tended to come and go as they pleased. He didn't blame them – they were only paid ten dollars a month. On the other hand, you didn't need a lot of money to hire an army in that part of the world, so why pay more? There were also the Americans and their Vietnamese Special Forces counterparts, the LLDB – the acronym for Luc Luong Dac Biet, but Redhorn told Lopez it really meant 'Low Lying Dirty Bastards'.

Lopez calculated that the CIDG got paid even less than the eleven and twelve year old black boys who helped Tom with the haying. He'd liked working in the fields with those kids. They used to sing the 'shortnin' bread' song over and over again as if it held some hidden ironic meaning. He wondered if those kids knew that Rideout's Landing, in any fair sense, really belonged to them. They liked coming to the farm but there was one place they wouldn't go near, a row of derelict sheds between the house and the hay barn, which used to be the slave quarters. Everyone thought they were spooky, particularly in the moonlight with the broken and charred roof beams reaching up into the sky like fingers. There was something about the CIDG bunkers at Nui Hoa Den – perhaps an odor, a feeling in the air – that reminded Lopez of those old slave quarters. It was a presence, not just of suffering, but of the silent suffering of those who would never have a voice to tell their story.

For most soldiers the army means early mornings. Lopez remembered almost fondly a winter of pre-dawn bayonet practice at Fort Benning. The sports stadium lights cast grotesque shadows as pairs of young officer candidates lunged, parried, learned to 'butt-stroke' – a rifle-butt smash to the face – and to 'slice', which involved slashing a bayonet blade through the angle where neck meets shoulder and slicing through the carotid artery and deep into the body. Then 'lunge, parry, butt-stroke, slice' all over again. After a while the movements were carried out with all the grace and precision of a corps de ballet. It was beautiful: the cadenced choreography of a death dance, each pair in the center of a penumbra of shadows.

One morning, while they were still in formation waiting to pair off, Travis asked for permission to speak. The instructor, still only a bit startled, barked, 'Granted.'

'There is a long tradition of musical accompaniment to military drill, and this stadium has an excellent sound system. Might I suggest the March of the Montagus and Capulets, from Prokofiev's *Romeo and Juliet*?' And he started to *pom*-pom-pom-pom *pom*-pom-pom-pom under his breath.

For a second the instructor seemed stunned and confused, then he fixed on the lowly vermin of a candidate who had dared interrupt his routine. Just as he was poised to pounce on Travis, Lopez called out, 'Surely the most apt piece is the fight scene between Tybalt and Romeo. It's a danse macabre.'

The bayonet instructor was now totally lost. He stared open-mouthed into space for several seconds, then turned to his assistant and said, 'What the fuck're these guys talking about?' For a few precious seconds, grinning at Travis, Lopez had felt deliriously happy – a tiny evanescent flash of civilization had suddenly glowed in the dark.

Redhorn was not an early morning soldier. He seldom stirred before eleven, and even then he tended to slouch around the camp half-dressed in shorts and sandals for hours. It was midday, and Lopez was going through the re-supply procedures and logistical record keeping when Redhorn appeared, wearing olive green jockey shorts and carrying his glass and a towel. Redhorn pointed to the paperwork. 'I'm glad I don't have to do that boring shit. Get Sergeant Clarke to do it – it'll make him feel important.'

'It's my job.'

'Oh, for fuck's sake, don't play at this boy-scout shit. Clarke'll do it and that's an order.' Redhorn went quiet for a few seconds – then looked around furtively. 'I have to tell you some real serious shit, but it's sensitive stuff – the kind of stuff the non-commissioned swine can't cope with and should never know.' Redhorn put his finger to his lips and bent under the desk where there was a cast-iron safe bolted to one of the wooden beams that supported the bunker. Redhorn twirled the dial back and forth five times, then pulled the door open. Lopez glimpsed a half-dozen files bound with black string and yellow Top Secret labels, thick piles of dollars and thicker piles of Vietnamese currency and, sickeningly – for he'd heard rumors but didn't realize they really existed – the white plastic tubes full of cyanide capsules.

Redhorn pulled out one of the top-secret files and closed the safe. 'Let's go someplace where they're aren't any ears – ears still attached to people, I mean.' Lopez followed Redhorn up the steps and into the hard glare of midday sun. It was siesta time and the camp seemed dead. Redhorn padded barefoot across the hard baked ground and climbed over the parapet of the .81mm mortar pit. Lopez followed him. The mortar pit was a five feet deep well of local stone and concrete surmounted by a parapet of sandbags. Redhorn stripped off his shorts and lay down next to the mortar tube, his cock lolling against a pale white thigh, the top-secret file next to him. The pit was a furnace of white heat – it must have been a hundred twenty degrees. Redhorn took his glasses off and basked in the bright dry heat. They might have been in the Sahara.

Lopez sat down and leaned back against the wall of the mortar pit. He remained fully clothed and the sweat began to pour off. The naked Redhorn, sprawled on the white concrete, looked like a homoerotic pin-up: the mortar tube, a phallic prop of blue green steel, tilted southwest at .45 degrees beside him. There was a certain counterpoint between the flawed vulnerability of Redhorn and the perfect beauty of the mortar – its lean athleticism, the delicacy of its aiming sights, its honed perfection of lubricated parts and readiness to respond – like an icon of some strange cult. Lopez closed his eyes and started to doze.

'Are you still there?' Redhorn had put his shorts and glasses back on and was sitting cross-legged. His lean body reminded Lopez of a photo-image of Gandhi.

'Why are we in this pit?' said Lopez.

'It's my Turkish bath. I come here to purify myself and sweat out all the poison of this shitty war.' Redhorn paused and bowed his head, then went on, 'To purge my hate for the cowardly generals and candyass politicians who have no stomach, no cojones, for killing and conquest. And you're here because I need to give you a counter-intelligence briefing – and this is the best place to do it. It's as far as we can get from the bunkers and there's something about this pit that absorbs sound. If you want to tell someone a secret always bring them here.' He handed the folder to Lopez. 'Look at this fucking stuff.'

Lopez undid the black string and pulled out a thick batch of documents. All the reports were marked TOP SECRET, NEED TO KNOW ONLY and NOFORN (access forbidden to foreign nationals). In the upper left hand corner of each document was a passport size photo of a Vietnamese soldier.

'This is the most heavily infiltrated camp in I Corps. And these are the fucking traitors – we know twenty-three of them, but I think there might be six or seven more.'

Lopez leafed through the pile and studied a few reports at random. 'I don't see anything that says these guys are definitely communist agents; they're described as suspects.'

'What's the fucking difference?'

'If you're so sure, why don't you arrest them? Or shoot them?'

'Why, Lieutenant Lopez? Why indeed? Because these little shits are the best soldiers in the camp. If we got rid of them, this camp would be a totally useless no-body-count waste of taxpayer's money.' Redhorn picked out a report. 'Take this little turd, for instance – Ho Cuc.'

Lopez looked at a face that seemed carved out of seasoned teak. The CIDG soldier had sunken eyes and badly cut hair.

'This guy has the highest individual body count in the

camp. He got five in one day – fantastic. If Ho Cuc were an American, LBJ would've given him the Congressional Medal of Honor on the White House lawn, and Cuc would now be a redneck hero poking whole trailer parks of white-trash pussy.'

'Maybe he's genuine.'

'No way. This devious little shit was a scout with the 173rd when they lost that battalion at Dak To. He claims he was captured after his company was cut to pieces in a crossfire. Bullshit – Cuc led them straight into it. Next, we have the great escape lie, about how he got away during a massive bombing raid, about traveling only at night, following watercourses towards the coastal plain and living on a diet of insects and roots until he met up with a patrol of ARVN paratroopers. His cover story isn't even a good lie, lousy pulp fiction; it's about as credible as promising Peggy-Lou and Charlene you're not going to come in their mouth.'

Lopez had another look at Ho Cuc's report. 'He originally defected to An Hoa.'

'That's right. He's a homeboy, a local. Cuc comes from a little village called Son Loi, up by the river gorge. Except Son Loi, as the froggies say, n'existe plus. It used to be an important river crossing for ferrying supplies. Now it's nothing but Agent Orange defoliation and craters: the most beautiful scenery in this fucking valley.'

Lopez looked at Redhorn and tried to find a note of irony, of jokiness. There was none: he really meant, really believed, every word he said.

'The S2 section spent four days interrogating this little fucker. They didn't believe his story – even S2 aren't that stupid – but they thought Cuc might be useful here, local knowledge etcetera, provided we keep an eye on him. I put him in the Combat Reconnaissance Platoon, thinking he'd get killed in a few weeks and end the security risk problem. But the little shit just won't die. Do you know about the

CRP? We pay them $2 extra a month to get killed quick. The CRP are the ones who walk point, who take the first AK burst and get blown up by the first mine. The slopes in the other platoons are scared shitless of the CRP, but they also like having them there. Our gooks are all mathematicians. They've worked out the odds and know that the CRP are buying them time, postponing the inevitable. Even the stupidest CIDG knows that sooner or later he's going to get it: ambush, sniper, fucked-up airstrike, booby trap, mortar. And even if he survives all that shit, this camp has always been a doomed and expendable write-off. This place is just another untenable fuck-you-Jack joke like Kham Duc. When the marines were here they were overrun twice.'

Lopez put Ho Cuc back in the folder and continued flicking through the reports. 'What about the rest of these guys?'

'What about them? They're just a bunch of murderous gooks waiting around to shoot us in the back or frag us while we're asleep.'

Lopez picked out a report and held it up. 'Shit, look at this one – he's an LLDB. I thought they were supposed to be the Presidential Guard of Honor.'

'The redoubtable Sergeant-major Dieu. He's a *real* honey.'

Lopez studied the photograph. There was something leathery and ancient about Dieu's face, like the preserved bog corpses from Denmark and Ireland.

'Dieu's the oldest guy in the camp, he's fifty-three. Lucky bastard, he's been through all three wars and never been wounded or captured. In fact, that old fuck even managed to survive Dien Bien Phu. He and three or four other gooks escaped somehow and made it back to the French lines.'

'Could that be just a cover story?'

'No, that bit's true. Dieu didn't become a Communist until '56, but then he shot up through the party ranks. He's an important guy. In fact, I don't know what the fuck he's doing here. Who knows – maybe this shit-hole is more important than it looks. In any case, Dieu's not an expendable piece of shit like these other agents. He's even got connections: his wife's brother's a minister in the Hanoi government. Let me have that.' Lopez handed over the report. Redhorn looked closely at the photo. 'I'm afraid of this bastard; Dieu's the only one in the camp that scares me. I'd really like to kill him.'

'Why don't you?'

'Because Sergeant Carson, the intel NCO, would go ape. By the way, Carson is the only other fucking creature who has access to these files. You realize – if Mendy and some of the other crazies knew about these guys, they'd just kill 'em. But, as officers and gentlemen, we of course see the broader picture.'

'Why's Carson on Dieu's side?'

'I think he loves the guy – they're both alcoholics and they've both been through as much bad shit as you can pack into one incarnation. Other stuff too. Aside from the friendship crap, Carson argues a good case for Dieu. One, Dieu is too important to waste and probably won't break cover until the final offensive, which could be five or ten years from now. Two, Dieu is irreplaceable. He's the most competent Vietnamese in the camp. Without him, the whole place would collapse – even the cooks would mutiny.'

Lopez had once heard someone say that when you go to Vietnam, 'you step through the looking glass.' He was beginning to understand just how true that was.

'But I'll tell you something else – if I get Carson out of the way, Dieu, irreplaceable or not, is going to be dead meat.'

'You're going to shoot him, personally?'

'You mean a field lobotomy with a .45 caliber scalpel? No, I'm doing this one by the book. The Group S2 is a good pal of mine and I don't want him to miss out. There's a name for the procedure – it's called "termination with extreme prejudice". I'll trick Dieu into leaving the camp, get him away from anybody that might help him; don't want a bloody gun battle like that one at Mai Loc when Louis Bowman fell out with his counterpart. No, we'll jump Dieu in some quiet place down by the river, put the handcuffs on him and call in a chopper.'

'Is there some kind of court-martial procedure?'

'Fuck no. They'll give him a lie detector test – which he'll fail – then an intravenous injection with enough barbiturate to drop a charging rhino, to keep him quiet during the boat trip. They always deep-six these guys, just wrap them up in ninety feet of half-inch chain and put them in a canvas sack. The last one woke up in the bag and started squirming around just before they threw him over. It was a stormy wet night, they were out of sight of land and everyone was seasick. The S2, a very kind fellow, felt around the sack to find the condemned's head and put him back to sleep with a couple of 9mm rounds. Not as easy as you'd think in a tossing boat on a pitch-black night. The Group Medical Officer was so impressed by the S2's humane intervention that he wrote out a death certificate describing the double agent's death as the worst case of suicide he'd ever seen. The S2 framed it to keep it on his desk.'

'Is there anyone else you have to keep an eye on?'

'Only you, Lopez, only you. Everyone knows you Ivy League guys are a bunch of pinkos. But maybe you're different.' Lopez could almost feel Redhorn staring.

'Yeah, maybe.'

Redhorn took the file and fished out one more report. 'You'll love Mister Kim. We call the CIDG unit commanders "Mister", like the British do their junior officers. Everyone loves Kim, he ought to be called Saint Nguyen Van Kim.'

Lopez looked at the photo. It showed a handsome man with fine ascetic features and the pale skin of someone who had spent little time toiling in a rice paddy. He looked educated.

'Kim was born in the North. He comes from a family of Catholic mandarins who sent him away to become a priest.

He must have realized that seminaries are not particularly good places for pussy, so he ran away. I don't blame him. Then his story becomes a bit muddled: Kim claims he worked as a railway clerk and married a girl with a nice dowry. Says he got pissed off because they wouldn't promote him because he had a bourgeois background. Bullshit – so does Ho Chi Minh. In any case, eventually Kim and his wife fled to the South in a leaky boat. They were given the usual post-defection interrogation by the Quan Canh and gave the usual answers: "We were victimized, sob, sob, threatened because of our bourgeois background and our religion, blah, blah." And all the rest of that refugee crap.' Redhorn put the report back and re-bound the folder. 'But you'll love Kim: he commands the Combat Reconnaissance Platoon and his men all adore him. We certainly can't get rid of Mister Kim – there's no one else who can control those guys. Funny, isn't it?'

'What do you mean?'

'The best people at killing Communists are other Communists. How're we ever going to catch up? Look at Uncle Joe Stalin – his body count was millions.'

Lopez knew that it was going to be like this. All the camps were riddled with infiltrators. It was having to watch their backs all the time that caused a lot of Special Forces troops to crack up or pull the trigger. Many of them ended up with a pathological hatred of the Vietnamese.

'Remember,' said Redhorn, 'don't trust these fuckers; they're just sleepers. Sure, as long as they're undercover, they'll smile in your face and kill VC and NVA like avenging angels. But when they get the wake-up call – tonight, next month, five years from now – Dieu and his fucking friends are going to booby trap our ammunition bunkers, sabotage our radio transmitters and frag us while we're still asleep. We know that one day, they're going to kill us – so we have to kill them first.'

ONE WEEK LATER the mountain mist wrapped itself around the camp like a shroud. The Vietnamese whispered that the mist was the icy breath of the unburied dead. They all believed in ghosts. Lopez took over the duty watch at two in the morning, when the mist was at its worst. Dusty Storm, the NCO who had the previous watch, was still decoding a message when Lopez arrived in the com bunker. Dusty's name was an alias: Storm was a Russian who joined the American army as a shortcut to getting US nationality. There were a lot of people like him in Special Forces – Hungarians, Cubans, Poles, East Germans, even one officer who claimed to have been a ski instructor in the Waffen SS – the deracinated professional traitors of the Cold War. Travis claimed they all had shifty eyes and a penchant for buggery.

After Dusty had explained to Lopez how to finish the decoding, he got up to go to bed. Lopez noticed he was wearing what appeared to be a Montagnard amulet on a silver chain around his neck: it looked like half of a dried peach. He asked Dusty what it was. 'Just a little souvenir,' he grinned. 'Something I picked up at Dak To.'

Lopez took it in his hand and examined it more closely. 'This is a human ear.'

'That's right, sir. It is neither metaphor nor symbol, but the thing itself. One needs a third ear. The medic at Pleiku had a gallon jar full of them, pickled in formaldehyde.'

Before he could say anything else, Dusty unclasped the ear from the chain and tossed it to Lopez. 'I can tell, sir, that you don't approve. Keep it.'

After Dusty had gone to bed Lopez studied the ear more closely: it really did look like a dried peach and even had the same texture. He didn't know what to do with it, so he put it in his pocket.

Lopez finished decoding the message: it gave the grid co-ordinates and dates of a Program Phoenix operation. Phoenix was a secret unit who dressed up in Viet Cong uniforms and traveled around the countryside executing enemies of the Saigon regime. The fake VC uniforms didn't fool anyone; they were a device to wipe US fingerprints off the murder weapons. There were other covert units wearing skull and crossbones insignia waging private wars in places that weren't even on the map. There didn't appear to be anyone in control. Lopez had heard that Phoenix reported directly to the White House. At least they reported to someone.

The Vietnamese commanding officer, Dai Uy Ky, came in and asked Lopez to accompany him on an inspection tour of the camp perimeter. The Dai Uy was in his mid-forties and wore a neat moustache and a blue silk cravat. All his uniforms were splendidly cut and tailored.

Redhorn claimed that Ky was a coward and a crook, even though the Dai Uy had been wounded three times. He was certainly a crook; he had to be. His expenses far exceeded his derisory pay as a Vietnamese captain – there were a wife, two teenage daughters, a widowed father and parents-in-law to look after. Ky's main problem was the landlord who kept raising the rent of his Saigon villa. Whenever he complained the landlord shrugged his shoulders and said, 'I can get twice your rent from an American.' And the daughters were expensive too, requiring silk ao dais and mopeds as well as the lycée fees.

All the CIDG had to pay a percentage of their own paltry salaries to Ky. Dai Uy Ky in turn had to pay a percentage to his commanding officer and so on. The most macabre thing about Ky's business was the phantom soldiers: when CIDG were killed, their names were kept on the camp roll and their pay was collected, via an impersonator, by Dai Uy Ky. There was already an entire platoon of ghosts.

It took half an hour to inspect the defenses. There was a raised sentry post every twenty meters. Ky spoke French to Lopez and complained about his financial problems. 'For Vietnamese people,' he said, 'it is necessary to provide dowries for one's daughters. In America, you do not have this custom?'

'No.'

'And yet your country is so rich. But still no dowries. Doesn't that strike you as being rather odd?' Before Lopez could answer, Dai Uy Ky halted and put his hand on his arm. 'Shhh.'

Lopez strained to listen to the night: the sound of measured breathing and snoring was coming from the direction of the next sentry post. He watched Ky tiptoe to the post. The guard's rifle was draped across his knees; his chin was resting on his chest. The Dai Uy reached up, grasped the muzzle of the rifle with both hands and wrenched it from the sleeping soldier's grip. The sentry woke with a start. His first reaction was to hang on to his rifle, but he lost his balance and landed at Dai Uy Ky's feet. Ky kicked the rifle out of reach, and then began to kick the soldier. The kicks landed without discrimination, but tended to favor the guard's face and thighs. The soldier took the beating in silence. After an *espèce de con* and an *espèce de cretin*, the only sound in the balmy night was the thump of boot against flesh. When Ky had finished, he told the soldier to report to the LLDB Sergeant-major in the morning.

'I apologize for that little unpleasantness, Trung Uy. I hope you do not think that I am a brutal man.'

Lopez didn't say anything.

'The French,' Dai Uy Ky went on a little coolly, 'would have had him shot, but that's another story.'

By the time they got back Lopez's watch replacement was waiting to take over. Lopez briefed him and went back to bed. As he undressed he found the ear in his pocket. He put it on his desk and decided to begin a letter to Rosie and Tom before turning in. Lopez found himself staring at the ear and wondering about the human head it had been sliced from and what thoughts had gone through that head in its last hours. The ear seemed to rehydrate like a dried mushroom left to soak. And then there was a pair of eyes – not human ones, but rat's eyes – that were watching from the shadows. The eyes were furtive and looking at him from the edge of the desk, as if calculating and measuring distances. When it happened the movement, if there was a movement, was so unexpected and swift that Lopez wouldn't have been able to stop it in any case. Perhaps it happened while he blinked, but both rat and ear were gone.

IT WAS ONE OF THOSE HOT LATE JULY AFTERNOONS when everything is quiet and still, as if stunned by the too-brightness of the sun. It was a perfect dry clear heat – so rare for a Chesapeake Bay summer. Tom was snoring on the porch, and everyone except them seemed asleep. They put a halter on Rosie's mare and took her down to the river. Ianthe rode her into the water while he backstroked over to the point. When the mare was out of her depth she began to snort like a sea monster, head arched back, teeth bared, nostrils flared, looking ferocious and dangerous. Ianthe clung to her neck, looking like a Rhinemaiden in a rainbow of spray. The mare was so close behind that Lopez could feel her breath hot and sticky on the soles of his feet. When they reached the firm sand of the shallows, the horse emerged dripping and tossing her head like a mythical beast from a lost Atlantis.

Lopez led the way into the beech wood where he'd built dens as a child and sometimes spent the night. It was always cool there. He looked behind and saw horse and maiden dappled with leaf shade and sunlight. 'Jump down,' he said. 'I'll catch you.' Ianthe swung her leg over the horse's head so that she was seated sideways on the animal's broad back. The river, brilliant with the midday sun, shone through the curtain of her damp hair and dazzled her eyes. Beads of water wreathed everything with rainbows. Ianthe balanced on the horse like a circus acrobat, her arms extended and palpating the air like wings. She felt the horse paw the ground and shudder beneath her bare thighs.

He was a barefoot apparition, sleek and dark in the shadow. 'Jump,' he said again. 'Trust me. I'll catch you.' His arms were open and his body flexed to receive her weight. She closed her eyes and let herself go, the horse's flank wet and glossy beneath her, like sliding down mossy rock in a waterfall.

She hurt him. Her forehead banged hard against his lower lip and split it open. He was bruised and dripping blood, but was only aware of her breasts, compact and hard as apples pressing against his naked chest, and their wet thighs touching. They were the same height and their bodies molded into each other. He felt her nipples turn rigid against the wet cotton of her blouse. For what seemed a long time they didn't do anything: they just stood there holding each other and listening to the other's breathing. Finally, she felt the blood dripping on her neck. 'Your mouth,' she said, 'is bleeding.' He held her closer and could feel her heart pounding. She began to kiss the blood away and then he felt her tongue against his tongue and the salty urgency of all that blood. They then pulled away from each other, ashamed at what they had felt, and never mentioned it. It began with blood – and ended with blood.

Lopez forced his brain back to Vietnam.

He lay on his bunk, fantasizing about showing her around Nui Hoa Den. 'This is where I live now. Do you like it?' He imagined her in her grown-up prissy mood. She would be wearing her white party dress, the one with the flounces and ribbons. He could see her twitching her nose at the latrines as he conducted her around the trenches, making a face as she bent over to rub a spot of mud off her stocking. How she would hate it – and how she would hate him for being here.

THE FUNNY THING ABOUT KILLING A MAN, the odd thing, the thing that really frightened Lopez, was that he hadn't felt anything. Just emptiness. At first he thought that there must be a delayed reaction, that the horror would eventually hit him. But it never did.

It was a typical patrol: a company of a hundred CIDG accompanied by two Americans. Their job was to do a reconnaissance in force in the mountains to the northwest of the camp. It was the same area where Redhorn won his second Bronze Star the previous May. He had managed to lure an NVA battalion into attacking his company: the North Vietnamese were then slaughtered by pre-arranged air strikes. Redhorn said it reminded him of Christmas because the surviving trees had been decorated with bodies and body parts tossed high into the branches by the 500-pound bombs. In the end about four hundred NVA were killed: Redhorn lost only one CIDG dead and six wounded.

Lopez had lain awake the night before the patrol worrying – not least about being unable to sleep. There were plenty of horror stories. Often the only people who failed to come back from a patrol were the two Americans. There were rumors that disaffected CIDG used the remote rain forests to assassinate Americans they didn't like – and there were lots of reasons not to like them. And there was the enemy to cope with too. Lopez was scared – scared to nearly-vomiting sick. His vivid imagination and a clinical appreciation of what happened when bullets and shell fragments hit human bodies made his fear intense. He threw aside his sheet and picked up a torch. He shone it on his feet, ankles and legs: for the first time he realized the beauty of the veins which crossed his instep and the complex of fine bone and tendon beneath. What would an AK-47 bullet or a landmine do to them? Or his spine or his eyes or his penis and testicles? All of him felt so soft and delicate and infinitely vulnerable. Lopez knew, in perfect honesty, that he only cared about what happened to his own body. If a leg or arm must decorate a tree, he wanted it to be someone else's.

The patrol was just a sweaty hike in the hills until the afternoon of the second day. They had halted for a break near the top of a mountain ridge. Suddenly, a small black dog jumped out of the undergrowth and started barking at them. Lopez was perplexed; small yappy black dogs weren't mentioned in the training manuals, and he didn't know what to do. Meanwhile, Dusty reached out towards the dog and said, 'Here, boy.' He started flicking his neckerchief at the pooch, like it was a game. The dog sunk his teeth into the cloth and Dusty drew him closer. The pup thought he was playing; a second later the little dog was impaled on Dusty's commando knife. Lopez thought it was a bad omen.

They continued over the ridgeline and down into the far valley, following a trail, but one that was overgrown and hadn't been used for some time. When Lopez heard the explosion, his first thought was that it must be a stray artillery round from an American battery – that was what he wanted to believe. They crouched and waited. It was half a minute before word was passed back that the front of the column had been ambushed by a Claymore mine. Lopez turned to Dusty and said, 'You shouldn't have killed that dog.' He knew it was stupid thing to say, an irrational reaction, like Jackie Kennedy trying to put pieces of Jack's brain back in his skull.

Dusty only said, 'We better go take a look.' They brushed their way past the Vietnamese to the point of the column. One soldier was squatting beside the trail with his trousers down having a shit. He was smiling with embarrassment. The other faces were taut and drawn, the trail was muddy and the vegetation damp and sticky. Lopez's heart was pounding with fear at what he was going to have to see.

One of the CIDG was dead; he was lying in a tangle of undergrowth and slender green tree branches which had been torn off by the force of the explosion. His eyes were open, his face was flecked with damp earth and his head lay loose on his shoulders as if his neck had gone slack. Lopez didn't notice any wounds other than holes in his face the size of small coins. There was another casualty behind him, still living, but with serious head wounds.

Lopez radioed a request for a medevac helicopter to evacuate the casualties while Dusty got the Vietnamese to make litters. The Forward Air Controller directed them to a bomb crater from where the casualties could be winched out. The most obvious places to land a medevac were booby trapped and targeted by anti-aircraft guns.

They left the trail and crashed through thick foliage, half dragging, half carrying the casualties in ponchos slung beneath long staves cut from young saplings. When they slid out of the undergrowth down into the yellow mud of the bomb crater, Dusty suddenly dropped the end of the stave he was carrying and said, 'What am I carrying this dead fuck for?' Lopez watched the dead Vietnamese roll out of the poncho into the mud, his eyes still open and staring.

Within minutes the medevac helicopter was hovering over the crater. Lopez could see the gunners staring intently into the jungle. At the end of the winch cable was a bullet-shaped device which unfolded into a seat, but it was jammed, so the wounded man had to be lashed awkwardly to the cable; he spun like a top as they winched him up. They did an even worse job with the dead man; he was winched up upside down with his head loose and gyrating.

The patrol left the crater and pushed uphill through thick undergrowth. After about fifty meters the column halted again. The lead element had stumbled on a North Vietnamese supply cache. Dusty and Lopez went forward to have a look. They found four raised bamboo platforms covered with rusty pieces of corrugated metal. The cache contained a number of large cone-shaped explosive charges intended for cratering roads. There were also boxes of blasting caps, hand grenades and spare parts for rifles. The cone-shaped explosives were too heavy and awkward to carry, so they decided to booby trap them instead. While Dusty was concealing hand grenades and rigging the supply cache with trip wires and other tricks, Lopez organized a perimeter defense in case the supply cache people came back too soon.

Lopez placed himself on a small trail leading up from the cache. The CIDG were posted at intervals in the undergrowth on either side. He had never experienced such absolute, such utter quiet. It was as if the world had stopped spinning. He went down on one knee, like genuflecting in church, and stared down the path which seemed to both disappear and not disappear. It was like looking into a black hole, a bottomless pit, down to a meaningless black vacuum of nothingness forever and ever. He felt a deep nausea, complete estrangement; he couldn't even recognize the backs of his own hands. It wasn't the natural fear of pain or danger or being maimed, but the vertigo of confronting utter nothingness. Death is for eternity. Lopez looked at the CIDG on his left, who had his hand down the back of his shirt, trying to crush an insect that was biting him. Suddenly, for Lopez, even the fear of dying no longer made sense – there was only a black emptiness that seemed to spiral out forever beyond the furthest stars.

Lopez saw something move on the trail. A man, dressed in stained khaki appeared. He looked about forty, perhaps older; his face was like wrinkled yellow parchment. He seemed completely unaware of the presence of an enemy, his rifle slung over his shoulder. He was smoking a cheroot. Despite the close range, Lopez's first shot missed. A look, not so much of fear, but of sheer astonishment, crossed the man's face. Lopez aimed again, breathed, and squeezed the trigger. His second shot hit the man in the stomach and he crumpled, making a sharp coughing sound as the bullet hit him as if trying to expel his spirit out of the hole. Then the CIDG on either side of the trail opened fire and for a while the body jigged up and down on the trail.

The shooting stopped. Lopez looked at the crumpled body. *Is that all? Is that all there is to it?* He looked at the CIDG on his left, surrounded by spent cartridge cases. The Vietnamese smiled at Lopez and reloaded his rifle. Before the soldier got up, he finally succeeded in fishing the troublesome insect out of his shirt, and crushed it between his fingernails.

Then it was time to move out.

Redhorn was drunk every night, and most days. As he became more drunk, his accent became more southern and more redneck. Lopez knew it was all an act. Redhorn came from a well off and educated background – his father was a doctor and his mother smoked little cigars and taught Latin and Greek at Sweetbriar Women's College. At first, Lopez wondered if Redhorn's being crazy was all an act too. He soon realized it wasn't.

The Group Medical Officer used to brag to his doctor friends that one in seven Special Forces personnel were clinically psychotic. 'Back home,' he said, 'this would mean a court order to the closed ward at Spring Grove and, if they behave, visitors from two to four on a Sunday afternoon. Here, they're valuable members of society. Psychopaths are extremely useful in a war. None of your Hamlet crap: they just do it.'

Not all the crazies were psychos; some were just war junkies looking for the ultimate mainline adrenaline rush. Unlike them, the psychopaths never got over-excited or turned on by it. They just went about their business coldly and unemotionally, calling in napalm, putting the wounded out of their misery, getting information out of prisoners, getting rid of prisoners, putting their colleagues in body bags – never traumatized, never depressed. They were in their element.

The psychopaths never wore necklaces of tanned human ears for they had no need to strike poses or show off. They were utterly self-contained. Their faces never betrayed emotion, except for impish half-smiles of satisfaction that never left their lips. Nor did they ever throw tantrums under stress and shout abuse at incompetent or cowardly comrades – they simply pulled the trigger. And best of all, though they had no physical fear, their names seldom appeared on casualty lists. Their antennae were always on the highest level of alert; their instinct for survival was almost psychic. Of course, they couldn't be trusted – the compulsive low cunning was always there, quietly evident in every act and word.

The first night that the generator conked out, Redhorn called Lopez into his cubicle for a drink. They started another bottle of bourbon just after midnight. Because there was no electricity they had to light candles. The atmosphere was more like Verdun in 1916 than Vietnam in 1967. Lopez thought that Redhorn, lying on his bunk, looked like an effigy of a knight recumbent on a medieval tomb, his profile grotesque as a gargoyle in the sputtering candlelight. Outside there was a terrific thunderstorm, louder even than the 175mm artillery from the marine base at An Hoa that was impacting on a nearby ridge. The senseless shelling of empty jungle loosened soil from the ceiling of the bunker and sprinkled them with earth, like next of kin at the edge of a grave.

The nonsense of the artillery got Redhorn going about the marines. 'Useless cunts,' he said. 'Look how they're fucking up at Khe Sanh. They *deserve* to be overrun.'

Lopez just nodded.

'Marines fuck everything up. When I was with the 8th in

Guatemala we had a liaison officer from the embassy – he was supposed to keep an eye on us. He was a Marine Corps major, good-looking guy who spoke fluent Spanish. He didn't turn up for a briefing one morning so they sent me to wake him. He was lying on the floor next to his bunk, dead meat, with a plastic bag over his head and a piece of washing line knotted around his neck. I rolled him over. At least he came before he died; there was spunk splattered all over a horny photo in his porn mag. I guess it was his favorite jerk-off picture: there was this Hispanic-looking girl simultaneously sucking off a soul brother and a white dude. The white guy still had his socks on – funny how you remember details like that – and the girl had a face full of semen, not just from the guys in the photo, but from the major too. It all had a certain symmetry, like a work of art.'

'Strange way to commit suicide.'

'Don't you know anything, Lopez? It wasn't suicide. It's called auto-erotic asphyxiation; it happens quite often to these who want to intensify their manual relief sessions.' Redhorn poured Lopez more bourbon. 'He should have used a slip knot. Marines are stupid. How can you send these guys to a place like Khe Sanh? They can't even organize a hand job without ending up in a body bag.'

Lopez was sitting in an old threadbare armchair with gilt legs, the kind of chair you'd expect to find in some nineteenth-century French sea captain's parlor in somewhere like Nantes. He wondered how it had found its way to a bunker at Nui Hoa Den. But Vietnam was one of those places where all sorts of junk washed up from all over the world, like lost keys and watches find their way to the dark side of the moon.

Lopez noticed that Redhorn was looking at him in a funny way. 'What is it?'

'Sergeant Storm, allegedly regarded in some circles as a toothsome morsel, tells me that you confiscated an item of personal adornment.'

'Human ears aren't jewelry.'

'Don't be a sanctimonious asshole. If there is a moral issue, it's about killing people in the first place. After they're dead, it doesn't fucking matter whether you eat them, fuck them, or turn them into lampshades.'

Lopez tried to contain his anger. 'Don't call me an asshole.' His voice was quiet and firm. He waited for Redhorn to answer, but for a while the only thing he got back was a blank stare.

'You know, Lopez, I once had a commanding officer who used to think he was a goddam Sunday school teacher. He used to talk about things like duty and honor.' Redhorn suddenly jumped up, grabbed a grenade launcher and slammed a round into the breech. 'Come on, Lopez, where's your fucking honor?' He pointed the grenade launcher in Lopez's face. 'Come on, man, pull honor's trigger and blow me away.'

Lopez finished his bourbon. When he looked at Redhorn again, he could almost see the aura of a Freudian death wish looping around his temples like an evil halo.

Redhorn sat down and disarmed the grenade launcher. 'If you want to play this moral shit, this Waffen-SS-man-with-a-conscience shit, you can get off this fucking hill. This isn't Hollywood, man. This is Viet-fucking-nam.' Redhorn replaced the weapon on its hook and lay back down on his bunk. 'Your problem, Lopez, is that you just don't understand. You just don't fucking understand.'

'What don't I understand?'

'The thing itself. The thing that is in the act itself. The act worships itself. Don't you understand?'

Lopez poured himself more bourbon. 'You're really impressive, Redhorn. You should get a job teaching philosophy at the Sorbonne.'

'You know something?' Redhorn suddenly sounded tired. 'Behind your mild mannered exterior, you're really quite an arrogant little shit, aren't you?'

Lopez fell into an alcohol haze while Redhorn gave him a lecture about how they were witnessing 'the end of the Western Empire', and how 'in a rotten society, that reeks putrefaction like a six-day-old body count, only the warrior is pure.'

After Redhorn had fallen asleep, Lopez left the bunker for some fresh air. He couldn't help thinking about the marine major in Guatemala. The dry season was ending with a vengeance, and the rain came in solid sheets. When the lightning flashed, Lopez could see that the downpour had turned the camp into a mudbath, disintegrating sandbag emplacements, collapsing trenches and letting loose a river of mud that carried barbed wire, mines and trip flares down the sides of the mountain.

It was three o'clock in the morning, but the camp wasn't asleep. There was always a low murmur of Vietnamese voices even during the darkest watches. The CIDG bunkers were faintly lit by oil lamps that cast soft yellow circles of light. The oily smoke that curled from the flames stained the bare earth walls and ceilings yellow brown. There was always gambling in one bunker or other, and the sound of cards and dominoes slapping on the hard earth floors until dawn. Sometimes the patterns of lamplight and shadow made the faces of the Vietnamese look fiendish as they squatted barefoot in tight circles staking what was left of their pay.

Phong was emptying out tea dregs prior to making another brew when he saw the new Trung Uy – the new lieutenant – standing in the rain. He called over to Lopez and gestured for him to come in. Lopez jumped down into the connecting trench and made his way to the bunker. Phong held open the door curtain and found Lopez a seat on an ammunition box while he made the tea.

Lopez liked the semi-domesticated fug of life in the CIDG bunkers, the cooling pots of tea, uneaten bowls of rice, even the dank curtains of washing hanging from a crisscross of clothes lines which made it impossible to walk upright. The air was scented with incense sticks and candles burning in front of pictures of the Buddha, the Blessed Virgin or a strange female deity who looked almost Hindu. Stains of tea dregs and spit discolored the yellow earth floors, and bandoleers of ammunition and weapons lay around everywhere.

Many of the soldiers had created little family shrines on shelves above their beds. These were 'the widower soldiers of Kham Duc' – there were about sixty of them. The shrines usually consisted of a few photographs, a poem written on a commemorative card, a toy, an item of cheap jewelry or an odd trinket inexplicable to all except the widower soldier. The grandest shrines had perforated brass ornaments for holding joss sticks.

Kim was staring at a photograph of his wife with the air of someone locked in a trance or in prayer. Lopez felt embarrassed, as if he were intruding on something. Ho Cuc stopped cleaning his rifle and said, 'No sweat, Trung Uy, don't worry. He does that every night: sometimes fifteen, twenty minutes, sometimes an hour. You wait, he won't be long now.'

The photograph had been taken when Kim's wife was seventeen. It was a formal studio portrait, contrived to be flattering and sentimental: the silk texture of the skin, the eyes like a sad young doe. But it was unnecessary, for the woman had been a natural beauty. There was a second photograph: his wife – a few years older – was holding their daughter, a girl of two, and the eldest son. There was no photograph of the youngest; the baby had only been seven weeks old.

After he had finished his meditation Kim noticed Lopez looking at his family photographs. It was polite for the Vietnamese to talk about their dead: they were still part of the family, just like the babies still to be conceived and born. Kim told Lopez the story in a voice that was calm and distant.

The accident happened when Kham Duc was being 'closed down'. It proved an impossible position to hold. Soon after the final siege began, it was decided to abandon the camp. A large C-130 cargo plane had been sent to bring the soldiers' wives and children out first. Lopez knew all about the evacuation of Kham Duc: it was part of the 5th Group's oral history. The operation was completely fucked up.

At the last moment there was a big argument on the airstrip between the camp commander, who wanted to get rid of the civilians because they were getting in the way, and the pilot, who thought his plane was already overloaded. The camp commander won the argument by sticking his .45 in the pilot's face. A lot of SF people sympathized: the aircraft in Vietnam always flew overloaded anyway – so why did the pilot go all regulation-strict at a time like that?

Kim and his family waited, while the propellers of the C-130 created a cloud of whipped sand that penetrated everything. Kim was concerned about the baby's eyes and held him tight against his chest with one hand gently covering his precious head. The baby had taken a fold of Kim's cotton field blouse into his mouth and was sucking it. The mistake made him laugh. 'I think he wants you,' he said, handing the baby to his wife. The crew chief finally gave in and signaled that there was enough room after all. Kim's wife and three children were among the last pushed into the packed aircraft. The hydraulics wheezed, the boarding ramp began to rise and the two-year-old clinging to his mother's leg disappeared from view. The last picture Mr Kim had of his family was that of his wife undoing her blouse and curling their hungry infant to her breast. Then the loading ramp shut.

The aircraft had just left the ground when it shuddered, turned its nose downwards and crashed just beyond the end of the runway. Kim and the others watched, stunned and uncomprehending, as everything that was precious to them was consumed in a fireball.

THE RAIN MOVED SOUTH and the dry season made a last-ditch attempt to reassert itself. The midday heat seared the soul; the sun burned away all coherence and purpose. Lopez watched some of the team fall into alcoholic lethargy as others turned to frenzied activity. Mendy took out his anger on a punching bag. Jackson sweated out his frustration repairing trenches and filling sandbags. The outpost smelled of sexual frustration, anger and boredom. The Americans became aggressive and bad tempered, the Vietnamese sardonic and increasingly furtive. Relations between the two were not good. Clark, the team sergeant, had to be sent back to Da Nang for accusing Dai Uy Ky of being 'a corrupt liar and cheat'. It was acceptable to shout these things behind their backs, so long as the Vietnamese could save face by maintaining the polite fiction that they didn't hear or understand. But Clark had crossed the line of no return by accusing the Dai Uy directly and in surprisingly fluent Vietnamese. Ky's letter followed the usual terse formula: 'Dear Captain Redhorn, I can no longer guarantee Sergeant Clark's safety at this location. Yours, etc.'

Carson, the team's next senior NCO, took over as team sergeant. He was in his mid-forties, but looked much older. At first, Lopez had found Carson difficult. The sergeant's behavior was surly, sarcastic and verged on disrespect. When Lopez complained about his attitude, Redhorn turned on the lieutenant. 'Listen up, Lopez, I know you didn't meet many Carsons at Harvard. But when the sewer backs up, the power lines are down or you're too ill to wipe your own ass – it's the Carsons of the world you call out. And, since they're dumb enough to do that for people who despise them, they're also dumb enough to obey orders – no matter how crazy. The Carsons moan and complain and don't like doing it, but at the end of the day they'll die for you. And, Lopez, that guy has a story to tell. You should listen; you might learn something.'

And eventually, during a long night in an airless bunker, Lopez heard Carson's story.

The sergeant came from an America that Lopez, before he joined the army, had only glimpsed through car or train windows. Carson enlisted in the army in 1943 as a seventeen-year-old from one of those places in Georgia where the dry hard clay nurtures only slash pine, scrub oak and dry hard people. The military was the only adult life that Carson had ever known. When he went home he always told his friends that the army was 'a shit job,' but paid better than the sawmill or sharecropping, and 'you didn't have to work so hard.' The problem was, according to Carson, that 'every time they send you to a foreign war it always ends up a fucking disaster.' He'd been captured twice: first by the Germans in Italy, and seven years later in Korea when the Chinese Army overran his unit.

Carson's first war ended in the olive groves of Italy. He was captured at Anzio in 1944 after his unit had been cut off and decimated. A week later, he was herded into a cattle truck and sent to a POW camp on the outskirts of Dresden. The following February, after the fire bombing, there wasn't sufficient manpower to bury and burn the dead; foreign workers and POWs were brought into the city to help. Carson remembered how the Wehrmacht had executed their fellow Germans for looting and tied signs to their bodies labeling them *Plünderer* – looter. He remembered the humiliation of marching past these corpses while the survivors of the fire bombing shouted abuse and spat at the Americans. They assumed that it must have been the Americans – not the civilized European British – who had carried out the bombing raids. But what Carson remembered most of all was the smell. The Germans had given the POWs large quantities of schnapps to blunt what was left of their human sensibilities, but it didn't work. In some cellars there was only a slimy green-yellow substance. Carson wrapped a cloth permeated with eucalyptus oil around his nose and mouth before he descended into a cellar with a rope and hook. As soon as the wave of stench hit him, he ran back to the surface and vomited up the schnapps and the morning's cabbage soup. In the end, the army was called in, with flame-throwers.

After the war Carson got married and tried to earn a living cleaning carpets in his wife's hometown – Raleigh, North Carolina – but it was too poorly paid to support his growing family. He re-enlisted, this time in the Marines, just in time to get sent to Korea. This time the Red Chinese captured him when his company was overrun at the Chosin Reservoir. Most of his colleagues had already been killed, so Carson had tried to hide under a pile of their bodies in a trench, hoping that he would be overlooked. The Chinese dug him out anyway and used him as a propaganda exhibit. They carted him around North Korean villages in a cage as an example of a depraved American. Carson unwittingly played the intended role: he made orangutan noises, dragged his knuckles across the floor of the cage and flung his own excrement at the gawking villagers. After being repatriated, he left the Marines and returned to the army. He reckoned that the army was 'more friendly and easy going.'

It seemed to Lopez that Carson was the only American who got on with his Vietnamese counterpart. The partnership between Carson and Sergeant-major Dieu was like a marriage based on mutual love and respect, while the other counterpart relationships were like blind dates that soon turned to loathing. For Carson, however, there was another factor: Dieu was his friend. They often got drunk together, but never said much. They were like a pair of lovers who had met in late middle age – they didn't need to talk about the past; history was written all over their faces. Carson knew there was a dilemma. He was just as certain as Redhorn that Dieu was an enemy agent. When the time came, Lopez wondered, would Carson betray his country or would he betray his friend? One night, Lopez overheard Carson saying a bedtime prayer: 'Please, Lord; please, sweet Jesus; let this cup pass away from my lips.' He walked away on tiptoe through the dark of the bunker corridor. He didn't want Carson to know that anyone had heard something so revealing, so tender.

Lopez was certain that, for Dieu, there was no such dilemma. Although Carson was the only American he had ever respected – and the only foreigner to whom he had given friendship – when the time came he would have no scruples about killing him too. Vietnam was his country and Carson was the foreign invader: no dilemma at all. And there was no need to explain this to Carson – he knew it already.

The ambush patrol had shot four rice carriers in the middle of the night. When they examined the bodies at first light they found that two of the porters, one of them a young woman, were still alive although shot through the abdomen. Lopez watched Carson's hand grip and ungrip the beer can as he described how Dieu had drawn his pistol to finish the victims off. 'The young woman was real pretty. I remember she had this little wisp of hair across her mouth. And Dieu just shot her: no regret, no mercy, just – just like he was doing her a favor. The way she was shot up anyway, I guess maybe he was.'

Afterwards they carried the dead to Xuan Hoa and left the bodies in the village square for their relatives to collect. 'I didn't like that,' said Carson. 'I know it's a dirty job, but just dumping them like sacks of rubbish . . . I said somethin' to Dieu about it, he said it didn't matter because the dead people had "bad luck" – what's that supposed to mean?'

The thing that annoyed Lopez most about Dieu was his smile – what Redhorn called that 'fucking sardonic smile grinning out of Judas' asshole'. Dieu's smile seemed to say, 'I watched the Japanese come and go, and then the French come back again and go again – and now, you have come, but not for long, for you will soon be going too. If one waits long enough, you all go – one way or another.'

Lopez found the Dead House eerie at night and unnaturally cold, as if icy draughts were rising from subterranean wells. The building, formerly the camp infirmary, was a squat windowless stone structure that proved more suitable as a morgue. The CIDG dead were wrapped in gray blankets and stacked on a long table until the coffin maker finished his task. There was always the sweet smell of incense sticks and the sound of wailing. The night after Ngo Van Linh stepped on a landmine, there was quite a lot wailing. Linh came from a large family: he was the youngest of three brothers, and had a twin sister, Co Lan, who was a camp cook. That afternoon Lan was laughing and joking with Hamchunk, the head cook, as she washed the pots. Then, for no apparent reason, she turned pale and ran for the door. Lopez watched her collapse on the doorstep and vomit up great lumps of green bile – her retching was so violent that he thought her insides were going to rupture. A minute later there was a radio message from the patrol saying that her twin had just been killed by a mine. Afterwards, one of Lan's brothers had to hold her arms to stop her from tearing out huge handfuls of her hair. That evening Linh's mother led the mourning with a keening so loud and piercing that Lopez could hear her in the depths of his bunker.

The keening reminded Lopez that he had to see Mr Kim, Linh's platoon leader, about details he needed to process the death gratuity. Death, even in war, carried documents and paper work in its wake. Lopez pulled on his boots, left his cubicle, went up the stairs and into the dank night torn by lamentation wails. He felt his way around the 81mm mortar pit and found the gap in the inner wire. When he got to Kim's bunker the keening seemed even louder: it was starting to make Lopez feel queasy. He was perhaps too brisk in asking for Linh's next of kin details and dates of service. Kim glanced at the photos of his own family and then said, 'Trung Uy Lopez, khong co' may dua con – Lieutenant Lopez, you don't have any children.'

Lopez didn't say anything, he couldn't say anything. He knew there were worlds, whole galaxies, of pain that he still didn't know – pain that diminished self to less than a pinprick.

That evening Lopez lay naked on his bunk and thought about the mental telepathy that had passed that afternoon between Co Lan and her twin brother. Linh's goodbye message must have shot out of his dying brain like a burning arrow. Lopez wondered if his dying would reach anyone like that. Was all closeness gone or was there still somewhere a mental frequency, an open synapse, that would receive his final message?

Lopez wanted to sleep, but for some reason could only think about Rideout's Landing. It was the river of his childhood that he missed the most. He loved it especially in the still summer evenings after the heat had died down. He always walked barefoot through the mare's paddock down to the jetty – past the chestnut tree and the Douglas fir – feeling the dew cool on his feet. Everything was soft and mellow, even the way the mare would sneak up behind him in the dark and nuzzle his back. It was the only time that he didn't feel an alien, a brown-faced intruder, when he knew that the river belonged to him.

It was on just such an evening that he heard Ianthe's news. Lopez had just come back from his exchange year in France. At dinner he had been on the receiving end of a good deal of Rideout's Landing teasing. Tom insisted on speaking to him in a French full of intentional mistakes and mispronunciations while Rosie stage-whispered to the guests that after his stimulating evenings with Jean-Paul, Simon and André 'he must find us all terribly boorish and unsophisticated.' After supper they went out on to the screened porch to drink and talk. The conversation turned into a terrible argument about Vietnam between Richard-the-diplomat and Michael-the-academic. It was totally dark, except for a weak yellow oval of light from the insecticide candle. The angry voices – disembodied from face and person – were like quarrelsome spirits hovering in the night. After a year in Paris, Lopez found Richard's support of US foreign policy hopelessly naïve, but he didn't get involved because the only thing he could focus on was being alone with Ianthe again. He was bursting with things to tell her, things he could share with no one else. The time he had spent in Paris had made him realize that he could never be as close to anyone as he was to her. His loneliness for her was made worse because all evening she had seemed troubled and detached. While Michael counter-attacked with something about how Dulles had reneged on the Geneva agreement, Lopez slipped out into the night and waited for her to follow him.

Lopez tried to stop remembering, but the past was like a murdered corpse and his brain like a dog that kept digging up the body from wherever he buried it. There was the sound of a rat rustling behind the plywood partition, a static broken radio voice, and a distant rumble of eight-inch artillery impacting in the next valley, but he couldn't stop his memory from hearing those other sounds and other voices: the swish of their legs through the paddock grass, hoofbeats in the dark as the mare spooked and cantered away. They found the mare and whispered to her that it was only they. Ianthe was beside him and he felt the back of her hand brush against his. She placed her hand in his hand beside the musky warmth of the mare's flank. 'Listen,' she said, 'there's something, something about me you ought to know.'

There was something in her voice that made Lopez freeze

and shake all over. Just then Rosie bellowed from the direction of the jetty, 'Hey, what are you two whispering and plotting about?'

They ignored her. Lopez gripped her hand and noticed how damp it was. 'Tell me,' he whispered.

'I think I might be pregnant.'

The words hit him like a sledgehammer blow between the eyes. He couldn't deal with change, not this sort of change.

Rosie was bellowing again: she had decided that Michael and Richard required a midnight sail to cool them off. 'I think,' she shouted, 'we have to go with them.'

So they cast off *Stormy Petrel* without using the motor and tacked down the St. Michael's River. Lopez and Ianthe were too closely huddled with the others to talk. He found the pain almost physical: his body was vibrating and his brain was burning. As soon as they left the shelter of the river the breeze from the bay made the boat heel and the water purr and gurgle along the hull. Lopez could feel the bump of each wave travel up his spine and explode against his brain. All his senses were humming with a sort of hysterical alertness. They sailed close-hauled to the first bell buoy. In the distance were the running lights of a tug towing an obsolete ship to the breaker's yard.

Later that night Lopez crept into her bedroom. 'Shhh,' she said. 'Rosie's still up.'

He got under the covers, but was careful not to touch her. Amid all the hurt, there was something absurd and comic. Lopez had thrown on a garish silk dressing gown that Tom's brother Harold had picked up on China Station in the twenties. The silk and the secrecy made him feel like a character in a pre-war bedroom farce. 'What really happened?' Lopez was desperately hoping that she was going to say it was only a tease. He waited. Nothing. 'Was it Angel?' he said.

She nodded and told him the story, so coolly and so

factually that she might have been describing a science experiment. For some reason, the fact that she had chosen someone of his own race made him even more sick inside. It was like there was some stupid sub-conscious thing, something that just made it all so complicated. Lopez was deranged by the idea that it was Angel, an over-dressed spoiled rich brat. The thought of that tailor's dummy driving his Mustang convertible back to his daddy's embassy and smirking under his pencil-thin pimp's moustache made Lopez want to kill. The image of Ianthe, her legs sprawled in the back seat, and Angel with his Brylcreemed hair shining like wet coal and his teeth bared in triumph, made him want to vomit.

When she had finished telling Lopez, she put her arms around him. 'What should I do?'

'You could marry Angel.'

Ianthe gently swatted Lopez on the back of the head. 'Don't be stupid.'

'There are only two choices: you either have the baby or you kill it.'

'Abortion's wrong.'

'So is letting a total scumbag put his sperm inside you.'

'I don't like it when you're crude. It doesn't suit you.'

'Yeah, I know, you told me that before – like a million times.'

'What's wrong, Francis? Are you crying?'

'No, I'm not.'

'Yes, you are. I can feel your tears on my cheek.'

'Ianthe, Ianthe. How could you?'

'I don't know, things just happen. What should I do?'

'I can't tell you. It has to be your decision.'

'Please, Francis, tell me.'

'No.'

'You still a Catholic?'

'No. I don't believe any of that nonsense. You know that; we used to argue about it all the time.'

'Will you help me get an abortion?'

Lopez turned away and buried his head.

'Please, Francis. Please.'

'Are you sure you want to do this?'

'Yes.'

'Promise you won't blame me afterwards?'

'I promise.'

'I couldn't stand to lose you; I couldn't live with you hating me.'

'Don't be silly, Francis. I'll always love you.'

'OK, I'll help you. I'll find someone.'

Ianthe curled up like, Lopez thought, the tiny fetus inside her and asked him to hold her. 'You haven't been so perfect yourself, you know.'

Lopez didn't say anything. She knew about how he went wild during his last year at school: the parties he used to go to in East Baltimore, the drunken brawls, the trouble with the police, and that Mary-Louise he'd taken to Ocean City. He had no right to condemn Ianthe.

The bunker was silent except for the sound of breathing in the next cubicle. Rat's feet ... quick scurry ... Must be sniffing, must have found the bait ... Then the loud crack of spring-coiled metal smacking down on flesh, bone and wood.

LOPEZ LOVED OTHER WOMEN TOO. Like the woman who hadn't seemed to realize that her hands couldn't stop bullets. Her first reaction had been to close her eyes and to raise her hands to fend off the rifle fire. She was struck in the left wrist by an M16 bullet which shattered that fragile complex of bones and left a gaping hole as an exit wound. One of the men escaped into the jungle, but the other two were shot down before they had a chance to surrender or defend themselves. They had been shot in the guts and lay moaning. They were local force Viet Cong who had been eating their midday meal at a supply cache encampment when the CIDG point element surprised them.

Later, as the CIDG carefully searched the cache, Dusty Storm heard the faint sound of soft breathing coming from beneath an oilcloth tarpaulin. Lopez watched as Dusty carefully lifted an edge with his rifle and said, 'Chao, Co Dep – Hello, Miss Pretty'. A young girl of about seven or eight was hiding beneath. As the child came out from hiding, Dusty wasn't able to stop her from seeing what had happened to her parents. He knelt down to comfort her and to wipe her tears away – but there weren't any tears. The little girl's eyes were nothing but black empty pools dilated by terror. It made Lopez afraid and queasy all over. This child had just been catapulted out of the normal world of children's tears to a burning planet where tears were banal understatement. Dusty hugged her, but there was no response, just dull, paralytic shock. Lopez remembered a war widow at Fort Benning who had an autistic son: that boy's fishlike unresponsiveness frightened him so much he had had to leave the house. 'Please, not her too,' he prayed. Dusty knelt down, placed his face close to the little girl's and took her by the hand. 'Chao, em,' he said – Hello, little sister. Dusty stared into her eyes, straining to make contact. Lopez watched a tear form and then saw her tiny hand clutch Dusty's fingers.

'Chao, anh – Hello, older brother,' she whispered.

As they made their way back to Nui Hoa Den, Dusty gave Co Dep a piggyback. The wounded men were carried in ponchos slung from stout bamboo poles. After they had walked a little less than a mile, two shots rang out. No one said a thing; it was as if nothing had happened. Twenty minutes later, when they stopped for a break, Lopez turned to his counterpart Trung Uy Tho and asked, 'How are the prisoners, Trung Uy?'

'I think, Trung Uy Lopez, they maybe drink too much water.' This was Tho's idea of a joke: there was a

Vietnamese proverb that drinking too much water brought bad luck, as well as cholera and dysentery.

'Or maybe,' said Dusty, using Vietnamese slang, 'they've been eating too much bronze candy.'

Later that afternoon, back at the camp, Lopez watched Co Dep's mother being interrogated. She looked forty, but was probably thirty. Her hair wasn't silken and shiny, but hard and wiry like steel wool; her skin wasn't soft and smooth, but cracked and brown from living rough. She wasn't pretty, but Lopez thought she was beautiful. She was wearing loose black trousers and a simple white blouse stained with blood. Lopez couldn't see her eyes because, like all prisoners, she was blindfolded. But he knew that she was more than beautiful; she was magnificent.

A Vietnamese medic cleaned her wound while Trung Uy Tho fired questions at her. Lopez looked at the wound and saw that all the bones in the wrist had been pulverized; her hand was attached to her arm only by ligaments and tendons. She showed no pain and seemed oblivious of the medic's attentions, as if the shattered wrist belonged to someone else.

'What does your husband do?' barked Tho. It was the fifth time he had repeated the question.

Finally she answered, but in a voice so low that no one could make out the words.

'Speak up,' said Tho.

'I said that my husband does nothing.'

'How can he do nothing? Tell the truth: is he a cadre, a guerilla? What does he do?'

'He does nothing.'

Tho sighed and made a face.

'He does nothing,' her voice was quiet, calm and sounded as if it were coming from far away. 'He does nothing because you have just killed him.'

Lopez wondered what it would be like to be Vietnamese.

He remembered a Jacques Brel song where a drunk staggers around in the early hours from nightclub to nightclub telling people *J'ai mal d'être moi*. It must be better to be a Vietnamese, he thought, because 'I'm sick of being me'.

He knew that in the morning Co Dep's mother would be gone, presumably to a Saigon government POW camp. They never inquired too closely about what happened in those camps. It was better not to know about the head-in-mud trick, the face-in-the-water trick, skinning, rack, orifice penetration, beatings various – or the electrodes attached to a man's genitals or a woman's vagina and breast. Lopez knew that, whatever happened, Co Dep would never see her mother again.

A week later, Dusty and Ly found a family in Nui Hoa village who offered to adopt her, a kind family who were involved with the local coal-mine. The mine, esteemed by both sides as a future natural resource, was respected as 'neutral ground'. So at least she would be safe. Lopez wondered why the girl was so warm and friendly. They had killed her father – probably her mother too – but the girl still smiled at their murderers. She should, thought Lopez, have hated them all, but instead she just wanted to be a little girl who was loved. Maybe, he thought, love was instinctual, but hate was learned. And maybe it was a good thing we did learn it.

The 5th Group commander escorted the American congressman, a fiscal conservative from the Midwest. The congressman was dressed in a safari suit, but donned a flak jacket and helmet so his photographer could take some pictures. Redhorn and Lopez gave briefings on the local situation and then the colonel gave a talk about the wider implications – the financial and political sides. He pointed out that Nui Hoa Den and the CIDG program were part of a process known as 'Vietnamization'. The congressman nodded approval: Americans in body bags were not vote winners, but Vietnamese stacked up in the Dead House didn't matter. The colonel went on to explain that the soldiers at Nui Hoa Den were part of a border screening force called the Biet Kich Quan, which translated as Special Commando Force. The congressman stopped him and said he was confused. He couldn't understand why the program was more widely known as the CIDG, the Civilian Irregular Defense Group. The colonel smiled and said, 'I suppose something got lost in that particular translation.' He didn't say that it had been a PR psy-op con-trick to fool people into thinking the CIDG was a peasant militia who had risen up spontaneously to drive the Communists out of their villages with light caliber weapons, pitchforks and hoes.

But the important thing – a point which the colonel emphasized by tugging on the sleeve of the congressman's safari jacket – was that CIDG soldiers were cheap, dirt cheap. It was the program's most important selling point. Whereas it cost thirty-five dollars a day to keep a US soldier in the field, a CIDG soldier could be flung against the enemy for a mere three dollars and fifty cents. His actual pay amounted to a small fraction of that – about thirty cents.

The congressman was satisfied. As far as Nui Hoa Den was concerned the American taxpayer had nothing to complain about. He was impressed that the CIDG cost even less than the chain gang he hired from the penitentiary to fill in the potholes in the lane to his farm.

On the other side of the camp Lopez saw Dusty Storm togged up in battle gear and posing for a British photographer who had arrived on the same flight as the congressman's entourage. 'What an asshole,' he thought. The Brit had hit it off well with Redhorn, even though Redhorn insisted on talking to him in a camp English accent. The guy was nothing like Lopez's idea of the English – smooth, debonair snakes in pinstripe suits riding around in black

London cabs in the rain. He had known an Englishman in Paris, seedy, drunken, a chronic victim of his sexuality who – despite his decay – had a voice as refined and clear as a Steinway grand. Later, Lopez found himself talking to the photographer.

'That Dusty Storm,' the man said. 'He seems like an interesting character – what's the story on him?' Lopez knew – they all knew – but he didn't feel like telling this British tourist any of it.

Dusty Storm had been born Pavel Kirillov, but changed his name when he enlisted in the American army. Part of him was ashamed of being Russian: he adored the Germans. He tried to impress Lopez by quoting Nietzsche and claiming that his mother was an ethnic German. He actually *succeeded* in impressing him by quoting from T. S. Eliot's 'The Waste Land', a poem Lopez loved. '"Bin gar keine Russin, stamm' aus Litauen, echt deutsch." That's me – not Russian but Lithuanian, a good German!' He bleached his dark hair Aryan blond to try to prove the point, but wore it far too long for a Prussian regiment. In fact, the long peroxide hair made Dusty look almost American, in a Californian-surfer sort of way. But his most striking feature was the enormous rose tattoo that he wore on his chest.

Dusty claimed to have been born in Moscow in 1940. His father disappeared in the war and his mother took on a drunken lover who used to beat her up. She got tired of the beatings and managed to get the necessary travel documents to visit her sister who was a translator in East Berlin. The visit was, of course, only a pretext to emigrate to the West. Dusty and his mother lived in the West Berlin refugee reception center for almost a year. The mother worked as a cleaner in a hospital, while Dusty played truant and became fluent in the argot of the Berlin underworld. He was a delinquent child who preferred the streets to the refugee center.

At first, Dusty picked pockets and played American pool during the day. At night he slept in the U-bahn – he found that the best places were on the hot air vents, but 'sometimes you had to beat up a tramp to get one.' By the age of fourteen Dusty had discovered how easy it was to make good money on the Ku'damm and around the Hauptbahnhof. There were always wealthy clients cruising the precincts in their Mercedes, a lot of ex-Nazi officers among them. Sometimes Dusty would beat them up and rob them, especially if they had lost an arm or a leg and couldn't fight back.

Once he beat up a client who was a black market racketeer and stole his Mercedes. The racketeer was a small plump man who wore thick spectacles and liked 'rough trade'. Dusty thought that he gave the guy what he really wanted – punishment, penitence. Dusty said that pummeling that soft pink face with fist and boot was a completely moral act: it was as if he was carrying out God's will, like a modern flagellum Dei. Throughout his perverted atonement beating the dealer kept pleading: 'Don't break my glasses; please don't break them – take everything, but don't break my glasses.' When he had finished, Dusty snapped the spectacle frames in two, and then stomped the thick concave lens to dust. Redhorn loved the story. 'People like Dusty Storm,' he said, 'enrich all our lives.'

Dusty found that the Mercedes' trunk was packed with medieval icons: virgins, saints, smiling infant Jesuses, sad-looking Jesuses hanging on crosses. The haul represented a small but irreplaceable portion of Poland's national heritage. In addition to the icons, there was a Renaissance oil painting of the Last Supper. Dusty had an uncanny feeling that he had seen the painting before, or something very like it. It proved to be the work of an itinerant drunk who roamed all over Poland doing holy paintings on commission for wealthy merchants. The artist was simply a whore with a paintbrush: for ten zlotys the purchaser's wife or mistress would be portrayed as the Virgin Mary; for a few zlotys more his enemy or a rival merchant might appear as Herod or Judas Iscariot.

Even so, Dusty bragged that he got enough money for the painting from his fence to rent a luxury apartment and get married. His bride, Frederika, was a seventeen-year-old orphan who worked on the cosmetics counter at the Kaufhaus. He was fond of flashing photos of her around – she had large blue eyes that were clear as crystal and as innocent as cornflowers. Dusty also liked to brag about how he taught Frederika to breathe through her nose and repress her gag reflex by using his thumb as a training aid. When the cash from the Mercedes' haul had nearly run out, Dusty began to evaluate his wife's possibilities. One evening he hinted as much and she tried to stick a bread knife in his face. He had a bad scar where he fended it off with his arm.

Their other arguments were always about America. Dusty wanted to stay in Berlin, but Hollywood and skyscrapers bedazzled Frederika. They finally made it to America under the Lodge Bill – which meant you could become a US citizen if you served a minimum of five years in the military. The Romans, Lopez thought, offered a harsher deal to their foreigners – twenty years in the Legion. He imagined that, on a quiet night, people could still hear the ghosts of those dead deracinated legionnaires squeaking and gibbering, from Scotland to Asia Minor, in bad Latin.

L OPEZ SPENT THE AFTERNOON helping Sergeant Jackson paint aiming crosses on the inside walls of the 4.2-inch mortar pit. By sighting on the cross and then leveling the two aiming bubbles, it was possible to quickly lay down mortar fire – after windage corrections – on a pre-planned target. Each cross had a description: Hill 60, Black Widow Mountain (east ridge), Hill 38, Xuan Hoa church, Phu Gia (bunker complex A). When they had finished, Lopez headed toward the team house to get a beer. Dusty appeared out of a bunker entrance and said, 'Can I have a word, sir?'

They walked over to the 81mm pit. Redhorn was right: it was the best place to have private conversations in the narrow confines of the camp. The sandbags seemed to absorb voices. 'What's up?'

'I don't like to cause trouble between officers,' Dusty looked around furtively, 'but I think you should know that Captain Redhorn's been going around telling people that you're "an arrogant gook-loving Ivy League bleeding heart" – or words to that effect.'

'I think *you* should mind your own business.'

Dusty looked hurt. 'I'm only trying to help you, just letting you know you ought to watch your back.'

'What's behind it all? Why are you doing this?'

'Don't you see, sir? We have a great deal in common.'

'What do you mean?'

'We neither of us belong. We're cut off from our roots, and just pretending, putting on a masquerade.'

Lopez turned and walked away. This had been happening for some time. It seemed that Dusty was always there, lurking in the shadows, turning up out of nowhere. He knew it wasn't a homosexual thing – he'd been pursued by men before – but this was something different, in a way deeper and more complex. Dusty always seemed to be watching him and listening, not just to his voice, but to his thoughts as well. Sometimes he could feel Dusty's eyes looking at him even when he was nowhere near. It was an uncanny feeling, as if Dusty could see his soul.

Redhorn's 'gook-lover' accusation was nothing new. It was an ongoing conflict. Everyone on the team had at least a smattering of pidgin Vietnamese, but Lopez had become almost fluent. This irritated Redhorn. 'It's just a typical Ivy League egghead affectation. What's the point? Might as well learn to bark and howl so's I can talk to my daddy's 'coon-hound.'

One night, when both officers were drunk, they actually came to blows. The fight started with an argument about 'free fire zones', areas where all living things – pregnant women, babies, water buffalo – were fair game, to be shot, shelled, bombed or napalmed on sight.

'It's a coward's charter,' said Lopez. 'And you know it.'

'There's a lot you need to learn about cowardice, Lopez. You're not a physical coward – it would be inaccurate to call you that – you're a moral coward, an ethical fucking coward. If people like you had ruled the world for the last thousand years, it would be even more overrun with üntermenschen than it already is. The whole fucking Western Hemisphere would still be a malarial swamp inhabited by disease ridden tribal creatures too ignorant to invent the wheel.'

'Like the Aztecs?'

'Exactly. Cortes certainly got *their* asses into gear.'

Lopez descended into a red mist, and suddenly he was on Redhorn, fists flying, and screaming, 'My people, you asshole! My people!' He had never felt anything like racial pride or anger before. Before that moment his ancestry had always been something distant, past and best forgotten. It was as if Redhorn had found a hidden button – and jabbed it hard. The fight ended when Lopez got his forearm across Redhorn's windpipe: for a few seconds he had seriously considered killing him.

In the morning, when they sobered up, it was all forgotten. No one paid much attention to fights at the border camps, or even the drunken brawls that occasionally broke out in the Headquarters' bars. There was an unspoken etiquette: if you only used your fists no one reported the fights and no one was disciplined.

Lopez did not hate Redhorn; in a way he respected him. Sure, Redhorn was evil, but his was an evil with integrity, conviction and even a certain intellect. Redhorn was, above all, no politician, no armchair warrior – he was the real thing. Lopez also knew that a part of Redhorn despised the free-fire zones and the high level bombing. Not for humanitarian reasons, but because it offended his ideal of war as something bloody, personal and close, where you could smell the blood and hear the bones crunching. Redhorn was, after all, a warrior.

Lopez knew that the free-fire zone policy, although it killed civilians, also attracted recruits into the camp strike force. The big advantage for the Vietnamese of being in the CIDG instead of the regular army was that they could bring their families with them, which was what Phong, Kim's RTO, had done. Phong's family used to farm in the Que Son valley. One day the Communists took over Phong's village: there was no one to oppose them, the nearest government outpost was miles away, and no one bothered to send in ground troops to eject them. A week later there was a leaflet drop, and then a helicopter with loudhailers, to warn the local populace that their homes and fields had been declared a free-fire zone and that they should evacuate the area. No one left: there was no other place to go. And even if they had left for the nearest refugee center they would have been turned away: the Saigon government had solved the refugee problem by refusing to accept any more.

A week later Phong's wife's eldest sister and her three children were busy in the paddy transplanting seedlings. When the gunships came over, she told her children to ignore them and not to run, otherwise they might be mistaken for Viet Cong. They continued to plant rice – holding the seedlings just at the root top, poking a hole in the mud with the thumb and then guiding the seedling into the hole – but all the while watching the shadows and reflections that the circling helicopters cast on the ankle-deep water. Phong's sister-in-law began to tell the children not to run even after they opened fire – she thought their innocence was merely being tested with warning shots –

but failed to finish her sentence when the machine-gun bullets snapped through her spine and her aorta erupted into a fountain of blood.

Phong had no problem dealing with the Communists, but the prospect of his family being used for target practice by American helicopter gunners was, on balance, worse than leaving the graves of his ancestors untended. So he packed up and left the village that had housed and fed his family for a thousand years. It was only because he signed up with the CIDG that Phong was able to move his wife and two children out of the free-fire zone into the Duc Duc District refugee camp. Once there, he built a house from cardboard boxes and plastic sheeting tacked to a bamboo frame. Few of his neighbors had anything better. He never stopped smiling and was known as Phong the Philosopher. 'Nothing,' he told Lopez, 'is completely bad. When the river floods, it may be bad luck for the farmers, but it's good luck for the coffin maker.'

Keeping the camp perimeter clear of vegetation was a lousy but necessary job. If you didn't keep it clear, you gave cover to attacking troops and obscured your fields of fire. Cutting grass and clearing brush from the barbed wire around the camp perimeter was hot sweaty work, and dangerous too, for not all of the camp's mines and booby traps were where they were supposed to be. It was the sort of job that made Lopez feel more *mal d'être lui* and culpable than usual. The ragged civilians were paid with Catholic Relief Agency food parcels, which Redhorn had promised the Monsignor in Da Nang he would give away to the neediest poor. The possibility of some widow refugee woman getting her legs blown off in order to collect a sack of rice paid for by a donation from some poor widow woman in Dublin had, Redhorn considered, 'a certain symmetry'.

Lopez wasn't happy that Redhorn had recruited refugees to do the job. He flinched as he saw an elderly woman pick up a 'Bouncing Betty' landmine. He turned and shouted at the interpreter, 'Ly, tell them to leave those fucking things alone. Just mark them with tape.' Suddenly the ground shook. Lopez looked around: no one was hurt, but everyone had frozen. The shaking was too enormous to be a mine explosion, and it had come from a distance. At first, Lopez thought it was an earthquake. The tremor lasted for a few seconds; it was as if a chill or spasm had passed through the loins of the mountain. The noise came as a low rumble, then rolling clouds of dust and smoke appeared like a genie above a nearby ridge line. Then another, even stronger, shudder passed through the mountain – a piece of corrugated iron clattered off a sentry post.

There was another tremor, but less violent. Lopez heard the thunder come again and saw more clouds of smoke and dust plume higher up over the mountain valley. He left the refugees and went to ask Redhorn what was happening. He even wondered if Lyndon Johnson had gone mad and authorized the use of tactical nuclear weapons.

Redhorn smiled. 'One of the horsemen of the Apocalypse is taking some exercise. His name is Arc Light.' Lopez had just witnessed the first Operation Arc Light raid – what was to become the saturation bombing of Vietnam by Strategic Air Command B-52 bombers. It was the first time the massive B-52s had been used in war. Until that afternoon the hulking bombers were for one purpose only: the game of the end, the thermonuclear destruction of the world. Their new mission, Arc Light, was to obliterate huge swathes of countryside with conventional bombs in the hope of destroying North Vietnamese troop concentrations. It was all worked out on computer: if the bombs completely demolished a thousand-meter grid square of terrain, then everything in it must be dead. There was no warning, and the aircraft flew so high that it was impossible to see or hear their approach.

When Redhorn was more bored and drunk than usual he used to tell Lopez about his plan to desert. Redhorn wanted to escape down the mountain of Nui Hoa Den and into the valley. Then he would journey west until he found the headwaters of the Son Thu Bon, then up over the Annamite watershed, past the ruins of Kham Duc and into Laos. 'Listen, there are valleys where no person, not even a Montagnard, has ever set foot, and they're teeming with wild animals and big game. This is where all the tiger, deer, wild boar and elephant have gone to escape this shitty war. And the waterfalls, Lopez, massive walls of water dropping from sheer cliffs to form clear deep lakes full of trout. And then we – because you're coming with me – are going to trek on to the Bolovens Plateau where the elephant grass is eight feet high and you have to burn great swathes through it to travel. There we'll meet the Kha people, who live in houses on stilts like Montagnards. We'll take native wives and help the Kha hunt down and capture their enemies to trade as slaves, or to offer as sacrifices to propitiate their angry gods. And after we have cast our seed into the most nubile of wombs and throats, and thrust spears into countless breasts, and have finally satiated our need for blood and fucking – then we will head west again to the valley of the Mekong. And then the final journey north – two thousand miles – to the river's source, where it spouts, an icy pure spring, out of a cleft in a Tibetan rock face. We'll drink the pure water and wash the blood from our hands and feet, and listen for the temple bells. The monks will be expecting us. They'll shave our heads and dress us in saffron robes. We will meditate and tend the temple gardens and meditate again until we have hoarded a whole incarnation's worth of good karma. Then death, rebirth, and back again and again to the service of the blood red god Juggernaut feeding for eternity his seven serpent heads and their inexhaustible hunger for human flesh stewed in human blood and human tears.'

That was the fantasy; the reality was going up into the mountains to count the bodies that Arc Light had left behind. Lopez thought Redhorn seemed vaguely amused by their orders. 'I guess we're not going to see much action,' said Redhorn. 'Those guys are no longer a military problem, they're a hygiene problem. If anyone crawls out of his hole after all that shit dropping on him, he's going to be walking around with his hat on backwards talking to himself.' Then he gave Lopez the equipment list: no extra bullets, just face masks and rubber gloves.

Just before three in the morning, Redhorn shook Lopez awake. At first, he thought there was a crisis, that the camp was about to be attacked or a team member had been assassinated. 'What's wrong?'

'Listen to this.' Redhorn wanted to tell him a joke. It was from the French war. 'During the siege of Dien Bien Phu there were these two foreign legionnaires – let's call them Jacques and Fritz – in a foxhole outpost. "Listen, my friend," says Jacques. "I have to take a shit or I'm going to burst." "Not here," says Fritz. "You want to take a shit, you use that abandoned trench line just behind us." So Jacques jumps out and runs off, through machine-gun and mortar fire, toward the trench. Several hours pass, Jacques still hasn't returned, and Fritz is beginning to regret that his being fussy might have caused a comrade's death. But finally, just after dark, Jacques scrambles back into the foxhole. Fritz says, "You had me worried. What took you so long?" Jacques kisses his fingers and says, "She was marvelous, wonderful." "What are you talking about?" says Fritz. "Just after having done my business," says Jacques, "I ran into the most beautiful army nurse I have ever seen. Tits like you can't imagine. So I got out my whanger and took her quickly from the front, and then I had her from behind two more times – and then once again from the front just before I came back." Fritz spitefully points out, "But you didn't get a blow-job, did you?" "I really, really wanted one," says Jacques, "but it was totally impossible. I tell you, my friend, I spent over an hour searching every centimeter of that fucking trench line, but I couldn't find her head anywhere!"'

THEY PATROLLED FOR NEARLY TWO DAYS back and forth through the bombed valley and found nothing. The raid had cost the US taxpayer tens of millions of dollars and had killed only trees and the few jungle animals that hadn't already fled the war. Redhorn thought it was funny. Every so often he would shout at the sky, 'You missed! You fucking missed! Can't you guys do anything right?' Sometimes Lopez wondered if Redhorn had become too mentally ill to function as team commander, and whether he should do anything about it. There was one place where his howling voice echoed – weird and uncanny – as if the desolated valley itself was mocking his words in a queer eerie imitation of those soft quavering Southern vowels. In a more sane moment, Redhorn told Lopez that he was certain that the Russians had tipped off the NVA: he said they had a fleet of trawlers off Guam that monitored flight paths.

In the late afternoon of the second day, the patrol came to a sudden halt. Lopez could feel fear shudder through the column, not just in the mind, but physically, up the spine. He turned to the interpreter, Ly, and asked him what was wrong. Ly said, 'Shhh,' and disappeared toward the front of the file. When he returned, he was frightened and breathless.

'What's going on, Ly?'

Ly said that there were voices, but that the voices 'weren't human.' Redhorn told him to shut up because he was 'beaucoup full of bullshit.'

Lopez noticed that Redhorn's hands were shaking: he'd never seen him like that before. They followed Ly back to the front of the column to see what had happened. It was necessary to crawl through a dense tangle of bomb splintered trees. When they reached the lead element they found a CIDG standing at the bottom of a bomb crater with a human skull in his hand. He was smiling. There was a stench, not so much of rotten flesh, but more like an open sewer. Then another wave hit Lopez. That one really was rotten: he had to cover his mouth and nose to stop from vomiting. Ly whispered in his ear, 'It's OK now, Trung Uy.'

'What's OK?'

Ly pointed at the skull. 'He stopped singing as soon as they found his friends.'

Lopez looked down into the crater. A half dozen soldiers were digging and scraping away like kids uncovering treasure on a beach. There were hip sockets, femurs, complete rib cages and skulls surfacing out of the red mud. The bomb had ripped open an old grave. The CIDG were laughing and smiling, not normal smiles, but nervous, embarrassed ones. Lopez thought they probably didn't know what else to do with their faces. The remains of some of the dead soldiers had been wrapped in plastic sheeting. These were the ones that stank most.

When the CIDG had finished exhuming and counting the corpses, Redhorn told Lopez to radio that the dead had been killed by the Arc Light bombing.

'I can't say that. Arc Light didn't kill those guys. Those bodies have been there for months, years maybe.'

'Oh yeah?' said Redhorn. 'Then how come that fucker was still singing?'

The Combat Reconnaissance Platoon thought that the skulls were splendid and, ignoring Mr Kim's orders, stuck them on the ends of their rifles. Lopez's first impulse was to stop it; it was obscene, but it was also thrilling. Lopez watched the parade of chapless skulls bouncing up and down as if impaled on spikes; it gave him a wild indecent sense of liberation, as if some primal instinct had been unburied with the singing dead. They continued to thread their way through a tangle of blasted, scorched and broken trees. As the twilight faded, the only objects visible in the evening shadows were the pale skulls which appeared to have floated free of the rifle muzzles and were dancing to a macabre rhythm of their own.

They spent the night surrounded by bomb-blasted desolation. It was wasteland – literally, land wasted. It seemed so empty that Lopez wondered if the war had ended and no one had bothered to tell them and they had been left behind alone with the dead. So what, he thought. They smoked opium and drank whiskey, then slept like drugged boar pigs after a night of rutting.

The next day they descended into the low hills which sloped down to the paddy fields of the river basin. At midday they slung their hammocks for a siesta. Redhorn was halfway through what promised to be a wet dream when Ly shook him awake. All was quiet except for a voice calling out in Vietnamese – a real voice this time, not a spirit one. Lopez rolled out of his hammock and grabbed his rifle. The voice called again, 'Chieu hoi. Khong ban – I'm surrendering. Don't shoot.' Lopez turned and saw Redhorn raise his rifle and start to take aim. He pushed Redhorn's rifle into the ground and called him an asshole.

Ly shouted instructions and a youth appeared out of the undergrowth with hands raised high above his head. He was dressed in civilian clothes – a clean white shirt and brown shorts – and looked too young to be a soldier. One of the CIDG crept forward and frisked him for weapons. He was carrying nothing at all, not even a handkerchief.

The boy's name was Hieu and he was fifteen years old. He said that he had run away from his village, Son Loi, because he was afraid that the North Vietnamese were going to shoot him. The NVA had come to his house three nights before and told him to come to Xuan Phuc the next night to help them carry rice. He didn't go. Redhorn asked him why he didn't go. Hieu just shrugged his shoulders like a village dolt. Redhorn asked why again. Hieu said he didn't know, but maybe he'd been frightened. Lopez could see that there was something about Hieu that wasn't straight. Maybe, he thought, he should have let Redhorn shoot him.

Redhorn sent for Ho Cuc to help interrogate Hieu. Cuc was also a Viet Cong defector and came from the same village. It quickly turned nasty: from time to time Ho Cuc stuck his rifle muzzle under the boy's chin to help his memory. When they were finished Hieu was sent away. Redhorn then got out his map and asked Ho Cuc for advice on the best places to spring ambushes.

They decided to set two ambush sites. Lopez's ambush was located in heavy brush beside a steep trail five hundred meters up the mountainside. He thought that the trail was more likely to be used by woodcutters than supply columns, in fact, he wondered if it went anywhere at all. He didn't like the idea of blasting away some early-rising woodcutter who had set off before morning light. There was no way they would be able to identify and spare a civilian in that vine-tangled murk. On the other hand, if enemy troops did come down that trail it would be a firefight at point-blank range: there would be no control, just chaos, noise and body tissue exploding all over the place.

Lopez pressed his hand into the dank mold of the jungle floor. He fantasized about finding an entrance to a magic tunnel, like Alice's. If he could find that tunnel, it would spin him through time and space until he tumbled out on the foredeck of *Stormy Petrel* as she glided on a broad reach down the St. Michael's River with the gentle gurgle of water against hull. Someone would suggest, 'Let's anchor in Eastern Bay and go for a swim.' They would say, 'There are soft-shell crab sandwiches in the wicker hamper and cold beer in the ice chest.' Lopez was sleepy. Sleeping on an ambush patrol was a court-martial offence, but what the hell. He was going to sleep anyway. Sleep was his only magic tunnel.

Redhorn also was sleepy. He had placed his ambush team in a position overlooking a place where a trail forded a stream. The trail sloped upwards from the ford and then formed a T-junction with another trail. The gentle sound of water flowing in the stream below the ambush site made Redhorn sleepy. Every time he began to doze he shook himself awake; he thought about taking an amphetamine, but he knew that would only make his opium induced constipation worse. Once, as he nodded off, he dreamed that he was hunting raccoons back home in Louisiana. Fully awake again, he tried to remember the dream. It was midnight and the hounds had treed a raccoon; someone was shining a powerful torch into the tree. The raccoon's eyes, framed by its black bandit's mask, reflected yellow-green and its mouth was open and snarling. For Redhorn, that raccoon at bay, magnificent as a medieval legend in its fatal glory, was the most beautiful thing he had ever seen. But a black youth shinned up the tree to saw off the branch where the raccoon was perched. The raccoon, as it fell to the ground, suddenly looked awkward and clumsy as it twisted in the beams of a dozen torches. The baying changed to growling, snarling and barking and within seconds the raccoon was dead. Many of the hounds were bleeding. Whoever wanted the pelt skinned the animal and the entrails were given to the dogs.

The gurgling of the stream below the ambush site reminded Ho Cuc of a waterfall not far from Son Loi; he was certain that this stream fed into the fall. When he was a boy he used to play there. The water cascaded out of a sheer wall of the darkest green, and had worn a smooth chute into the rock below. Cuc used to slide down this chute which ran for forty meters before dropping into a deep pool. It wasn't long before he had perfected the art of body slalom. He even improvised a repertoire of artistic gestures – mercurial attitudes, mournful arabesques – as the music water flung him towards the distant sea. The water chute, along with his wife, had been the great sensual pleasure of his life. He had dreamed of teaching his children how to shoot their bodies through the water slide. When he closed his eyes he could almost hear the joy-laughter of their spirits.

Redhorn had found from experience that the best time for an ambush was between just after dark and midnight. He knew that the enemy preferred to reserve the dark watches of the night for sleeping. Redhorn waited and, when nothing had happened after several hours of darkness, he allowed himself to fall asleep.

It was a tunnel dream; he often had tunnel dreams. The tunnel was full of people. At first there were refugees, carrying all their belongings on poles. There was something sinister about the way their faces were shadowed by their conical straw peasant hats. Then came the soldiers. All had lost their weapons and were barefoot. They shuffled forward with their eyes fixed on the ground, except for those who had blank black holes instead of faces. They shuffled forward – from the A Shau Valley, from the Ia Drang, from the hills around Dak To, from the Iron Triangle, from Lang Vei, from Nong Son, from Khe Sanh, from Con Tien, from a thousand places known only by the elevation of a hill in meters or by grid co-ordinates. They kept coming. Redhorn tried to force his way back, back through this bloodshod host, but the tunnel was so narrow and there was such a crush that the momentum of this army of the night was impossible to resist. There were so many, and they said nothing, just swayed forward. But Redhorn still continued to elbow, claw and push his way back against the retreating shuffling column. Suddenly one of the soldiers raised his face and looked at Redhorn. It was Sergeant Clements who had been killed at Plei Trap the same day that Redhorn had been wounded. Clements stared through Redhorn with dead eyes that had lost their points of reference. 'Go back, sir,' he said. 'It's no use. Go back, sir.' Redhorn ignored him and tried to push past, but Clements had grabbed him by the arm. His grip was like cold iron and Redhorn couldn't shake it loose. 'No, Clements,' he said aloud. Redhorn suddenly awoke to find Ho Cuc shaking his arm and Cuc's fingers stopping his lips from saying more.

'Shhh,' hissed Cuc.

Redhorn heard the sound of someone splashing through the ford. He was fully awake at once. The party of rice carriers had learned that the CIDG were operating in the area and were being more cautious than usual. A stream crossing is an obvious place for an ambush, and for that reason they had stopped short and sent two scouts ahead to reconnoiter the opposite side of the ford. The scouts had waded through the shallow water and had just begun to ascend the trail when they stopped. Perhaps they had heard the sort of metallic noise that can never be a natural night sound, or perhaps they had simply felt the presence of their enemies through a sixth sense. There was no time to run back or to seek cover; they were shot and killed immediately.

Redhorn knew that most of the carrying party had escaped because he heard shouting from the far side of the stream. He could actually feel the adrenaline pumping. He felt that he was on the brink of an incarnadine apotheosis, he felt he was becoming a god. He stood up and tried to get the CIDG to pursue the survivors. 'Let's go. Di mau di!' Redhorn had reached his life's pinnacle, he felt transformed into sheer power. At that moment Ho Cuc lifted his rifle and put a bullet through the base of his spine.

THE MARINES fished the body out of the river near the bridge at An Hoa three days later, and sent it on to the I Corps mortuary at Da Nang airfield. Lopez had been designated Redhorn's 'Survivors' Assistance Officer'. He hated the whole business: it meant he had to identify the body, bundle up his personal belongings and answer awkward letters.

Lopez found the mortuary visit like the day he arrived in Da Nang, but in reverse, like a film spooled the wrong way round – the drive back through the desolate peninsular sand flats, the RMK yard piled even higher with scrap, and the RMK girls more than ever bloated with the semen of foreign soldiers, then the sleepy guards on the bridge, the NO INDIG notices at the entrance to the Da Nang airbase and, finally, the hum of the refrigerator condenser units at the rear of the dead meat parlor.

He had to stop at the entrance to the mortuary compound and wait for a guard to let him through. It struck him that it must be one of the most heavily defended compounds in I Corps: the mortuary had the best barbed wire he'd ever seen – concertina, razor wire, tangle-foot. But it wasn't the Viet Cong they were worried about; it was their fellow Americans. Everyone hated the Graves Reg personnel – all those embalmer types and mortuary attendants. And every time another pal got killed they hated them even more. People were always chucking grenades into the compound and the one in II Corps – at LZ English – even had a rocket attack. No one would talk to anyone who had anything to do with Graves Registration: they had their own barracks, their own mess hall, even their own chaplain. And they need barbed wire and bunkers – for their own protection.

Lopez parked the jeep next to a Graves Registration Platoon truck. Some ghoul had written: URGENT PRIORITY – DON'T DELAY – I CORPS MORTUARY on the front bumper of the truck. The lettering was done in fancy Gothic script like an advertisement for a horror movie. He wanted to turn around and go back, and later he wished he had: Lopez was sure he was going to have nightmares about it for the rest of his days.

He explained his business to the inner perimeter guard, who had long fingernails painted purple, and was led into a long prefab building with no windows. An embalmer in a stained lab coat consulted a clipboard and asked Lopez to follow him. There was a sharp acid stink of disinfectant and chemicals. There must have been thirty tables on either side with nude carcasses who wore a waxy glassy look. Some of the bodies had tubes stuck into their necks and crotches that were sucking the blood out of their veins. Other corpses, already drained and bloodless, were festooned with similar tubes that pumped embalming fluid into the arteries. Many of the dead had ugly purple black blotches on the backs of their hands: evidence of some ham-fisted medic in a blind panic trying to find a vein to start a drip. It all made Lopez feel sick and greasy. On one table were charred pieces of pilot.

He was finally led to a loading bay where six dark green body bags were lying next to each other on the cold concrete floor. A stockpile of aluminum coffins, stacked in rows six high, towered over them. The embalmer checked the tags until he found the right bag and then asked Lopez to give him a hand.

They lifted the body bag on to a white porcelain-clad table with blood gutters. Lopez watched the embalmer undo the clamp that sealed the bag and peel back the plastic. The face was bloated and decomposed, the eye sockets empty except for the brown cracked husk of a withered eyeball, but he knew it was Redhorn. A thick swollen finger had burst like a cooked sausage around his wedding ring.

Afterward, Lopez felt no pity or sorrow, only a sense of having been defiled by the corpse and the ghoulish mechanisms of the mortuary. His only desire was to be cleaned, to be purified. He wanted to be stretched out naked on a sunny beach in winter, being scrubbed clean, like a piece of bleached driftwood, by the icy wind.

There was a custom at Nui Hoa Den that whenever anyone did anything for the first time they had to buy a case of beer for the rest of the team. On Lopez's first evening back after identifying the body, Dusty Storm stomped into the team house and chalked up a case of beer next to Redhorn's name. 'What the fuck are you doing?' asked Carson.

'He sure as fuck never got himself killed before.'

Lopez asked the team what they thought: they agreed that the beer cash be appropriated from his personal belongings before they were packed up and returned to the next of kin. It was usual to make macabre jokes in the face of death, but the mood was still miserable and depressed. Everyone hated it when a team member got killed: it wasn't just mourning and grief for the person killed; it was mourning for one's self too, the reawakening of the queasy fear of becoming 'dead meat'.

Before leaving Da Nang, Lopez had been told that he would be acting camp commander until Redhorn's replacement arrived. It could be a long wait. There was a shortage of captains because they were grinding up infantry lieutenants faster than they could turn them out. The lieutenants, who didn't get ground up, didn't want to become captains either; they just wanted to say 'Fuck you, Uncle Sam' and get out as soon as possible. The army was so desperate they started giving direct commissions to sergeants. Even Dusty Storm had been put forward for one.

Lopez couldn't sleep that first night back: he just lay on his bunk and stared into the blackness and sweated into the sheets. The mortuary visit kept flashing back. And besides that there were rumors – convincing ones – that the camp was going to be attacked. He tried to listen through the usual night sounds – the crackle of the radios, the dull whump of distant artillery – straining to hear something different. He hated responsibility.

After a while he got up, poured himself a slug of bourbon and lay down again. He tried to blot Vietnam out of his mind by recalling all the women that he'd ever been with and fantasizing he was doing all sorts of crazy sex things.

That even made him more miserable because – cruelly and incongruously – the image of Redhorn's corpse kept floating up in the middle of his sex romps. The body-bag scene kept reminding him that he was likely to die without ever having sex again.

Lopez fell asleep. There was an insane dream: somehow his bedroom at Rideout's Landing had been transported to a house in Da Nang. He looked out the window and there were rickshaws in the wet night and a hearse parked at the curb. Ianthe came into the room: she was dressed in mourning. She told him that everything was all right. Lopez found her black dress, her black stockings and black shoes, incredibly erotic. Something was different. She was no longer a step-sibling that had shared his bathtub until the age of six. Ianthe, in death, had turned into an object of intense erotic desire. She put a finger on his lips and told him that they must be quiet. Then they lay down together and began to make love – silent but hard, breathless and passionate. Just as Lopez was about to enter her he woke up. He hugged the pillow tight and whispered soundlessly, 'I loved you so much, I adored you. Please forgive me.'

Someone was sitting on the side of his bunk. Lopez could smell cigarette smoke. When he opened his eyes he saw a dot of red ash glowing in the pitch black of the bunker cubicle. He felt a hand resting on his thigh. 'Who's there?'

'It's me, Trung Uy.'

It was Tho, Lopez's Vietnamese counterpart. 'What's wrong, Trung Uy?' Lopez liked the formality of the relationship with his counterpart. They always called each other Trung Uy, first lieutenant, regardless of the situation.

Tho sat smoking and moved his hand further up Lopez's thigh. 'I think, Trung Uy, VC come tonight.' Tho's voice sounded so calm and soft that Lopez wasn't certain that he had heard correctly. 'How do you know this, Trung Uy?'

'There are many intelligence reports from our agents in the

valley. But that's normal: agents always saying VC about to attack. But this time, I think, the reports are correct.'

'Why?'

'Trung Uy, our outposts and perimeter bunkers are mostly abandoned.' It sounded like Tho was sobbing, but Lopez soon realized his counterpart had the giggles. Tho found the situation so unbelievably awful that it had turned into a comedy of the absurd. 'When,' said Tho, 'CIDG soldiers heard VC supposed to be coming, they bugged out. No bullshit, Trung Uy, they checked out PDQ. They goddam legged it.' Tho spoke English with an exaggerated New York accent that he had picked up while chained to a POW from the Bronx during two years in a jungle prison camp.

Lopez asked Tho if he was teasing. It was too dark to see his face, but he could almost sense his counterpart's half-hooded eyes and the ironic knowing way he tilted his head.

'Of course not, Trung Uy. Go take a look around the bunkers yourself.' Tho laughed his hangman's laugh. 'I think the CIDG said, "I wasn't born yesterday, Uncle Sam, I get the hell out of here PDQ."' Tho wiped his eyes. 'PDQ, that means pretty damn quick, Trung Uy, just in case you didn't know.'

Lopez got out of bed and dressed. He knew that many Vietnamese were secretly contemptuous of the Americans, but Tho was one of the few who were completely open about it. Tho had been held in a POW camp with four Americans and twenty South Vietnamese captives. Every one, POW and captor, was given the same frugal rations and lived in the same conditions. The Americans alone were unable to cope. Eventually, there were three Americans left, then two, and then only one. A short time before Tho escaped, or was released – the facts surrounding his return were pretty murky – the remaining American expired from pneumonia. Tho giggled when he told that story too.

Lopez asked Tho if they had any soldiers left at all.

'Yeah sure,' he replied more Bronx than ever. 'You can bet your bottom dollar, Trung Uy, there will always be people too stupid even to come in out of the rain.'

Tho's open sarcasm was getting on Lopez's nerves. 'Stop patronizing me, Trung Uy.' Lopez wasn't sure that Tho knew what the word meant – he didn't imagine they used it too much in the Bronx. But Tho surprised him.

'How can I possibly patronize you?' he said, 'You're only a ... only a boy.' Tho had a talent for retorts to which reply was impossible.

'How many CIDG are still in the camp?'

Tho said there were about forty.

Lopez woke up the American team, put the camp on full alert and made sure there were Americans in charge at all the key points. He almost told them to shoot anyone who attempted to leave, but was afraid he'd sound like a B-movie villain and that they'd laugh at him.

Lopez got a chair and radio so he could sit on top of the .50 caliber machine-gun bunker. The position gave the best view of the camp, but made him a sitting duck. He didn't care: if it was going to happen you might as well get it sooner than later. And he didn't like the idea of being handcuffed to Tho in a POW camp either.

But he knew that when it did happen, it would be an inside job. The CIDG who didn't run away wouldn't be staying because they were 'stupid' – they'd be there to do a job. The loyal ones would take off; the double agents would stay behind to kill the Americans and their counterparts.

The villages and hamlets of the river valley were still populated, but at night there were never any lights – only the moon reflecting on the river. But that night there was no moon, which made endgame even more likely.

Lopez tried to cheer things up by firing illumination flares from the 4.2-inch mortar. He had already dropped the first one down the mortar tube before he remembered that he should have checked to see if the mortar had been booby-trapped to explode. It hadn't.

It was fun sending up illumination rounds, like fireworks on the Fourth of July. After three or four seconds the river valley was washed in a spectral pale green light as the flare, suspended from a tiny parachute, swung back and forth drifting, back and forth descending, casting stalking shadows which ran like ghosts across the trenches and bunkers.

After a time the air turned damp and chill, the stars were extinguished, a bank of mist rolled down the river, licked the base of the mountain, liked it, and ascended the slopes. The mist veiled the camp in a shroud so dense that visibility was a question of feet, not yards. Lopez continued to fire illumination, but the light of the flares only turned the black impenetrable murk into a milky green impenetrable murk. This was, he thought, the place where the boundaries of death's kingdoms came together, so close together.

Lopez heard someone moving in the trench line behind the bunker. He flicked the selector switch of his rifle from safety to semi-automatic. Him first, he thought. Someone was singing:

> *Two little children lying in bed,*
> *One of 'em sick and t'other one dead.*

'Hello, anybody home?' Sergeant Jackson sounded drunk. 'Ain't nobody back at my place; even the chickens done gone to roost in an old crab apple tree.'

'It's me, I'm up here.'

'Well, that's somethin'. It was gettin' mighty lonesome over there. I was startin' to think I was the only person left in the whole goddam camp.'

'Are there any CIDG left?'

'Soon as the mist rolled in, they rolled out. Well, I better get my ass back and mind the store. Good night to you, sir.' Jackson had no body, no substance: he was only a voice, a spectral sound in the dark mist. Lopez listened to him go. It had been so long since he'd heard that song.

> *Call up doctor, doctor he said,*
> *Feed dem children on shortnin' bread.*
> *Mama's little baby love shortnin', shortnin',*
> *Mama's little baby love shortnin' bread.*

A few minutes later there was a sound of an explosion on the western perimeter of the camp. The explosion was followed by the sound of small arms fire; it lasted about two minutes, then came the sound of a grenade going off, a few more sporadic shots, then complete silence once again. Lopez braced himself and waited for more, but nothing – only silence. After half an hour, the mist lifted just as suddenly as it had appeared. From time to time he illuminated the camp and valley with flares, but all appeared at peace. Whatever it was, had passed.

At first light, they found that some barbed wire had been cut and a few trip flares dismantled. There was also a human leg dangling from the concertina wire near where one of the camp's mines had exploded. Nothing else was amiss. The CIDG began to trickle back. By mid-morning everything was normal. Soon all the CIDG were back, everyone pretending, like civilized adulterers, that nothing had happened.

'YOU KNOW SOMETHING, Lieutenant Lopez...' Lopez and Captain Boca were standing on top of the .50 caliber machine-gun bunker and looking out over the valley of the Son Thu Bon. Redhorn's replacement had finally arrived.

It was hate at first sight. Lopez hated everything about Boca: his opinions, his voice, his face, his body, his tastes, his mannerisms. A lot of the officers in Special Forces were like Redhorn – crazies, deviants, psychos, crypto-fascists, closet Klansmen, sociopaths – but Boca was worse; just dumb faceless humorless dull brutality. It wasn't the Redhorns of the world who stoked the ovens of the Holocaust. Murder as a routine industrial process would have bored them to death; they would have begged a transfer to Stalingrad. The great killers are dull, they are without imagination. They are not psychopaths: they are the gray technocrats of death, pasty faced from lack of sun, ready and waiting in missile silos and nuclear submarines.

After several weeks in command, Lopez was surprised how resentful he felt at handing over to Boca, and it wasn't just because he loathed the man. He had begun to feel that Nui Hoa Den was his, that he owned it. The morning was exceptionally clear and fresh. Despite everything, the view continued to thrill Lopez with its beauty. The valley was a place where, despite the crater scars of war, the paddy fields were still green mirrors which rose in terraces on the lower slopes of the almost perfect pyramid of Black Widow Mountain. And beyond that mountain lay the broad valley of Que Son and then more mountains, wildly cragged and blue-gray in the morning.

'You know something,' repeated Boca, 'all these goddam countries look alike.'

This was Boca's first time in Vietnam, but he'd already had tours in Taiwan, Korea and the Philippines. So, presumably, all those other 'goddam countries' had patterns of paddy fields etched into the contours of the land by generations and generations to reflect the sky like inlaid glass set in lacquer frames.

A week after Boca's arrival, Sergeant Carson was shot during a sweep through the village of Phu Gia. The village had been Communist since the beginning of the war, but was tactically worthless. Redhorn had ignored Phu Gia – there was nothing there except for a handful of ragged local force guerrillas. Most of population had left the village when it became a free-fire zone. Nothing was left of their homes except for the bamboo frames. The remaining population lived in forlorn hovels roofed with rotten thatch, prone to infestation by obnoxious larvae. The people of Phu Gia learned to ignore the black worms falling from their roofs into their rice bowls. It was more important to dig deep and solid underground bunkers than to repair the roofs. The remaining population comprised a hundred or so women, children and old men, and about twenty-five guerillas who disappeared into the hills or tunnels as soon as a patrol approached the village. The people were gaunt and ragged. Many of the old suffered from trachoma – the eye disorder which causes the eyelashes to turn inward, causing excruciating pain and blindness – and all the children had running leg ulcers.

As soon as they were outside Nui Hoa Den's barbed wire, Carson turned to Lopez. 'This isn't just a waste of fucking time, sir, it's a dangerous waste of fucking time.'

Lopez pretended he wasn't listening. He found that the best way to deal with Carson was just to let him talk, let him get it out.

'This, sir, is one useless operation. Ain't nothin' in Phu Gia worth shooting or blowing up, but some of our guys always get shot or a couple of legs blown off. Attacking Phu Gia is like picking on the saddest ragamuffin in the schoolyard. You start callin' him names, pushin' him around, you think he's real chicken – then all of a sudden he hammers you in the testicles, then he goes and knocks your eye out when you bend over in pain.'

Carson was wounded just before nine in the morning the next day. Poor visibility made tactical control of the troops impossible. The CIDG emerged out of the morning mist laden with plunder attached to their rucksacks: marrows, bunches of bananas, a few live chickens. Carson turned to his Vietnamese counterpart to complain. 'Listen, Trung Si; this is supposed to be a combat patrol, not a shopping trip.'

The Trung Si simply shrugged.

Carson started to lose his temper. 'Listen up, Trung Si, stealing is wrong. Looting is a court-martial offence. You better tell them to leave that stuff where they found it.'

The Trung Si shrugged his shoulders again.

Carson turned back and tried to find Lopez in the mist. 'In the last war,' he shouted, 'I saw soldiers who were *shot* for looting.'

As if on cue – like a reply from a looter's ghost – a shot rang out from the mist and Carson collapsed like an old man on sheet ice. His voice had startled a squad of NVA who were also lost in the morning mist. There was a chaotic firefight at close range which lasted about a minute. The only casualties were Carson and a CIDG who was killed by a bullet through the head. Carson had the luckiest wound possible: the bullet struck him just below the buttock and passed through the fleshiest part of his thigh well clear of bone or tendon. Lopez slit his trousers leg from knee to waist with a commando knife, and was relieved to see that the bullet holes were small and neat, though the color was an ugly purple. It looked exactly like someone had pushed a pencil through Carson's thigh.

During the next few weeks Lopez watched his new commanding officer become obsessed with Phu Gia. Boca spent hours gazing at the village through a pair of ship's binoculars mounted on the roof of the command bunker. He logged every movement and numbered each hut and paddy field. Dusty claimed that he'd even done a census of the village's water buffalo and dogs. It was no use telling Boca that Phu Gia had no military significance, that the village was nothing more than a sad ribbon of derelict houses and fields that followed the serpentine twists of the Son Thu Bon as far as the mountain gorge. For Boca, Phu Gia was the enemy – that elusive and invisible enemy that the Americans seldom even glimpsed. Boca couldn't bear to see the people of Phu Gia and not act. To him it was like finding cockroaches on his kitchen floor – he just had to stomp on them.

A week after Carson was wounded, Boca spotted a man in a tiny boat. The man had just embarked from Phu Gia to paddle to a hamlet on the opposite bank. Boca jumped down into the command bunker hoping to blast the boat with the .50 caliber machine-gun, a comic-strip weapon that fires bullets the size of zucchini. Boca swung the weapon towards his target only to hear the gun's barrel crunch against the edge of the bunker's firing slit. The slit was too narrow to allow the machine-gun to fire anywhere near that part of the river. Boca bellowed for help.

Jackson materialized wearing flip-flop sandals and holding a can of beer. 'How can I help you, sir?'

'Help me get this goddam machine-gun moved.'

'You can't move it, sir, the tripod's bolted to the floor.'

'Then get your ass on the 4.2-inch and start putting out mortar rounds.'

Jackson went into the mortar pit, put his beer down and started to adjust the aiming mechanisms in response to Boca's commands. The boatman was still in the middle of the river when the water spouted and exploded about a hundred meters in front of his boat. The next round landed a hundred meters behind. The boatman was paddling like mad. Jackson looked up and saw Lopez who mouthed an instruction. The third and fourth rounds landed well wide of the boat. Two seconds later, the boatman reached the bank and went running and dodging through a maze of palm groves and bamboo thicket. Two more rounds landed on the riverbank, but by then their target had disappeared. Boca scowled at Jackson for having done a lousy job and stomped off. The boatman probably wasn't transporting ammunition or rice, but merely taking medicinal herbs to his father who was old and unwell, or some such errand.

Jackson's casual attitude and poor aim with the mortar

irked Boca. The next day he decreed an end to flip-flop sandals and T-shirts and ordered the team to have 'white-wall' haircuts. The Vietnamese barber assumed that the Americans were being humiliated and punished for something. Dusty Storm highly resented having his hair cropped, but couldn't see the sense of being allowed a token inch of hair on the top – so he told the barber to shave that off as well. His overdoing it infuriated Boca even more than his beach-boy mane had. 'Storm,' he shouted, 'you're supposed to be a soldier, not a goddam Buddhist monk.'

Lopez was grateful for one thing. Hating Boca gave him an emotional life, almost a purpose. He especially hated his looks. He'd never seen a person whose outward appearance so suited his inner being. He found it difficult to believe that Boca – slab faced and protein-glutted – and the Vietnamese – swarthy, fine-boned and taut with lean sinew – belonged to the same species.

THE M-79 GRENADE LAUNCHER is designed to protect idiots. The rounds it fires require a minimum number of rotations before they are armed to go off. This means that, for example, if someone fires an M-79 without checking his overhead clearance and the projectile bounces back off an overhanging tree branch it won't blow up the idiot who's just fired it. It also meant that there were a lot of unexploded M-79 rounds lying all over Vietnam. They weren't harmless duds; they just hadn't had sufficient spins to be armed. It suited the Communist 'use war to feed war' doctrine. The Viet Cong paid people a bounty for collecting them so they could use them to make booby traps.

The M-79 round is about the size of a hen's egg. A ten-year-old girl found one beside a busy cart track near her village. She was delighted: her find was worth enough to buy her family a bottle of fish sauce. She teased her younger brother and his friend, who were eager to examine it themselves, by tossing the dud explosive from hand to hand, pretending that it was too hot to handle. It was a good joke, and they were all laughing. She didn't realize that by tossing it she had added the number of spins required to prime the arming mechanism. Then she dropped it. She hadn't meant to.

The children were carried to Nui Hoa village where there was an infirmary and a radio link. The village nurse radioed the camp and explained what had happened. She was upset, crying and begging for a helicopter to evacuate the children to a hospital in Da Nang.

Boca refused. He said he wasn't convinced that the wounds were as serious as the nurse had reported. Lopez had just come into the comm room. Boca looked up, 'You can't trust gooks; they all exaggerate.' Lopez found himself shaking and almost deranged with anger and hate. He told Boca that he would go down and find out for himself. He didn't wait for Boca to answer: he just turned and left. He had to get away from Boca, to stop himself from smashing in that gross self-righteous face.

Lopez was so angry that he nearly killed himself as he drove down the hairpins of the mountain road. He wasn't paying attention and almost ran over one of the camp's own anti-personnel mines that had been washed down the hill and on to the road by a recent storm.

The village infirmary was a stucco building with gray shutters. The shutters were closed; it was dark and cool inside. The room was packed with people. It seemed to Lopez that the whole village was there: there was hardly space to stand. In a room so crowded with humanity, the utter silence was unnatural. Without anyone saying a word a path was cleared so that Lopez could make his way to the children. The three were lying next to one another on stretchers placed on two tables which had been pushed together. A middle-aged woman with a heavily lined face held a cloth to her eyes and swayed backwards and forwards groaning. There was no other sound, except for rasping labored breathing from one of the boys. The girl was completely swathed in bandages from head to foot. For a second Lopez was confused, not realizing that this thing, bound like an Egyptian mummy, was a child. Then he saw that in places the mummy's bandages were stained with blood. Her death was real; it was fresh too. The boy with the rasping breath was struggling against death, barely conscious, and his face was as gray and pale as moonlight. Lopez placed his hand on the boy's forehead: it was damp with sweat, but so cold. He wanted to stroke him, to hold him tight, anything to make him warm again. The blast had caught the boy full in the middle of his body. There were severe abdominal injuries, and he had lost his penis and testicles. The other boy lay beneath a coarse gray blanket and stared at the ceiling with dull eyes which never blinked. Lopez radioed for a helicopter.

Boca was boiling with anger when his lieutenant got back. The captain looked like a freshly steamed crab; his face was pink and beaded with sweat. Lopez knew that Boca liked being angry: it made him feel that he was in charge, that he could really kick ass. He was seething and shouting at Lopez for calling in an emergency priority medevac.

Lopez tried to explain what had happened, even though he knew it was a pointless on-deaf-ears exercise. Boca said that it 'didn't fucking matter, because you only request emergency priority medevac when there are American casualties.' He went on to tell Lopez that it wasn't his job to run 'a fucking gook ambulance service.'

By this time Boca had ceased to be a person, he was only a thing with sound coming out. If it had been a human being, Lopez would have walked away or hit it with a stick. But it was a thing like a radio or television that you want to turn off but can't find the switch. So he kept foolishly, mechanically, responding to the sounds coming out of the thing hoping that it would eventually turn itself off. 'And the girl was dead.'

'Then she sure as fuck didn't need an emergency priority medevac,' said the object.

Lopez then tried to explain how one of the boys had horrible abdominal injuries and had his lost his genitals.

'So what?' said the thing. 'Fucking Vietnamese don't know what they're for anyway.'

Lopez gave up – it just wouldn't stop making noise – and walked away. The sun was beating on his bare head. He tried to remember where he had left his hat. A hammer was beating behind his forehead. He turned to say something, but Boca was only a blur. He needed to get out of the sun.

It was better in the cool of the bunker. Lopez poured himself a glass of bourbon, took off his boots and lay down on his bunk. He looked at his .45 hanging on its hook and prayed that Boca wouldn't come looking for him. Then he tried to remember what had happened, but he could only remember the bloodstained bandages. He remembered, perfectly clearly, that he had spoken to the nurse, but couldn't recollect any of the words. He closed his eyes and tried to conjure up a single face or word, but his memory was blank – except for the spreading stains of blood oozing through the bandages.

Nothing else mattered. Not Redhorn's death, not all those waxy bodies at the I Corps mortuary. None of them mattered. No soldier's death could ever matter again. Never. The child's blood was only that thing counted, that blood seeping through – spreading, staining – her bandages. Lopez forced back the tears. She deserved more than tears. She deserved action.

It was a dream in which the layers of time and the boundaries of space had dissolved into a lunatic synthesis. They were alone in the kitchen at Rideout's Landing. It was late at night and she had just come down from New York – she was all right now, everything had turned out fine. Lopez was still in battle dress and boots, as if Vietnam were only a few miles away – perhaps someone had towed it up the Chesapeake Bay. He told her how much he loved her and how he needed to do penance. She looked at the floor and began to cry. Lopez started to kiss her, to feel her mouth moist and hungry against his – and then Dusty Storm woke him up.

Lopez wanted to kill him. He grabbed Dusty's T-shirt and threw a punch, but somehow Dusty managed to duck and swerve. 'Why, you fucking shit, why did you take her away from me?' Dusty told him to calm down, that he was only waking him up because he was next on the watch rota. Lopez told him to go away, then got up to dress. When he got to the comm bunker, Lopez saw the date in the duty log – and it all came back again. He put his face in his hands and prayed for God to punish him. He cried for a while and then went up to inspect the perimeter defenses.

He took with him a secret night vision device called the Starlight Scope – they were supposed to test it and write a report. Boca had volunteered Nui Hoa Den as a site for testing prototypes in 'an actual combat environment'. The device was the size and shape of an ordinary telescope. Lopez sat down on top of the .50 cal bunker and removed the lens caps. When he looked through the eyepiece he saw the dark void of night mutate into a too bright world of luminous emerald. It polluted the sweet night and changed the sleeping world into a submarine horrorscape in which the only colors were shades of green putrefaction. Lopez searched the perimeter for enemy sappers, but the only creatures he spotted were rats foraging in the wire – queer puke-green creatures, like bottom-feeding fish snouting through seaweed fronds and blissfully unaware of his techno-eye.

The next morning another R&D prototype arrived for testing. It was no more than a plain metal box, about sixteen inches square. It looked like something a high school student might have knocked together in a sheet metal craft class. Other than a jack for an antenna and an off/on switch, it was just a plain metal box. It was called 'the beacon'.

In the afternoon, Boca brought the team together for a beacon training session. The box was supposed to beam highly accurate and calibrated signals. Aircraft could then fix on the beacon and deliver precision bombing patterns called 'beacon runs'. The advantage was that the bombers could fly so high that they were virtually invisible and totally safe from ground fire. Then suddenly, with no warning and for no apparent reason, a quiet green landscape would erupt into fire and smoke. Efficient, accurate and safe.

Boca explained that the only thing you had to do was radio a compass bearing and distances to the pilot, then a description of the type and shape of the target. The pilot's on-board computer took care of the rest, even ensuring that the bombs fell in geometrically spaced patterns, thus avoiding any wasteful overlapping of the kill-zone radii.

To demonstrate, Boca set up the beacon on the roof of the command bunker. It was the best place to view the valley below. Lopez regarded a pattern of riverboats, water buffalo and brimming silver paddy fields while Boca tried to make radio contact with the bomber pilot. It took several attempts and Lopez could see him getting red in the face and beginning to perspire. If the beacon failed to work, Boca knew that he would look a fool. When he finally did make contact with the pilot, the transmission was weak and garbled. Boca announced that he was going to bomb a rivulet in some foothills where there were supply caches of ammunition. He radioed the necessary information.

The pilot's reply was so distorted and static-broken that Lopez feared that he was about to witness a horrible bombing error. He thought there was a distinct possibility that the pilot had been so confused by Boca's instructions that he had mistaken the beacon location for the target location, that at any moment 750-pound bombs were going to rain down on their own heads. Nonetheless, a few seconds later the precise spot that Boca had indicated erupted into a chaos of flame and broken earth, vindicating him and his metal box.

'Did you see the secondary explosions?' Boca asked. He wanted Lopez to endorse his claim that there had been ammunition caches in the rivulet.

Lopez said no. Boca said he needed to get his eyes tested.

ONCE A MONTH Lopez had to go the C-team HQ at China Beach to pick up the CIDG payroll. While he stood next to Travis at the latrines, Travis asked if he had noticed that most of the gecko wall lizards had their tails amputated. He explained this was because a number of officers amused themselves while pissing by swiping at the lizards with their commando knives. 'Wouldn't it be funny,' said Travis, 'if, when these officers die, they discover that God is an almighty giant celestial wall lizard who will chase them through the ether for all eternity slashing at their dangling dicks with a gleaming machete?'

There were often brawls in the C-team officers' club bar. The sheer hatred between the officers who came in from the field and the China Beach staff officers was legendary. Many of the field officers spent their entire stay drunk and shouted 'rear echelon motherfucker' at any staff officer who crossed them or even made eye contact. The staff officers, many of whom had been badly wounded during their time in the field, often answered with a left hook or an empty bottle.

When Lopez entered the bar he saw that Eric Rider, the CO at Tien Phouc, and two other field officers had handcuffed the Protestant chaplain wrist to ankle over the back of a chair. They had already pulled the chaplain's trousers down and Rider was shouting, in a falsetto imitation of a desperate bar girl, 'Who wants to brown the padre – only ten dollar MPC? He no butterfly, he faithful bride, Trung Uy. He got virgin asshole, he cherry tight. Where's Murphy? Hey, Lopez, get your papist ass over here: Catholics get a second poke for free.' The chaplain was screaming for help in thin high-pitched wails, as if he really did believe his anal virginity was in peril. An officer with an Alabama accent said, 'Thaat thang sounds like a hawg in a castration clamp.' A number of other field officers had started to practice parachute-landing falls off the bar and there was broken glass everywhere. Two officers having a fistfight over the favors of a bar-girl had slipped on the broken glass and were rolling around on the floor trading punches. Travis was trying to cool the situation by spraying them – and everyone else – with a foam fire extinguisher. An alert siren from the next compound was wailing a mortar attack signal. Lopez was sitting in a corner with his feet propped up on an unconscious second lieutenant and quietly drinking a quadruple Scotch and soda. Lieutenant Colonel Cale came in and was immediately doused with extinguisher foam. Someone shouted, 'Hey, chocolate sundae with whipped cream!' Cale decided it was time to call in the Chinese Nung guards. The last thing Lopez remembered was having his neck clamped in a blackout restraint hold by a massive Nung known as Beaucoup Kilo. Considering the circumstances, Lopez found Beaucoup incredibly gentle – he thought he'd be great as a nurse in the high security ward at Spring Grove. When he woke up in the morning Lopez found himself handcuffed to a bunk and lying in his own vomit.

Lopez left on the morning chopper, but then had to spend another night at China Beach because the flight was diverted to Tra Bong for a medevac and limped back to China Beach packed and overloaded with CIDG who had been shot up in an ambush. Lopez was crushed next to a soldier whose face was the color of stale milky coffee. At first the CIDG's pulse was faint and rapid, then fainter, then there was nothing, except occasional gasping breaths, like a fish that had been lying for a long time on the deck of a boat. There was also a black American sergeant who had been wounded in the arm and had his good arm around an elderly Vietnamese woman who was racked with grief and whose blouse was stained by blood – not her own blood, but still her blood. Her dead son's.

Lopez didn't mind having to spend another night at the C-team. He enjoyed swimming away his hangover in the South China Sea and being away from Boca. He swam and swam until the sun was lower than the slopes of Monkey Mountain. He toweled himself dry with his uniform, dressed and went back to the compound. As he walked through the beach gate, a Nung guard carrying an ancient carbine began to prepare for the night by dragging a roll of concertina wire across the opening. The evening was closing in all at once. There were no languid pastel summer evenings in Vietnam, just an abrupt shutdown every evening at six all year round.

It was Happy Hour in the club bar. Lopez decided to get drunk while the whiskey was still half-price. The mood in the bar was subdued and quiet. A small group of officers and someone in civilian clothes were talking in low voices at the end of the bar. Lopez suspected that the civilian was CIA. He wasn't one of those Ivy League Rhodes Scholar mandarins who ran the Agency in the 1950s. He was one of the new fox-faced kids from the trailer parks, in mirror-reflective sunglasses and Hawaiian shirt, long black hair greased and slicked back like a country and western singer. Lopez wanted to drink alone and avoided eye contact, but the deputy commanding officer was in an expansive mood and drew him into the group. 'How's Sergeant Storm getting along?'

'He's an outstanding NCO,' Lopez began the litany of praise: no one would ever criticize a team member in the presence of outsiders. 'He shows initiative, ingenuity, leadership potential and effectiveness under fire.'

Then the CIA man butted in. 'What's Storm's personal body count, Lopez?'

'He's got some kills, but I don't know how many. He doesn't brag about that sort of thing.'

'I didn't mean,' said Krueger, 'how many men he'd killed.' There was muffled laughter around the bar.

'You know,' said the deputy CO, 'that we need to put some NCOs in for commissions. Both you and Redhorn recommended Sergeant Storm. Would you still endorse that recommendation?'

'Completely. He's intelligent, adaptable, shows sound judgement under pressure...'

'Oh, shut up, Lopez. Are you supposed to be Storm's executive officer or his fucking PR agent?'

'Sir, I...'

'Don't waste your breath, Lopez. I know exactly what you're going to say next. It's going to be all that shit about how an officer has to be loyal to his men, or some such crap. Don't bullshit me about Storm – real name Pavel Kirillov – he's a faggot who used to peddle his butt on the Ku'damm. Comrade Kirillov's not just a fruit, he's a cunning psychopath of a fruit. Isn't that right, Krueger?'

The CIA man nodded. He wouldn't take his sunglasses off and hadn't taken advantage of Happy Hour to tank up on cheap booze. He was drinking orange juice. 'I met Storm a long time ago. He thought he could scare me, get me real scared. No way man, no way. Then I checked him out.'

A captain who spoke with a slight lisp, winked at the deputy CO and said, 'Krueger, you ever been to Dallas?'

'Course, I been: I was on the grassy knoll. I thought everyone knew that.'

Lopez had had enough of their teasing. He finished his

drink and ignored their catcalls as he walked back to his billet in the beach house. He felt bored and cheated of a good drinking session. As he crawled into bed he looked at the luminous dial of his watch: it was only eight o'clock. He hung a flashlight from the frame of the overhead bunk. He was trying to read an Agatha Christie that he had found in one of the secondhand book boxes that the Red Cross sent to Vietnam. It was a murder mystery set in Sussex, England. There was a Griselda and someone else known as Colonel Protheroe. After a few pages Lopez had forgotten the plot and couldn't keep his eyes open. He switched off the flashlight and fell asleep.

Lopez felt he'd been asleep for decades when the alert siren awakened him. There were often mortar attacks, but usually targeted on the Marine Air Wing close by. Lopez liked watching them. The chance to enjoy a spectacle of exploding helicopters, flaming aviation fuel and general mayhem was well worth the slight risk of being hit by a stray fragment. Lopez pulled on his trousers and padded out on to the veranda barefoot and half-clothed in the balmy night. No luck. The soft purr of the South China Sea was disturbed only by a few explosions which were too mute and muffled to be those of a mortar attack. There were also bursts of small arms fire from what seemed a mile or two away.

The sounds were from the direction of the Command and Control compound at the base of Marble Mountain. It didn't sound too serious. Lopez wondered if one of the Montagnard tribesmen who C and C used on their missions into Laos had drunk too much rice wine and run amok. He was surprised that it didn't happen more often. The Mongtagnards were taken from a forest world where each tree, rock, stream and animal had its own spirit – sometimes a good one, sometimes an evil one, but the familiar spirits were always there. Then one day the Montagnard was seduced from his forest to a witchcraft world of fire-spitting sticks and metal birds where everything from drinking tins to tobacco leaves were covered with messages to strange gods called Coca-Cola, Hershey Bar and Lucky Strike. Then one day he could no longer connect: nothing led to more nothing. So he picked up his rifle – to him a black magic crossbow – and an American ended up with a bullet between the eyes. The Montagnard always seemed to choose a mortar pit for his last stand. They always brought in a tribal elder who tried to get him to surrender. He never did. Eventually someone would crawl up close enough to lob a grenade into the pit.

The small arms fire became more intense and then there were sharper, louder explosions. Lopez changed his mind about the mad Montagnard. Something else was happening.

'Get your gear on, this could be serious.' Lopez recognized the voice, it was the captain from Lang Khe – a camp that everyone knew was truly in the shit. The captain's face was hidden in shadow beneath his helmet. He was armed to the teeth and fully kitted out with flak jacket, webbing and ammunition. He hadn't, however, bothered to find his trousers and his legs shone knobbly and sickly white between his boots and combat jacket. 'Get your weapon and report to your alert position.'

'Where is our alert position?' said Lopez

'I think it's the bunker. Get your stuff and follow me.'

It was a pointless exercise, but Lopez was too tired to argue. He stumbled around in the dark – the captain wouldn't let him use a light – until he found his rifle and webbing.

'Hurry up,' said the captain. He beckoned for Lopez to follow and led the way in a half crouching run to a sandbagged bunker half sunk in the ground. Lopez found it hard not to laugh, but he reckoned that being at Lang Khe had made the captain paranoid and a bit crazy. He followed him into the bunker; the interior was dank and utterly black. Lopez felt his shin brush against a bench and sat down.

'Hello, hello, anybody home?'

There was no answer. The captain told him to keep quiet.

'Do you realize,' whispered Lopez, 'that we're the only people in here? I don't think anyone else is on alert.'

'I still think we should stay here until the All Clear.'

They waited five more minutes. Neither said anything. Finally, the absurdity of sitting alone in a dark bunker while everyone else in the compound was going about as normal got through to the captain. He cleared his throat. They got up and emerged into the open. The small arms fire and explosions had ceased, but a helicopter gunship was pouring a stream of mini-gun fire around the base of Marble Mountain. The mini-gun had a rate of fire so rapid that its tracers formed an unbroken ray of orange light from sky to earth. Lopez found its laser-like death rays a bizarre, almost a beautiful sight. He left the captain, who was gazing mesmerized at the gunship's tactics, and returned to the beach house.

One of the other transient officers had taken advantage of Lopez's brief absence to discard his prostitute into his bunk. She was plump, had oily skin, and her breath smelled strongly of nuoc mam sauce. Lopez tried to push her to one side so he could get into bed too, but she responded by sticking her bottom out even further to occupy the whole mattress. When he tried to lever her against the wall with his knee, she snarled, spat and jabbed him with her elbow. Lopez responded by grabbing her shoulder and forcing her on to her back. As he was about to enter her, she scissored her legs shut, nearly crushing his testicles to pulp, and at the same time raked his back with her nails – the scratches later turned septic. Once again she turned her back and stuck her bottom out like an army of occupation. Lopez tried the knee-in-the-back tactic once more, but this time when her elbow came ramming back he was ready and grabbed it. He got hold of her wrist and twisted her arm up into her shoulder blade until she conceded a thin strip of mattress. A separate war, a separate peace. Lopez, to stop falling out of bed, had to clasp her in his arms like the fondest of husbands.

The captain from Lang Khe, who had prowled the compound for a while after leaving the bunker, finally returned to his bed where he tossed and turned until dawn. Despite the noise of the captain's bedsprings, the whir of mosquitoes, the heat, the smells of sweat and nuoc mam, the snoring of the girl and of an adenoidal helicopter pilot in the top bunk, Lopez held his partner close and fell into a blissful sleep.

The news at breakfast was that the Command and Control compound had been hit by enemy sappers the previous evening and sixteen US personnel had been killed. The sappers had landed on the beach from tiny round fishing boats, like Irish coracles. They had then cut their way through the wire. Someone, probably an insider, had already done 'silent kills' on the sentries by muffling their mouths and sticking a commando knife up their rectums. The sappers proceeded to throw satchel charges into the billets, killing most of the sixteen Americans while they slept. The survivors quickly became aware of what was happening and managed to shoot down four of the sappers before they escaped.

Lopez had known one of the dead Americans and recognized the names of a few others. The captain from Lang Khe, who was sitting next to him at breakfast, had known most of the dead. One had been a roommate of his at West Point, but that didn't stop the captain from gobbling his scrambled eggs and sausages.

'What did you think of all that?' said Lopez.

'Of all what?'

'The C and C sapper attack.'

The captain from Lang Khe took another mouthful of

scrambled eggs. 'If your security is lousy, you deserve to die.'

If anyone deserved to die, thought Lopez, it was Boca. He was determined to kill him. The ideal opportunity would be on a patrol, but Boca was too aware of the enmity to risk being on the same rota. Sometimes the best idea seemed to be fragging – blowing him up with a hand grenade – but the narrow confines of the camp made getting Boca alone difficult. Simply shooting him was the easiest option, but also the most likely route to four years in a military prison; and Boca just wasn't worth it. Lopez knew he was becoming obsessed and started to fear that one evening he'd have too much to drink and would just do it. Lopez found it best to keep out of the way; he started to volunteer to go on patrols. If he spent too much time in the camp he'd either kill Boca or go crazy.

IT WAS AFTER THE DAI BINH PATROL that Lopez first became aware of the blood smell. No matter how much he washed, scrubbed and even burnt his hands with disinfectant, he still couldn't get rid of it. Each time he sniffed, the blood smell was still there. In the past, when he had gutted game or cleaned fish, the smell always went away after a day. Why not this? Maybe he really was going crazy.

Dai Binh was a prosperous village that sold supplies to the enemy. It was such a beautiful village that Lopez expected to be greeted by harp music and showers of lotus blossoms. Dai Binh was protected from floods by high river banks and curled itself like a lazy cat into a bend of the Son Thu Bon.

Lopez's patrol arrived on market day. The center of the village was all color, spice smell and movement. Baskets of live chickens and ducks, piglets for fattening, trays of dried shrimp, cured tobacco leaves twisted into plugs, rice wine, tin utensils, woven baskets and endless bottles of nuoc mam – all were on sale. Cool shaded lanes radiated from the village where lovers could stroll through mature plantations of palm and banana trees. Here the children had fewer running leg ulcers, the people were better fed, and the eyes of the old were less likely to be blinded by trachoma or milky with cataract than in the upper valley.

The Communists were excellent customers – they paid cash for everything and bought rice at double the market price. No one wanted to lose their business. For this reason, none of the patrols from Nui Hoa Den ever made enemy contact at Dai Binh. The VC and NVA were always warned well in advance and withdrew to the foothills.

The village chief, a smiling man with gold capped teeth, invited Lopez and Dusty to spend the night in his own house. They would have preferred slinging their hammocks between a couple of palm trees. Vietnamese beds were just hard wooden platforms – even the pillow was a plain block of wood – but turning the chief down would have caused him to lose face.

In the morning there was a breakfast of fruit, oven-warm bread and café au lait. The coffee was prepared in an ancient gray metal cafetière and dripped on to a two-inch-thick layer of sugared milk in the bottom of a glass. As Lopez watched the coffee drip he wondered if the Communist officers received the same hospitality.

The rest of the day was spent providing security for a veterinary team who were inoculating water buffalo against rinderpest. Two Americans in civilian clothes accompanied them. They were CIA agents pretending to be officials from the Agency for International Development. Lopez recognized the one who seemed in charge – he had seen him drinking orange juice in the club at China Beach. After deploying the CIDG in a secure perimeter, Lopez and Dusty made their way through tall sharp grass to liaise with the vet team. The morning dampness of the grass soaked them to the waist. The China Beach agent was talking to the veterinarian in fluent Vietnamese.

'I know that bastard,' said Dusty.

The agent looked at Dusty over his mirror sunglasses. His eyes were cold, dead. 'Listen up, Kirillov; I hope you're not talking about me, 'cause I don't take that kind of shit.'

'You listen to *me*, punk!'

Lopez saw the confrontation leading to fists or bullets. He grabbed Dusty by the arm and pulled him away. He was surprised to see Dusty so angry, so close to really losing it. Lopez half dragged and half pushed him through the damp grass. Dusty started shouting, 'The guy's not just a drama queen, he's a fucking *faggot* queen! Who does that fruit think he is?'

The agent pretended not to hear him.

Dusty tried to pull free. 'Let me go, OK. I'll cool it, OK. I'll tell you about it someday, OK.'

Lopez let him go, and they rejoined the others.

The agent pretended that Dusty wasn't there and addressed himself to Lopez. 'I think we met before. My name's Krueger, Launcelot Krueger. We're going to be spending a lot of time in your area of operations. And the only thing you have to know is the following: we are not – I repeat not – required to clear our ops with you or to liaise in any way. Is that clear?'

'I'd like to make something clear too. Don't you ever speak to me or any of my NCOs like that again.'

Krueger didn't say anything, he didn't move. The sun reflected off his lenses and made Lopez shield his eyes. The other agent, a red faced balding man in his forties broke in, 'Lieutenant, if you'd been brought up on an Alabama farm like I was, you'd know what we're doing. You see, you just got to keep the stock healthy. This means you got to inoculate some of 'em.'

Krueger pushed his sunglasses back on to the bridge of

his nose and added, 'And it means you got to cull, thin out, the rest of 'em.'

The rinderpest inoculation was only their cover story. Dai Binh had been targeted by Program Phoenix. This meant that Phoenix assassins disguised as Viet Cong guerrillas and carrying Kalashnikov rifles would come to the village in the dark watches of the night. They would kill the village chief, and all the farmers who had been selling rice to the North Vietnamese – and many who hadn't. The bogus Viet Cong uniforms would fool no one; they were just a fig leaf to 'sanitize' the American involvement.

Lopez heard from Krueger again in the evening. One of his 'veterinarians' brought an intelligence report about a supply unit of local force guerillas and rice carriers who were camped in the lightly wooded hills overlooking the rice fields. The VC were waiting for the patrol to leave before returning to Dai Binh to fetch more supplies. Lopez decided to act on the information. Part of him hated the war and hated the killing, but another part of him thrilled to it and needed the catharsis of action.

They set out two hours before dawn. The CIDG column entered the wood just as the damp grayness of pre-dawn twilight began to sketch individual trees from the dark mass of night. Lopez was having an adrenaline rush for breakfast – heart pounding, pores open, goose-bump skin, his mouth dry and copper tasting. He knew it was wrong, but it was exciting.

The platoon was strung out in single file and moving fast, then it slowed to a crawl, then it stopped. A message was passed back: there weren't any words, only fingers on lips. Everyone crouched like cats about to leap. Lopez watched Dusty thumb the selector switch of his rifle from safety to semi-automatic. 'This time,' whispered Dusty, 'we're gonna get some.' A second later the wood in front erupted into a clatter of automatic weapons fire. They all started running towards the noise. The trees were just saplings, the undergrowth was sparse. It was easy to move. The platoon fanned out from single file into a sweeping assault line. Trung Uy Tho was smiling and lashing about with a baton like a mad conductor bullying a tired orchestra. He was hitting CIDG in their faces – some were bleeding – and he was making them run faster. Lopez felt like a halfback sprinting towards a winning touchdown. But when he reached the goal line, the shooting had already stopped. It had been all over in less than a minute.

The body of a dead boy was sprawled in the center of a small clearing, the only casualty. He was wearing black shorts and a white shirt, and seemed too young to be a soldier. None of the CIDG had been hurt. The clearing was about twenty meters in diameter; there was a cooking fire and two bamboo lean-to's with rusty corrugated metal roofs. Lopez asked if there were any captured weapons. There weren't any. The dead boy was unarmed: he had been left behind by the others to rig booby traps, but hadn't had enough time to conceal the trip wires. The CIDG had easily discovered the two booby traps he had set. One was made from a captured American fragmentation grenade slipped inside a Coca-Cola can, which was fastened to a stick hidden in the undergrowth. A trip wire had been attached to the grenade so that if someone caught the wire across his instep it would be yanked out and explode.

The soldier who had dismantled the booby trap was looking for a piece of wire narrow enough to replace the missing safety pin. He found himself in a dilemma – he had a live grenade in his hand, but no means to make it safe other than the pressure of his grip on the spring-loaded handle. The other CIDG were laughing at him.

Afterwards, Lopez realized he ought to have told him to fasten the handle with rubber bands or surgical tape. But at the time he had been too busy arguing with Trung Uy Tho. Most of the CIDG were strung out in assault formation on either side of the clearing. It seemed logical to sweep further up into the foothills in pursuit of the survivors, but Trung Uy Tho was using his veto. He was angry and would only speak to Lopez through the interpreter. Ly tried to explain and mediate. 'Trung Uy Tho says there are too many mines up there, and he thinks we might get trapped in an ambush as well. Please, Lieutenant, don't make him lose face.'

Dusty said, 'Tell the little...' but an explosion cut him short. Lopez threw himself on the ground. He lay there for a while checking for pain or the sickening wetness of blood. When he realized that he hadn't been hurt he got up to see what had happened. The soldier who had found the grenade was lying on the ground and steaming. Half his face had been torn off, and part of his shirt had been burned away and was mottled with dark blood and pieces of burned flesh. He wasn't making any noise, but his body was quivering.

The CIDG had tried to get rid of the live grenade by throwing it into the undergrowth. He didn't know that booby-trapped grenades sometimes had their fuses altered so they exploded immediately instead of after a three-and-a-half-second time delay.

The LLDB medic was kneeling over the wounded CIDG. The soldier was still alive, but the medic confined his treatment to a useless show of straightening the casualty's legs and covering him with a poncho. It was the medic's first patrol and he had received little training in first aid, he had never seen a field casualty before. He looked sickened by it all and completely confused. Dusty opened a tin containing a bottle of serum albumin for intravenous injection and placed it in the medic's hand. He started searching for a vein in the CIDG's remaining arm. The medic inserted the needle several times, but his hands were shaking too much to have any success.

Sporadic small arms fire had begun to rattle somewhere up on the hillside. The soldier's rib cage was shuddering with ugly sucking spasms. His face was a mess – most of the jaw was missing. Dusty grabbed the medic by the arm and tried to show him what he needed to do. He took the medic's hand and tried to make him put his fingers down the wounded man's throat. The air passage was blocked by pieces of tongue, teeth and flesh – it needed clearing. The medic jerked his hand away, his eyes were glazed. He started crying, then he began to throw up. Dusty pushed him hard in the back, so hard that he fell into his own vomit. There was quite a lot of firing by this time.

Lopez started picking the obstructions out of the casualty's throat, but couldn't get his finger far enough past what remained of the tongue to clear an airway. The missing part of the man's face had so filled with blood-swollen tissue that it looked like a slab of raw liver. Dusty searched the medic's satchel for a forceps, but the bag was stuffed with bandages and useless bottles of pills and ointment. A squad of CIDG were lying on the edge of the clearing and firing bursts into the trees. Dusty finally found what he thought was a tracheal tube – it had been used as a spool for winding loose bandage. He unwound the bandage and tried to push the tube down the CIDG's throat. It wouldn't go any further than Lopez's finger had. Dusty handed Lopez a pocket-knife and put his finger on a spot just above the casualty's Adam apple. Lopez pushed the blade in between the cartilage rings – he was surprised that it went in so easily – and noticed that he was wearing a rosary around his neck: another Catholic. He thought it peculiar that the explosion hadn't blown the rosary away.

The plastic tube still wouldn't go in, so Lopez rotated the blade to widen the opening. While he was doing so the soldier jerked his stump upwards and scratched Lopez's face with the jagged ends of charred and splintered bone. Lopez pushed the scorched stump away, but it popped back and scratched his face again. At first it seemed a reflex action, but then Lopez realized the dying soldier was doing it for some purpose. Lopez pushed the arm away again and fitted the tracheal tube into the windpipe.

The popping sound of bullets passing close overhead had become intense. Lopez placed his finger over the end of the tube, but it wasn't drawing breath. Dusty saw the problem; he leaned over, put his mouth to the open end of the tracheal tube and sucked out a small mouthful of blood and mucus. He spat. 'Salty,' he said. Lopez was doing the cardiac massage – cruel rib cracking thumps. Dusty checked the tube and said the soldier was breathing. Lopez put his finger on the opening of the tube; there was a slight suction, like the breath of a wounded bird.

During a lull in the firing they dragged the casualty out of the clearing and into the cover of the wood. Lopez had to crawl so close to the dead enemy soldier that their faces were only inches apart. He was only about fourteen years old; one of his eyes had been shot away, but the other stared dully. There was no more adrenaline rush, only a dead boy wearing clear plastic sandals and a pair of shorts with the sort of sewn-in elastic waistband you see in children's clothing.

When they were a safe distance from the clearing, they called in artillery support and rigged a litter for the wounded soldier, but by this time his respiration was marginal and his pulse undetectable. A few minutes later he was dead, but every so often a ghostly wheeze of trapped air escaped from the blood-stained plastic tube. Lopez looked at Dusty. 'What a waste of time! Why did we bother?'

'Because he wanted us to.'

'Why?'

'Because he needed time to confess his sins.'

Lopez didn't believe any more. Rome had only been the faith of childhood. But for a second it all came back: the whole ghastly horrible awe of being a Catholic. That no matter how much you fuck up your own life and the lives of others, it's always there, glowing and sparkling: forgiveness and redemption.

Lopez found that, if he put his hands under the pillow and away from his face, the smell of blood was fainter. That way he could sleep. The morphine helped too. He had started with the synthetic tablets that the medic had recommended for a cold and a bad cough; they weren't a cure, but they stopped him from making noise on night ambushes. He continued taking the tablets even after the cold had gone, and then started to experiment with the injectable syrettes.

The morphine also helped him deal with what had happened to her. Everything was his fault, and there could be no redemption from that sin because there was no penance searing enough to burn it away. The image would always be there: Ianthe sprawled naked on a rumpled bed in a seedy New York hotel, the sheets and the insides of her thighs smeared with blood. He had known that the guy was weird, even for a back street abortionist. One of the pre-med students had suggested him, told Lopez the guy was a final year medical student at Columbia, so he thought he'd know at least how to do the job. He didn't think he'd turn out to be a sick and incompetent pervert.

On the way to the hotel Ianthe had said, 'I'm not sure I want to do this. It's a sin; it's killing a baby.'

Lopez didn't say anything. He just looked out of the rain-smeared cab window at the greasy bleakness of Manhattan. At the time, he was annoyed at her last minute vacillation. She must, he thought, have known.

She leaned on his shoulder. 'But I can't back out now. Let's get it over with.'

If only, if only – the bitterest stupidest words in the language. He could have told the driver to turn around, could have taken Ianthe in his arms, told her to forget Angel, to have the baby – the child would have been Ianthe and Peter and Tom and Rosie too. But he'd killed them all;

he'd wiped out the line. Why? Because he was jealous, that was the simple shameful truth. Maybe, thought Lopez, that was why it had been so easy that day on the mountain path – he had murdered before.

The hotel was vile, a place where no one would choose to stay the night. The abortionist was a young man dressed in black with a pale white face and long greasy black hair. He looked more like a piano tuner than a medic and spoke with a lisping New York accent. He explained to Ianthe that wouldn't be able to complete the abortion – he could only start it – and that she would have to go to a hospital for a dilation and curettage where they would scrape out the rest of her child. Then he turned to Lopez. 'Do you mind,' he said, 'if you leave us alone? I can't work with anyone watching.'

Ianthe had already taken off her skirt and underpants, and was sitting on the edge of the bed covering her nakedness with a blanket. She looked at Lopez, her eyes seeming to say, 'Don't go. Please stay. I need you here.' But Lopez left anyway. Later, in the ambulance, she told him what had happened.

'Why did you leave me alone with him?'

He was holding her hand in both of his, too shocked and frightened even to cry. 'I'm sorry.'

'I didn't want you to go. He frightened me. And when you walked out the door, you didn't even turn around to smile and wish me luck. All I saw was your back.' She freed her hand and tugged at his sleeve. 'This old gray sweater – so many holes – and black hair over your collar. I thought how much you needed looking after since you left home – and you seemed so crumpled and furtive when you went through that door.'

The paramedic looked at the blood pressure gauge, then said something to the driver. The ambulance lurched forward.

'When you'd gone, he took my face in his hands and told

me not to be afraid. I didn't want him to look at me, I didn't even want him to touch me. Then he started to examine me. He took a long time. I just wanted him to get on with it, but he just kept talking, telling me how pretty I was, how sad it all was. He put his arms around me and tried to kiss me. I pushed him, and I shouted for you but you weren't there – you weren't anywhere. Then he put his hand over my mouth, it was dirty and it smelled of stale cigarettes. I flipped and I started hitting him, then he started saying, "Look I'm sorry, I won't try anything – I'm sorry, OK." I could tell he was scared. He said, "Please don't scream. I promise I won't hurt you." He took his hand away, he was shaking. He put a towel under me and laid out his instruments. It hurt a little to start with, and then a whole lot more – it was unbearable. Then he put the towel in between my legs. And he said, "I'm sorry, I have to go now" and he just ran out of the room. I started screaming..." Lopez remembered the plump black woman with a red wig, a prostitute at the end of her working days, who had called the ambulance, following the stretcher into the street and saying, "God bless you" as they closed the ambulance door. God wasn't listening.

The trip to the hospital seemed to take forever. Ianthe stopped talking. Her hands felt so cold. The towel between her legs was soaked with blood; Lopez wondered why the ambulance crew hadn't started a blood transfusion. She had stopped moving, and looked so pale and washed-out that Lopez tried to hold her, to make contact with her. When they got to the hospital, she opened her eyes again and said 'Why?', and they wheeled her away. Lopez tried to come with her, but they wouldn't let him. He started to push past, but a huge black porter blocked his way. 'Sorry, man, it's staff only can go in there.'

'You can't stop me.'

He felt Ianthe's fingers touch his wrist, faintly as a butterfly's wing. 'No,' she whispered. 'Please, don't.'

He just looked at her. He reached for words, but they weren't there. He watched her being taken away, through the double doors.

Lopez remembered walking the streets all night trying to find him. He bought a kitchen knife in all-night grocery. He planned to kill him North African fashion – his organ shoved down his throat. He wanted him to die real slow. Once Lopez saw someone who resembled him. He shouted, 'Hey you, you fucking bastard!' and chased him half way across Central Park – it was two in the morning – before he finally caught the guy by his coat collar and threw him down on the grass. It wasn't him. Lopez apologized and started to cry and ask forgiveness. He remembered the way his victim started to run away, then looked back and shouted, 'Hey, man, you're sick, you're crazy. You need to see a doctor.'

The only other people on the street seemed to be dangerous addicts in torn leather jackets and sneakers stained black by gutter grime. Occasionally a figure would slide out of the shadows and call him 'chico' or 'hombre' and say something in Spanish that Lopez – even more deracinated than they – couldn't understand.

When dawn came he threw the knife in the East River and checked into a hotel full of car salesmen who were having a convention. He showered, shaved and tried to fall asleep, but it was no good – he just lay in the bed staring at the ceiling. He dressed and went back to the hospital. He arrived on her ward just before noon and asked a nurse if he could see her. The nurse gave him a cold starchy look and disappeared. Five minutes later she came back. 'I'm sorry,' she said. 'You're not allowed to see her.'

'Can you just tell me how she is?'

'We're only allowed to give information on a patient's condition to the next of kin.'

'I am the next of kin.'

Lopez felt the nurse's eyes on his brown face. 'Somehow, I don't think so.'

'Fuck you, I'm going in there now.'

The nurse put her hand on his arm. 'Hey, listen, I'm going to have to ring for security. And that's just going to make things real bad.'

Two huge dark shadows had already appeared. Lopez knew that it was all over, that he had destroyed everything. He asked if he could leave her a note. The nurse gave him a funny look, then said, 'Yeah, sure.' It was a simple message: he loved her and it was all his fault and everything he had done was selfish and wrong. The nurse folded the paper and promised to give it to her.

Lopez needed to be with someone, anyone. His nearest acquaintance was an advertising copywriter named Andrea whose daddy had bought her an apartment on 12th Street. They had once had a one-night stand after a drunken party on Beacon Hill. Andrea gave Lopez a drink, but said she had to go out that evening with a doctor from Belle Vue. At that moment, Lopez was full of hate for all medics, real as well as fake. He asked her date's name, then grabbed her address book, looked up his number and started dialing. She grabbed the phone and told Lopez he was an asshole. He started crying. Andrea rang the doctor and cancelled the date herself.

Then they started to have sex. They had sex over and over again that night and the next morning. Lopez needed to pour all his anger, hate and self-loathing into someone, and also to forget. He emptied his mind of everything but a writhing orgy of erotic images that fantasized him into orgasm after orgasm inside Andrea. That evening they went to see an arty Italian film about a beautiful young woman who killed off her wealthy businessman husband by constantly demanding her conjugal rights. Lopez bought a half-bottle of whiskey and carried it into the cinema in a paper bag. He started to drink himself into oblivion while Andrea sucked him off.

The next afternoon he bought some books and flowers and went back to the hospital. The starchy nurse had been replaced by a sympathetic young nurse with acne. When Lopez explained why he was there, the nurse asked him to come with her. She led him to an interview room and asked him to sit down. 'I'm so sorry, but it's very bad news. She died of hemorrhaging two hours after she was admitted. Her folks were here this morning.' Lopez turned white and started crying. The nurse brought him a glass of water and put her arm around him. She seemed to know everything.

Lopez wandered the streets all afternoon and all night. At midnight, he woke up his roommate at Harvard with a telephone call and told him to take whatever he wanted of his books, clothes and belongings and to give the rest away. In the morning he found a recruiting office and signed up as soon as the doors opened. There was no other place to go. He just wanted to disappear and not have to face anyone or answer any questions. The army gave him that. No one knew who he was or what he had done. And, although it could never be penance enough, the US Army of the sixties still provided routes to those dark places where repentance and suffering were possible.

WHEN LOPEZ was in the basic training barracks at Fort Dix the recruit in the upper bunk was a Christian fundamentalist named Jethroe, who came from a remote hamlet in the mountains of Tennessee, the sort of place that few people other than oral historians doing dialect recordings for the Appalachian Project imagined could exist in twentieth-century America. From time to time Jethroe tried to impress upon his bunkmate the importance of scriptural revelation until Lopez lost his patience. 'Shut the fuck up, Jethroe, there isn't any God – only cretins like you believe in Him.'

Jethroe's trump card was the fact that Lopez hadn't actually read the Bible. He was sure that if he did read it he would see the light. There wasn't much else to do, so Lopez offered him a deal. 'OK, if I read the f–...' he stopped himself from saying, "the fucking thing," because the pain in Jethroe's watery blue eyes behind his pale translucent lashes seemed so acute. 'If I read it, will you stop trying to convert me?' Jethroe agreed. So Lopez read the Bible, Jethroe's personal Bible, his own nicely bound King James Version written in the same Elizabethan English that Jethroe and his family still spoke. It took Lopez a week to finish it. He found much of the language beautiful, but also made notes of divine contradictions and injustices for taunting Jethroe. 'Hey, Jethroe, do you love your mother?'

'Course ah do.'

'God doesn't. God hates women.'

Lopez started to quote from the Bible's rich feast of misogyny, but got no further than Leviticus before Jethroe put his hands over his ears and shouted, 'You talkin' about Jezebels and whores of Babylon. My mama ain't no Jezebel or whore of Babylon.'

Lopez could see that he was really upset and suddenly felt ashamed of himself. He put his arm around Jethroe and said that he was sorry. He could see that Jethroe was fighting hard to hold back the tears.

When Lopez was sent out to find the missing marine reconnaissance team, he kept thinking about the Old Testament miracles he had read about in Jethroe's Bible. The mission was a useless exercise; there had been no contact for three days, and the recon team were, barring a miracle, dead meat. Lopez's search party was on the verge of turning back when an aerial recon reported a mirror signal. It was highly suspicious since there was still no radio contact, so Lopez was asked to check it out. No one wanted to take responsibility for sending a helicopter rescue team into a fiery death trap.

When they were within a hundred meters of the location of the mirror signal, Lopez sent Ho Cuc and Phong forward as scouts to see if it really was the marines. A few minutes later Phong came back smiling. 'It's the Americans,' he said. Lopez could almost hear Jethroe's voice, triumphant – 'Though ah walk through the valley of the shadow of death ah will fear no evil...' But it wasn't God that saved the marines, it was their smell. The lactose-intolerant Vietnamese never eat dairy products; to them, Americans and most other Westerners have a smell like babies, a sort of sour-milk cheesy smell. Phong and Ho Cuc found the lost marines by following their noses.

The marines were hiding in a poorly camouflaged shelter in a bomb crater. The team had, literally, been struck by lightning. The radio operator had been using a long whip antenna during a tropical storm. The lightning bolt might have been hurled by Zeus himself: it was two miles long and carried a punch of over 200,000 amps. It killed the radio operator and roasted the radio. The lightning lit up the whole jungle and made their hair stand up on end.

It was soon dark. It was going to be a long night before the evacuation helicopter arrived at first light. They were surrounded by North Vietnamese, but had lots of air support on call if things got rough. As the night wore on it started raining; the loud patter muffled voices. Lopez found out that the recon team was a lieutenant named Quentin Grey, a Virginian with a soft gentle voice who had majored in French at the University of Virginia, and who had also done a year at the Sorbonne. 'How bizarre can this war get?' said Quentin. 'I mean, how likely are you to meet in Vietnam – in the middle of God-only-knows-where, in a *bomb crater* – another guy who had an exchange year in Paris? When I write my dad about this, he'll think I've been smoking grass.'

'Shhh.'

'What?'

'I heard someone cough.'

'Maybe it was an animal.'

'There are no animals in these mountains. No birds either. They've all been poisoned by defoliant. Don't worry – let's talk about France instead.'

They talked. They talked about Stendhal and de Maupassant, about Simone de Beauvoir and Jacques Brel, about getting drunk on pastis and eating moules et frîtes after midnight, about standing at a zinc bar on a cold morning and ordering un p'tit crème, watching the steam escaping from the coffee machine. And the faces of the regulars, like animated paintings, who talked about Paris St. Germain or the horses at Auteuil. And the buttery aroma of warm croissants.

'What was that?'

'Only artillery.'

'No, that crackling sound.

'The wind? A broken tree falling into a bomb crater? Maybe a rat taking a bite out of your RTO?'

'My room was in a garret in the rue St. Paul. Freezing in winter. But remember those old Paris houses with steep pitched roofs and mansard windows – all the different chimney shapes? I liked the way the roof tiles gleamed on a frosty morning, the shady roofs still sleepy with white frost or light snow, others gleaming and steaming in the sun.'

'Remember how in the spring the Seine flooded the quais and lower promenades, and how the trees shook in the current? And when the water was too high for the boats carrying gravel and coal to pass under the bridges, how the crews just sat around reading newspapers, playing cards or staring at the river? I'd have liked to work on a Seine barge.'

Quentin told Lopez about the sweet sadness of coming back to the Gare d'Austerlitz on a Sunday evening, for he had fallen in love with a girl from the Auvergne – he and she still wrote letters to each other almost every day – and how it was important to the Auvergne girl that their parents met. But it was difficult, for Quentin's father was old and seldom traveled. He was a widowed judge who used to do the gardening in a panama hat and a white linen suit. After Quentin's mother died, he took on a woman named Florence to look after the boy, a tall black woman with high cheekbones who looked like the Queen of the Nile. 'When I was a little kid, I used to be really afraid of thunderstorms. I used to run to Florence and bury my face in her apron. She always smelt of oak, seasoned oak. But during these thunderstorms her aprons and skirts seemed to have the odor of oak smoke. That first night here I buried my face in the jungle floor, in that dank mold, trying to smell oak, trying to find that strong oak scent that would take me back to Florence. Because as long as she was there nothing could harm me: no Viet Cong, no atom bomb!' And there was no one else in the family except him and Florence and his old dad.

The night grew colder and colder and eventually they had to stop talking because they could hear NVA soldiers who seemed to be searching for them. The NVA were so close that they hear them stumbling about and cursing in the total dark of the rain forest night. It was nerve racking, and Lopez wondered how acute was their sense of smell. They were lucky: the NVA soon get fed up and moved on.

At first light the surrounding jungle was thumped and pummeled by bombs and helicopter rockets in preparation for the arrival of the extraction helicopters. As soon as the smoke cleared a huge marine Chinook hovered into position over the teams. There was a ladder hanging from the belly of the helicopter: Quentin hooked the dead Marine to the bottom rung and then clambered up. Lopez and the others followed him. It was impossible to winch them in: the teams that were extracted this way simply attached themselves to the ladder by snap-links and swayed in the breeze until they got back to base.

They ascended through a swirling maelstrom of throbbing noise, whipped dust, earth, leaf and wood. Everything, thought Lopez, seemed to be working to plan. The down blast of the rotors had blown away the poncho that the marines had wrapped around the corpse. The seat of the dead marine's trousers had been burned away when the lightning bolt had passed through his body into the damp earth, Lopez could see the burn marks on his buttocks.

For the first time Lopez started to relax and feel how wonderful it was, what a relief it was, to get out of that place. Just as he was getting use to the idea of being safe and alive, he heard something go 'pop' – and saw a stream of yellow smoke billowing in the wake of the helicopter. He looked up. The smoke appeared to be coming out of Quentin's chest. He was wildly flailing about with his arms and legs in every direction, attached to the ladder only by his shoulder harness and snap-link. The pin of a smoke grenade had snagged on something and pulled out. There wasn't any explosive in the grenade, but there was a phosphorous element that was emitting a scorching scalding white flame. Lopez could see that Quentin was going wild, his face distorted with pain and his mouth screaming, but the cries were lost in the wind. Lopez unhooked his snap-link and started to climb up to help him. He ducked when Quentin's rifle slipped off his shoulder and fell into the jungle. There wasn't enough time. The flame burnt through the rest of Quentin's harness webbing. Lopez watched him fall – it seemed to take such a long time – still trailing a plume of yellow smoke, into the green sea of vegetation. Meanwhile the radio operator's corpse was twisting in the wind like a rag doll; it was attached to the ladder by its feet, and the arms seemed to be waving a grotesque farewell. Smoke continued to billow from under the trees. One of the gunships made a low pass over the spot, then flew on.

Lopez thought of Quentin's father, in his white linen suit, emerging like an apparition from the dahlias and honeysuckle to receive a telegram from hell.

NUI HOA DEN was cold in the winter monsoon; everyone was wearing field jackets. The morphine made Lopez feel even colder. He had been called from the warmth of his bunk to help interrogate a Viet Cong who had just deserted from the wretched village of Phu Gia. When asked why he had left, the deserter simply shrugged his shoulders and said that he'd 'had enough'. Lopez found all his answers vague and unconvincing; he seemed shifty and depressed at the same time. To prove his sincerity, the deserter offered to lead them to a secret arms cache near Phu Gia. The fact that he didn't even bother to ask how much they would pay him for the information made Lopez even more suspicious.

The next day a patrol led by Mr Truong, the best of the CIDG company commanders, set off with the deserter to find the cache which was supposed to be in a cave near the base of Black Widow Mountain. Truong was just as suspicious as Lopez about the deserter. He sent out flank security to check for ambushes and made his column stay off the main trails, even though it meant slow going through thick brush. When they got near the cave, Truong gave the order to halt and went forward alone with the deserter to investigate the cache. At the mouth of the cave someone tripped a booby trap and both Truong and the deserter were killed instantly. When they finally searched the cave there was nothing other than a few obsolete World War One bolt action rifles and some useless and decayed explosives.

The two bodies, wrapped in coarse gray blankets, lay unclaimed in the Dead House. Truong had relatives in Da Nang, but no one knew what they intended to do, if anything. As for the dead deserter – if he was a deserter –

no one was going to mourn for him. It seemed almost certain that he had blown himself up in order to kill a CIDG company commander. Lopez found it all so predictable, so stupid, so pointless.

That evening he went to the Dead House to light incense sticks for them. Peace, he thought, and remembered Eliot's lines, *He who was living is now dead / We who were living are now dying* ... He saw that Truong and the deserter were lying close together, their bodies gently touching, like an old married couple on a stormy night. He listened to the rain drumming on the corrugated iron of the roof and breathed the perfume of the incense smoke. It was pitch dark except for the tiny red dots of the incense sticks glowing like a tiny pair of lizard's eyes. He felt very at peace, like the resigned damned of Dante's ninth circle, the ones whose very tears have frozen. Maybe, he thought, this was where he was meant to come and why he was there.

Later that evening, Boca called Lopez into his cubicle and said they were going to have to do 'something serious' about Phu Gia. They'd argued about the village before. Lopez always maintained that airstrikes ought to be used further up the river where supplies were ferried across or on the trails in the mountains. This time Boca told Lopez that he had his head up his ass and that Truong's death proved that Phu Gia wasn't an innocent village, but 'a running sore that needs to be obliterated.'

Morphine induced lethargy made Lopez disinclined to anger but candid. 'If you do that, you should get the civilians out first.'

'The dumb fucks want to go on living there, that's their fault!'

The following night there was an attack on one of the camp's outposts. From the relative safety of the .50 cal bunker Lopez found the attack a pretty sight. Rocket flashes followed by green tracer poured into the outpost, and red tracer spat out and ricocheted off the mountain rocks, and then the sky was full of parachute flares. The show only lasted a few minutes, but Sergeant-major Dieu managed to get shot in the leg. He was lucky, in that the bullet struck him in the shin, but managed to pass between the tibia and the fibula without damaging either bone. But there were ugly purple holes both back and front, which soon began to fester.

A few days later Lopez went to see Dai Uy Ky about a new directive from Saigon. Ky and all the other Vietnamese commanders had been instructed to give up their extortionate monopolies over camp canteens. At Tien Phouc there had nearly been a mutiny when the Vietnamese CO tried to pay his soldiers in canteen vouchers instead of money. It was common knowledge that the American high command had finally given the Saigon government an ultimatum about blatant corruption in the Vietnamese Army. The American aim was to get the Vietnamese officer corps to spend less time running business rackets and more time being soldiers. Instead, the ultimatum set off a last-chance feeding frenzy of graft.

Dai Uy Ky was shrewd enough to deduce that the Americans were preparing to leg it. He had already started to collect gold Rolex watches; it was a way around the import controls on gold bullion. And Ky had known, long before Lopez, that he was going to have to turn over the canteen to a civilian entrepreneur. Indeed, he had already made a short list, including a Chinese merchant named Chou. The concession had to be awarded on a competitive tender approved by a US officer, in this case Lopez. In reality, the final decision hinged on who would offer the biggest bribe to Dai Uy Ky.

The evening began with dominoes in the Dai Uy's private quarters. It was past midnight and Lopez found it difficult to focus. After a few games, Ky put the dominoes back in their case. 'You're not concentrating, Trung Uy. I can't take your money.' He tried to give back what he had won, but Lopez refused to accept it. 'You make me feel guilty.' Ky took a bottle of cognac out of an inlaid cabinet and poured his guest a large drink. He called his servant and told him to lay the table for supper. The first course was lukewarm rice gruel with pieces of pig intestines. Afterwards there was cold pickled pork wrapped in vine leaves. Ky poured more cognac and asked, 'Is it true that everyone in America has a car?'

'Many, but not everyone.'

'Not everyone?' Ky looked doubtful.

Lopez asked about his daughters and the Dai Uy said they were well and often asked about him. Lopez noticed that Ky was looking at him in a strange way – he wondered if he was being considered as a potential suitor. Ky pinched his arm and said, 'You have skin like a Vietnamese.' Then he smiled and picked up a deck of cards. 'Shall we play poker?'

Lopez nodded and Ky dealt the cards for seven-card stud with aces and one-eyed jacks wild.

As they played Lopez asked if there was any news of Sergeant-major Dieu. There wasn't. Lopez tried to keep the conversation on Dieu; he wanted to see if Ky knew that the Sergeant-major had been a Communist agent. But he couldn't ask directly: there were categories of intelligence information that neither team would share.

Ky knew that Lopez was probing him. He didn't want to appear evasive and impolite so he told him about Dieu's sex life instead – it was OK to talk about that. Dieu had quite a reputation. Soon after arriving at Nui Hoa Den, he had seduced the cooks, moved on to the camp nurse, and then talent-scouted the surrounding villages. A recurrent nuisance had been shouting matches at the camp gates between the guards and hysterical husbands, weeping women, and homicidal mothers. 'Did you know that Dieu is fifty-three years old?' asked Ky.

'He looks younger.'

Ky went on to describe Dieu's wife – 'a very patient woman' – and her business interests in Da Nang and their two children. The son was an army officer, Ky said, but didn't specify which army. It was difficult to gather how much Ky really knew about Dieu's double life, and about how much it really mattered. Perhaps, for them, thought Lopez, the barriers between friend and foe were permeable membranes rather than iron curtains.

Dieu wasn't at all well. Lopez and Carson arrived just before he was carted off for his second amputation. Carson had brought a bottle of Scotch as a present, but knew that it would disappear if he left it on the ward. He held Dieu by the hand – it was dry and feverish, and there was a sickly sweet smell of corruption from the gangrene. Carson told Dieu that he would keep the whiskey in safekeeping until after the operation. He also told Dieu that he was pissed off to see him getting such a rotten deal. They had tried to get him transferred to an American hospital, but it couldn't be done. Carson's own wound had been very similar: an uncomplicated puncture wound that had missed bones and organs. He had complained at first when they doubled the diameter of the bullet path by running a drill through his thigh to bore out all the dead and damaged flesh, but he was back on duty in less than a month.

The staff at the Vietnamese Army hospital didn't drill out Dieu's wound; they made no attempt to debride it at all. Maybe they didn't know how, maybe they didn't have the equipment. In fact, they did nothing but paint the surfaces of the wound with antiseptic and then put a dressing on it. Septicemia set in, and then they didn't give him enough penicillin – if it was penicillin at all (the Harry Limes of the medical supply corps were selling it on the black market where Viet Cong agents paid excellent prices). Then gangrene set in and they amputated his leg just below the knee – but not high enough. So now they had to amputate again, leaving just enough thigh to fit an artificial limb.

While Carson was flying back to Nui Hoa Den, clutching the whisky he had wanted to give his friend and hoping that no one could see his tears, Lopez was drinking pastis on the balcony of Le Grand Hôtel in the old port quarter of Da Nang. He was waiting for Mr Chou. As he drank, Lopez fantasized that he was back in France. The illusion was helped by the presence of the only other customer, a tall dapper Frenchman wearing wraparound sunglasses and a white linen suit. The Frenchman sat a discreet two tables away, drinking a café crème and reading the financial pages of Le Figaro.

The balcony of the hotel was screened, not against terrorist grenades like other restaurants, but merely because of the mosquitoes which rose from the river which ran parallel to the street. Le Grand Hôtel didn't need anti-grenade mesh on its windows – the management paid protection money.

There were few Americans in Da Nang. The city had been declared off limits after two pilots, who went off to find girls, found their throats cut instead. Their bodies later turned up on a rubbish tip with their hands bound and their amputated sex organs shoved down their throats. Lopez wasn't worried – the pilots had just been unlucky, and maybe careless too. Still, he wished that he were wearing a white suit like the Frenchman instead of a green US army uniform. Then he could ask him about the latest rubber prices on the bourse and everyone would think that – with his skin – he was, say, from Marseilles and had an Algerian mother.

Lopez liked sitting on the balcony amid all the fading

elegance of peeling shutters and Art Nouveau ironwork, watching beads of sweat form on the ice-water jug and listening to the music of the street and river. A world, a civilized world, away from Boca and the Americans.

Lopez was too preoccupied to notice Chou's arrival. The merchant was wearing a white shirt, light blue trousers and the sort of smart white canvas shoes worn by 1930s yachtsmen. Chou bragged about being the last in a line of Chinese merchants who first arrived in Da Nang in the 1890s. The rest of his extended family had long since moved on to Singapore, Malaysia, the Persian Gulf, Canada. Chou alone had remained in Vietnam, and now he realized it was almost time to go. He knew that one day the Americans were going to leave and that, no matter which Vietnamese won, that his *carrottes*, as the French used to say, would be cooked. So he had to pile up lots of loot, an escape fund for bribes, exit visas and the cost of setting up again in whichever backwater of the Pacific he could buy himself an entrance ticket.

Chou immediately spotted Lopez on the hotel balcony and introduced himself. The merchant ordered a round of drinks. There was half an hour of small talk before Chou started the process of negotiation and bribery. They drank another round of pastis before they left the hotel. Their first destination was a jeweler. His shop was full of stuff other than jewelry, weird things which had mysteriously found their way there from all over the world. On the wall hung an English bowler hat and a rolled umbrella. Lopez, unable to imagine how it had got there, took the hat down, blew the dust off it and looked inside; it had apparently belonged to a P.W. Long, Esq., and had been supplied by Medler and Gower, Gentlemen's Outfitters, of Norwich.

Chou asked what the lieutenant would like for his wife. Lopez said there wasn't one. Chou then asked who was the most important woman in his life. Lopez felt the pain come back, sharp, sudden, in the center of his being.

'Your mother? A sister, perhaps?'

Lopez thought of Quentin. He wondered if the girl from the Auvergne had learned that her lover was dead – or if it mattered. 'A Frenchwoman,' he said.

'Not an American? How interesting.'

'No, not one of them.'

'What is her name?'

Quentin hadn't said. Lopez picked the first French name that came to mind. 'Sophie.'

'Is she blonde and fair?'

'No; au contraire, she has thick black hair and smooth olive skin.'

'Then gold would suit her. Is she of the town?'

'No, the country. Her father is a herder in the Cantal, the highest mountains of the Auvergne. In the winter, she has to get up two hours before dawn to milk the goats and to break the ice in their water troughs.'

Chou lit another Gitane. 'She sounds a most extraordinary young woman.'

'She certainly is. Her passion is music. She plays the cello – so much concentration, her eyes become bottomless dark pools. A man could drown in them.'

The jeweler meanwhile kept fetching trays of rings, bracelets and anklets, all of which Chou waved away as not being worthy of the Trung Uy's 'shepherdess'. Lopez found the jewelry on offer flashy and vulgar, but after twenty trays of tat there was one piece – diffident and almost inconspicuous amid the brassy brooches and necklaces – that caught his eye. It was an antique hair clip made from Vietnamese gold. Chou congratulated Lopez on his good taste. The hair clip was a beautiful piece, simple but elegant and engraved with the Chinese symbols for happiness and long life. Lopez tried to imagine what it would look like in the thick black tresses of his imaginary girl from the Auvergne. He tried not to imagine what it would have looked like on Ianthe.

While the jeweler wrapped the hair clip, Chou asked Lopez what he would like for his favorite concubine. When he explained there was no concubine, Chou became distraught. He looked so upset that Lopez was tempted to invent a second woman.

That evening they went back to Le Grand Hôtel for dinner. There was fish followed by roast duckling and braised pigeons. Chou ordered the most expensive white Burgundy on the list. He restricted himself to a glass of beer and insisted that Lopez finish the wine on his own. As his honored guest, Chou offered Lopez the heads of the birds. Chinese etiquette meant that Lopez had to suck out the brains, which he did.

After coffee and liqueurs, Chou drove Lopez to a house on Trung Trac Street where he had arranged an appointment with the beautiful concubine of a Vietnamese general, who had learned to be entrepreneurial in his absence. She did to Lopez – only with consummate skill and subtlety – what he had done to the duck and pigeons.

The next morning Lopez watched the most remarkable monsoon rain squall he had ever seen sweep in from the South China Sea. The rain came in solid sheets at a forty-five degree angle, the surf was being pounded so hard that it was simmering over the beach like boiling milk, the sand had turned into wet pastry. The rain made Lopez think about Sergeant-major Dieu: it was as if his ancestral spirits were foaming out of the void to greet him.

Lopez knew that it was going to be his last visit to the hospital. This time there weren't even sheets. Dieu's stump bandage was stained with dark fluids. Lopez found the stench of gangrene putrefaction overpowering. Dieu already knew the truth, he knew that he was going to die. Lopez asked him if he wanted morphine.

'No.' His voice was soft and faint, almost like a child's.

'You've always been a Communist cadre, haven't you?'

Dieu's eyes were fixed on a lone fly buzzing above his face. It wasn't envy, just regret that the fly was still going to be alive when he was dead. The fly, drawn to the smells coming from the stump, disappeared to the other end of the bed.

'Maybe,' said Lopez, 'it was the right path to follow.'

'Some water, please.' Lopez held the cup to Dieu's lips. He drank. 'You ask me these questions even when I'm dying.'

'Because now we can't hurt you: you can tell the truth.'

For a long time Dieu stared into nothingness. He was so still and quiet Lopez wondered if he was already dead.

'Maybe,' said Lopez, not knowing whether the man he was speaking to was alive or dead, 'maybe, I want to follow that path too. Tell me how.'

Dieu stirred with all the strength and anger of death, and turned his eyes on Lopez. 'You want their names, so you can torture them to find out more names, so you can kill them.'

'No, I would never hurt them. I might help them. Trust me.'

'Trung Uy Lopez, when an interrogator says "trust me" he really means "fuck you".'

Lopez reached under the sheets and touched Dieu's arm; it was hot and dry, like a kindling twig. 'For months I protected you, for months Redhorn and Boca wanted you arrested. They knew all about you.'

'Tactics, not protection. You wanted to see where the thread would lead.' He closed his eyes and lay back breathing deeply. After what seemed a long while and many thoughts Dieu reached out and took Lopez's hand. 'But – but – I will give you one name and no more.' Passion and madness had begun to glow in his eyes, he drew Lopez to him and whispered a name in his ear, the name of his wife.

'Whatever you think, I won't betray her. It is our secret.'

Dieu's whisper was barely audible. 'It doesn't matter.'

'Why her? Why expose her and not the others?'

Dieu used all his strength to raise himself on his elbow; his voice was full of bitterness. 'Is she here? Is she here now?'

A week after Dieu's death Lopez went back to Da Nang so he could pay his condolences to the widow. She was known as Madame Nguyen Thi Binh – Lopez wondered why she hadn't taken her husband's name. He found Madame Binh's house by turning off Doc Lap Street into a dingy alley where there was a bicycle repair shop. Someone, probably Ky, had told him that Madame Binh owned the lease. There were three greasy hard-looking men in the bike shop who stared at Lopez as if trying to intimidate. The alley then opened unexpectedly into a small sunny courtyard with a fountain and miniature trees; Madame Binh's house was on the left.

She greeted Lopez with poise, dignity and a limp handshake. Madame Binh was an imposing full-breasted woman of about forty. Lopez found it difficult to imagine her and Dieu rolling around in the sack together; she seemed too stately for his tastes. The widow was wearing a formal ao dai with a high stiff collar, and her hair was pulled back into a bun revealing delicate ears pierced with small jade earrings.

She placed Lopez in a small stuffy room next to the entrance hall and left him there while she went to arrange tea. On one wall was an out of date Bank of Hong Kong and Shanghai calendar with a color photograph of a modern bustling harbor, all gleaming cranes and container ships. The only other decorations were two silk screen prints depicting lonely mountain crags with a bird or two clinging to weather-blasted branches. There was also a live bird in an ornamental cage.

A servant girl in her teens brought the tea. She was slight and pretty except for a damaged and blind eye that was shriveled to the size of a pea. Conversation with Madame Binh was difficult because every time Lopez tried to speak, the bird – a type of canary – burst into a song so melancholy and beautiful that interrupting would be ill mannered. Meanwhile, Madame Binh seemed so detached that Lopez wondered if she had forgotten that he was there. When she did speak Lopez wasn't certain whether she was talking to him or to the bird – and sometimes she seemed to be speaking to both of them or to no one at all. There were many silences. Finally, Madame Binh caressed the birdcage, cooed at its inmate and then explained to Lopez that the bird sang so much because it had lost its mate. She then looked at the floor and added, 'The bird and I, Lieutenant Lopez, are very much the same: we have both lost our mates.'

Lopez started to tell her how much he had admired and respected Sergeant-major Dieu. She stopped him from saying more – 'Not him, not him.' Lopez wondered what to say next; he decided to keep quiet. Madame Binh looked at the floor. Lopez looked at the floor too, waiting for the passage of minutes to dilute the embarrassment. After a while, when he realized that he could spend the rest of the day studying the cracks in Madame Binh's floor tiles, he said, 'War and lost love are very sad things.'

Madame Binh said nothing – she merely moved her head slowly from side to side, very slowly. She was in a different world, in an almost catatonic trance.

A minute later she snapped out it, poured more tea and told Lopez that she and her friend often went to see movies at the Institut Français on Bach Dang Street. The last one she had seen was *L'Année Dernière à Marienbad* – she had found the story difficult to understand. Her favorite movies were *Singin' in the Rain* – which made her feel happy – and *Brief Encounter* which, despite having to read the French subtitles, she had seen four times.

When Lopez rose to leave Madame Binh shook hands again and said, 'When you return to Nui Hoa Den, please give my best wishes to Nguyen Van Kim.' For a second or two Lopez was surprised that she knew Mr Kim. Then something jogged his memory. Was it an unguarded remark or a facial expression? Things were connecting.

When Lopez went back to his jeep the bicycle shop gang stopped work once again so they could stare. They watched Lopez as he crawled underneath the jeep to check for booby traps. He could hear them laughing. His final check was inside the fuel tank. The Viet Cong sometimes used young boys to slip grenades wrapped in surgical tape into the gas tanks of American vehicles: after a time the solvent property of the gasoline dissolved the adhesive, allowing the tape to unwind and release the arming lever of the grenade. The resulting fireball would turn the driver into a human torch. Lopez thought the jeep seemed clean, but the grins from the bike shop worried him and made him check again.

Lopez turned left into Bach Dang Street – he had decided to make a detour to see what was on at the Institut Français. As soon as he completed the turn, a white-canopied Japanese jeep swerved in front of him and made him stop. How, thought Lopez, did he know where to find me? He must have his own spy network. Mr Chou got out of his jeep and feigned surprise: 'Ha, ha. Is it not funny, Lieutenant Lopez, that we meet again so soon? But I am so glad.' Lopez felt his elbow clamped by a bony tentacle of a hand. 'Only yesterday I was thinking: Lieutenant Lopez needs a new wristwatch; that one's good enough for a soldier but not for an officer...'

It soon became evident that the canteen deal had been a success and that Chou wanted to show his gratitude. Lopez was escorted to another jeweler where an officer's Rolex replaced his soldierly Seiko. Afterwards there was lunch at the Club Select where Chou asked Lopez if he knew anything about the canteen franchise at Lang Khe. The merchant had heard that the concession was still open for bidding. Probably, thought Lopez, because the camp was under siege. In any case, he promised to help. Chou showed his gratitude by buying Lopez another blow-job (not as good as the general's concubine) and 'souveniring' him a bottle of Pernod.

Lopez averted his eyes from the I Corps mortuary as he drove past on his way back to China Beach, but couldn't block his ears to the funereal hum from the Graves Reg refrigeration condensers. After all, they had to keep the boys nice and fresh. Lopez remembered that he still had to pick up December's pay for the CIDG, and was annoyed with himself for forgetting to ask Madame Binh if she had received the death gratuity for Sergeant-major Dieu.

Christmas passed unobserved and unlamented at the C-team HQ. They had been spared Bob Hope, but were visited by a famous actress in her mid-fifties who, owing to her status as a reserve colonel in the Nursing Corps, was dressed in full combat gear. Lopez was drunk when she arrived unannounced in the officers' club bar, and he found the whole thing surreal. The last time he had seen the woman was on film – in a flag-waver Second World War movie playing a nurse trying to cheer up battle wearied troops somewhere in the Pacific – and now here she was doing the same thing all over again. He wondered where the cameras were.

It got more bizarre still. When she had finished her comedy routine, she started hugging and kissing. Lopez got a bit of tongue. The actress told him, 'You Latino boys are the greatest lovers.' Travis got her to autograph his underpants. She ordered drinks all around, downed a double whiskey, and said that she loved them all 'to bits', but apologized for not being able to do more. 'Because,' she said, 'if I fuck one of you, I'll have to fuck all of you and a bunch of studs like you would be too much for an old girl like me.' A second later she was gone, blowing kisses like crazy, on her way to visit some 'fly boys'. Lopez thought he could still smell her perfume clinging to his combat blouse.

Later, Travis and Lopez got even more drunk. Stinking drunk. Travis had just been discharged from the hospital at Monkey Mountain – he had managed to get shot through the hand during an altercation with his Vietnamese counterpart. In order to save face all around, Travis been re-assigned to Lang Khe, the northernmost camp, the one that was 'truly in the shit', and where Chou wanted a canteen concession.

When he got really drunk – 'hawg-whimperin' *assholed*' – Travis stripped off his bandages and flourished his wounded hand. 'This here, you guys, is a gen-u-wine stigmata. I want you all to know – it appeared the day I renounced sexual sin.' Later, after even more drink, he started claiming to be 'Jee-sus Christ, crucified and risen from the daid.' Lopez was surprised how many officers found his behavior offensive. Maybe there were more closet Christians in the unit than Lopez had supposed.

The next morning, while Travis was trying to sober up, Lopez sat on the side of his bunk and started to tell him about Mr Chou and his interest in Lang Khe. Travis said he didn't give a fuck who got the franchise. 'The only thing I want,' he buried his head in the pillow, 'is to stop that sledgehammer wrecking what's left of my brain.'

'You should be grateful. I'm trying to do you a favor.'

'Gracias.'

'Chou's a useful guy to know. Nice food, nice girls, nice ... whatever you want.' Lopez often wondered if Travis had secret vices.

'Look, when I get better I'll really regret not doing this, but I have to go out to Lang Khe on the next chopper. So how do I meet this guy?'

'I'll bring him out to see you.'

'Great idea. We can have us a nice coffee morning with angel food cake and lemon meringue pie.'

Two days later Mr Chou arrived at China Beach, dressed in

tan slacks, a white shirt and a panama hat. Lopez signed him through the security gate and drove him to the helicopter pad. Lopez realized he had made a mistake as soon as he saw the other Lang Khe passengers: they were wearing helmets and flak jackets and looked nervous. He took Chou aside and suggested they postpone the trip, that Lang Khe wasn't 'open for business.' The merchant simply made a dismissive hand gesture and said, 'War is good for business.'

As the helicopter climbed to ten thousand feet above the Hai Van Pass, Chou started to turn sickly pale with cold. Narrow-chested and dressed for a garden party, he looked like a porcelain ornament mislaid in a lethal crate full of the chunky green and black paraphernalia of war. Lopez felt guilty. He took off his helmet and flak jacket and gave them to Chou.

After half an hour Lang Khe appeared out of a thin mist. The camp lay at the top of a narrow valley and was surrounded on three sides by dark mountains with jagged ridgelines. The helicopter came in high and dropped towards the square of green steel planking which marked the camp's helicopter pad. It was a feint. At about two hundred feet the pilot banked sharply away and veered towards the outer perimeter. Lopez looked behind and watched a pair of gray puffs appear dead center on the steel planking. The exploding mortar rounds looked as transparent as fine gauze.

The helicopter glided over an outer line of barbed wire defenses; the body of a naked man impaled on stakes flashed by; the door gunner fired a long burst at the tree line, then the pitch of the rotor blades suddenly changed. They were in a stationary hover a few feet above the sandbagged roof of an outer perimeter bunker. The helicopter was unloaded in a blur of sand-whipped turbulence: mortar tube and base-plate, mail bag, Mr Chou, ammunition, cases of beer, personnel replacements were out; and an indistinguishable flurry of figures, some being carried, were in.

The new arrivals were already inside the bunker when the helicopter pulled pitch and headed back to China Beach, clean sheets, and half-price drinks in the club during Happy Hour. No one moved; they were all crouched down and waiting with their hands over their ears. The re-targeted mortar rounds finally impacted – ten seconds too late to catch the helicopter, but near enough for Lopez to hear the sudden whoosh of air being sucked into the explosion.

What was visible of Mr Chou – most of him was hidden beneath Lopez's helmet – looked confused. Lopez grabbed him by the arm and led him, speechless and dazed, down a section of trench line to the LLDB communications bunker. He left Chou with two NCOs who were playing cards in front of a radio receiver which emitted a stream of static interspersed with unanswered but urgent messages in Vietnamese. Chou was invited to play a third hand. Lopez continued on alone to the command bunker, hoping to find Travis. It was a clear beautiful day. After the dull mugginess of Da Nang and the coastal plain the mountain air was invigorating.

The half of the command bunker that was above ground was a smooth concrete dome, nearly five feet thick. Lopez tripped over something as he entered. A bottle of serum albumin dangled on a stick above it; a medic reached underneath, pulled out the needle and said, 'He doesn't need that any more.' There were a number of Americans; most of them were shouting into radios or arguing over maps. No one paid any attention to Lopez – his being there was silly and senseless, he felt invisible. Lopez leaned down and lifted the corner of the poncho that covered the dead man's face. It was Travis. He felt sick; he just wanted to leave. He finally managed to find the team sergeant, and told him that he needed a flight back to the C-team 'urgently'.

The sergeant replied, 'Ain't going to be no more choppers today, sir. But if you got a dime, you can call a cab.' Someone threw Lopez a quilted poncho liner and told him that he'd have to bed down in an ammunition bunker.

That night the mountain seemed to wink at Lopez. Each wink was the back-blast of a rocket being launched. Two or three seconds later it would impact with a shatteringly loud crack. The noise was the worst thing about rockets. They didn't throw out much shrapnel and seldom found their ways into mortar pits or trench lines. Rockets were intended for penetration, for use against armored vehicles, bunkers or buildings. Because Lopez was in a sunken mortar pit at the time, he wasn't too worried about watching the mountain wink in the night. Mortar rounds, on the other hand, were lobbed in a high trajectory and could, theoretically, land in the bottom of a well shaft. They didn't penetrate; they splattered. Mortars were intended for 'soft targets', which was what the weapons manuals called humans. A mortar round leaving its tube makes a sound like a bottle of wine being uncorked. Whenever Lopez heard eternity's wine waiter opening another bottle, he ducked back into the bunker.

His companions were two Bru Montagnard tribesmen and an American sergeant. The Montagnards smiled and giggled continually, their way of expressing nervousness. The American grumbled continually – that was *his* way – until Lopez told him to shut up. The sergeant had been complaining bitterly about the poor quality of support they were receiving from the C-team. He had the impression that Lopez was personally responsible for a missing mortar tube – 'I requisitioned two tubes, sir, not one tube and a base-plate. Why do we need a fucking base-plate? What did you send it for? We sit out here getting our ass shot off, people back there don't give a fuck. What the fuck we want a base-plate for? Can't shoot it, can't shit it. Goddam thing weighs a ton, can't even throw it at them. What we fucking supposed to do? Drop it on their goddam toes when they walk in the door?'

Lopez explained for the twentieth time that he was only there 'as a tourist' and had nothing – 'absolutely nothing whatever' – to do with the supply section. He wanted to order the sergeant to shut up, but he hated pulling rank. Someone sent up an illumination round from the 4.2 pit. Suddenly the voice became a person. The sergeant's face, illuminated by the greenish light of a parachute flare, had the twisted features of a medieval saint carved in stone and lit by Lenten tapers.

The previous evening a shell had dropped into the mortar pit. The explosion had killed a Montagnard and bent the mortar tube, but hadn't damaged the virtually indestructible base-plate at all. Earlier in the evening Lopez had noticed a bit of 'soft target' – a piece of brain, barely enough to fill a teaspoon – lying next to the side of the pit. A fly was crawling on it. When he looked again, it was missing. Presumably it had been carried away by a rat, probably one of the same rats that had run across his body in the dark watches of the night after he had wrapped himself in the poncho liner and settled down to a fitful sleep between two rows of stacked boxes of 81mm high explosive.

The morning was strangely quiet. Lopez was waiting for the helicopter in a perimeter bunker with two Americans and a number of Vietnamese. An LLDB officer, who had been wounded in the hand, wore his arm in an elaborate sling. One of the Americans was Eric Rider, who had been transferred from Tien Phouc to the Mobile Reaction Force and was visiting Lang Khe to report on the feasibility of sending reinforcements. The other was Captain Carlsson, the chaplain. Carlsson had recently replaced the previous chaplain – the one Rider and Redhorn had handcuffed over a chair in the officers' club. The new chaplain had porcelain blue eyes, smoked a pipe and wore a tranquil smile which radiated reassurance. He came from a place in Wisconsin where there were a lot of dairy farms, and where the girls – clean-limbed blue eyed descendants of Scandinavian immigrants – made their boyfriends wear condoms.

Chou was nowhere to be seen. The last time Lopez saw the merchant he had been playing dominoes with the Vietnamese camp commander, negotiating the canteen buy-out arrangements. Chou had told Lopez 'not to worry'.

The sound of distant helicopter blades began to echo, intermittently at first then steadily, against the mountainsides. Outranked and unwounded, Lopez realized that his chances of getting a place were slim. He decided to wait for the next one. The staccato beat of the rotors became louder and more intense. A sergeant pulled the pin of a smoke grenade, but waited until the helicopter was nearly overhead before he dropped it outside the bunker. The pilot homed in on the smoke and the sound of the blades suddenly rose to a crescendo as the helicopter landed on the roof. The hopeful passengers scrambled out into a maelstrom of stinging sand and acrid yellow smoke. After a second or two there was a great vibrating noise as the blades changed pitch, and then the clatter of the rotors decreasing into the near distance.

The smoke and dust settled and the ones who had failed to get a place returned below. There was a lot of cursing in Vietnamese. Lopez was surprised to see Rider still there. 'Couldn't you get on?'

'There was room for only one more.' Rider's deep-set eyes gave his face a sinister skull-like quality. 'The chaplain offered me the place, but I somehow felt he deserved it more.'

Lopez watched the helicopter as it gained height against the backdrop of still crystal-clear blue sky. Soon it was a small dark silhouette, gradually losing form and diminishing. Then it appeared to cough – it shuddered and released a puff of black smoke. The helicopter spun slowly downwards until it disappeared behind a stark and jagged mountain ridge. Something about it reminded Lopez of Madame Binh's forlorn silk-screen birds.

He finally managed to get a place on a helicopter in the afternoon. They were all terrified, all thinking the same thought: 'How many more heat seeking missiles do they have?' No one said a word, not even after they got back.

EVERYONE HAD TO ATTEND the eight o'clock morning briefing at the C-team, even if they were 'just visiting'. Lopez always sat in the back row hoping that he wouldn't be noticed and asked any questions. He had celebrated his safe return and mourned Travis until well after midnight. He would have had a thumping hangover if it hadn't been for the morphine.

When Lieutenant Colonel Cale strutted in he was obviously in one of his don't-fuck-with-me moods. The staff snapped to attention. Cale was followed by his deputy and the adjutant, both with gray serious faces. The colonel plumped himself into an armchair positioned a few inches forward of the ordinary folding chairs in the front row. He coughed and the staff sat down again. The adjutant drew back a curtain that was stenciled SECRET, to reveal a huge topographical map which covered all of I Corps. Lang Khe, inconspicuous in the top left-hand corner, had been reduced to a small blue rectangle surrounded by several red rectangles. Each section leader marched to the map – each officer a brisk automaton with left hand open against the small of his back, left forearm parallel to ground, pointer firmly grasped in right hand – 'never reach untidily across body' – and reported as appropriate on the intelligence, operational or logistical developments of the past twenty-four hours. The supply officer was given an impressive grilling about Lang Khe in particular and about his inadequacy as a human being in general. After he was permitted to return to his seat, the colonel twisted around in his armchair and scanned the rows of well-scrubbed staff-officer faces to find his next target. It was Johnson, the medical officer.

'Captain Johnson.'

'Sir.'

'Have the chaplain's dental records been forwarded to Graves Registration?'

'No, sir. But will do ASAP.'

'Do it now.'

The doctor excused himself and trotted off. Archer, the lieutenant from Tra Bong, leaned over and whispered to Lopez, 'Is he dead?' Archer's eyes were sparkling with mischief. He wanted Lopez to pass the message on so that everyone in the back would be squirming and trying not to laugh at the grotesque understatement.

'It's not funny.'

'Oh, come on. When you got back from ID'ing Redhorn, you got drunk as a skunk and went around singing the Baggy Song.' The Baggy Song was sung to the tune of 'Camptown Races': *Sonny got killed in Vietnam, doo dah, doo dah.* Lopez didn't like being reminded that he had been like that. It seemed such a long time ago.

'It wasn't funny then, and it's not funny now.'

'Something's wrong with you, Lopez, you ought to see a doctor.'

Lopez was sick, sick of the army, sick of war. He didn't want to be with any of them. He wanted to be in a meadow that sloped down to a slow river lined by willows. He wanted someone to hold him tight and breathe on his neck; he wanted to fall asleep with his head in her lap. He felt as if someone had pushed 'fast forward' on a tape recorder – everything seemed to be coming apart all at once.

When Lopez got back to Nui Hoa Den there was a new medic. He had replaced Huber, who had only been at the camp a month, and who had to return to the States because his wife had become depressed and suicidal. The chaplain, the one who had just been reduced to dental records, had managed to get Huber sent home for compassionate reasons.

The new medic, Bobby Hatch, was a conscientious objector. He came from a place in northern Vermont near the border with Quebec. When the team first heard about the new medic, there was a lot of grumbling. 'Last thing we need is some fucking anti-war peacenik creep.' But Hatch turned out to be a tall blond athlete who drank, told rude jokes, didn't believe in killing but didn't mind using his fists, and had the looks of a film star. He was big, self-confident and gentle. He became the most popular team member. But Lopez didn't want Bobby Hatch at the camp – he was too innocent, too clean.

Bobby's family were descendants of a nineteenth-century Utopian New England sect famous for their handmade furniture. When he was drafted, he claimed exemption as a conscientious objector. The tribunal turned him down because there was no evidence of his having a coherent religious or philosophical belief that opposed war. He just wanted to keep making chairs and cabinets, and play in his rock band at weekends. So they drafted him anyway, but conceded that he wouldn't have to 'bear arms' if he became a medic.

While he was in basic training, Bobby was talent spotted by one of the army's slickest PR operators. He told him how much they respected him for being a conscientious objector. It was, in fact, 'a cherished right of every American' and wouldn't prevent him from playing a valued role in the army. Bobby was naïve enough to take the bait, and ended up volunteering for Special Forces. The PR types knew he was a keen outdoorsman, and they managed to make all the parachuting, scuba diving and outdoor living irresistible. The PR people loved him and at first Bobby was flattered by all the attention. There were lots of news articles about 'The

Green Beret Pacifist' – just what was needed to counter SF's psychopath image. Later Bobby found it all embarrassing and realized that he had been used. But he had gone too far to quit, and he still rationalized that being a combat medic was 'doing good'.

What happened to Bobby was proof of what Lopez had learned only too well. The military industrial complex were not all dumb shits like Boca – they had brains too. And those brains knew so well how to twist and re-package everything, they could market dog shit as baby food.

It was three in the morning and Lopez was sweating and murmuring in a twisted morphine-induced dream. He was having straight sex with one of Mr Chou's girls. Just as the girl started to have an orgasm, her face shriveled into a pale skull, eye sockets full of maggots. 'No,' he said. 'No.' Then there was a tunnel and Lopez was running down it, and he tripped, and there was a ditch full of bodies . . .

'Hey, Trung Uy. Trung Uy Lopez, wake up.'

Someone was whispering and shaking his shoulder. It was Dusty Storm. Lopez felt so relieved, he wanted to embrace Dusty for releasing him from Hell.

'You awake now?'

'Yeah, what's happened?'

'Shhh, listen – I found out a few things.'

Lopez didn't ask what, he just let him talk. It wasn't the first time that Dusty had passed on gossip and information. He knew that Dusty ransacked all the files and document packets whenever he was on duty in the communications bunker late at night. But he didn't know that he'd also cracked the combination to the top-secret safe – only the commanding officer was supposed to have access. Lopez was slightly impressed.

The first file that Dusty had gone through was Covert Operations, which detailed the extent to which the assassination group, Program Phoenix, had been let loose on the local population. Lopez had already suspected as much from meeting Krueger at Dai Binh. Dusty then told him what he'd found in the Counter Intelligence file. 'Listen to this, Trung Uy, it's estimated...'

'Hey, keep your voice down, man.' Lopez was worried about Boca and his spies.

'... there are twenty to twenty-five sleepers in the camp, all hardcore agents. And your pal, Mr Kim, is one of them.'

'Those reports are full of shit.'

'Not this one, Trung Uy, it's got the Top Reliability rating – the stuff on Kim comes from "multiple and independent" sources.'

Lopez grabbed Dusty by his T-shirt. 'Don't say a fucking word about this to anyone else. Kim is clean; I know that for sure. You can't trust those counter-intel agents – they're all doubled. It's called orchestrated misinformation.'

'Keep your cool, Trung Uy, none of this spook shit matters to me. It doesn't matter at fucking all, it's just fun and games for boy scouts. And it's not why I woke you up.'

'What then?'

'Boca has put in a request to G3 Air for a grid destruct beacon run on Phu Gia.'

'So what?'

'You know so what, Trung Uy Lopez, you know so what. Dead babies, man, dead babies. Another wasteland of overlapping craters. But it'll be good for the mosquitoes. Mama Anopheles and her daughters'll turn the stagnant water of those bomb craters into a bacterial soup. Won't need to drop no more bombs, the malaria'll kill what's left of them. At least,' Dusty went on, 'King Herod's soldiers did it on the ground, with smoking swords and aching arms. Here it's just a radio message, a bearing fix, and five seconds later – paddy fields, babies and village are churned into hot stinking mud.'

'You sound like a fucking book. What's this chapter called: "Dusty the Humanitarian"?'

'What's your chapter called? "Lieutenant Lopez: self-pitying pill-popping drunk"?'

'Go fuck yourself.'

'It's a waste of time talking to you. You just don't care about anything.'

'You can't say that.'

'Yes, I can. You came down on me all moral and serious like some kind of holier-than-thou priest because I was wearing some poor fuck's ear. The guy was dead; he doesn't matter any more.'

'Why don't you just shut the fuck up?'

'You think that I'm all bad and corrupt, don't you? You know I used to be a whore and a thief, and you think that I only care about myself and will turn Judas whenever there's a profit to be made. Well, you're right, Trung Uy Lopez, that's me. But there's a limit: you don't hurt little kids and old people, you protect them. The others – I don't give a fuck about them; they can look after themselves.'

'Why don't you leave me alone?'

Dusty didn't say anything. He wasn't looking at Lopez, he was more interested in studying his cubicle: the bottles of drink, his books, the helmet and flak jacket he never bothered to wear, the web gear heavy with grenades and ammunition, the battered AK-47 Lopez had taken as a souvenir from the man that he killed. 'You're the only one on the team,' said Dusty, 'who doesn't have any pictures. Don't you have a family, or a girlfriend – a dog or a parakeet, even?'

'It's none of your business.'

'If I, Trung Uy, can't make comments about you, then maybe you shouldn't go around judging other people – like me, for instance. Something's died inside you – and it wasn't the war that killed it – so that now you can only see bad in other people.'

'You don't know anything about me.'

'That's right, Trung Uy. But I do know something about

a little girl in Phu Gia. She's only about eight or nine, and she has to look after this enormous water buffalo. When she rides him it looks so funny, like a tiny kid on a big old hairy couch that just got up and walked away. And she has this incredible smile; it's like a lamp. What keeps that smile glowing in that miserable village? Her smile is worth more than...' Dusty stopped. He got up and turned to leave. '...more than your life, more than my life too.'

Lopez remembered Vargas once saying, 'Why doesn't everyone hate gringos? Why don't gringos hate themselves? And you know something, chico? I hate you when you try to be a gringo – which is almost all of the time.' Lopez promised himself next time he saw Vargas he was going to tell him how wrong he was, how very wrong. If he'd ever been a gringo, he certainly wasn't one now. But he hated himself.

The American consul was the ultimate gringo, from his Brooks Brothers tropical light tan suit down to his fine handmade, but thriftily re-soled, English brogues. He was a civilian in his mid-fifties, tall, gray, aristocratically slim and flowing with all the effortless superiority of Harvard and the diplomatic service. He was part of the New England where 'the Lowells speak only to Cabots, and the Cabots speak only to God'. His name was Archibald and he was, in fact, related to the Cabots, but he still condescended to speak to Lopez. 'Thank you for your memorandum, Lieutenant Lopez. It was powerfully argued and, by military standards, surprisingly well written.'

Lopez was tempted to say that he modeled his prose style on the later novels of Henry James. But he didn't want to alienate Archie by coming across as a smartass spic, so he just said, 'Thank you, sir.'

Archie told him not to bother with 'that sir business'. He said, 'Call me Archie – even my son used to.' Then he looked at the memo to see what he should call Lopez. 'Francisco?'

'No, no one's ever called me that. My step-parents anglicized it to Francis when I was still a baby.'

Archie poured coffee from a silver service on a large mahogany sideboard, made small talk and then offered Lopez a little tour. The US consulate was a graceful French colonial villa with fancy wrought-iron balconies and tall windows with gray shutters. It used to be the residence of the French Sureté chief. The State Department ought, confided Archie, to have chosen a building with fewer colonial associations. During the French war the villa was notorious for the torture sessions carried out in its cellars. Lopez knew that, unlike the French, the Americans didn't have to get their hands dirty: they had their Vietnamese puppets do the torturing for them. The bloodstains in the consulate's cellars had long since dried and the torture chambers were used only for storing wine and boxes and boxes of Johnnie Walker Black Label.

They returned to the office – Archie told Lopez it used to be the main dining room. He showed him a wall cabinet containing enamel bell buttons – cuisine, poste de surveillance, garage, salle de police – from which the chef de La Sûreté used to summon servants and guards between courses. Behind Archie's desk french windows opened on to a garden with manicured lawns, flower borders and croquet hoops. A gardener, dressed in khaki and smoking a cheroot, was picking up blown blossoms from under the frangipani trees. Lopez started when he saw the gardener's face. He was the very double of the NVA soldier he had killed last July. It was as if the ghost had followed him there.

'If I might summarize,' Archie propped a pair of gold half-frame spectacles on to his Yankee eagle nose and referred to Lopez's report, 'your main point is a condemnation of the free-fire zone policy. You then refer to the village of Phu Gia as a specific example "where civilians may be killed and injured for no rational military purpose". In support of this view, you cite the Geneva Convention of 1949 on the protection of civilians in wartime – which is, of course, totally irrelevant.'

'Why's that, Archie?'

'Because, dear boy, the United States government doesn't give a fuck about the Geneva Convention. If we did, we wouldn't be using napalm, plastic flechettes, defoliants or CS gas.'

'I'm sorry, I thought international agreements were legally binding. I guess I'm a bit naïve.'

Archie looked hurt. 'There's no need to be sarcastic, I only want you to see things from a wider perspective.' He sipped his coffee and made a face. 'Sorry about this stuff; Hoang makes terrible coffee.'

Lopez hadn't noticed.

'The truth of the matter, Francis, is that the military are being given a free hand to run the show the way they want. We in the State Department are still regarded in some quarters as Anglophile, Ivy League, liberal pantywaists. Therefore our bosses in the diplomatic service are trying to be even more macho than the generals. In any case, the Ambassador genuinely believes that Westmoreland can pull it off by sheer brute force. This means endless artillery, carpet bombing, defoliation, bulldozing swathes of jungle and a whole land subject to relentless penetration by firepower. As you, no doubt, have already noticed.'

Lopez nodded.

'I hope you don't think that I'm patronizing you, Francis, but you should be aware of the monumental cynicism that imbues my job – and which ought to be the flavor of your job too, if you want to survive.'

Lopez didn't say anything.

Archie chewed on the end of his spectacles and stared out the window for a few seconds. 'How old are you?'

'Twenty-three.'

'My son would have been twenty-three. Car crash in Vermont two years ago.' He paused. 'Driver fell asleep. My son had a girl friend at Bennington – Hillary, fine girl – and tried to make it back to Cambridge for lectures on Monday morning. He was all, all, I had. Scotch? It's safer than the coffee.'

'Thank you.'

'So frankly, Francis, I don't care. As a matter of fact, Francis – ice? Say when – as a matter, of fact, I would roast alive every single inhabitant of your precious Phu Gia if that act would bring my son back to life for five minutes. Can you understand that?'

'No.'

'But you will, Francis, one day you will.'

To avoid eye contact, because he was finding all the dead kid stuff embarrassing, Lopez glanced around the office. It was untidy like a university professor's study. There were shelves full of books and reports, and a table piled high with newspapers and journals from all over the world.

'OK,' said Lopez, 'I know that Westmoreland's strategy is attrition and firepower, but why not evacuate civilians before you obliterate their villages?'

'Ask the President of South Vietnam. It's the policy of the Government of Vietnam to accept no more refugees. No – more – refugees.'

'Why?'

'Why? Oh, there are lots of reasons: refugees are a security risk, a means of infiltrating agents into government areas; social problems, overcrowding, disease risk; they're a source of disruption, the people in the safe areas don't really want them around – would you want a refugee camp in your back yard? And the cost, Francis, the cost. And besides, the civil re-structuring program is already stretched beyond the limit even with the current number of refugees.'

'And you – not you the State Department official, but you

personally, you the bereaved parent – go along with this policy?'

Archie paused and looked at Lopez as if he were a greasy mechanic who had crashed a family party on Martha's Vineyard. 'What do you want? Why have you come here? I don't really see what you're trying to accomplish.' The mask was off. Archie was only a suave mandarin on the surface. Underneath he was just another ruthless cog in the massive stone and iron juggernaut of pitiless empire.

'I want to accomplish as much as I can. In fact, I've already written to Robert Devereux about the matter.'

'Is he your congressman?'

'No, he's a good friend of my step-parents.'

Lopez knew he had started what West Pointers call 'ring knocking'. When things aren't going the way they want at a meeting, they softly tap their class rings on the table to remind their fellow West Pointers that they are all members of the same club. Lopez wasn't a West Pointer, but he was doing the same sort of thing and it left a foul taste in his mouth.

'Who are your step-parents?' Archie had given up being subtle.

'Tom and Rosie Ardagh.'

'The same Tom Ardagh that used to run Panama before the war?'

'Yes, but he retired a long time ago to look after the family farm. He likes doing that, I'm not sure why.'

'He had a reputation as a keen botanist. He used to go off on expeditions to Mexico,' Archie paused, Lopez's brown face was slotting into place, 'looking for rare orchids.' Archie reminisced a little more, 'Pity about the sons.' The slotting was now complete.

Lopez didn't say anything. He hated himself for mentioning Tom and Rosie – and he hated himself, once again, for not having recognized their pain until it was too late to comfort them.

'So, then. What, Francis, do you think you can do about all this?' Archie's tone was softer, but more cautious.

'Well, as a last resort, I guess I could go to the press, resign my commission. I could refuse to obey orders, get myself court-martialed as a matter of principle, anything – all publicity's a power lever. If it weren't, you wouldn't spend millions on PR reptiles.'

'I can see the headline, GREEN BERET OFFICER WHO GAVE UP HARVARD TO FIGHT IN VIETNAM COURT MARTIAL LATEST.'

'Yeah, something like that.'

'Two column inches on page four of your local paper. No one cares, Francis, no one cares. If Muhammad Ali refusing induction can't hold the front page, I don't think you're going to be too much of a *cause célèbre*.'

'Thanks.'

'But that's not important. In another place and time your youthful idealism would be almost touching.' Archie paused and pressed the tips of his fingers together. 'How many civilians are we dealing with?'

'Around a hundred.'

'Let's do a deal, Francis. If you keep quiet, don't cause any trouble, we'll see if we can get those civilians into a resettlement center before any bombing. OK, a deal?'

Lopez agreed. He was being fobbed off, but it was more than he expected.

'Come back to see me in couple of weeks so I can give you the details. In any case, there's no hurry.'

'Why's that?'

'There's big trouble brewing at Khe Sanh. For the next few weeks, all spare capacity for air strikes is going to be diverted there. Johnson's worried sick, paranoid. If he loses that base and its marine battalions, he can kiss the White House goodbye.'

It started to rain as soon as Lopez left. There were US

Information Service Agency posters on the consulate railings depicting scenes from the NASA space program. On one side were huge color photos of the Gemini capsules orbiting an earth lustrous with bright oceans and wreathed by cirrocumulus clouds. On the other side were artists' impressions of the proposed Apollo missions. The posters were getting sodden and bedraggled, but it didn't matter. It was obvious that not a single Vietnamese had ever stopped to look.

As Lopez drove back to China Beach, he thought about what Archie had said about Khe Sanh. It tied in with rumors he had heard and intelligence reports he had read. Something big seemed to be in the offing. Would it be an attack against the cities and the big bases or a push to grab more countryside? Lopez thought it must be the countryside. How could they dent the massive defensives of the coastal plain: the huge bases ringed by barbed wire, mines and massive bunkers; the lumbering armored hulks and the skies full of bombers and gunships? Or Saigon itself? No way.

Lopez wondered what Ho Cuc, Kim and the other sleeper agents in the camp knew – and what they were up to. Were they about to break cover and sabotage the camp in a late night bloodbath? There would, of course, be an external attack too, but the key to success was the 'inside job' part of the operation. Lopez thought of Ho Cuc's face – those hollow eyes, that taut brown skin, that grim asceticism. He was ready – he was always ready – aching for that final apotheosis of revenge. For Kim, thought Lopez, it must be otherwise. It would be nothing more than duty, an impersonal unselfish carrying out of his historical role. Kim took no joy in blood and slaughter, it was a form of social contract – like the epitaph for the Greeks who fought to the death to stop Xerxes at Thermopylae: 'Traveler, if you go to Sparta, tell them that we lie here in obedience to their laws.'

The thought of returning to Boca and a Nui Hoa Den that might be about to be overrun depressed Lopez. He decided to get drunk and party – might be his last chance – before going back to the camp. Despite the war, there was a festive atmosphere and most of the Vietnamese army seemed to be on leave: it was the beginning of Tet, the Vietnamese New Year. Dusty had persuaded Lopez to visit a house that he considered – 'from a professional point of view' – to be a very superior brothel. They were accompanied by the lieutenant from Minh Long, a shaven headed Croatian Yugoslav named Husac who, like Dusty, hoped to become an American citizen by doing military service. Then later, as soon as Tito died, Husac intended to return to his native country so he could kill Muslims and Serbs. While they were held up at an intersection in Da Nang, an old woman, half blind with milky cataracts, importuned them with a tray of cheap watches. Lopez explained to her in Vietnamese that they already had adequate watches.

'Why, Francis, did you learn to speak the language of dogs?' said Husac.

'If they're dogs,' said Lopez, 'then we're vermin.'

Co Hai, a Vietnamese woman of forty, ran the brothel. At first sight she seemed beautiful: her body was spare and graceful, her hair long and silky. But when you looked at her more closely, you could see the pockmarks, the ravages of smallpox inexpertly covered by cheap cosmetics, and the tired eyes. Dusty loved her, he thought she really was beautiful. Hers wasn't the beauty of a possible life, of hope, of children, of a future. It was the beauty of dignity staring out of wreckage.

A single bare fluorescent tube lighted Hai's place of work. A curtain separated the waiting room from her hard planked bed. Hai had done well: there was a Japanese television and a stereo. She had paid for all of this by taking the penises of thousands of foreign soldiers into her mouth. According to Dusty, who ought to have known, she did it exceptionally well. He praised her virtuosity like a connoisseur of wine who had just discovered a new claret. 'I bet you, Trung Uy,' said Dusty, 'that the day will come – twenty, thirty years from now – when a whole generation of bored American men, thick and obtuse with middle age, will lie awake next to their antiseptic American wives and long once again for Co Hai.'

Co Hai poured whiskey for Dusty and Lopez before taking Husac behind the curtain. Hai kept her drink in a glass display case beside the pathetic keepsakes of a life apart. She had, thought Lopez, come so far with so little: a bronze perfume burner, a greeting card bearing an invitation to a Tet celebration of many years before, china ornaments decorated with the symbols for happiness and long life. There was also a framed photograph of herself; she must have only been seventeen or eighteen, and had skin like silk and eyes like a young doe. There were no other photographs or objects to link her to any other life, family or friend, other than the narrow world of her customers and her hard bed.

Just as Husac emerged, doing up his flies, there was a commotion in the street outside. The Quan Canh – the Vietnamese military police – were out looking for deserters. The Saigon Government, under heavy pressure from Washington to sacrifice more of their own soldiers, had launched a series of deserter hunts that tended to turn nasty. The street was loud with the noise of running boots, shouting and doors being battered on. Someone was shooting tear gas.

A CS canister landed in a courtyard beside the house, and the girls and their clients had to flee upstairs to escape the gas. Lopez crawled up the steps, feeble and short-breathed, as the CS stung his eyes and burnt his lungs. Dusty was wheezing and rubbing his eyes while two of the girls were hammering on his back with their fists. 'It's not my fault,' he kept saying. 'Why are you blaming me? It was the fucking QC.' Then he saw the baby.

The baby, who was a year old, had stopped breathing, and had turned a blue-gray color; the tips of his fingers were purple.

'Help me,' Dusty shouted 'Please. Help me!'

Dusty thumped the child's back, but nothing came out except for a little clear fluid. They needed to do something fast, even though Lopez seemed to be coughing up his lungs and Dusty's eyes were two dripping pink pin-pricks.

'You do the massage,' said Dusty.

He put his mouth over the baby's mouth and nose and breathed gently twice, while Lopez put two fingers on the baby's breastbone and pressed firmly but gently four times. Then they did it again. They kept it up – it seemed a lifetime – until finally the baby started moving, then he threw up over Dusty's shirt and began to cry. Lopez was shaking and his eyes were still full of tears from the gas. 'I didn't press too hard, did I? His rib cage felt so fragile.'

'No, he's fine.' Dusty used his little finger to clear the last of the vomit out of the child's mouth. Then he hugged the child close. 'We're not always vermin, Trung Uy, not always.'

They hadn't planned to go back to China Beach that night; they'd arranged to get a lift in the morning with the truck that fetched mail sacks from the air base. But they hadn't expected the QC to go on the rampage. The girls hid them in a loft that was rank with damp straw and rat droppings. The QC wouldn't have bothered with them, but for some reason jeep loads of US MPs were also careening around. Outside, the night was loud with Tet firecrackers and the sound of drunken voices. One of the girls brought them a gourd of rice wine.

The first rocket attack started at 3 a.m.; it sounded like the air base was being given a pasting. Husac said it was more prolonged than anything he'd ever heard. A few minutes later a 122mm rocket passed close overhead – Lopez thought it sounded alive and breathing like a dragon – f'ollowed by a shatteringly loud impact in the dock area.

He wasn't really frightened until he heard small arms fire

– some of it from the next street. Lopez removed a couple of pantiles from the roof so he could peep out into the night. Arcs of tracer crisscrossed the sky in the direction of the bridges; the area around the air base was so bright with flares that it looked like an early dawn. Then one of the girls came up and told them to keep absolutely quiet. A minute later there was hammering and shouting at the door, and the sound of Co Hai arguing with an excited male voice. The only words Lopez could make out were Giai Phong Quan – Liberation Army. He was terrified, close to urine incontinence. There were other men's voices, also nervous and urgent. Lopez thought he heard someone say Hoa Ky, an impolite term for American, then the voice of one of the girls, the baby's mother, sounding angry and hysterical. A voice from outside shouted something. There was more arguing downstairs, and then the sound of footsteps running in the street. More shooting, then a pause followed by the sound of armored personnel carriers and heavy machine-guns. The street battles continued until first light, but seemed further away.

By dawn the neighborhood was back in government control. Some buildings were pockmarked by heavy caliber bullets and a few places were burnt out and still smoldering. It was obvious there would be no mail truck, so they hitched a lift with a truck full of Vietnamese paratroopers. They told Lopez that they were being sent to Hue as reinforcements. All the soldiers seemed to be laughing and smiling, to be exhilarated by the whole thing. Many were wearing brightly colored scarves of exquisite and transparent fabric, as if, thought Lopez, they were medieval knights carrying their ladies' favors into battle.

Lopez was stuck at China Beach for two more days. All the helicopters had been diverted to Lang Khe. The news was awful. The story came out in bits and pieces. The team-sergeant at Lang Khe had been woken up in the middle of the night by a loud grinding, clacking noise and assumed that the gasoline generator that provided power for the camp's radio transmitters and other electrics had thrown a flywheel belt. When he went out to inspect the generator, he realized that the noise was coming from outside the camp. He was totally confused – he couldn't imagine what sort of machine could make such an infernal gear-grinding metal-shearing racket. Then he realized that tanks were coming through the barbed wire.

This was the first time that the enemy had used armor of any kind. For this reason, the camps were not supplied with anti-tank weapons. The CIDG at Lang Khe were Bru Montagnards, usually good reliable soldiers, but they decided that fighting tanks wasn't part of their contract of employment. By first light the perimeter bunkers had been abandoned, and the Americans and Vietnamese that were left had sealed themselves into the dome-shaped command bunker.

When Lopez was at Lang Khe, the team engineer had told him that the command bunker's four-foot-thick concrete walls could withstand 'anything non-nuclear'. But 'anything' did not include the small handmade grenades which the North Vietnamese infantry, who managed to scramble on top of the bunker between air strikes, dropped down the ventilation shafts. The first grenade blew the foot off a Vietnamese sergeant, the second didn't detonate. By the time the third grenade was dropped the defenders had grabbed broomsticks and were using them to block the overhead vents. The grenade concussion, however, knocked the broomstick from the grip of the man holding it; he ended up lying on the floor, without any face and without any hands, making gurgling noises, and still alive.

In the early afternoon, a series of intense air strikes managed to sweep away the North Vietnamese and opened up the chance for a helicopter evacuation. The survivors left the bunker and made a dash for it, leaving the footless

Vietnamese and blood-gurgling American behind. A pair of Cobra gunships hosed down the area with covering fire, the rescue helicopters dropped to a low hover at maximum power. The survivors jumped on and that was the end of that.

The fall of Lang Khe made Nui Hoa Den the northernmost camp. When he finally got back, Lopez and everyone else had the same thought: 'Does that mean we're next?' The mood was bad tempered and nervous. Boca had developed irritable bowel syndrome. Lopez had started to use one of the Vietnamese two-holers in order to avoid the indignity of listening to Boca's colonic rumbles. Latrines were dangerous places. The American latrine at Thoung Duc was rocketed while the commanding officer was defecating; he lost part of his penis.

It was early evening and Lopez was lying on his bunk reading *Three Men in a Boat* by Jerome K. Jerome when the door curtain moved and Boca's sweaty red face appeared. 'I want a word with you, Lieutenant, now. Outside.'

He was annoyed at being disturbed. He was reading Jerome K. Jerome because his was a world so far from Vietnam, from America: a strange damp island where people gave dogs names like Montmorency and rowed the wrong way up the Thames. He reluctantly put England aside and came back to Nui Hoa Den. 'Can't we talk here?'

'No. What I have to say to you is strictly private.'

Lopez followed Boca outside. The camp felt deserted.

Boca turned and started jabbing a finger in Lopez's face. 'Have you been reading classified documents that have nothing to do with your job?'

'I don't know what you're talking about.' Lopez knew that Boca didn't have any proof.

'You know something, Lopez, you really are an asshole. You thought you were being a real smartass when you went to see the consul. Well, he told me all about your whining little visit.'

Lopez ignored Boca's verbal abuse and calmly and plausibly lied about his knowledge of the Phu Gia bombing plans, but at the same time he was furtively looking around for a metal stake or a rock, anything he could use to smash in Boca's face and beat him to death. But there was nothing handy: only sandbags, corrugated iron and barbed wire.

Meanwhile, Boca was droning on, 'What happens here is for me, *me*, to decide, you fucking asshole. And I'll tell you another thing, Lopez, you are not, I repeat, you are to have *no* further contact with civilian officials unless you have my express permission. And that, Lieutenant, is a direct fucking order.'

'Are you finished?'

'If it's the last thing I do, I'm going to get your ass off this hill.' Boca jabbed the finger again. Lopez wanted to grab it and break it off, but let Boca carry on. 'I've had a gut full of your bleeding-heart gook-loving shit. And by the way, since you're such a fucking gook-lover, you can go down to Phu Gia yourself to move your little slope friends. And when you start getting your ass shot off, don't go screaming for air strikes or 155 artillery – 'cause some little mama san with a little baby gook san might get in the way.' Boca finished ranting and started to walk away.

'I have something to say.'

Boca turned and affected to look bored and uninterested. 'Yeah, what is it?'

Lopez just stared at him. It was at least a minute before he said, 'You are a piece of shit, Boca, if you . . .' He was too angry to finish the sentence. Lopez stared at him again and waited for Boca to start shouting and begin the process of reprimanding him for insubordination. But nothing happened. Lopez tensed up: he wondered if Boca was going to throw a punch or, more likely, go all calm and professional and say that he was relieving him of duty for misconduct.

But Boca did none of these things; he just turned his back and walked away without a word. Lopez knew then what he had suspected for some time: Boca was a coward.

But he also knew that being a coward wouldn't stop Boca from getting revenge or annihilating Phu Gia and the people who lived there. Those were the things that cowards did.

The putting forward of the evacuation plan for Phu Gia meant that Lopez had to see Archie again. As soon as Lopez got to China Beach, he realized that he'd left his morphine behind at Nui Hoa Den. He discovered that he'd forgotten the tablets as well as the syrettes while unpacking his things in the transient officers' billet next to the beach. He sat on his bunk and hissed a litany of 'fucks', then threw his rucksack across the room. The noise woke up a helicopter pilot, who started crying because it was the first time he had been able to fall asleep for a week. Lopez was too pissed off about forgetting the morphine to apologize.

The transition to alcohol alone was a rough one and he felt pretty nasty the next morning. All the aches and pains of normal life – headache, sore throat, diarrhea, nausea, insect bites, crotch rot from jungle fungus, toothache – so easily obliterated by the magic poppy, came back in a flood of unwanted reality.

Things were a lot different since the offensive. After he signed in the adjutant took him into the CO's office to show where a mortar fragment had gone straight through Cale's armchair and splintered the plywood wall behind. 'Unfortunately,' said the adjutant, 'Catfish wasn't sitting there at the time.'

The next day, on his way into Da Nang to see Archie, Lopez thought the RMK girls seemed subdued and fewer in number. Driving was a pain because the Quan Canh had set up checkpoints all over the place. It seemed to Lopez that every duck or chicken had to have its backside fingered for hidden explosives before it could go to market. As he drove past the I Corps mortuary he noticed a construction team erecting a prefab extension.

Archie looked different too. Lopez noted that a flak jacket and a pair of oil-stained trousers had replaced his Brooks Brothers suits. He was, however, still wearing the same brown English brogues, polished like the varnished woodwork of a classic yacht. Lopez noticed that, beneath the decades of highly polished veneer, the leather was cracked and worn, like the patina of 'distress' that gives value to antiques. It occurred to him that Archie's shoes were an emblem, a seal of social hierarchy – you couldn't 'buy' shoes like that, you had to inherit them. Lopez supposed that they were a bit like Cinderella's slipper: if you weren't related to the Cabots or Lodges you wouldn't even be able to get them on your feet.

Archie noticed that Lopez looked unwell and poured him some whiskey. 'How are things at Nui Hoa Den?'

'Not too bad. We seem to have been bypassed for Hoi An and the district capitals. But now that Lang Khe's gone, we feel that we might be the next border camp to get knocked off.'

'I shouldn't think so: you look pretty impregnable on that mountaintop – unless, of course, it's an inside job.'

'How were things here?'

'Not too bad. We knew it was coming. I was woken up by my marine guards about an hour before it began. They bundled me into an armored personnel carrier and carted me off to the airbase just in case. Later, an ARVN parachute company secured the consulate. Not much happened; this place hasn't got the same propaganda value as the embassy. But the QC did arrest my gardener, and I still haven't been able to find out what's happened to him. In any case, he wasn't a very good gardener.'

'Seems a pity he should end his days in a tiger cage because he didn't look after the borders well enough.'

'I am,' Archie's voice was cold and firm, 'doing everything possible to find him and secure his release. Which, considering the fact that he might have led an assassin into my bedroom, is more than generous.'

'Your security here strikes me as pretty minimal; aren't you worried?'

'Not too much. You see, I've got good intelligence, the best in I Corps. The trick, Francis, is to use the agents that you can't trust, the ones you know are doubled – they're the ones who can really let you know what's going on.' Archie poured himself more whiskey, then offered Lopez a refill as an afterthought. 'I suppose you've come here about that village business – Phu Gia, wasn't it?'

'That's right. We shouldn't bomb it if we don't get the civilians out first.'

'You realize that the policy is still the same – no more refugees. And I don't think I need to tell you that the offensive, and our response to it, has left a helluva lot more people wandering around homeless than before.'

'Are you reneging on our deal?'

'Circumstances have changed.'

'Then we'll just bring those people out anyway, and march them into the resettlement center at gunpoint.'

'You're talking crazy, Francis. By the way, did you know that your Captain Boca thinks you ought to see a psychiatrist?'

Lopez didn't rise to the bait. 'Listen, you made a deal.'

'Listen to *me*, Francis; refugees are defined as people fleeing a disaster or war voluntarily. If you remove them by military force – as you intend – they're classified as Displaced Persons.'

'What difference does that make?'

'It means you're in serious violation of international law. If you kill civilians in a war, it means they just got in the way. If you round them up and march them out of their ancestral homes at gunpoint, you've violated a basic human right.'

'That's worse than killing them?'

'Legally, it is – and maybe it is in other ways too.' Archie poured another whiskey.

'I'm not going to back down. You know that, don't you?'

'Only too well, Francis. But I want it to be perfectly clear that this thing is your responsibility and, if it goes wrong, you're going to carry the can.'

'Agreed.'

'Rule number one. Whatever you do, Francis, don't call the Phu Gia people "civilians". You're not removing civilians, you're bringing out prisoners of war.'

'But some of them are only babies.'

'What do the Jesuits say – "Give me a child before the age of seven..."? In any case, when you get to Que Son, you'll meet the District Chief. Remember to keep insisting that the Phu Gia people are POWs no matter how much he argues. He'll know that he won't be able to send them to a POW camp, because they'd only send them back again. Ergo, the District Chief will just have to find room for them in the resettlement village.'

'This sounds devious and complicated. I'm not sure I like it.'

'That's all there is, Francis. Take it or it's off to bed and no supper.'

For a second Lopez imagined Archie as a knobbly-kneed child self-righteously digging clams on a family holiday on Cape Cod. 'What's your role? What are you going to do to help?'

'I'll have someone there to do some arm twisting just in case. But, as far as I'm concerned, this conversation never took place.'

Lopez finished the whiskey. 'Thanks for being so helpful.'

'You disappoint me, Francis. I thought I told you before that I don't care for sarcasm. But I have been helpful and I want you, for my own satisfaction, to know why.'

Archie had been leaning forward with his hands on his desk; he slipped imperceptibly, then regained his balance. Suddenly Lopez knew why the conversation was so bizarre – Archie was drunk, stinking.

'Because, Francis, it's obvious that you're a troublemaker, the sort that writes letters, learns which ropes to pull and which ears to bend. You know how to play people's personalities, you can be charming. Someone bought you a good education and taught you a few urbane tricks, but they left out the loyalty lesson. I know a lot of people in the State Department, and in the Agency too, who are completely cynical and ruthless shits, but at the end of the day I can trust them. I don't trust you. I've helped you for time management reasons – it's the quickest and easiest way to get you off my back.'

Lopez picked up his beret. 'I'd better be going.' As he walked to the jeep he felt so flushed with pride that he wanted to sing. They really weren't worth it; they were all sham – all the way back to the Mayflower and beyond. An echo of Vargas's tasteless joke about the gringo and the onion echoed in Lopez's memory. He'd been dismayed by the crudeness of the joke then, but now – oh, now he could cut up this particular gringo and never shed a tear.

Lopez had the midnight to two o'clock watch. He managed to drag the French gilt armchair on to the top of the command bunker with a view to enjoying the tranquillity of bourbon and cool night air. He was trying to stay off the morphine. He slumped into the chair and sipped his drink, and tried to block out the sounds of maternal lamentation coming from the Dead House.

Somehow the armchair had found its way from nineteenth-century Nantes to Nui Hoa Den. Vietnam seemed to be the final resting-place for the obsolete, the incongruous and the sloughed off. Some odd remnants of colonialism, like the jerky nineteen-twenties' porn film with French sub-titles that did the camp rounds, had a certain logic. But what about the marble bust of Immanuel Kant in the teamhouse at Ba To? The last time Lopez had seen it, the author of *The Critique of Pure Reason* was wearing a jungle hat, sunglasses with a lens missing, and had a marijuana spliff stuck in his mouth. And how could pure reason explain why an English bowler hat and rolled umbrella were on display in the Da Nang jeweler's where Chou had unknowingly bought Lopez the hair-clip for Quentin's fiancée? It was as if, each night, an occult procession of lost and *démodé* objects set off across sea and continent to Vietnam. And the people too. Lopez remembered his one and only visit to what the Vietnamese called 'the German cemetery'. It was at Phu Bai, astride the Route Nationale that the French used to call the Street Without Joy. There weren't just German legionnaires, but also graves with Algerian and Senegalese names. And now he, Francis Lopez, half or two-thirds Aztec Indian, hybridized by the seed of every Spaniard who had raped or bought his female ancestors, cradled in the language and culture of the next wave of conquerors, was looking out, as had the Prussian and African dead of Phu Bai, into the Vietnamese night with a rifle in his hand.

From time to time Lopez searched the camp perimeter with the starlight scope, but found nothing of note except for a sentry peeing over the side of his guard post – the scope magnified the urine to such exceptional brightness that the sentry looked as if his prick were on fire. There were footsteps in the shadows. Lopez went down on one knee and put his finger on the trigger. He was worried by his increasing paranoia but didn't know how to control it, or even if he should control it. He heard a voice; it was Bobby Hatch, wanting to talk about a 'confidential matter'. But there were too many small spaces and too many big ears. Lopez led him to the 81mm mortar pit.

'What is it?'

'I've heard rumors, sir, that you smoke dope. I know that they can't be true, but I thought you ought to know.'

'Have you got some good shit?'

'Not bad.' He started to pass Lopez a joint.

'Not here. We'd better go to a CIDG bunker – if Boca smells the dope we can pretend it's theirs.'

They went to Mr Kim's bunker; from the entrance Lopez saw Kim lying in bed trying to sweat off the last stages of a bout of recurrent malaria. Ho Cuc was sitting at a small table writing a letter by the weak light of a smoking oil lamp, and at the same time arguing with poor Kim. Lopez could hear Cuc's voice rising and falling, exaggerating the tonal nature of Vietnamese; it was a rhetorical trick they used in speeches. He tried hard to understand what Cuc was saying but could only pick out a few words, some names of people, one of whom was 'an idiot' who 'talked too much'. When Ho Cuc saw them he shut up and turned over what he was writing.

They all shook hands; it was like going to your local café in France. Kim was glad to see Lopez and asked if he had read the Vietnamese poems he had lent him. Lopez felt ashamed, like an idle student, and apologized for being too busy. They shared the joint with Kim; Ho Cuc sat in a corner scowling and refusing to smoke.

'Where'd you get the dope – it's excellent.'

'Massachusetts.'

Lopez started to laugh. '*Massachusetts?*' The marijuana made him light-headed and juvenile.

'What's so funny?'

'Hatch, you must be the only fucking person in history ever to have smuggled dope *into* Southeast Asia. My admiration knows no bounds.'

Lopez felt good. Despite Kim's malaria, the sounds of mourning from the Dead House, the earth floor and the dank oiled presence of weapons, it was all so normal. For a few minutes they were no longer soldiers, but ordinary young men talking about motorbikes, girls, which bands they liked and swapping stories of wild beach parties.

Bobby rolled another joint. 'By the way, Captain Boca says that I have to go on some kind of "humanitarian operation" with you.'

Lopez tensed up. 'Did he say Phu Gia?'

'That's the place.'

'That fucking asshole.' Lopez wanted to kill Boca more than ever. It was wrong to send someone as inexperienced as Bobby on an operation like that. It was wrong in other ways too: Bobby was the only one on the team who didn't have blood on his hands, the only one who didn't deserve to get hurt.

'What's wrong? Is there a problem?'

'Boca's made a mistake. You're not going, I'm changing it.'

'I wish you wouldn't. I don't want to be treated any different from the others. No special privileges. I may be a peacenik pacifist, but I'm not yellow-bellied.'

'Listen – you see this?' Lopez touched the lieutenant's bar on his collar.

'Don't make a fool of yourself.'

'OK – that's the way you want to play it?'

'That's right.' Bobby paused and looked directly at Lopez. 'Don't, Lieutenant Lopez, use your rank to take away my dignity, my right to make choices.'

'Thanks for the dope.' Lopez went back to his armchair on top of the command bunker.

After a while an American reconnaissance plane appeared and began to slowly quarter the nearest ridgeline. The aircraft was a 'people-sniffer', fitted with highly sensitive infra-red instruments that could detect human body heat. The North Vietnamese thwarted the people-sniffers by hanging up pots of urine, which caused the infra-red detectors to go wild and often tricked the air force into obliterating vast tracts of empty jungle.

Lopez watched the aircraft inscribing ever-tighter circles over the nearby ridge. He wondered if it had found a whole regiment of *pissoirs*. Suddenly, a line of green dashes rose from the jungle and followed the aircraft as it banked and turned. It took Lopez a few seconds to register that the plane was being fired on by a .51 caliber machine-gun. It was odd, because there wasn't any sound, just the graceful pyrotechnic arc of the tracers. After a while, the plane wriggled its wings and flew off apparently unscathed and perhaps unaware. The machine-gun stopped, and then, after a few seconds had passed, Lopez saw the tracers coming towards himself. He felt perfectly safe – there still wasn't any noise – and the green line of tracer burnt out well before it reached where he was sitting. Something went *pop* past his right ear: Lopez remembered that the phosphorous element that made tracer bullets glow burned out long before the bullets stopped flying. He still, enthralled perhaps by the night air and the marijuana, felt no sense of panic or urgency. He finished his bourbon and calmly dragged his chair and radio link to a less exposed place. What had happened seemed secret and unreal, like an intimate conversation between strangers on a train late at night.

Suddenly everything seemed pointless, empty and lonely. Lopez almost wanted the machine-gunner to find him again, then guilt, responsibility and decisions would vanish into the void. Decisions were the worst thing: they were never perfect, they were always tainted, but you always had to choose. He still wanted to kill Boca – it would be personally satisfying – but it wouldn't solve the problem. Or would it? Killing people like him wasn't like cutting off a Hydra's heads: Bocas were finite. But it was really the pilots and the air war planners who needed to be killed. It was still a court-martial offence, still murder, to shoot unarmed civilians – especially babies – on the ground, but it was all right to incinerate them or blow their bodies apart from the air. Especially if the babies were non-white and lived in places with names like Hiroshima, Nagasaki and Phu Gia; then it was OK to roast their smiling little faces into yellow goo under a layer of black ash. Pilots were the Herods of the skies. You could even make a Freudian joke of it by naming the bomber Enola Gay after your mother, and calling the bomb Little Boy.

There were signs that the infantry were getting into the act too. And there were some pretty sick rumors going around, about something terrible that was supposed to have happened in a village in Quang Ngai, on the coastal plain. Its name made Lopez think of the Roman sea victory that led to the destruction of Carthage. He remembered that T. S. Eliot had used it in 'The Waste Land':

> There I saw one I knew, and stopped him, crying: 'Stetson!
> 'You who were with me in the ships at Mylae!...

THE NIGHT BEFORE THE PHU GIA EVACUATION Lopez got the shivers. Morphine withdrawal had messed up his body's temperature control. At three o'clock in the morning, he pulled on a sweater – he was feeling really awfully cold – and wrapped a blanket around himself, feeling like an addict huddling in a 126th Street doorway. He was suspicious about Boca's willingness to let him evacuate the civilians, and wondered if Boca had hidden motives, a hidden plan. He knew that he could only sleep if he used morphine. But he wanted to keep a clear head, so he was going cold turkey. He was more frightened than he had ever been before a patrol.

Lopez had ignored Bobby's plea and tried to get him replaced with someone more experienced, like Carson or Dusty; but Boca had insisted that a medic was more appropriate because of the 'humanitarian nature' of the operation. Lopez suspected that Boca's real reason was that he wanted him to fail, wanted to discredit him or even get him killed. He knew that the operation had only a slim chance of success. Casualties had reduced the number of CIDG troops available to just ninety – not enough for the job. He needed twice as many soldiers as well as air and artillery support to secure the high ground on both sides of the river, especially Hill 110.

Lopez could hear Boca snoring two cubicles away and, closer, the rhythmic sound of furtive masturbation. It was, he thought, not one of the details that Homer had mentioned in the *Iliad*.

Earlier in the evening Bobby had given Lopez a piece of fruitcake that his mother had baked and sent in a tin. He wondered what it must be like to have a family like Bobby's. They were so young and so full of the future. His mother was hardly forty and his father not much older. Tom and Rosie were in their seventies; in fact, Tom was nearly eighty. Lopez had been adopted into the past; it didn't bother him, it made it easier to see how it all linked together. He finished the cake, washed it down with a glass of whiskey, and then, as if he had swallowed a potion, fell asleep.

An hour later, he woke again. Something soft and gentle was nibbling at his fingertips. It was ever so delicate, more gentle than the touch of the most considerate of lovers. It was a rat, which had scented the cake crumbs under Lopez's fingernails and was lapping them out with its tongue.

THE HILL OVERLOOKED PHU GIA AND THE RIVER. It was bare of trees and sparsely covered with grass and low scrub. Lopez knew that if they lost the element of surprise they were going to be in trouble, were going to get 'wasted'. When he spotted a couple of CIDG silhouetting themselves against the evening skyline he grabbed Trung Uy Tho and shook him so hard that he thought he could hear his brains rattle. 'Tell those dumb fucks to get down.' It was a lousy start.

Lopez wrapped his poncho and poncho liner tight around his body and lay down. He had been asleep for ten minutes when the noise woke him. There had been three shots. The shots were quite near; it sounded like they had come from the base of the hill, no more than a couple of hundred meters away. Bobby grabbed his arm. 'What were those?'

'Don't know. Could be signal shots.'

'They know we're here, don't they?'

They did, but Lopez didn't want to tell him that. He took a half-bottle of whiskey out of his rucksack and passed it to Bobby. He was longing for morphine. Bobby drank, and curled up in his own poncho. He looked, thought Lopez, so out of place: tucked up like a little boy with his fair skin and blond hair. Lopez's dark skin and compact body had, at least, the advantage of making him a less obvious target for snipers.

Lopez fell asleep again, but then the dream came again and spoiled it. *A coffin is sliding out of a hearse, it falls to the ground and splits open. There is something tiny wrapped up in a shroud that rolls out and spills on to the wet gravel road. It's always a child – this time it's a little girl with a pretty smile, the one Dusty described riding a water buffalo* ... Lopez woke in a cold sweat, like he always did when the dream came back. Then, relieved that it was only a nightmare, he went back to sleep. Why was there, he wondered, always such a big coffin for so small a child?

They rose at 4 a.m. Lopez had nearly two hours of darkness to get the company into their start positions. They descended the hill as silently as possible. At the base of the hill, the company divided into three. The sweep element headed for the river where they would enter Phu Gia at the upstream end; their job was to move through the village in assault formation rounding up the civilian population and flushing out any Viet Cong or NVA. The second element were to form a blocking force at the other end of the village and to shoot any enemy who fled before the sweep. The third element – including Bobby and himself – were to occupy Hill 38, the high ground overlooking Phu Gia. From Hill 38 they could cover the flank and rear of the sweep element.

Lopez knew that the big problem was Hill 110, an ugly lump on the opposite side of the river which was pitted with camouflaged firing positions. The frustrating thing was that Hill 110 was just a few meters beyond the maximum range of Nui Hoa Den's biggest mortars, so that once the enemy got dug in they were impregnable.

Lopez and his element moved quickly along the paddy dykes and arrived at the base of Hill 38 well before the other elements were in position. He knew that they had to secure the hill quickly. If the enemy got there first, they would all be chopped to pieces in a crossfire between Hills 38 and 110. It was still dark as pitch when Lopez and his element began to ascend Hill 38. The point of his column were three abreast so they could shoot their way out of trouble. Nothing happened. It was, thought Lopez, going to be OK.

The point had nearly reached the summit. Then a flash of light illuminated the top of the hill. For a split second there was the silhouette of a detached limb etched against the dazzling white light.

Lopez's first thought was that the light was the back-blast of a rocket and they were about to be chopped to pieces in an ambush. He knew it was the end. He hugged the earth as if it were the sweet mother that he had never known. He waited. Four seconds passed and he opened his eyes. All was quiet, except for the low moaning of the wounded. Bobby was the first to move: he started to crawl up the hill to tend the casualties.

One of the CIDG had tripped a booby trap and had lost a leg and three fingers. Another soldier had lost an eye. Bobby covered the torn face with a field dressing, but there were even worse wounds staining the CIDG's uniform with treacle-dark blotches. For Lopez there was no sense of reality. It was less than a dream; it was like a film of a dream. He sensed a camera zooming in on a close up of Bobby's left hand as he felt for a pouch over his left hip, unsnapped the pouch and took out a morphine syrette. He watched the film of Bobby removing the plastic cover from the syrette and plunging the needle into the remaining thigh of the worst casualty. A voice-over was explaining that Bobby was squeezing only just over half the morphine out of the tube 'because the smaller body size of a Vietnamese cannot tolerate an American size dose.'

The third wounded man was Ho Cuc. There was a liquid gurgle of air escaping from a hole in his chest cavity. Lopez held a piece of plastic wrapper against the hole while Bobby pulled the dressing tight. Cuc was also badly wounded in one hand and had a leg full of fragments. He was in excruciating pain: Lopez could see pain-fever sweat beading his face. But he still refused to groan or utter a word. It reminded Lopez of a tableau from the Stations of the Cross, and how when he was little he used to imagine he was a Roman soldier watching the nails go into Jesus. In that misty gloom of pre-dawn twilight, nothing was real. Lopez felt like he had stumbled on to a stage where some primal nightmare had to be acted out all over again. And it was so dark, as if daylight would never come. The other two wounded moaned and pleaded in counterpoint, 'Cho toi may bay, Trung Uy, cho toi may bay – Get me a helicopter, Lieutenant, get me a helicopter.' They kept chanting it, like the mind-throbbing litanies of early morning Lenten masses – *Cho toi may bay, Trung Uy, cho toi may bay*.

Lopez blocked out the noise and suffering of the wounded. He had to think clearly, had to get the facts straight, to decide what they were going to do next. He knew that most of the platoon were still strung out and exposed on the slope of Hill 38. The top of the hill was heavily mined and booby-trapped.

If they tried to occupy the hilltop in the dark they would blow themselves to pieces. On the other hand, if the platoon remained exposed on the slope of the hill they would be slaughtered at first light by fire from enemy positions on Hill 110. One of the casualties moaned again for a helicopter – Lopez almost told him to shut up.

He didn't know what to do – that was why he had wanted someone like Carson on the operation, so he could have passed the buck. Lopez looked around for Tho, but couldn't find him. He had to do something. He told Ly, the interpreter, to get the CIDG to come up the hill – carefully – on their hands and knees, feeling for trip wires. He knew there would probably be land-mines as well. The drill for finding them was to probe every square foot of ground with a bayonet lying loosely on the palm of the hand, but there wasn't time for that.

As soon as Ly started translating the instructions, Ho Cuc said, 'Khong – no.' Lopez asked him what he meant by 'khong', but Cuc ignored him. The top of Hill 38 was crisscrossed by a network of shallow trenches. Without another word Ho Cuc slid into the deepest trench like a snake and emerged a few minutes later with four hand grenades that had been attached to concealed trip wires. Cuc was naked except for his dressings and bandages; his clothes and boots had been cut away to tend his wounds. His drained body was pale against the dark; as he searched the trenches his paleness rose and fell like a hovering wraith in a cemetery. When Cuc had finished clearing the hill his sling and bandages were stained with mud and blood. He dragged his shattered leg delicately behind him like a cat crawling away after being struck by a car. Ly gave a signal and the remainder of the column slowly moved forward and occupied the hilltop.

Lopez and Bobby lay in a section of monsoon-eroded trench that was only eighteen inches deep and hardly provided protection for one person. The hilltop was virtually bare of vegetation or other cover. As day dawned it began to drizzle. The moaning of two of the wounded had become an incessant antiphonal counterpoint that ground in Lopez's brain like the unset ends of fractured bones. Cuc maintained a stoical silence, but his face was as pallid as stale cold coffee. The medevac helicopter was taking forever. Vietnamese casualties were always low priority. And if there were no Americans with them, they were no priority at all.

It was nearly an hour after first light before they heard the helicopters. Nothing had happened since the explosion. It seemed to Lopez to have happened a century ago, in a different country, the country of the night known to the ancient Greeks as Chaos. There were two helicopters, but they were both escort gunships. The big Chinook helicopter for evacuating the wounded was nowhere to be seen. Lopez radioed the gunships. They told him that because it was Sunday the Chinook pilot had slept late and hadn't finished eating his breakfast. Lopez shouted into the handset, 'Who does that cunt think he is?'

'Say again, over,' said one of the pilots. There was laughter in the background.

'Our casualties are serious – dying, in fucking fact. They can't wait.'

Lopez listened to the pilots arguing with each other and complaining about Foxtrot 58 not having his 'ass in gear'. Finally one of the pilots offered to pick up the wounded with his gunship even though he had no medical facilities on board. The helicopter landed on a grassy saddle that linked Hill 38 to a neighboring hill. The wounded were carried in poncho liners, except for Cuc who crawled on under his own strength. The two most seriously wounded had serum albumin drips. Bobby handed one bottle to a door gunner and said, 'If the tissue around the needle starts swelling up, the fluid isn't getting into the vein. You need to pull it out and start it again.' The gunner grinned and nodded, but he obviously had no intention of doing a thing if the drip went wrong. His job was putting 7.62mm bullets into Oriental people, not plasma substitutes. Lopez gave the other casualty's drip to Ho Cuc. Just before the helicopter pulled pitch to take off, he grabbed Cuc's free hand and said, 'Why did you do it? Why did you save us?'

There was no contact. Lopez felt Ho Cuc's blank stare pass through his head and out the back of his skull. Cuc was more than a person – he was, it seemed to Lopez, a whole culture. His unrelenting stare held more than bravery, something other than words. Lopez felt the down-blast of the rotors as the helicopter began to take off. It only lasted a fleeting fragment of a second, but Lopez had felt Ho Cuc squeeze his hand. It was so fleeting and subtle that he might have imagined it.

As the helicopters left the river valley Lopez requested some fire support. There was a bamboo thicket along their withdrawal route from Hill 38 that he was worried about. He asked the pilot who hadn't picked up the casualties to give the thicket a strafing run. There was little risk involved, but little risks accumulate. The pilot replied, 'Go fuck yourself, dipshit.'

After the helicopters flew off, Lopez took out his binoculars and watched the column of refugees and soldiers as they threaded their way eastward along the river. They seemed to be meeting no opposition. Mr Kim's platoon had been given the task of searching and clearing Phu Gia village while Lopez's element secured Hill 38. The platoon were making a lot of noise as they swept through the village, firing their weapons blindly into hedges, banana plantations, thickets, and any other places likely to provide cover for enemy troops. The idea was to panic concealed enemy into giving away their location by firing back. The tactic never worked, but was popular because it vented frustration and allowed the soldiers to lighten their load of heavy ammunition.

Lopez was worried about looting. Mister Kim usually controlled it, but discipline and morale were getting worse and worse. He scanned the column and began to see that many of the CIDG had already loaded their rucksacks with marrows, fruit, chickens, ducks, and any other plunder that came to hand. Lopez was more worried about the civilians. It looked like Kim's troops had rounded up just over a hundred. There were, of course, no men of military age in the civilian column, only the old, the young, and women with children. He scanned back along the column again, and paused, focusing on a little girl carrying her younger brother on her back. Even in the chaos of the evacuation, she was laughing, her face alight. Probably Dusty's water buffalo girl, he thought.

Lopez was sure that Kim's CIDG would treat the civilians well. The soldiers themselves had been uprooted by war and the faces of the Phu Gia civilians probably reminded them of their own families. But Lopez also knew that if there were a firefight, the civilians would be human shields; if they came across land-mines, they would be human mine detectors.

There still wasn't any resistance. Maybe the enemy were afraid of shooting their own families. Progress was slow because most of the civilians were too old, too young or too ill to move quickly. And too burdened with the weight of all their worldly possessions – rolls of bedding, sleeping mats, pots, bowls, chopsticks, blackened kettles, and all the other sad baggage of the war homeless. Lopez put down the binoculars. He didn't want to see any more, it was too depressing.

As soon as the sweep element were clear of the village, Lopez's position on Hill 38 came under heavy fire. At first it all seemed to be coming from Hill 110, but then one of the CIDG spotted movement on the next hill, less than a hundred meters away. It looked to Lopez like the people on Hill 110 were trying to pin them down so that another element could close in for the kill. He knew he and Bobby had been picked out by the snipers. Lopez hated being shot at; it terrified him. There was a big difference between being 'under fire' and being 'shot at'. One is general, the other is personal. There was something nauseating, like unwanted physical intimacy, about the knowledge that a few hundred meters away a complete stranger was lying in a well concealed hole and taking careful aim at his body in the hope of puncturing its soft organs, rupturing its arteries and shattering its bones.

The bullets were making a sharp popping noise as they passed overhead. Lopez curled himself even tighter into the trench. A bullet cracked so loud past his ear that it must have missed by only inches – then a few seconds later two more bullets cracked twice as loud as they whip-snapped past. Lopez's RTO was scrunched up in the trench behind him. The radio antenna was making the RTO a target too. Lopez grabbed the handset and requested fire support. 'We're under heavy fire. Put some ordnance on 110 ASAP.'

Boca told him they couldn't do it. '110's out of range!'

Lopez wanted to smash his stupid face in. 'For the mortars, I know. I meant, get some artillery from An Hoa'

'You'll have to contact them direct.'

'We tried – both frequencies – but they don't answer.'

'Did you try six-seven?'

Lopez tried six-seven, but there was still no reply. He was shaking with fear and frustration. 'Seeing action', he thought, was such a funny phrase to describe being in a war: the only thing he could see were the soles of Ly's boots. The noise from the CIDG had stopped again. Lopez shook Ly by his ankle.

'What you want, Trung Uy?'

'Ly, tell them to keep shooting back.'

The first CIDG to uncurl from the fetal position were the machine-gun team. They fired a few bursts at Hill 110 and then at a squad of Viet Cong who were running across some paddy fields towards the base of Hill 38. Suddenly their firing stopped; a bullet had struck the machine-gun's breach and jammed the gun. The gunner had been slightly cut below the eye by a shard of metal. He was smiling, the machine-gun was now useless and he had nothing left to do. He and his assistant crawled out of the trench and took off in a crouching run down the side of Hill 38 toward safety. Lopez watched them as they raced down the hillside like schoolboys released early from a tedious lesson.

Lopez looked back towards Nui Hoa Den and saw a plume of black smoke rising from the camp. They were burning the shit. The latrines were wooden seats placed above 55-gallon drums cut in half and filled with waste oil. Twice a week, on Sundays and Wednesdays, the drums were wheeled out and the shit and oil burnt off. For Lopez, that smoke signaled their own utter insignificance: they were pinned down on a barren hill and likely to die, but three miles away it was just another Sunday morning and they were burning the shit.

Lopez told the others that they were going to have to run for it. He leapt out of the trench and ran crouching and weaving off the crest of the hill to the relative safety of the rear-facing slope. He looked back and saw Bobby kneeling upright on the top of the hill trying to see what was happening. 'Get down here. *Now*, you stupid fuck!'

Bobby slid down next to him. 'We're trapped. They're coming up the other side of the hill. If we run for it, they're gonna pick us off before we get to the bamboo thicket.' The safety of the thicket, their nearest cover, was a dash across three hundred meters of open ground.

'We need some fire support.' Lopez looked around for the radio, but it was nowhere to be seen. 'Where's the RTO?'

'There.' Bobby pointed down the hill. The RTO had lightened his load by leaving the heavy radio behind and was bounding along gaily in the wake of the other two CIDG.

Lopez looked back up the hill. The RTO had left the radio on the crest of the hill in the middle of an open space. Lacking human targets, the enemy had started firing at the radio instead. Lopez ran back up the hill. He no longer felt that he was inside his body: his body was playing a role in some corny war movie and Lopez was watching it. The bullets couldn't really hurt because it *was* only a movie. It was all an adrenaline blur. When he grabbed the radio, it seemed weightless.

Lopez started shouting into the handset while still scrambling back to Bobby: 'Hill 38, white phosphorus, fire for effect and repeat.' White phosphorus had been outlawed by the Geneva Convention because, not needing oxygen to burn, it seared into the flesh and continued to burn its way through the tissues like acid. Lopez was hoping that they could get off the hill before the shells impacted, and that the enemy and the white phosphorus would arrive on Hill 38 at the same time.

It started to rain as they ran down the hill towards the thicket. 'Please,' he prayed, 'please.' As the first shells exploded Lopez could hear the sound of air being sucked into the fireballs, like he had at Lang Khe. The white phosphorus spewed plumes of white billows on and around the hill as they ran towards the bamboo thicket. He thought it oddly pretty: the barrage of white phosphorus was decorating the hill with white floss, like an insane wedding cake.

The only thing left to do was make their way over low bare hills towards Hill 60, the rendezvous point where they would join up with the other two elements. As they made their way up the valley, a lone CIDG turned around and emptied half a magazine at Hill 38 in a gesture of pointless bravado. A few seconds later Lopez received a radio call from the marine artillery battery at An Hoa offering fire support – equally pointless, and late. He gave them the grid co-ordinates of a hill behind them where there might be snipers. The 155 shells passing overhead sounded like

Volkswagen Beetles being slung out of a giant catapult.

Lopez felt drained. The exhilaration of escaping from Hill 38 had quickly worn off. It seemed that Bobby had also gone quiet. They trudged along in silence. Lopez thought he heard something, but wasn't sure. He noticed Bobby had stopped and was listening.

'Did you hear something?' said Bobby.

'Not sure. What about you?'

'I don't know. It sounded like a dull thud from the direction of Hill 60.'

A few seconds later there was a radio call. Kim reported that a CIDG had stepped on a mine near the top of the Hill 60, and there were three casualties. Lopez put the handset back on his webbing. 'Just what we don't fucking need.' They hurried their pace. A short time later there was the sound of another muffled explosion and another radio message. This time three civilians, including a young boy, had been injured. Lopez now understood the signal shots of the previous evening: the Viet Cong had known they were coming and had spent the night laying minefields.

Half the blocking force element were waiting at the base of Hill 60. They had decided not to go up the hill when they found it was mined. It was obvious to Lopez that everything had turned into a mess again. That the CIDG and the Phu Gia civilians had managed to get trapped in the middle of a minefield. That they badly needed a medevac. That Kim's troops were close to mutiny and had probably started using the civilians as human mine detectors.

Lopez didn't want to go up the hill, but there was no other way. He knew that American medevac pilots wouldn't land if a Vietnamese directed them. He explained the situation to Tho, who somehow had ended up with the blocking force. Tho provided ten volunteers who had experience of clearing mines. Ly also agreed to come. Lopez found it bizarre: the CIDG were all laughing and miming macabre jokes about getting blown up. Just before they started up the hill there was another explosion from the top: two more CIDG had managed to blow themselves up. 'Why the fuck,' said Lopez, 'don't they just sit still?'

Nothing happened until they were two-thirds of the way to the top. It was a small mine. It blew off the foot of the CIDG who was leading the way and slightly wounded the man behind him. Bobby injected the amputee with Lopez's last but one morphine syrette. They tried to improvise a litter out of a hammock, but it was difficult for the hillside was bare and there were no bamboo or other trees for poles. In the end, they had to drag him like a sack of potatoes.

The next point man was more observant. He detected another mine only a few minutes after taking over. He dug it up, defused it, and popped it into his rucksack. They carried on for another fifty meters and the column halted again. The point man had discovered another mine. By now he was quite near the top of the hill. He quickly unearthed that mine as well, defused it and stowed it in his rucksack. Lopez was becoming annoyed with the delays. He wanted the point man to lead on, but instead he was digging up yet another mine. Bobby said, 'This is stupid, really stupid. This guy is supposed to be finding a way around the mines, not through the middle of the them.'

'Maybe he needs the money. He gets a 200-piastre bonus for each one, almost a week's wages.' Boca had introduced a system of prize money for captured weapons and explosives. An anti-personnel mine was worth about the equivalent of a can of Coca-Cola.

Lopez saw that the point man was holding the mine against his chest and struggling with what seemed to be a safety slide. It must have been rusty and stiff. Lopez shouted at him to leave the mine. Just then, the CIDG stepped back with his right foot to steady himself for another go at whatever was wrong with rendering the mine safe. The hill shook and the soldier disappeared in a dark geyser of earth. The concussion set off the mine he was holding as well as the ones in his rucksack.

Lopez didn't want to get up from the ground. He just wanted to go on lying there. Bobby shook him to see if he was all right. Lopez was splattered with blood and pieces of flesh from the victims, but he wasn't hurt. He took off his glasses to try to clean them, but his hands were shaking too much to wipe them. He handed them to Bobby who cleaned them and handed them back.

A minute passed and no one did a thing. The less badly wounded were crying for help, but they would have to wait. Lopez turned to Bobby and gave him his last morphine syrette and one of his field dressings. He had no intention of helping the wounded. He didn't even want to look at them: they were Bobby's business. Lopez knew that his business was to find a way to the top of the hill and call in a medevac. He shuffled forward past the casualties; he tried not to look – there was only an impression of lumps lying on the ground.

Lopez found Ly beside him. They took turns leading and together groped their way to the crest of the hill like a pair of drunks. It began to drizzle again. Two of Kim's men came down to lead them the rest of the way. Lopez found it all so absurd: it was like a game at a children's party – they were all holding hands and each person had to put his feet in exactly the same place as the one before. When they got to the top the guides went back down to help Bobby bring up the dead and wounded.

Phong, Kim's RTO, led Lopez along a cleared path to where the Phu Gia civilians were herded close together and squatting on the edge of the hill. There must have been a hundred of them, all motionless, faces hidden by straw hats, the huddled mass exuding a low murmur. How, thought Lopez, do you say you're sorry? Kim was squatting next to an old man and talking to him. A squall of rain blew in over the valley and the mass of displaced people swayed and flattened like tall grass in a summer storm. Lopez explained to Kim that they needed to clear a landing zone that was absolutely safe before he could call in a helicopter.

Bobby had managed to get the casualties to the top of the hill. He arranged them alongside the rest of the wounded. They were all lying in a row under ponchos, most had serum albumin drips dangling next to them from sticks or rifle butts. Bobby asked Lopez if he had spare water. Lopez turned so that Bobby could get a canteen from a rucksack pouch. Bobby got the water, then stopped and stared at the canteen. There was a fragment of gray flesh with hair attached stuck to the canteen cap. Bobby flicked the meat off with his middle finger, unscrewed the cap and offered the water to one of the wounded.

Some of Kim's CIDG had begun to clear a landing zone. They were down on their hands and knees probing for mines with knives and pieces of stiff wire. They were making slow progress and had uncovered only four mines, none of which seemed to be part of a logical mine laying pattern. Lopez was concerned about the mines, but also concerned about the time it was taking to clear them. Some of the wounded were hemorrhaging to death and others were going into terminal shock. The rain pattered down. They had finished burning the shit at Nui Hoa Den.

Lopez sat down, got out his map to see if there was a safer place to bring in a medevac. Kim was standing above him studying his own map. His feet were straddling a tuft of grass directly in front of Lopez's face. Lopez didn't know why, but something in that tuft of grass drew his eyes like a magnet. Then he saw it. Concealed in the grass between Kim's legs and half buried in the ground was a 'Bouncing Betty' – a World War II mine that leaps four feet into the air before detonating, thus much more efficiently scything the area with shrapnel than an ordinary land mine. Ly saw what Lopez was looking at and grabbed Kim by the shoulders. 'Don't move, not even a centimeter.'

Bobby came over. He looked anxious. 'When are we going to get this medevac in. Some of these people are looking really bad.'

'Listen,' said Lopez, 'this place is fucking lethal. No way are we doing a medevac here. No way. It's all a fucking mess.'

'So let's try the other end of the hill. Phong says he thinks it's pretty clear.'

Lopez hadn't considered that part of the hill at first because it was too exposed to ground fire from Phu Gia, but his concern for helicopter pilots was waning. They couldn't wait any longer. He got on the radio and said that they were ready for the medevac.

It didn't take long to move the casualties – some had wilted to a pale etiolated color – to the place Bobby had suggested. The ground was rougher and looked as if it had been ignored by the minelayers. There hadn't been time to check it out, but a number of CIDG were walking around the area without getting blown up. Lopez thought it was stupid they hadn't tried there sooner.

Twenty minutes later the river valley was echoing with the racket of the medevac helicopter and her escort gunships. Lopez marked the LZ with a yellow smoke grenade. There was a small hitch when the smoke blew back over the wounded and it looked like the helicopter was going to land on the casualties, but he radioed corrections in time. It took only a few seconds to load the wounded, dead and dying on the helicopter – the pilot made it clear he wasn't going to hang around – and soon the dust had settled and all was still again.

Lopez was asking Kim the best way to get the civilians to the refugee camp at Que Son when Bobby brushed past and said,

'Can anything else go wrong?' Lopez watched Bobby walk back across the landing zone to where he'd left his rucksack. He shouted at his back, 'Could have been a whole lot worse.'

Bobby was at the very spot which had been directly underneath the belly of the helicopter. The pilot had been lucky: the medevac's landing wheels must have straddled the mine. This was a mine designed to destroy vehicles, not just foot soldiers. It probably contained enough explosive to make a jeep turn a somersault or blow the track off a main battle tank. It blew Bobby's legs off and tossed what was left of him ten feet into the air. But it didn't kill him.

The medevac pilot refused to return for Bobby; he said the landing zone had not been properly cleared and marked. When, however, they realized the casualty was an American, one of the escort gunships turned back and picked him up.

It was, in the end, easy to find a way out of the minefield and down the hill. The Phu Gia civilians showed them a safe route. They had known the whole time.

Lopez got the civilians to Que Son in the late afternoon. He had expected to be met by the Duc Duc district chief and his adviser, but the only official there was Launcelot Krueger accompanied by his two Korean bodyguards. Krueger was wearing tan chinos and a shirt decorated with bright tropical birds. He was leaning against a bamboo gate at the entrance to the refugee camp. Lopez went over to him: 'I'm supposed to see the senior district adviser.'

'Who're these fucks?' Krueger nodded towards the swarm of Phu Gia civilians.

'They're not your problem.'

'That's right, they're not my problem, because I don't go around breaking international law by using military force to remove civilians from their homes. You're in fucking trouble, Lopez, big trouble.'

'Keep your nose out of this, Krueger. It's none of your business.'

'Who authorized you to move these people?'

Lopez didn't say anything.

'Go on, tell me. Was it my pal Archie? Did Archie tell you that you could get away with this?'

'I brought these people out as POWs. If the district chief doesn't agree with that, he has to accommodate them in the resettlement center or in a refugee camp.'

'Who told you that? Did you get it in writing? Didn't you at least take minutes of the meeting?'

'You are one prime fucking asshole, Krueger.'

Krueger gave a signal and one of the Koreans took Lopez down from behind and starting choking him in a hammerlock. The other bodyguard had grabbed his rifle.

'Let him up.' There was the sound of a helicopter in the distance. 'I'm not going to waste any more time on you, Lopez: you're too insignificant. I just want you to know one thing: it's GVN policy, and US policy too, to accept no more refugees. No more refugees. So send these fucks back.'

The helicopter was circling to land on the soccer field. It had the red, white and blue livery of the agency's fake civilian airline, 'Air America'. Lopez knew that he was a fool, a completely powerless fool. Krueger and the Koreans boarded the helicopter and took his rifle with them. After taking off the pilot hovered at about fifty feet above the ground; Krueger picked up the rifle and threw it to the ground. Lopez wondered what other infantile gestures he had in his portfolio.

It was getting dark and too late, Lopez hoped, for the civilians to try to make their way back to Phu Gia. He had to warn them that they would be killed if they went back. It was raining again and they had no shelter. There was a wide sandy river beach at Que Son where a number of boats had been pulled up. Lopez saw that a lot of the Phu Gia people had gathered there to find shelter by huddling in the lee of the hulls.

Lopez saw Mister Kim sitting beside a boat with an old man dressed in white in his arms. 'Kim,' he said, 'what are you doing?' The old man he was holding seemed completely limp. 'Kim, can't you see the guy's dead? Just leave him.'

Kim, still cradling the man like a Pieta, looked at Lopez. 'He thought I was his son, Van Troi. But he also knew that Van Troi was killed years ago. I think this old man was very confused.'

Someone had found some ragged plastic sheeting. The stronger of the Phu Gia people were making shelters to protect the weakest and oldest.

'He looked after the ducks,' Kim went on, as much to himself as to Lopez. 'He was eighty-two years old and had no one, so he looked after the ducks. When I told him he had to leave, he got very upset. He asked me, "Did you ever keep ducks? Because if you did, you would know that you can't just leave them – they are constant trouble, and such careless parents." I told him I had a soldier who was a renowned keeper of ducks, and promised to leave him behind to guard his flock. "When are we coming back?" he said. I lied. I said, "Very soon". He got up, then suddenly sat down again in the dust, "I have seen eighty-two years and am very tired." I had to carry him most of the way. I gave him water and food, but he couldn't keep it down. He got weaker and weaker – and he started calling me Van Troi. He was very cross that I had been away for such a long time. I told that I had come back to do my duty as a true son. And I promised that I would never leave him.'

'So what will you do now, Kim?'

'In the morning, I'll see that he has a proper burial, and I will look after the shrine myself.'

Lopez sat down next to Kim. The old man's eyes were half-open, showing dull white, his mouth gaping and dry.

'Is something wrong, Trung Uy Lopez?'

'You are, Kim. You are.'

Lopez looked up and saw Ly, the interpreter, hauling a

heavily pregnant woman towards him. The woman was full of anger and spitting at Ly, waddling and stumbling as he dragged her along.

'Ly,' shouted Lopez, 'what the fuck are you doing?'

'Trung Uy, Trung Uy Lopez, this is Xuan Houng. Famous Viet Cong family. Everyone in Phu Gia knows about them. Her husband is a sniper, probably same sniper who tried to kill us.'

It all seemed so stupid, so irrelevant. Lopez couldn't understand why Ly was so intense. There had been so much death and mutilation already that arguing about this angry red-faced eight-months-pregnant woman was merely tiresome. Lopez was sitting cross-legged like a Buddha. He could no longer hear Ly's voice or make sense of his angry gestures. Finally, Lopez shouted, 'Stop.' Ly froze and the woman was suddenly silent too. Lopez felt like a potentate in a tiny shitty kingdom. All was stillness. 'Let her go.'

Ly flung the pregnant woman in the dust in front of Lopez. Her blouse was torn and he could see her breasts, firm and swollen with maternity.

Lopez leaned on his rifle, although broken and useless, as if it were a scepter. 'Is your name Xuan Houng?'

The woman raised herself, thrust back her head and then spat in Lopez's face. Ly lunged forward to strike her with his rifle butt.

'No,' shouted Lopez. He was beginning to like being a god. 'When did you first know we were going to attack?'

The woman frowned and counted on her fingers. 'Three days.'

'How did you know?'

'We always know.'

'Did you know where the land-mines were buried?'

Xuan Houng stared for a few seconds into Lopez's face, then blushed and giggled like a girl admitting to a stolen kiss. 'Yes, it's the job of the women and children.'

Lopez looked at her, a plump unremarkable woman –

ridiculously pregnant – making admissions that, uttered in front of Redhorn or a lot of other officers, would have left her disemboweled. Was she mocking him, his weakness? 'What happened on the way up the hill?' he said.

'Your soldiers made us walk in front, to step on the mines. We lost my cousin Linh Hai, and my nephew Kieu had his foot blown off.'

'And you knew all the time where the mines were – you just walked over them to pretend you didn't know?'

Xuan Huong nodded.

'What made you show us where the mines were, so we could get off the hill?'

Xuan Houng smiled. It seemed to Lopez that her face was flushed with pride. 'When the big American was blown up, we knew that we had done enough. We had to kill at least one American.'

Ly stepped forward again with his rifle butt raised to smash in her face.

'Ly!'

The interpreter paused, then chambered a round in his rifle. 'Don't worry, Trung Uy Lopez. I'll take her down to the river and shoot her. No rape, no torture, just shoot her.' Ly smiled as if he understood what was required.

'No, Ly, just let her go.'

The interpreter lowered his rifle and watched Xuan Houng waddle back to her people. He smiled at Lopez and patted his own stomach. 'I could have killed two VC with one bullet.'

The bombers came the next day, but Phu Gia was not totally obliterated. In the aftermath of the Tet Offensive there weren't enough planes available. Nonetheless, more than half the village had been 'craterized', and the remaining fields sprayed with waste sump oil. As soon as the aircraft had gone, the Phu Gia people went back to their village for they had no place else to go.

For the next few days Lopez closely monitored all the agent reports. The sniper husband was still alive, and the Duc Duc district Communist *cadre* had provided emergency supplies of rice, tinned Russian mackerel and cooking oil while the people cleaned up the fields and dug new bunkers.

'I GUESS HE SHAT HIMSELF as soon as he felt his foot depress the plunger on the mine. They often do – shot-down pilots are especially notorious for losing bowel control. But we cleaned up your young sergeant, and we didn't do such a bad job – considering.' The doctor was still in light green theater dress. Lopez thought he sounded like a car mechanic describing a smashed-up car he had lovingly restored – except that cars that badly wrecked went straight to the breaker's yard.

'The fireball from the explosion caused third degree burning – total charring – of his sex organs and anus. If you like, I'll show you the pre-op photos'

'No thanks, I'll take your word for it.' Lopez noticed that the doctor, a small wiry man with glasses, had a slightly deformed earlobe, as if someone had slit it with a razor.

'We had to remove what was left of the penis and testicles. Then we had to do a double hip disarticulation. One of the stumps was a total mess and definitely had to go. We thought about trying to save the other one, but it would probably have turned ischemic – and, in any case, what was left would have been unsuitable for fixing a prosthetic device. We also had to remove a piece of large intestine.' The doctor held up his fingers as if describing the size of a small fish. 'Not much. By the way, did you ever see one of these ops?'

Lopez shook his head and wondered why the doctor had even asked.

'You have to work at an awkward angle – almost like gyno or obstetrics – in what we call the "head-low position", with the table tilted at forty-five degrees and the buttocks hanging over the edge.' The doctor continued talking and miming the procedures with his hands as if Lopez and Dusty were medical students. 'I'm awfully glad he wasn't a rare blood type; he used up twenty-six pints of O positive. Must have been one hell of a mine.'

A woman nurse arrived wearing the silver rank insignia of a first lieutenant. 'They're ready in number five, doctor.'

'Bombing error on the road to Hue. Splattered a platoon of ARVNs.' He turned to the nurse. 'These men have come to see Sergeant Hatch. Can you take them down to Intensive?'

The nurse led them along a corridor that smelled of disinfectant and was littered with push-chairs, trolleys and soiled linen bins. There was something zombie-like about her. She spoke without looking at either man, her eyes fixed on some invisible point in the distance. 'Sergeant Hatch has been a very naughty boy. He tried to kill himself last night.' She showed them into a six-bed ward.

There were two drip-stands next to Bobby's bed. A urine catheter connection tube led from under the covers and emptied into a bottle fixed to the side of the bed. The liquid was cloudy and bloody. Bobby seemed to be sleeping, but his lips were moving. Lopez put his hand on Bobby's arm – it was hot and dry. Both arms had been tied down with restraint straps. 'Hey, Bobby, it's me. Dusty's here too.'

'I want my daddy, please, I want my daddy.' Bobby twisted and strained against the straps. His voice was piercing. *'Where's my daddy?'*

Dusty gently touched Bobby's face with his fingertips. 'Bobby, look at me. What's my name?'

'Daddy, you promised we'd go for that canoe trip soon as the weather got better. You said we'd go in May – before anyone else – when it's still nice and fresh and the river's full of melted snow. And you said we wouldn't turn back. We'd go all the way to the sea, *all the way to the sea!*'

The nurse was replacing one of the drips. 'They hallucinate,' she said, 'as the morphine wears off.'

Bobby seemed to have fallen back to sleep, but Lopez could see rapid eye movement behind his lids. He hoped that they were happy dreams.

The nurse looked hard at Lopez. 'Did Sergeant Hatch kill anyone?'

'No.'

'He thinks he did and he's really upset about it. Last night he was talking to some little Vietnamese girl. He kept asking, "What's your name, little sister? Why do you want to talk to me? What's your name?" Then he sat up and started screaming "No, no, no!" I asked him what was wrong. He said he looked under the girl's hat so he could see her face, but there was nothing there – just darkness. He said he heard her say, "I have no name, you killed me". Later he smashed a bottle of saline solution and tried to slash his wrists. That's why he's tied down.'

Lopez thought of the water-buffalo girl with the beautiful smile. He had seen her on Hill 60 with the Phu Gia people.

Suddenly Bobby was awake again. He was staring at the ceiling and shouting, 'Daddy! Please, daddy!'

'It's me, Bobby, Dusty. And Lieutenant Lopez.'

Bobby focused on his real visitors. Reality flooded back and Bobby was racked with tears – they weren't his family, this wasn't Vermont. He was in the 95th Evacuation Hospital at Monkey Mountain, in the Republic of Vietnam.

Another nurse arrived to wash Bobby and do his mouth care, Dusty grabbed her tray and said, 'We'll do that.'

The nurse tried to pull her tray back. 'You're not qualified.'

'Yes, we are. He's our comrade and we're going to do it.'

Bobby looked into Dusty's eyes. 'Please kill me. Please, *please*, kill me.'

'You're going to be OK, partner. Me and Lieutenant Lopez are going to look after you.'

Bobby's tears turned into high-pitched howls of despair. The nurse looked Dusty straight in the eyes. 'Now look what you've done.' Her pupils were dilated from the

Benzedrine that she had to take to stay awake and alert. The wounded had been flooding in since Tet.

Still Dusty wouldn't let go of the tray.

'OK, Sergeant, you do the care if you want to. You might learn something.' She flicked back the sheet from the bed cradle. What was left of Bobby looked and smelled like it had been blow-torched. There hadn't been enough skin to close the wounds, so they had been left open and covered in tulle gras, a cotton net material impregnated with Vaseline. 'Perhaps you'd like to change the dressings as well?'

Bobby's body felt hot, dry and feverish. When they were finished, Dusty said, 'We'll try to see you again before you get shipped back. You're going to be OK.'

Bobby turned his head away and didn't say a thing.

As they left the ward, the nurse followed them out. They were halfway down the corridor when she ran up to Dusty, grabbed his collar and threw him against the wall. 'You fucking asshole! This is a hospital, not a film set for *Beau Geste* auditions. Both of you – fucking *assholes*! Going back to play soldier now? Going back to zap some more gooks? You see what it's like here? This is good, man, this is the best fucking trauma care in the world – and it's pretty, isn't it?' She turned on Lopez and flicked his Special Forces shoulder insignia with her fingers. 'I know what your job is, it's changing the color of the corpses. What do think happens when a Vietnamese soldier gets fucked up? You been to one of their hospitals? No problem with changing the sheets, there *aren't* any fucking sheets. If they ran an animal hospital like that, the SPCA would close it down.' She turned away and started to walk back to the ward. 'Just go,' she said tiredly. 'Just go away.'

On the way out, they passed a ward where a body with a tag tied to a big toe lay on a trolley. The empty bed had already been stripped, carbolized and remade.

As they drove back to the C-team Lopez told Dusty to take a

detour into Da Nang. He wanted to visit the consulate. He wanted to see Archie. Lopez wasn't sure why he wanted to visit, but he was wearing his .45 and there was a round in the chamber. He didn't know what he intended to do. Part of him was saying 'stay cool'. Lopez knew that if he could only manage to shoot one person before getting arrested, it ought to be Boca. The going tariff for killing a colleague in the field was three years at Leavenworth. For shooting diplomats it might be more. And there was also a good chance of his getting shot by one of the guards.

When Lopez walked into the consulate, the layout had been rearranged. The villa's entrance foyer had been turned into a reception area staffed by two typists and two marine guards. He told the nearest typist that he had come to see the consul. A white-shirted civilian, in his early thirties, was leaning over her desk signing letters.

'How can I help you?' he said without looking up.

The new consul told Lopez that Archie had been 're-assigned'. No reason was given.

Two days later Lopez went back to the Monkey Mountain Evac Hospital and was told that Bobby had died the night before. The zombie nurse told him everything: how Bobby had managed to break loose and pull out all his drips, screaming, 'Kill me, kill me,' over and over. They sedated him and tied him down. The next day it became apparent that he wasn't responding to antibiotics and his urine output began to diminish. The nurse told Lopez how she smoothed Bobby's pillows and moistened his lips while he was dying. She told him about how guys in the path lab had joked – 'You're not gonna believe *this*' – about the levels of bacteria in his last blood sample. Two hours later, Bobby was in a body bag in the back of a truck on his way to the mortuary at Da Nang Airfield. She told Lopez she had cried, and said how much she hated it all. When he asked her why she still did it, she just said, 'It's my job.'

The worst thing, absolutely the worst thing, thought Lopez, was identifying the body. The new regulations were really strict about that. The 199th Light Infantry had recently sent back a dead GI to the wrong family – their kid, in fact, was still alive – the sort of thing, thought Lopez, that would have caused Redhorn endless mirth. But at least the Redhorn experience had taught him the trick of going to Graves Reg: you just didn't get curious about what was there, you just didn't look. This time Lopez kept his eyes focused on his boots and on the floor until the attendant told him he had found Bobby's coffin. He listened to the sound of it popping open and then looked. Bobby was naked in a shroud. It was the first time that Lopez had really looked at him. His chin seemed weaker than it had been in life, and the other features too were more pinched and delicate. He looked like a child martyr. One eyelid was slightly open, Lopez touched it with his finger to try to brush it shut, but it wouldn't move. The attendant handed Lopez a clipboard and he signed the necessary documentation – twice, because one of the carbons was too faint.

Once again Lopez had been appointed Survivors' Assistance Officer. The procedures had been tightened up since Redhorn's death. You had to draft a letter of condolence for the signature of the group commander. The letter had to be tactful and full of praise for the deceased. There was even a list of useful phrases – 'so-and-so's selfless personal bravery reflected great credit upon himself and his family', etcetera. It reminded Lopez of an Infantry School instructor who wasn't famous for tact and sensitivity. His way of inspiring military competence went: 'Ah hope ah nevah have to write a letter to your poor mama sayin' "your son is daid because he was one stupid fuckah". Hopefully that letter'll just say, "your son is daid".' There were also strict guidelines about dealing with the deceased's personal belongings. You had to use discretion: you weren't to send condoms, drugs, pornography or letters showing evidence of adulterous affairs back to the next of kin. You were supposed to destroy them in front of a witness.

When Lopez got back to Nui Hoa Den, he had to pack all Bobby's belongings into a footlocker for sending back to his family. There were quite a few letters from his family, from school friends and a girl named Jennifer. There was a cheap camera, a radio cassette and tapes – Joan Baez, Dylan, Julian Bream, Country Joe and the Fish, *Sergeant Pepper's Lonely Hearts Club Band*, The Supremes, Tchaikovsky's *Swan Lake* and Beethoven's *Moonlight Sonata* – and family photos too. Lopez knew it was prying, but he wanted to piece things together. He started turning the pages of Bobby's photo album. They were an outdoor family, fond of cross-country skiing, canoeing, picnicking and swimming in lakes. There was a picture of Bobby and his mother on a sled – 'Chiputnetcook, December 17th, 1954' – and with his father in a canoe – 'Moosehead Lake, July 1st, 1959'. It was a canoe that Bobby and his father had built together: it had beautiful curved ribs gleaming with layers of varnish. The father was wearing a gray sweatshirt and a floppy white canvas hat; Lopez could almost hear him saying, 'Hold the paddle like this, Robert.' Lopez closed his eyes. For a second, he became Bobby. He could feel Mr. Hatch's hand around his own, showing him how to grasp the paddle just above the blade. The sun was so bright and the water so clear. There were dragonflies, and a brown trout somersaulted in the shallows.

Lopez heard the muffled sounds of artillery impacting on a nearby mountain ridge. The marines at An Hoa, he thought, still had shells to waste.

Bobby's books were piled next to the footlocker. There were a half-dozen paperback novels, some natural history texts, a manual on how to build your own birch bark canoe and Robert Frost's *Collected Poems*, a fourteenth birthday present from his mother. She had written in the cover: Dearest Robert, I hope that over the years these poems will give you as much pleasure as they have your father and myself. Then she had copied out one of the poems:

> The Pasture
> I'm going out to clean the pasture spring;
> I'll only stop to rake the leaves away
> (And wait to watch the water clear, I may):
> I shan't be gone long. – You come too.
>
> I'm going out to fetch the little calf
> That's standing by the mother. It's so young
> It totters when she licks it with her tongue.
> I shan't be gone long. – You come too.

LOPEZ HAD HEARD THE RUMORS BEFORE, but at first he didn't believe them. It would require too big a conspiracy; they wouldn't get away with it. But every month in Vietnam peeled off another layer of naïveté: rational thought became obsolete; the boundaries of the credible spiraled into infinity like expanding galaxies; the bizarre became routine, gothic nightmare a commonplace; the most grotesque perversions too banal for comment.

Dusty told Lopez about it during an ambush patrol. It was a wet black moonless night and they were lying in a cemetery on the outskirts of Xuan Hoa. The individual graves were landscaped into circular plots, representing the cycle of existence, and from the air it was easy to mistake them for shell craters.

'Poor Bobby, with his reamed-out asshole they'll be sure to use him for a mule.'

'So how'd they get the stuff out of Laos?'

'The Agency have their own choppers, but a lot of the shit comes out on the unmarked Sikorskis that SOG use for out-of-country insertions.'

'And then the embalmer freaks take over. Someone should rocket that place.'

'No, Trung Uy, no. Graves Reg and the mortuary are totally out of the loop. The heroin's passed on to an air crew flight chief who sticks the stuff up the dead guys' asses after the coffins are loaded on the daily C-130 flight that takes the stiffs to Cam Ranh. This guy, Trung Uy Lopez, is one badass black motherfucker. He used to be a professional basketball player, one of those enormous black dudes whose hands are so big he can actually palm a basketball. They call him Fingers – his middle finger is twice the size of a white boy's dick. You need someone with big strong fingers to get the condoms up past the sphincter deep into the lower colon. They put about six ounces of heroin into each condom – priceless stuff, priceless – cut and processed from Golden Triangle opium, the purest and finest shit in the world.'

'Shhh, Trung Uy.' Phong whispered. 'Something moving, up in the tree line.' Lopez had arranged the ten-man ambush team to cover a trail coming out of the trees with paddy fields on either side. He doubted they were going to get any kills, the trap was too obvious. Phong had probably heard a stray water buffalo or an escaped pig.

Lopez wrapped his arms around himself tighter to keep warm; it had stopped raining and turned cold. He laid his head on his rifle stock and began to half-doze while still listening to the night. Images rolled through his brain like a slow motion porno film – the cargo-hold full of aluminum coffins, the wheeze of hydraulics, the internal aircraft guts of tubes, conduits, wires and perforated metal ribs. He visualized a big black American checking the documentation on each coffin until he found Bobby's, snapping open the spring-loaded levers with a slight pop, for the coffins were hermetically sealed. *Bobby's body, pale, waxy and naked in its shroud, is rolled on its side, the wad of cotton wool inserted in his poor burned-out ass to stop seepage removed. And then commences the final violation as Fingers breaks Bobby's virginity with a quarter-million-dollar drug phallus* – women, thought Lopez, aren't the only rape victims of war.

Lopez sat up, woken suddenly by the sound of small arms fire and explosions from the camp. He looked back toward Nui Hoa Den and saw tracer fire streaming from the machine-gun positions. It was suddenly as bright as day as parachute flares illuminated the surrounding valley.

'I'm glad we're not back there,' said Dusty. 'Do you know that, statistically, you stand a better chance of getting killed inside the camps than you do going on patrol?'

'Tell that to Redhorn, tell that to Bobby.'

'But, Trung Uy, when they knock off a camp, they kill lots of guys all at once.'

The firing began to peter out and then stopped altogether. 'Looks like just a couple of mortar rounds and a ground probe,' said Dusty. 'Not the real thing.'

'Are you part of this drug thing, Dusty? Straight answer, please. Remember, I can't prove what you say without a witness.'

'No, I'm not part of the inner circle. It tends to be the older NCOs, SOG guys mostly. Remember when you were back at Bragg? Did it ever occur to you, Trung Uy, how the fuck those guys – E7s on $5,000 a year including jump pay – were driving Porsches and wearing enough personal jewelry to make a Vegas whore look like some Mormon hausfrau?'

'Don't know. Guess I thought they had rich wives, or stupid bank managers.'

'But the big honchos aren't SF at all – they're in the Agency. And that bastard Krueger is one of the biggest of all. Whenever there's a big shipment, he disguises himself as a Medical Supply Corps major – false ID, false travel docs, the works. All the dead guys are shipped in the baggage holds of the chartered airliners that take the live guys back as well. Krueger pretends to be this major at the end of his tour so he can follow his heroin mules back to Travis Air Force Base – all the corpses go through Travis.'

Lopez thought he could hear small arms fire from the

other side of Black Widow Mountain. It was too far away to worry about.

'Krueger controls the whole California supply chain – most of the guys are his personal catamites. He beat the shit out of one of them a few months ago, might even have killed him. Poor fuck was a medical technician in the warehouse where they store the bodies. His job was draping American flags over the coffins and making sure they were put on the right onward flight. By the way, your family gets to keep the flag, but they have to send the coffin back. They're government property, have to be sprayed with disinfectant and re-used. So, this guy's other job was to find the bodies with the heroin and remove the drugs. One day this stupid fuck managed to split a condom, leaving a hundred thou's worth of heroin in some corpse's lower alimentary tract. Any decent SF medic would have extracted the stuff with a pair of blunt toothed tissue forceps. Needless to say, Krueger was not a happy bunny. I heard he took the guy up into the hills and beat him to death with a shovel, then spent the weekend celebrating in his favorite Frisco bath house.'

'How do you know these things, Dusty?'

'You remember that corny line from a Peter Lorre film, "Ask me no questions, I tell you no lies"?'

'Do you really hate Krueger?'

'Not completely. He's an evil shit, but he's also one fucked-up guy. There's this really funny story about him on one of those repatriation flights. Twelve hours after take-off, a soldier breaks into convulsions. Of course, it's the stewardess's first time on a Vietnam charter run and she's never seen heroin withdrawal symptoms before. So she wakes Krueger, who's the senior ranking officer on the aircraft, to tell him she's going to ask the pilot to divert to Hawaii. Krueger just looks at her without blinking. "You do that, you're going to have a fucking mutiny on your hands. Let the degenerate fuck die, he deserves to die." So the stewardess has a confab with the pilot and by the time she comes back to Krueger, two more guys have started to twitch and the first one looks like he's having a *grand mal* seizure. So she asks Krueger to go talk with the pilot. Five minutes later Krueger's on the PA asking any medics on board to report to him. There're six of them, and Krueger tells them, "You are responsible for these assholes. Do whatever is necessary to keep them under control – sit on them, smack the shit out of them, but keep them quiet." Meanwhile the stewardess says the pilot's radioing ahead to have an ambulance waiting. This *really* pisses Krueger off. "No fucking ambulance! You radio for the MPs, these assholes are going straight in the slammer. Do as I say, I take full responsibility for the decision".'

'What's funny about this story.'

'Krueger is. Guy's got no sense of fucking irony. He really does hate drugs and the people who use them. In his own twisted way, he's an American puritan. I think that's really funny.'

Lopez started thinking about the tactical situation again. He knew they weren't going to get any kills where they were, and it was too late to move to another position. Earlier in the evening, before they left the village, an old man came to see Lopez and gave him the location of a small Viet Cong unit. Lopez studied his map and saw that there was another trail, one that branched off behind Black Widow Mountain, where the Viet Cong were more likely to be caught. He tried to get the Vietnamese squad leader to move his men there, but he flat-out refused. Lopez tried to pull rank on the obstinate Vietnamese by radioing Dai Uy Ky, but Ky made some feeble excuse about their needing an Area of Operations extension. You were supposed to stay within certain map-grid squares, otherwise you might shoot up another friendly unit. Lopez was annoyed, because he knew this was just a stupid technical quibble and there weren't any 'friendlies' within miles. He should have gotten Boca to twist Ky's arm, but he didn't want to have to talk to Boca. He now felt guilty, because he had put personal loathing before professional duty. Was it is just duty? Why was it that, after all the senseless heartbreak, a part of him still wanted – ached and longed – to kill enemy soldiers? He remembered how, a few days before, thumbing the selector switch on his M16 to fully automatic, he had run towards a stream junction where they had surprised a group of bathing Viet Cong. He had felt no fear or doubt, only adrenaline-rush excitement and the desire to kill. Was he just another murdering Krueger?

The next morning the patrol went back to Nui Hoa Den. Lopez learned that a Viet Cong platoon, probably the one he failed to ambush, had overrun the Regional Forces outpost at the base of Black Widow Mountain and killed sixteen soldiers before withdrawing.

LOPEZ WAS EATING BREAKFAST in the C-team mess hall next to a major wearing the twin snake insignia of the medical branch, but it was somehow different from any that he had seen before. The major was completely bald, but had a splendid dark moustache with curled and waxed ends. Lopez thought he resembled the actor in the teamhouse's jerky old 1920s French porn movie: *'Madame, je suis médecin. Allongez-vous sur le divan, s'il vous plaît...'*

The major looked up from his scrambled eggs. 'Are you on the staff?'

For a second, Lopez was surprised to hear the major speaking English. 'No, sir, I'm from one of the camps. I have to come here once a month to pick up the pay for the CIDG Strike Force.' The major was wearing the shoulder patch of the Saigon HQ. 'You're from MACV, aren't you?'

'Yes, but I don't spend much time down there. My job means I have to move all over the country, but I seem to spend a lot of time up here in I Corps. In fact, I'm here right now to deal with your chaplain. There seems to be a bit of an identity problem.'

Lopez wasn't surprised. As far as he was concerned all chaplains were weirdos. He tried to imagine what the problem might be – marital, mid-life, sexual orientation – or maybe the chaplain had simply wised up to the fact that God doesn't exist and felt guilty about drawing his pay under false pretenses. Lopez was trying hard not to smile, but he also suddenly missed Travis – he would have loved this story. He looked closely at the major and tried to sound sincere. 'You've got a really interesting and important job. I don't know many of my colleagues who appreciate the psychological strains and damage that this war is causing people.'

The major wiped his mouth and looked at Lopez in a curious way. There was a look on his face that hovered between suspicion and total incomprehension.

Lopez leaned forward and said, 'You are a psychiatrist, aren't you?'

The major frowned at Lopez for a second. Then his face softened and broadened into a smile. 'My dear boy, I am neither a psychiatrist nor a psycho-therapist of any sort. I am Vietnam's one and only dental pathologist. The chaplain's helicopter flew right into a mountain. I'm trying to match up a piece of charred jawbone recovered by a marine recon team with his dental records.'

Suddenly Lopez remembered the helicopter that was lost near Lang Khe – it seemed so long ago.

Lopez met the replacement chaplain later that day. The new padre was an intense looking Roman Catholic priest with bushy eyebrows. The chaplain confided to Lopez that he suspected his presence was pointless. 'I don't know why they sent me here. There don't seem to be any practicing Catholics among the US personnel.' The only serious Christians were a small band of fundamentalist Southern Baptists, one of who lost no time in telling the priest, 'Rome is the whore of Babylon and your Pope is the Antichrist.'

When it became apparent that the chaplain was the only

staff officer who had nothing to do, the adjutant suggested that he could help draft letters to the bereaved families of dead soldiers – since Tet there had been a lot of them to write. He was sure that the priest's experience with funerals would be useful. 'It's nice,' said the adjutant, 'if the letters have a personal touch, like we'd actually *known* the poor fuck: you know – kind of music he liked, position he played on the baseball team, the name of his dog. Now, padre, you've buried lots of folks and always had to give a nice little talk about the departed, and I bet you knew less than diddly-shit about them...'

The priest agreed to help, but was still reluctant to accept that he had no pastoral mission. He knew there were a large number of Vietnamese Catholics among the local population. Eventually, he sent a letter of introduction offering his services to the bishop of Da Nang.

Lopez was about to go back to Nui Hoa Den when the priest told him that he had been invited to the cathedral for "an audience". 'The adjutant says I can use his jeep, but I don't know my way around Da Nang. Is there anyone...?'

'No sweat, Father, I'll be your driver.'

Lopez had begun to like Da Nang. He liked its seediness, its secretiveness, the decaying ambience of its French past. As they drove past the RMK girls – Suck 'em Silly Sally and company – Lopez was tempted to make a crude comment to embarrass the priest, but held his tongue. The chaplain was, he thought, just a harmless fool and not worth baiting; he probably had more than enough of that from the C-team.

'Lieutenant Lopez, your name suggests a possible Catholic past.'

'You mean because I'm a spic? And spics, like micks and dagos, are almost always Papes?'

'Well, I guess it wasn't the most tactful way of asking if you were a Catholic.'

'Not any more, not at all. I gave up all that mumbo jumbo years ago.'

'Why did you offer to help me then?'

'Because my commanding officer at Nui Hoa Den is a total shithead and I will use any excuse I can to stay away, because if I spend too much time in his proximity, I will eventually shoot him. And killing that piece of scum is not worth three years in Leavenworth. I hope that answers your question.'

The priest laughed. 'God's grace works in funny ways.'

'Where'd you get that line, father? Out of some Graham Greene novel?'

'I know you, Lieutenant Lopez, perhaps better than you know yourself. You're too sophisticated to believe, but not sophisticated enough to have faith in something that lies beyond your own intelligence.'

'Can't you do better than that, father? You make me feel like I'm arguing with a Mormon.' Lopez used to say the same thing when Ianthe nagged him to go to Mass. 'It's like going on believing in the tooth fairy after you're grown up,' he would tell her. 'All that God stuff'll get you a closed cell at Spring Grove.' In the end, he thought, Ianthe had gone against her religion; she'd had sex outside marriage and an abortion, and she'd died.

The cathedral was a grotesque monstrosity of too-bright red brick and pinkish stone. Lopez pulled over, jumped out of the jeep and pressed a buzzer on a locked rusty iron gate – it didn't work. He shouted through the railings, 'Hello – chao – bonjour – anybody fu–...' Then he noticed a gong with a length of steel rod hanging on a string; he gave the gong a few solid strokes which shook the mid-day peace. A pedicab driver shouted something rude as he passed. Lopez made an obscene gesture with his thumb and shouted, 'Hôn dit toi – kiss my ass!' at the driver's back. An old woman on a bicycle laden with bales of coriander leaves grinned and called something bawdy.

'You seem very at home here,' observed the priest.

Lopez just said, 'Someone's coming.'

A plump laughing nun came hurrying across the sunny courtyard with short quick steps; she carried a set of keys so huge and ancient that they might, Lopez thought, serve to open the gates of heaven and hell. They followed her into a mock-gothic cloister with scrubbed tiles and then into an inner sanctum heavily curtained with red velvet and smelling of incense and stale tobacco. At first Lopez thought they were alone, but then he heard a cough. As the chaplain's eyes adjusted to the gloom, he saw an elderly, wizened Vietnamese priest who introduced himself as Monsignor Chuyen. He apologized for the bishop being unavailable, and added that the bishop was likely to remain unavailable for the foreseeable future. The monsignor's speech was punctuated by a racking chain-smoker's cough that seemed to rattle his bones almost audibly. He begged his visitors to sit down and offered his hospitality with such fervor that they felt obliged to accept for fear that the old Monsignor would otherwise collapse into a heap of brown sticks. A servant was summoned and laid out a silver coffeepot, a crystal decanter of cognac and a tray of sticky rice cakes.

Monsignor Chuyen spoke in French, but it was obvious that the chaplain was finding it difficult. Chuyen apologized for not speaking much English. Lopez was about to offer to translate when the chaplain said something in Latin. The Monsignor smiled and answered in Latin. He spread out a map of the diocese on the table, and continued to speak in Latin as he drew his fellow-priest into the Byzantine web of Vietnamese Catholicism. Lopez looked on, abashed. He felt he'd fallen into a time warp, as if the two priests were naturalized Roman pro-consuls, of different tribes, charting frontier provinces in the language of their common conqueror. The Monsignor pointed out Hue, Quang Tri, Hoi An, Tam Ky and An Hoa as he traced the web of influence of another Roman power that spun its threads down river valleys and across mountain passes, threads that wove in and out of political loyalties and bound together opposing armies as though the continuing bloodshed was almost irrelevant, war simply a vulgar and profane distraction that belonged on a lower plane.

A few weeks later, one of the padre's invisible threads led him back to Lopez and the camp at Nui Hoa Den. Things had deteriorated: every night now the Communist battalions flowed past the camp as though it were merely a small rock in a large stream. Despite the bombardments and displacement, a large number of Vietnamese Catholics still lived in the villages of the river valley.

Although Phu Gia had been almost obliterated by high altitude carpet-bombing, the hollow ruin of its church still stood on a small knoll just outside the village. Its function as a place of worship was long forgotten. For years its only function had been as a reference point for directing air strikes and artillery fire – 'See that church? Lay down the napalm just behind it.'

Boca was annoyed that the priest wanted to say Mass in Phu Gia. He had no intention of providing a security force to protect him. 'You go down there, padre, you're on your own.' On the other hand, if the priest were captured or killed, it would make him look bad. Even worse, he might have to organize an operation to get the priest back, alive or dead. Either way, the whole thing was 'a pain in the ass and a waste of fuckin' time.'

But the priest was determined. 'I've spoken,' he said, 'to the people in the valley, and they say there hasn't been a priest in the village for years. Leave it to me, Captain Boca; I take full responsibility.'

'You gonna go by yourself, padre?'

'If no one else will come with me.'

'Padre, I don't think you're gonna find anyone stupid enough to do that.'

Lopez, who was busy writing an after-action report, rapped the table with a beer can for attention. 'I'm stupid enough, father; I'll come along.'

'Well done, padre, you've brought Lieutenant Lopez back to the faith. How about that?'

A half-dozen Vietnamese also agreed to come. Lopez drove down to the river in the two-and-a-half-ton truck, the priest beside him and the others in the back. At Nui Hoa village, they hired a boat to carry them down the river as far as the landing at Xuan Hoa. Something about the journey reminded Lopez of Easter in a warm spring. But it was still a stupid and dangerous thing to do.

As they walked up from the landing, the priest asked, 'Have you changed your mind about the church since our last conversation?'

'Fuck, no!'

The priest kept quiet and smiled.

Lopez wanted to see what was left of the village after the bombing. A shortage of aircraft meant that they had only half done the job. Most of the village had been cratered, but the derelict church, a handful of outlying houses and the paddy fields furthest from the river had escaped. The church had been built on a flat mound that dominated the surrounding paddy. Its thatched roof and beams had been burnt away by napalm, but the stone walls remained intact. The Catholics of the valley had prepared for the mass by building an altar and communion rail from freshly cut bamboo. The local Viet Cong and a North Vietnamese patrol had looked on at first, and then joined in to help. The sanctuary was decorated with jungle ferns and perfumed with dried herbs and spices. Bright flowers and palm leaves had been woven into the communion rail. Instead of bells to signal the elevation of the Host, a large ox-hide drum was suspended from a bamboo frame.

The priest donned a purple chasuble and began the

service. It had to be an old fashioned Latin mass: it was the only mass that the villagers remembered. Lopez found the whole thing – ragged Vietnamese peasants chanting *Domine non sum dignus* and *Et cum spiritu tuo* – surreal, the Mass of his own childhood refracted through a maze of broken mirrors, and all around him the too-human vestiges of an antique faith.

The sexton, a dried and shriveled man – Lopez wondered if he had been unwrapped from a dust-sheet for the occasion – struck the ox-hide drum once as the priest raised the Host, and again as he elevated the chalice. Lopez had no intention of receiving the Eucharist. He didn't believe in it, and, even if he did, his soul was not in the necessary state of grace. Besides, he wasn't certain that he even had a soul. But he knew that if, supposing Pascal's divine lottery ticket was a winner, he did have one, it was black and pitted with murder, selfishness, deceit, willful cruelty, lies, blasphemies and – the worst sin of all – hurting someone that loved him.

When it came time to approach the altar to receive Holy Communion, Lopez was the only one who didn't move. He closed his eyes and lost himself in a daydream of flesh that was a million miles from the austere penance of Phu Gia. He was jerked awake when he felt a hand on his elbow. Lopez tried to pull his arm free, but the grip tightened like a vise. He turned and looked into the hollow eyes of the elderly sexton. The old man was pushing him towards the communion rail. Lopez was amazed that there was so much power in such a frail body. He couldn't stop that ancient strength from pushing him forward, and the sexton knelt at the rail beside him as if to block an escape. Lopez closed his eyes and waited for the Host to land on his tongue.

When they returned to their places, the sexton was murmuring Hail Marys in the lilting singsong accent of Annam and counting the thick beads of his rosary. It was an elegant rosary – large beads of polished hard wood and a silver crucifix. Lopez felt nauseous – rosaries were bad omens, Old World voodoo relics. He remembered a black rosary, with beads like cockroaches, wrapped around his mother's cold stiff fingers. They had packed the coffin with ice – it was a hot August – to preserve the body, to keep it uncorrupted pending his late arrival in Vera Cruz from the States so that he could see his mother, for a once and only time, before they buried her. It was a mother that he had never seen – at least could not remember – in life. And there she was, stiff and frozen for him to see and remember. Lopez's first impression was of an old Indian squaw in a cowboy film: brown skin drawn tight over high cheek bones and black hair pulled straight back. The comparison was banal. He felt ashamed; he wanted to think of her as otherwise – this woman's face belonged to a stranger.

Many of his Vietnamese soldiers wore rosaries, as if they were magic charms to ward off bullets. One had been blown up at Dai Binh, when a booby trap took away half his face and most of his right arm. The cheap plastic beads were soaked with blood, but the rosary was still in one piece and hadn't been torn from the soldier's neck by the force of the blast. Lopez sat beside the soldier and watched him die. During the pitiful minutes before losing consciousness the man kept trying to make the sign of the cross. But his hand was no longer there – it had vanished in a flash of fire and shrapnel. Lopez remembered the jagged ends of two blast-blackened bones protruding from the stump, their futile reaching for forehead and shoulder. It was a horrible reflex, unbearable to watch.

Lopez was conscious only of the cold empty sky, and a pair of fighter-bombers – trim, gleaming silver darts – intersecting the perfectly clear blue above the church. He tried to empty his mind of everything but the dry, bland taste of the Host dissolving on his tongue, but the infinite suffering of stupid vulnerable human beings kept spinning in his brain, and he began to cry. The sexton put his arm around him and tried to press rosary beads into his hands. Lopez pushed the sexton away; he felt nauseous and wanted to be alone. The chanting – *Agnus Dei, qui tollis peccata mundi, dona nobis pacem* – was echoing inside his head, reminding him of masses half-heard in childhood, and of Ianthe dragging him to mass on hot summer Sundays. *Lamb of God, that takest away the sins of the world, grant us thy peace.* Oh, please.

Afterwards everyone shook hands and bade one another farewell. As they departed Lopez looked back and saw the Phu Gia Catholics still smiling and waving, framed against the backdrop of blackened stone, until the closing matrix of young bamboo, banana leaves, and palm fronds shut them from sight.

Just as they reached the river, Lopez felt the earth shake under his feet. A thousand meters away high explosive bombs were screaming into the church. Boca had called in an airstrike to massacre the congregation before they had a chance to disperse. The priest's face turned pale, he looked at Lieutenant Lopez; his lips kept mouthing 'why', but no sound came out. He finally found his breath and whispered, 'This is sacrilege. This is blasphemy against God.'

Lopez's face was soaked with hot tears. He couldn't believe what the priest had just said, couldn't believe he was still babbling superstition and nonsense. 'It's worse than any of your fucking sacrilege.'

The priest reached out towards him. 'I care about these people too.'

Lopez pushed his hands away. 'You understand nothing, priest, you make me sick.'

The napalm came next. Lopez hadn't expected that. But he wasn't surprised either – it was part of the pattern. He watched the thick gray smoke billow above the tree line, and something began to roar inside him, something so deafening and so just that he would never again hear anything else.

Lopez got into his jeep and roared off back to the camp.

He screeched to a halt, jumped out, chambered a round in his M16, and went to find Boca so he could kill him.

He looked in the teamhouse, the comm bunker, in the captain's own quarters, but Boca just seemed to have disappeared. He started to search the CIDG positions, the ammo bunkers, all the trenches, everywhere. No one said anything, but Lopez attracted a crowd of Vietnamese who followed him around though keeping their distance. Finally, he heard a voice behind him, put his finger on the trigger and turned around.

'Lieutenant Lopez, what the fuck are you doing?' It was Dusty.

'Where's Boca?'

'Gone. Left on the mail chopper. Didn't he tell you? He's got a week's R&R with his family in Hawaii.'

The next day they brought Xuan Huong and her newly-born baby to the Nui Hoa Den infirmary. She had gone into labor when the napalm exploded and the liquid fire poured into the bunker where she had gone for cover. She had suffered third degree burns over most of her body. The baby was fine. But it was a baby who would never suck milk from her mother's breasts, because those breasts had been burnt off, a baby who would never bring joy to her mother's eyes because the jellies of those eyes were melted. Nor would that mother ever caress her baby, because the hands that would have held and caressed were so ruined by American napalm they had to be amputated.

At first Lopez was ashamed to be back on the morphine. He had progressed from tablets to injecting the syrettes intended for battlefield wounded. He had managed to steal a whole box from the infirmary. He felt ashamed because his pain was so much less than the pain of others, less than the wretched blinded Xuan Huong's, less than poor naïve

Bobby's, or that of the human beings they used as mine detectors. He thought about all the limbless kids. The eyes were the worst things about those kids. No accusation, no hate, just bottomless black pools of acceptance and pain. Lopez would have preferred anger, a flailing attack with a crutch. Anything would have been better than those hollow-eternity eyes. Was it Nietzsche who said something about staring into the abyss, and the abyss staring back? Lopez couldn't take it; he didn't even want to try to comprehend it – the endlessness of that pain, the eternity of that acceptance. Was this all that most of humanity would ever own? He didn't need more knowledge of this: he needed a drug.

Lopez pulled the plastic top off a morphine syrette. He looked at the needle that glistened gold in the candlelight and remembered the first time he had used one, not on himself, but on a Vietnamese casualty. The CIDG soldier, so slightly built, had looked like a child of fifteen. A mine had blown off his leg to just above the knee. The meat of his thigh was flayed and shredded, ragged flaps of skin hanging like ribbons, the bone sticking out splintered and charred like someone had taken a blowtorch to it. Lopez radioed the team medic for advice. 'Don't let him go into shock,' said the medic, 'or he's a goner. If he's still conscious, give him a morphine jab.' Lopez injected the drug into the good thigh, then radioed back for more advice. The medic said, 'You didn't give him the whole syrette did you?' 'Sure I did.' 'Uh-oh...' The dosage was designed for beefy Americans, not diminutive Vietnamese. Lopez regretted that he hadn't stayed with him till he died, wished that he'd held him in his arms, had whispered, 'I'm sorry.'

There were other evasions too. He knew that he had to stop saying 'they'. It wasn't they – it was *he*. He had been in command and it was his responsibility that those awful hills had been strewn with body parts. Lopez stared at the needle: he still had two legs and was big enough for a full American dose. He hated to remember that he held a position of authority. Lopez didn't want to be reminded that, compared to a CIDG soldier, in the tiny world of Nui Hoa Den he had all the power of a Medici prince. But then, as the sweet numbness crawled up his body from the intra-muscular syrette that he had squeezed into his thigh like a tiny tube of toothpaste, it no longer mattered. He poured a whiskey and lay back on his bunk. A paperback copy of Rimbaud's poems that Rosie had sent him jabbed into his back – he tossed it on the earth floor and watched the candle light flicker on the cover. The cover design was a chaos of broken lines and splattered paint reproduced from a Jackson Pollock. 'Why the fuck?' he thought. Why the fuck indeed?

Lopez watched the candle flicker on his desk. He was starting to feel good – nothing much mattered. He no longer wanted to kill Boca, no longer wanted to kill anyone. It was a quiet night: no artillery, no keening from the Dead House – even the radio seemed asleep. The drugged silence reminded him of a lieutenant that he had roomed with at Fort Benning. The lieutenant had lost the use of a leg when a white phosphorus grenade had accidentally exploded during a helicopter insertion on the Cambodian border. The phosphorus had melted all the tendons, cartilage and ligaments that made up his knee joint. There was no treatment: the lieutenant was condemned to watch the muscle of his leg slowly wither away until it was nothing but a bony stick. The medical board awarded the lieutenant a big fat disability allowance. His mother said he had to forget the past and think about the future; she pleaded with him to use the disability money to buy a fast food franchise that he could run with his sister – she'd do most of the work. Instead the lieutenant bought a return ticket to Asia. The last Lopez had heard was that he had set up home in an opium den in Taiwan where he was spending every last cent of his disability pension. Lopez could see the point – it was a way out, a way to get rid of the pain. And it wasn't just the withered leg.

Lopez felt cold, so he took off his boots and got under the blanket. He looked up. There was a face next to the candle – Dusty Storm. At first he wondered if it was an hallucination. Lopez hoped it was: he wanted there to be a separate universe. There was also a voice – what was Dusty saying? – which seemed to be echoing from the other end of a tunnel – yualola, yualola. Lopez wanted to turn it off: he didn't like the way Dusty was laughing, mocking. Suddenly the words became loud and clear, as if someone had pulled cotton wool out of his ears. 'You're Lolita. All of you, you're Lolitas.'

Lopez closed his eyes and opened them again, but Dusty was still there. He leaned forward and showed his teeth, tiny and stained. 'But *I'm* not Lolita, I'm Humbert.' Dusty lifted the edge of the blanket and looked at Lopez's feet. 'Hey, Lolita. Want me to paint your toenails, Lolita?'

The morphine seemed to be wearing off. Lopez wanted to make Dusty disappear. He tried closing his eyes, but when he opened them again the apparition was still there. 'Why the fuck don't you leave me alone?'

'Why? Because then you wouldn't know how disappointed I was to find out who you are. You'll always be Lolita – American – and I'll always be Russian. Your brown face and your French education don't change a thing.'

'You're an asshole.'

'And you speak the language of the high school locker room. I'm disappointed. I thought you were different. But you're just a Disneyland fake with the keys to your Daddy's car in your pocket.'

'Go 'way.' Lopez couldn't begin to imagine what Dusty was on.

Dusty had been reading Nabokov. Every month or so the Red Cross sent to the camp a crate of second-hand books, all with their front covers removed to prevent their being resold on the black market, as if, in a cratered landscape scented by napalm, this posed a serious moral problem. Part of Lopez, the part that was still a preppy snob, wanted to let Dusty know that he had actually met Nabokov, that the author had been a houseguest at Rideout's Landing. But he knew that would only prove Dusty's point: that he really was a Lolita. A spoiled privileged Lolita with car keys and culture too.

He could see why Dusty liked Nabokov – both were stranded in supercilious adolescence. Lopez remembered, one morning at Rideout's Landing, finding the author studying a portrait of one of Rosie's ancestors, a Confederate major who had been killed at Shiloh. Lopez had always found the dead officer fascinating; with his goatee beard and shoulder length hair he looked more like a poet than a soldier. Nabokov, on the other hand, was regarding the sacred portrait with his head cocked to one side and a mocking smile on his lips. At the time Lopez was only fifteen. He felt a thrill when the writer looked at him like a fellow conspirator and whispered, 'C'est drôle, n'est-ce pas?'

Dusty disappeared as inexplicably and suddenly as he had appeared. Lopez was sweating and feeling sick. He wondered when he had first started hating America. Was it just a snobbish thing – that when he first came back from France he had winced at the huge cars and the loud vulgarity? Or was it deeper? He resented Dusty for reminding him that he was, in essence, American: rich, self-indulgent, shallow. Fuck up a country? Sure, fuck up as many countries as you like. Who's going to firebomb *your* Dresdens, *your* Hamburgs – who's going to send your leaders, your generals, to the gallows at Nuremberg? Being American meant not having to pay the price.

Fuck history – and fuck the supercilious Russians too. Why *should* he pay the price? It wasn't his problem. He would start over. He had to stop punishing himself for *her* death. By doing so he had only hurt more people, killed more people. He had to survive and start to live. As soon as he left the army, he'd be back in the loop. The connections were still there, he just had to plug in.

Lopez wrapped the blanket tighter round himself, sipped

the whiskey and wondered what he should wear for his first interview. He knew how to buy smart understated suits that made him look good. He looked good in gray – it complemented his dark skin. Where would he live? New York? Paris? Why not both? He preferred the life in Paris, but found American girls more erotic – fetishized, depilated Lolitas. Maybe he could have the best of both worlds – he could fuck American girls in Paris!

Lopez realized that he only had to survive eleven more weeks and his Vietnam duty tour would be finished. He already had plans to pick up a new Triumph Bonneville straight from the factory in Birmingham, England for a motorcycle tour of Europe. Then five easy months at NATO HQ in Brussels before leaving the army. Lopez knew that tomorrow belonged to him: sleek offices, nice clothes, fragrant women, laughter and the clink of glasses on the yacht club terrace, freshly pressed tennis whites. He wanted a bedroom with tall open windows and a sea breeze and sheets that smelled of lavender – a bedroom that he didn't have to share with rats.

The candle was nearly spent. Lopez knew that he couldn't live like that. He loved sensual comfort, and wanted to have all those nice things, live in those nice places, but he feared that he never would. There was something inside of him that would always fuck it up.

The next morning was a day so clear and beautiful that it almost hurt the eyes. The mountains were in sharp focus against the sky, rumpled green blankets so near in the perfect air you wanted to reach out and stroke them. The river, a living thing, writhed through the valley like a ribbon of shining blue foil.

Boca had set up his ship's binoculars on a tripod and was scanning the valley for targets. The binoculars, bearing the nameplate of a battleship sunk at Pearl Harbor, were another of those objects that – like the armchair – had found their way to Vietnam. Squatting behind the binoculars, Boca looked like a toad; Lopez wanted to stick a sharp spike through the back of his neck and into the brain stem, the way a Paris chef kills a frog. Boca had the radio beside him and seemed to be in communication with the .155 artillery at An Hoa. Lopez left him to his murderous games; his very presence polluted the place. Later that morning, Lopez heard shells impacting in the valley, but couldn't imagine that there was much left to destroy.

An hour later, the first casualties arrived at the Nui Hoa river landing. Among the chaos of shattered limbs and multiple fragmentation wounds was a tiny little bundle – the little water buffalo girl of Phu Gia. She had been hit in the stomach by a single shell fragment and had died in the boat crossing the bright river. Lopez folded her in his arms and held her for a long time. 'I'm so sorry,' he told her. 'Tell them all – I'm so, so sorry.'

There were no tears when he laid her down again, only a terrible pulsating in his head, which spread from his brain through his entire body. Every cell was screaming as if he had been wired to a lightning bolt, and no amount of morphine would silence that screaming. It went beyond words like 'justice' and 'retribution'. He needed just to kill, and punish, and kill again.

He was still a soldier – perhaps more of a soldier than he had ever been before – but no longer an American one.

LOPEZ PRETENDED to Madame Binh that he had come to see her about Sergeant-major Dieu's death gratuity. As before, the one-eyed girl servant brought the tea. Madame Binh told Lopez that she had received everything to which she was entitled. He thought she seemed nervous and apprehensive, as if she had the impression that he was there for other reasons. Maybe she was wondering if he was interested in drug trafficking or illegal currency transactions, even something to do with sex. If so, she was probably offended that he had come to her, that he might even think she could help. She most likely just wanted him to leave.

Lopez tried to make small talk about films and the courses on offer at the Institut Français. They had recently shown *Jules et Jim*; he asked Madame Binh if she had seen it.

'Sadly, no. There has been so much to do recently.'

Lopez could tell that she was looking for an opportunity to end his visit. 'Madame Binh, I have not come here to talk about your late husband or the films of François Truffaut.'

She let out a breath. Her visitor's directness made her feel ill at ease, but she did not want to seem impolite. She covered her mouth with a small blue notebook to hide her embarrassment.

Lopez knew that it was rude to be bold and direct. He knew that the Vietnamese regarded time as cyclical, knew that there would always be another day, another season. But he felt that the time for waiting, for subtle suggestion, had passed. 'Madame Binh, I know that you are associated with the National Liberation Front, although you may not be a cadre at present.'

She couldn't stay seated; she got up, her hands shaking. Lopez felt he had violated her. 'Lieutenant Lopez, you are suggesting things about me which are very dangerous.'

'Madame Binh, I hate this war and what the Americans are doing to your country.'

'All of us hate this war – but there are certain things one must never say.'

'Hating the war is not enough. I want to help the NLF and the Liberation Army in whatever way I can.'

'I cannot help you. I know nothing about them.'

'You wouldn't be involved, Madame Binh. I do not want you to be involved.'

'Please keep your voice down, my servant may hear.'

'Just tell me how I can make contact. Just a hint would do.'

'I do not know what you're talking about.'

Lopez could tell that she was extremely upset; he could

almost hear her heart beating. 'I am sorry to have caused you so much distress.'

'I think you have mistaken me for someone else. Maybe someone has told you lies about me.'

'Good-bye, Madame Binh. I wish you well.'

Lopez returned to his jeep and began the usual security checks. Perhaps, he thought, Dieu had lied to him; perhaps he had sought some form of posthumous revenge. Lopez was parked next to Madame Binh's kitchen window. He could hear the servant singing as she went about her chores. She was summoned; a moment later she appeared, hiding her face behind her hair as she walked past Lopez and disappeared into a narrow passage at the back of the bicycle shop. The shop was padlocked shut, and Lopez wondered what had become of all the dangerous looking types who had stared at him the last time he was there. He went over to the shop and peeped through a broken shutter; all the tools, bike parts and bikes were still there. Something felt uncanny – he had the feeling that he was being watched.

Lopez decided to take a look around before he went back. He left the jeep and walked along the tiny dark passage where the servant had disappeared. There was no sign of her. The passage came out through an unlocked gate on to Doc Lap Street. Lopez turned left to see if he could find her. He saw a soup café and a pharmacy, separated by a dark and malodorous alleyway which, it seemed to Lopez, must lead to the back of the bicycle shop. It was dark, dank and smelled of fish sauce and kitchen waste. He followed it until he was within ten feet of the bike shop. Suddenly a voice greeted him from the shadows in English. 'Who are you looking for, Trung Uy?'

Something inside Lopez – it was just a hunch – made him say, 'Ho Cuc?'

The voice just said, 'He isn't very well.'

Lopez could just make out a dark figure, more shadow

than flesh, leaning on a crutch. He was sure it was Cuc.
'Chao anh,' he said.
'Welcome home, Trung Uy.'
The figure coughed and disappeared into the darkness. Lopez heard the crutch scrape, then a door slide closed, a key turn. He waited for ten minutes, but there was no further communication. He made his way back through the alleys to the jeep. There was a note lying on the driver's seat. Someone had written, in an elegant hand, 'Tomorrow, 1300 hours, stone bench near ferry landing.'

Lopez arrived at the ferry landing rendezvous fifteen minutes early. He didn't know who or what to expect. It even occurred to him that he might, as a suspected agent provocateur, be shot by a passing assassin riding pillion on a Honda. A languid Vietnamese soldier and his girlfriend were sitting on the next stone bench eating lime ices. Lopez's presence seemed to make them uneasy. They began to whisper and giggle after he sat down. A minute later they got up and strolled away, laughing, under the flame trees along the river promenade.
Lopez continued to wait on the stone bench – the ends were carved dragons – and listened to the sound of boats churning against the harbor current. He kept checking his watch: his contact was already five minutes late. A class of lycée girls dressed in billowing white ao dais flung by on bicycles, their silken hair and laughter flowing behind them. They looked like a flock of swans. One of the girls stopped to pump up a bicycle tire. Lopez saw her pull back a braid of hair and look around. The girl was flat-chested and looked incomplete, unfinished, like a fine china vase that an artist had left half painted. Her hair was plaited into pigtails: it made her look so young and vulnerable. Lopez walked over and asked her in Vietnamese if he could help.
She answered in English, 'If you betray me, they will kill you.'

'Trust me, I won't.'

'I don't trust anyone who hasn't proved their commitment. You may come to my home this evening.' She handed him a slip of paper with the address, then got back on her bicycle. 'Don't look at me when I cycle away.' Lopez turned and walked away. He heard the white train of her ao dai flutter and snap in the sea breeze as she pedaled off. He didn't even know her name.

Lopez set off just after dark. To get to the address he had to pass through one of the poorest quarters of Da Nang. The roads were unpaved and pitted with deep potholes and mud baths. The poor leered at Lopez in the light of the jeep's headlamps; their eyes seemed to be mocking him. He continued to a level crossing over a railway line that went down to the docks. The connecting bridges had been blown up long ago and there were no more trains. The line was covered in rank vegetation. On the other side of the crossing, there were no more slums: this was the precinct of the officers and profiteers. The address was a single story stucco villa with a courtyard, and an ornamental pond. A Vietnamese Army jeep was parked inside the wrought iron gate.

Lopez parked outside and was padlocking the steering wheel when the gate scraped open and a man's voice told him in Vietnamese to park inside. The man was middle-aged and wearing the uniform of a Vietnamese Army captain. He shook hands and told Lopez that he was 'Nhung's father'.

He led Lopez into the house, which was too bright with overhead fluorescent tubes. Nhung was seated next to her mother. He formally shook hands with both of them. Nhung's mother struck Lopez as a humorless woman who looked as though she should be chairing a school governors' meeting. The father was an officer in the Transportation Corps, a good job that kept him out of battle and provided lucrative opportunities for selling army gasoline.

Lopez didn't understand why Nhung had invited him to

her family home. The evening was a formal and claustrophobic one. They drank tea and carried on polite stilted conversation. Lopez found out that Nhung was studying modern languages at Saigon University and had taken a year out to be a teaching assistant at the lycée in Da Nang. He soon became aware that Nhung had spun her parents a cover story that involved Lopez giving a talk to her students on 'American civilization'.

The mother was saying fretfully, '...and when the trees were all dead, the Americans came with chainsaws, and cut them down. Such a beautiful city.' She sighed. 'But Saigon is so ugly now, without the trees.' Lopez did not point out that it was the Vietnamese municipal authorities who had let the trees die in the first place.

Meanwhile, the grandfather, with his loose white clothing, white hair and a wispy beard, sat cross-legged in an alcove off the main living area. He seemed unaware that there was any one else in the room: his business was being the eldest, the link with their ancestors. The grandfather impressed Lopez: he seemed outside time. He sat as still and as silent as a meditating monk. He had far too much dignity to engage in meaningless polite conversation.

Just before curfew Lopez began to say goodbye to Nhung and her family. Suddenly the grandfather stirred from his alcove. It was uncanny, like seeing a saint's statue come to life. The old man climbed out of the alcove and shuffled towards Lopez on bare feet. He could see that the parents were embarrassed, but Nhung looked as if she were trying not to laugh. As the grandfather approached, Lopez bowed his head. He thought he was about to receive a blessing or a profound Confucian maxim. The old man stretched out his hands. His gnarled arthritic fingers were clutching soiled and wrinkled banknotes. He wanted to do a black market currency swap.

Nhung accompanied Lopez outside to open the gate. He tried to take her hand. She pulled away. 'Don't touch me.

My mother is watching, Any suggestion of impropriety is going to cause me a lot trouble.'

'Why did you ask me to come here?'

'I wanted to get to know you better, I also wanted you to know my situation. My parents, as you can see, are bourgeois Catholics.'

'Do they know?'

'They know nothing. It's difficult for me – I have to protect them as well as carry out my obligations as a cadre.'

'When can I see you again?'

'Wait at least two weeks: there are things I have to check. I can't act on my own.'

It all seemed so unreal to Lopez, but also so exciting. It was like waking up from a nightmare. He imagined that being a traitor must be like committing serious adultery. Living with your lawful spouse would become more and more irritating, but it was also easier because you could see the way out – a future, even a dangerous one, with the person that you really loved.

When Lopez got back to Nui Hoa Den, he found that Boca had insulted and pissed off all the Vietnamese. In a fit of paranoia, he had constructed an 'inner perimeter' in which only American personnel were permitted. The American sector was cordoned off with eight-foot-high barbed-wire barriers and command detonated Claymore mines. There was also another machine-gun bunker aimed, not outwards, but directly at the center of the main Vietnamese areas of the camp. The most insulting gesture of all was the padlocked steel grating that blocked off the American half of the underground bunker from that of their LLDB counterparts. Dai Uy Ky was so irate that he refused to speak to Boca.

Lopez met Dusty for a private word: 'What's provoked all this?'

'Something or someone's persuaded Boca that the camp

is in serious danger of being overrun and that it's going to be an inside job.'

'Guy's crazy. Hey, aren't we supposed to be imbibing copious quantities of Scotch right this very moment, to speed Sergeant Carson on his way?'

'Guess so. Do you realize it'll be the first time in the guy's long and distinguished military career that he's gotten through a war without being taken prisoner?'

'I hate it when it's my turn to be duty officer.' Lepreux shuffled the dominoes and looked enquiringly at Lopez. 'Another game?'

Lopez shook his head. He had flown back to China Beach with Carson on the pretext of resolving a supply problem with the S4 – it had become obvious that Boca didn't give a shit what Lopez did – and had wasted the day requisitioning supplies that he hoped would never be delivered. It was now nearly midnight and he was ready for sleep. Beaucoup Kilo, the leader of the Chinese Nung platoon who provided the nightly perimeter guard, was snoring on a chair in the corner of the orderly room. 'Hey, Kilo,' Lepreux shouted. There was no response. 'Wake up, you fat fuck!'

The Nung finally opened his eyes and looked blankly at Lepreux.

'If I can't get any zee's, neither can you. Understand?'

The Nung nodded; it was obvious he hadn't understood a word.

'I really hate this duty officer shit,' Lepreux said again. 'You have to stay awake all night and then they expect to carry on as normal with your staff stuff next day. And whenever it's my turn, things always go wrong. First time I had the duty, some guy drowned messing about in the surf; that must have been before your time –'

'No, it happened my first night. We were in the same replacement levy. Guy called Whiteford.'

'Hey, you been out here a long time, Lopez. You must be the only guy left from that bunch.'

'But you've been here even longer.'

'Yeah, but I don't go out in the field any more. And I keep my ass away from helicopters. I try to lead a quiet life, and I sure do hope this is going to be a quiet night.'

Lepreux was about to start sharing out the dominoes for another game when they heard the sound of running footsteps outside. A young sergeant ran into the orderly room, shouting, 'Someone just got shot!' Afterwards Lopez wondered why they hadn't heard the gun. The sergeant's eyes were wild and dilated, and he was shaking with fear. He had just arrived in Vietnam – a 'new kid' – and couldn't believe that the madness had begun already.

'See what I mean? Whenever it's my turn! Last time it was the Tet shit, now this.'

Lepreux picked up his M16 and chambered a round. They followed the sergeant to the transient NCO billets, an old French beach house built of gray clapboard. Lopez listened to the soft soughing of the South China Sea that filled the night. Lepreux, by his wide, whined, 'Why does this always happen to me? I just want a quiet life...'

The medical officer, barefoot, in a T-shirt and trousers, was already there. 'Dead,' he said. He pulled back a sheet; for a second Lopez glimpsed the blond features of a twenty-year-old helicopter gunner. The boy-child gunner had just completed a full tour without a scratch and, until fifteen minutes before, had been on his way back to his Mom and Dad safe and sound. There was a hole in one temple and the mattress beneath his head was soaked with blood.

'OK,' said Lepreux. 'I don't need to see any more. Cover him up.'

The medical officer drew the sheet over the shattered head.

'Don't let anyone come in and don't let anyone leave. Seal the building.' Lopez thought Lepreux looked embarrassed, as if he knew his words sounded trite and over-dramatic in the context of real tragedy and loss. He looked at Lopez. 'This is a goddam-awful mess, and I feel ill. Can you help me?'

'Sure. What should I do?'

'Wake Catfish and the adjutant, and tell them I'll be in the orderly room.' Lopez nodded. 'I'm going to try to get the MPs out here – I think that's the procedure. Hope I can get them on the landline.'

An hour later, Sergeant First Class Albert Carson was sitting in the orderly room in handcuffs. Lopez, as his unit officer, was allowed to be present and to take notes. A Military Police major took Carson's statement; meanwhile, a bored-looking Judge Advocate General's Corps captain was jotting notes on a yellow pad.

'What exactly did you say to Sergeant White when you first spoke to him?'

'I said, "I'm trying to sleep, please turn the music down".'

'Then what happened?'

'He turned the music down and I went back to bed. But five minutes later – just as I was starting to doze off – he turned it back up again.'

'Did you ask him to turn it down again?'

'Didn't see the point, he wasn't going to listen. So I went back and shot him.'

'Then what did you do?'

'Turned the damned thing off, went back to bed and went to sleep.'

On the table in front of the MP major was a sealed plastic bag with the suspect's personal effects. Among the effects was a Zippo lighter that Carson had managed to hang on to through three wars and twenty-four years. While waiting to be repatriated from a POW camp in Germany in 1945 he had had engraved on it: *Fuck God, Fuck Uncle Sam, Fuck the Army, And fuck you too.*

Lepreux told Lopez he had known Carson for some time and found the whole thing depressing. 'Carson reminds me of an old tomcat me and my wife adopted when we were first married. That old tom suffered from arthritis, rheumatism – you could never pick him up without being scratched. Sunny days, he liked to warm himself on the stone flags of the yard between the married quarters. Well, one day a young kitten who just wanted to play skipped over and batted a gentle swipe at him. Our old tom opened one eye and hissed. The kitten thought it was part of the game and did the same thing again. The old tom jumped up, sank his teeth into the kitten's neck and just shook him till he was dead.'

Lopez had to go back to the C-team to deal with the incident. It quickly became obvious that relations between the helicopter crews and Special Forces were poisoned. In any case, the crews had seemed embittered and strange for some time. There had been some sort of incident in Quang Ngai province involving a company from the Americal division. The supporting helicopter crews had seen things that they shouldn't have seen and photographs had been taken. The rumors were obscene. Now everyone was telling the pilots and crew to shut up or they'd be 'shat upon from a great height'. Lopez had been at Fort Benning with a lieutenant who was a platoon leader in the division concerned, and who had struck him as a weak incompetent with a streak of sadism.

In the early evening Lopez went to see Nhung. Her father was out and her mother was busy in the kitchen so they could talk freely. Her grandfather chaperoned them from his perch in the alcove, but as he knew no English and was deaf in any case, they could still talk. Lopez found Nhung angry and terse, as if she were dealing with him against her better instincts. She asked him to draw a map of Nui Hoa Den's defenses. Lopez found it difficult to stop his hands from shaking as he drew the diagram. Suddenly, it was no longer idle talk and game playing; he really had become a traitor and was committing the sort of crime that had sent the Rosenbergs to the electric chair – and they were probably innocent. She asked Lopez to include the locations of the escape tunnel and the emergency radio link and its underground antenna. Lopez did so and handed her the completed sketch. There was no turning back after that – he had handed his life to her.

'When,' he said, 'should we meet again?'

'At the end of the month. Can you come back to Da Nang then?'

'I hope so, I will.'

'Don't come here. I'll meet you at the visitors' gate to the China Beach compound at ten in the morning on the last Sunday of the month.'

Carson's court-martial began the next day. Lopez had to attend as an observer as well as a character witness for the defense. He found it difficult not to imagine himself on trial. Carson had only killed one of his fellow soldiers – how many, thought Lopez, was *he* going to kill? He realized that betraying people in a war wasn't at all like 'serious adultery': sleeping with someone else didn't explode your wife's aorta with a concussion blast and lacerate her body with shrapnel.

On the last day of Carson's court-martial Gary Linden, one of his former officers, was called as a character witness. Lopez listened while Linden gave his testimony. It turned out to be an earnest, dignified and articulate account of Carson's 'high moral character, selflessness and devotion to duty.' The three majors and two colonels who made up the board – effectively judge and jury – were impressed. Lopez was impressed too, for he knew Linden to be an unpredictable and dangerous psychopath. He remembered how when Linden first heard news of the murder, he had pounded the club bar with glee and shouted, 'Carson done got some round-eye body count!' At the court-martial, however, Linden spent an hour giving a complex and sensitive testimony about how the horror and stress of war had finally caused a soldier of 'innate human decency and sensitivity' to have 'a momentary aberration'. Lopez knew that everything he said about Carson was true, but was amazed that Linden was the one saying it.

That evening the board members went to the officers' club bar and sat in a dark corner by themselves to confer. They had to decide Carson's sentence in the morning. Linden, meanwhile, unaware of their presence and roaring drunk, was bragging in a loud voice to a group of new arrivals about a Viet Cong officer whom he had tracked down and killed. He explained, in clinical detail, how he had cut out the Viet Cong's heart, carried it on the end of his dagger into the market place of the nearest village and, surrounded by an audience of shocked Vietnamese, fed the heart to the village dogs. The next morning the board decided to discount Linden's testimony and sentenced Carson to three years' hard labor in Leavenworth.

THE END OF THE MONTH CAME. The hours just ticked away, an inexorable countdown to eternity blast-off. Lopez wondered if there were clocks and calendars on prisons' death rows. His cover story for coming to Da Nang was to pick up the CIDG payroll. Pay day, he thought – pay day.

Lopez also had to visit the PX, the Post Exchange. He hated going there, but when anyone came to Da Nang they were expected to go shopping for the rest of the team. The list was mostly booze, but also cassette tapes, toiletries and a punching bag for Mendy to practice flicking jabs. The PX was located at Da Nang airfield, not far from the mortuary. The Exchange was a massive warehouse. You could buy anything from duty free Chanel No.5 to flavored condoms, from exercise bikes to excise-exempt Cadillacs to drive, if you still had legs to work the pedals, when you returned to the States. At first, Lopez thought it was bizarre to have a bursting shopping mall amid the bloodiest battlefields of Vietnam. Later he realized the goods in the PX were the whole point. The sale and distribution of all that crap was why the war was being fought.

Lopez found the PX just as nausea-inducing as its neighbor, the mortuary. When you walked into the Post Exchange the cryonic chill of air conditioning overload grabbed your testicles. There were no windows, but the building was tinsel bright with the light of a thousand neon tubes. Lopez stopped by the magazine racks and picked up a free copy of *Stars and Stripes*, the official army newspaper, and turned to the back page which always had a list of those killed in action the previous week. He found the names of two line infantry officers, Tadeusz and Williams, who had been in his company at Fort Benning. He didn't recognize any of the other four hundred names on the page.

Lopez tucked the paper under his arm and walked past stacks of electric fans, tape decks, amplifiers, speakers, refrigerators, cameras and televisions to the counter where they sold clocks and watches. He had to get a watch for Sergeant Jackson, who wanted it as a present to make up with his counterpart. The air conditioning chilled Lopez's sweat to ice-water and the ticking displays of clocks triggered a sense of nausea that turned his legs to lead and drained the blood from his face. A hideous reproduction Swiss cuckoo clock went *tick tick, whir*, then *tick tick – cuckoo, cuckoo*. Time. He closed his eyes and saw the images of past and future slaughters pasted on the insides of his eyelids. *Tick tick, whir*. He opened his eyes. Nausea rising. The gleaming displays of stereo systems and cameras – cool, subdued and seducing in the artificial chill and neon light – were suddenly mixed up with a dying soldier trying to make the sign of the cross with a handless arm; a dead girl in dirty blood-sodden bandages; Bobby's stumps – lots of stumps, stumps scorched and shredded; the proud woman with her hand nearly shot off; the destruction of Phu Gia, the blind breastless Xuan Huong; the dead boy at Dai Binh wearing those gray shorts with the elasticized waist – and then the accounts of the massacre at My Lai and of the ditches filled with dead babies and raped women – *I had not thought death had undone so many.* Lopez leaned against a counter and willed himself not to vomit. He counted to sixty, then to a hundred, and felt himself steady. Then he finished the shopping – for those he was going to kill.

Nhung arrived at the entrance gate to the HQ compound as promised. She had borrowed her mother's Honda and was wearing a yellow ao dai and her hair unbraided and free. Lopez signed her in. She then had to proceed under the watchtower, past a machine-gun bunker and through a hut with infra-red lights for checking identity cards. Despite being his guest, Nhung still had to pass through a dressing cubicle where a female guard strip-searched her for weapons, while another guard inspected the Honda's fuel tank for explosives.

They left her bike near the C-team squash courts. 'It's nice here,' said Nhung. She looked surprised. There were palm trees, manicured lawns and neatly kept paths. The sleeping quarters were long low buildings with verandas; everything was tidy and freshly whitewashed, even the rocks that lined the paths were painted white.

'It's very quiet. Where are the Americans? Have they decided to go home already?'

'They're down at the beach for the Sunday barbecue. Are you hungry?'

'Yes, a little.'

Lopez led her to the beach where several Americans were already drunk. The air was full of the smell of burning charcoal and meat, and the loud laughter of the Americans and the nervous laughter of prostitutes. Two officers, muscular and well endowed, were emerging naked from the South China Sea.

'I'm sorry,' said Lopez touching Nhung on the arm to guide her away. 'I didn't know they'd be like this.'

Nhung had her hand over her mouth and was laughing. 'It doesn't matter, not in the least. I think they're very funny.' Her voice seemed to Lopez so refined, almost English.

They walked a short distance up the beach to a quiet place in the dunes. 'Shall we sit here?' said Lopez.

Nhung took a straw mat out of her bag and spread it neatly on the sand. She tucked her ao dai to her thighs and sat with her legs folded under her.

'Would you like something to eat? I think there are burgers, sausages, steaks and spare-ribs.'

'Perhaps I will just have an orange drink.'

Lopez wasn't hungry either. Hill 60 had left him with a distaste for the smell of burnt meat. Sometimes eating meat made him sick; there were too many associations. He brought Nhung an orange soda, and a beer for himself.

They finished their drinks and strolled along the beach towards Marble Mountain. The mountain was a squat turret of jagged rocks that looked strange, somehow mislaid, on the flat coastal plain. When they were out of sight of the others, Nhung told Lopez the plan. The camp at Nui Hoa Den was going to be attacked 'from within and without' between ten and eleven o'clock on the night of 11 May. Lopez's job was to disable the radios and to put explosives down the mortar tubes in the Americans-only inner perimeter. As soon as someone dropped a round down the mortar tube, it would blow up the entire mortar pit and kill everyone in it. Lopez suggested that he could also lay charges in the ammunition bunkers.

'That would be a terrible waste,' said Nhung. 'The attacking forces will want to take away the ammunition to use themselves – "One uses war to feed war".'

It seemed to Lopez that a part of the plan had been left out. 'What's going to happen to me?'

'What about you? Why do you think you're so special?

When the sappers go in, they're just going to kill everyone. It'll be too dark and too confusing to tell friend from foe.' Nhung stopped to shake sand out of her shoes. 'But fortunately for you, the cadre thinks that you might not have outlived your usefulness. If you want to live, get out of the camp by eight o'clock. There's a place on the river where the barges from the mine used to load up with coal in the days when they sent it down to Hoi An. Someone will be waiting for you in the shadow of the second derelict barge. If necessary, say that you are the agent of Phoung Hoa – that's my alias.'

'Phoenix flower?'

'I know, it's really corny – it's the cadre's idea of a joke.'

They were in the shadow of Marble Mountain. There was still a US Marine observation post on the top of the mountain, but the rock below was porous with caves and caverns that sheltered hard-core guerrillas. No one knew how the guerrillas got their supplies. No attempt to clean them out had ever succeeded. Maybe, thought Lopez, the dark rock was the gateway to an underworld that stretched forever. 'What's it doing there?' he said. 'No other rocks, otherwise a flat coastal plain. It's like a hulk washed up from the sea.'

'It's the Turtle's Egg. Do you know the story?'

'I don't know anything.'

'You're still young enough to learn,' said Nhung.

'Teach me then.'

'Listen carefully, and don't ask questions until I'm finished. A long time ago a young fisherman was caught in a storm at sea and his boat sank. He tried to swim for shore, but was swept farther and farther out. Just as he was about to give up and drown, he was rescued by a giant turtle who carried him to the shore. The fisherman asked the turtle how he could show gratitude for having his life saved. The turtle gave the young man a large egg which he was to care for and protect against predators.' Nhung paused. 'Surely, you don't want to hear a Vietnamese fairy story?'

'Please don't stop, it's getting interesting.'

'Well, the fisherman covered the egg with sand and watched over it day and night. One day the egg cracked open and a beautiful young woman emerged.'

'I thought that was going to happen.'

'Be quiet and listen, or you will have to leave the class. The young woman said, "I am the spirit of the turtle. Thank you for protecting me." The two married and were very happy, but also very sad.'

'Why were they sad?'

'Why? Because they both knew that one day the woman would have to return to the sea. The sad day came: the beautiful woman changed into a turtle and crawled back into the sea. And,' Nhung pointed to Marble Mountain, 'that is what remains of her cracked eggshell – so the story must be true.'

Lopez looked away. A US Navy destroyer was anchored a mile out to sea. Its silhouette against the horizon was low and sleek, with the promise of speed – like a racing yacht. He remembered a fast beam reach down the bay, and Ianthe hauling hard on the jib sheet and leaning back over the gunwale in a haze of spray and sunlight.

'What's wrong?' Nhung touched his face. 'You're crying.'

'Nothing's wrong.'

She put her hand on his arm. 'It's not such a sad story – they had some time together before she returned to the sea.'

Lopez didn't say anything: he knew that nothing he said or felt would make sense to her. They continued walking along the beach until the barbed wire barriers of the C and C North compound blocked their path. After the attack that had killed sixteen Americans, the compound's wire had been extended all the way to the sea.

A boat was coming toward the beach. The sea was high and it was wallowing in the swell. The boat was a big broad-beamed motor whaler, a traditional lifeboat and ship's tender, about thirty feet long. It reminded Lopez of regatta week at Annapolis, with midshipmen in starched dress whites taking parties from shore to yacht. When the whaler got near the beach, one of the crew threw out a stern anchor; he paid out the anchor warp and the boat slowed, the engines still churning slowly as the whaler mounted the beach. *USS Richard E Kraus DD849* was stenciled on its bows.

An officer jumped out of the boat into the surf while two crew carried an anchor up the beach. It was all so smartly done, so text-book perfect. The officer spotted Lopez and Nhung and walked up the beach toward them. He seemed uncertain, confused perhaps by Lopez's brown skin and tiger-stripe CIDG uniform and Nhung's traditional ao dai, and kept his hand cautiously on the .45 automatic that swung from his hip. 'Do either of you speak English?'

Lopez was tempted to a wisecrack, but simply said, 'Yes.'

The naval officer, wearing the silver bar of a lieutenant junior grade and an Annapolis ring, was as handsome as a film star, with an uncanny resemblance to James Dean and a still-uncorrupted purity. 'I'm trying to find the Marine Air Wing. A classmate of mine is a jarhead Chinook pilot, and we brought some stuff for him.' The crew were piling up boxes on the beach. 'Things you can't get here: filet mignon steak, Maryland crab cakes, couple of gallons of Tabasco sauce. It took some convincing to get the skipper to come in close; we've already taken some hits from counter-battery fire. I allowed for a south-running tide, and my coxswain kept to the compass bearing, but we still seem to be –'

Lopez heard voices. Four marines were running along the beach, and one of them – presumably the classmate – was shouting, 'Hey, Frank old buddy! You missed us by about three hundred yards! Cast off again, and I'll con you in.' The marines and sailors re-loaded, and pushed the boat back out. Has there ever, thought Lopez, been another war like this?

As the boat floundered through the surf, Lopez and Nhung turned back toward the compound. They didn't need a compass or a pilot; they knew where they were going and what they were going to do that afternoon. Theirs was a silent understanding conveyed by a touch, a look, a closeness. They left the beach and went back to Lopez's quarters in the transient officers' billet. The billet was another low gray beach house of weathered clapboard, with shuttered windows and louvered doors leading on to a veranda, that had been left behind by the French Army. It reminded Lopez of the holiday cottage on Cape Hatteras where he had stayed with *her* all those years ago – bare floorboards grainy with sand and the constant sound of the sea. Lopez was sharing a large airy room with two helicopter pilots and the captain who used to command Lang Khe – they still hadn't decided what to do with him. The pilots weren't there, but the captain was lying on his bunk clad only in shorts and dog tags. His face was beaded with sweat and he seemed to be struggling for breath. His skin looked clammy. Lopez gently asked if he was asleep.

'I can't sleep.'

'Are you sick?'

'Yes. And so are you.' He looked at Nhung. 'And so is she. I guess you want me to leave?'

'No, we'll go someplace else.'

'Don't bother, Trung Uy Lopez.' The captain got up and began to dress. 'You and your girlfriend stay here. It's the honeymoon suite. I'll have room service send a bottle of champagne and a dozen cherrystone oysters on the half-shell – you come buckets when you eat oysters.' The captain put his arm around Lopez and put his face close. Lopez could smell his breath, alcohol-sweet with bourbon. 'Get the hell out of this place, Lopez. If the slopes don't kill you, our guys will.' Then he clumped out on to the veranda, his boots still loose and unlaced.

Lopez pushed aside the mosquito netting over his bed to make room for Nhung.

'What's wrong with him?'

'He doesn't have a job. His camp was overrun, but he managed to escape and now he just mopes around, drinking and feeling guilty about even being alive.'

'Guilt is a useless emotion.'

Lopez held her close. Her mouth opened against his. There was no coquetry, her body started to writhe as soon as he touched her. She suddenly stopped, but only to slip off her clothes, neatly fold them and pile them beside the bed. Her breasts were little more than buds, her arms slender as lotus stems, but her legs were strong and well shaped. At first she seemed so fragile, but when she wrapped herself around him Lopez felt a body as supple and taut as steel cable. He knew that she was stronger than he, stronger than all of them put together.

When they began to make love, Nhung arched her pelvis and stroked the back of his neck. Without coyness she showed him how to touch her, when to be gentle, when to be passionate. He felt her hot breath panting in his ear and saw her brown legs entwined with his own brown legs. He knew that he was no longer a stranger, that he was coming home. He moved, lost deep in her, so deep. Lopez could feel her gripping him hard and pulling him to where it gave her the most pleasure. Afterwards, she curled herself into a ball, alone again. She whispered a song. Not for him, but for herself.

> *She walked home to face the night alone,*
> *While her lover fared the long, long way.*
> *Love split their moon. Half swayed down and slept*
> *By her lone pillow, half lit his far road.*

She stopped singing and held Lopez's hand to her face. 'Are you disappointed that I wasn't a virgin?'

'Of course not, that's a silly question.'

'Some families are very traditional. There are many Vietnamese men who would never have me as a wife.'

'Do you still have a lover?'

'Not any more. It happened when I was at university in Saigon. I had a friend – just a friend at first – who was also a student at the university. He was studying music.' She turned away and didn't say anything else.

'What did he play, what instrument?'

'He's not a musician, he's a composer. But he does play most stringed instruments. He's a good violinist, but he prefers an old Vietnamese lute called the ty ba. I used to accompany him on the sao truc, a form of flute. We were both members of a traditional music group.'

She went quiet again. It seemed to Lopez that part of her wanted desperately to talk about it, but another part wanted to forget it all. 'Why did it end?'

'He didn't want me any more.'

'Because of your activities in the National Liberation Front?'

'No, all that came later.'

'Why then?'

'I don't have to tell you that.'

Lopez could feel her freeze. He caressed her and held her to him.

'Don't you see that worrying too much about the past – especially being jealous – is a waste of emotion? You should use the past as a book from which to learn, not as a knife to cut yourself.'

They lay together, silently entwined. Lopez felt Nhung's body loosen as she began to sleep. He lay awake next to her constructing images of her life. He visualized the composer lover wearing thick spectacles and having long Brylcreemed hair brushed straight back from a high sensitive forehead. He imagined them strolling along the boulevards as if Saigon were Strauss's Vienna, talking about music and the fleetingness of their love. Strolling beneath the dead trees that an American construction battalion later cut down with chainsaws.

Then there was nothing but the sounds of the sea and the

rise and fall of Nhung's breathing. Then no dreams, no more images – just the sweet deep after-sleep of love. It seemed hours before Nhung shook him awake. 'I must go, it is late.' As soon as they were in public Nhung assumed again her modest air. Lopez knew that she would regard a public farewell kiss as the height of vulgarity. Despite everything, she was a reflection of her class and culture. Nhung was searched again prior to leaving to ascertain that she was smuggling no wristwatches, no bottles of whiskey or fragmentation grenades out of the compound. She emerged from the search cubicle and kick-started her Honda.

He found it awkward to say goodbye. 'Are we going to meet again?'

'Have you already forgotten? You have to come to the lycée on Tuesday morning to pick up the explosives.'

'Don't worry. I'll be there. That's not what I meant.' It was impossible to talk here, among the watch towers, barbed wire, clouds of dust swirled by trucks and armored vehicles, and the clatter of helicopters.

'Is something wrong?'

'No, that sort of thing doesn't matter.'

'I don't know what will happen,' she said. Her face was hidden in the shadow of her straw hat. 'When you come to the lycée, you'll have to wait for me in the Mother Superior's office if I'm still teaching.'

Nhung rode off without waving or looking back. Lopez watched her disappear into the dusk and walked back to the beach house alone.

The adjutant had an unusual surname, Glasscock. He quickly became known as 'Crystal-prick'. On Tuesday Lopez had to borrow his jeep to go to the lycée. The adjutant tossed him the keys. 'Bet you want some more of that gook pussy, you lucky bastard.'

'That's right, Crystal.'

The closer Lopez got to the lycée, the more uncertain and frightened he became. By the time he had got as far as the RMK scrap heaps, he'd already concocted a story to tell the C-team Intelligence officer. He knew, of course, that Nhung would be arrested and tortured. He himself would be reprimanded for running a DIY intel op on his own, but he'd still get a pat on the head for turning her in and exposing the plan to overrun Nui Hoa Den. Lopez decided to let the tide decide. If when he got to the river the tide was flooding, he would stick to the plan; if ebbing, he would betray Nhung. When he got to the bridge the stern of the moored guard boat was pointing seaward – the tide was ebbing. For a second or two Lopez felt relieved, but then he realized that an ebb tide meant that it was time to go to sea, to take the chance. He would go through with it. He had to.

The lycée was a large stucco building on Quang Trung Street, with red roof tiles and surrounded by high walls. When Lopez walked in there was a lot of giggling, but the amused ones vanished before he saw them. The corridor tiles were dark and highly polished, the ambience was as Spartan and clean as a barracks. Against one wall was a statue of the Virgin Mary with silver rays beaming from her fingers and a serpent being crushed under her bare foot. On either side were plaques naming in gold lettering all the head girls since 1902. Until 1940, all the names were French ones. Lopez found a door engraved *Mère Supérieure*, knocked and was told to 'Entrez!'

The Mother Superior was a small dark nun of about sixty dressed in a white habit, who looked and sounded more Cambodian than Vietnamese. She asked Lopez to sit down and continued to speak in rapid French which he had difficulty in following. She offered him a drink – the choice was mineral water or beer. Lopez said beer and a servant was summoned to bring two chilled bottles of '33'. The Mother Superior had been expecting him and said that Co Nhung would arrive 'bientôt'. While Lopez waited, she told him about herself: she had been born in Phnom Penh, but educated at Ste. Fleur in the Auvergne and then at university in Aix-en-Provence. She was very fond of Aix: she especially loved the tree-lined boulevards where she had strolled, arm-in-arm and singing, with her fellow students.

When Nhung arrived the Mother Superior shook his hand and left them alone. Nhung had chalk dust on her nose. Lopez brushed off the dust and kissed her.

'I wasn't certain that you were going to come,' she said.

'Listen, Nhung. I will never lie to you. To everyone else, but never to you. I must tell you the truth: I'm frightened, I don't want to die. And I'm not sure that I want to kill others.'

Nhung froze for a long moment and looked at the floor. For a second, she looked almost angry, disappointed. Then she began to speak, slowly and deliberately. 'You've been brought up in a society that teaches people to be afraid of death. It's a fear that you can unlearn.'

The hard steel in her voice unsettled Lopez. 'Are you,' he said, 'ever afraid?'

'Not of death.'

'Of what then?'

'Of losing love.' Nhung turned away. 'The explosives are in this book cupboard.' She undid a latch and slid up the roll-top cover, to reveal shelves with sets of texts for Géographie, Lettres Françaises, Sciences Sociales and Instruction Réligieuse. In the bottom of the cabinet was a cardboard box with the explosives. She picked it up and handed it to Lopez. The explosives were heavy.

He said, 'Will we ever meet again?'

'I would disappoint you.'

'No, you wouldn't.'

'Yes, I would. You don't know everything about me.' He wanted to hold her, to kiss away the silliness of her self-deprecation, but his arms were full of explosives.

'I have to go back to my class. It's very difficult teaching them tenses. You see, we don't have them in Vietnamese.'
'Of course, I know that. I love your language. Why don't you ever speak Vietnamese to me?'
'Because my English is far better than your Vietnamese.'
'Anh yeu em gio lam. Did you understand that?'
She kissed him. 'Em yeu anh gio lam.'
He put down the explosives and held her close. He felt the fine silk of her hair against his face. He whispered the final words of the Vietnamese love pledge – 'All the days, all the nights and all the years.'
She walked with him to the entrance porch. Lopez carried the explosives to the jeep and looked back, but Nhung was already gone.

Lopez lay on his bed in the beach house and listened to the sound of the sea. There were two hours to wait before the helicopter to Nui Hoa Den. He got up and opened the shutters. The weather was hot and sticky, even the breakers looked low and lazy. Lopez looked at the box of explosives once again. They had been wrapped to look like bottles of whiskey and were mixed in with real bottles of whiskey. He couldn't stop looking at the box and touching it. It was like when, as a boy of eleven, he had caught a twenty-pound striped bass while casting along the weed beds on Love Point. It was five times the size of any fish he'd caught before. As he rowed back to Rideout's Landing he kept stroking it and looking at it. The fish was so magnificent that he couldn't believe it was his. It fed the family for a week. The box of rigged explosives wouldn't feed anyone, but it might help end a war.

If only, Lopez thought – *if only*, the saddest and most futile of all words. It was so odd, he thought, that a spy could face the death penalty for betraying his country, but walk free as a glorious May morning if he betrayed the person who loved him.

He turned the gold hair-clip that Chou had insisted on buying for him in China Beach over and over in his fingers. It was of modest unaffected design, but crafted from the purest Vietnamese gold, probably from the mine at Bong Mieu. He had no idea how old it was, only that it was old, and he tried to imagine the many women who might have worn it – beloved wives, abused concubines, maybe a French planter's daughter who died of fever, a guerrilla fighter's wife, the imaginary dark-haired girl from the Auvergne ... A few hours later he woke up, wrote a short letter, wrapped the hair clip in a neat package, and addressed it.

'You seem mighty anxious to get me away from the camp. What are you up to? If you're gonna kill Boca, you still have to get eight other witnesses out of the way. And for fuck's sake, I'm one of the guys who would lie for you. You should send Mendy instead – that guy *really* hates you.'

Lopez had convinced Dusty to take an R&R to Hong Kong. He was supposed to be leaving the next day, but still seemed reluctant.

'You'd be a fool not to go. You'll have a good time and make at least a thousand dollars' profit on the watches.'

Dusty still looked suspicious. 'If it's such a good deal, Trung Uy Lopez, why don't you do it yourself?'

'I'm going to, next month. I want you to go first and recon the best jewelers. Try Kowloon first, Hong Kong island itself will be a lot pricier. But don't mess around with fakes; we need certificates, the real stuff.'

Lopez had set up a deal with Dai Uy Ky and some other Vietnamese officers which involved smuggling gold Rolex watches from Hong Kong to Vietnam. Gold Rolexes had become a form of hard currency. The Vietnamese officers could either sell them for double their purchase price on the black market, or use them as an emergency reserve to flee the country when the time came. The deal was a genuine one, but also a cover story devised by Lopez to save Dusty's life by getting him out of the camp.

'And by the way, there's something else.' He handed Dusty the small package with the enclosed letter and the gold hair-clip. 'Could you post this?'

Dusty looked at the address: Judge Grey, father of First Lieutenant Quentin Grey USMC, care of State Attorney's Office, Richmond, Virginia. 'Shouldn't there be a street name or something?'

'Don't worry, it'll get there.'

Lopez liked playing God; it was exhilarating. There were two other team members he intended to spare: Jackson and the medic who had replaced Bobby, a Puerto Rican named Fernando Castro. Castro was young and a little naïve, but something about him struck Lopez as kind and thoughtful. It had been easy to rig the patrol rota so that Jackson and Castro would be far away from the camp on the night of the attack. Jackson was a natural born survivor who would look after the young medic. Unless their luck was very bad, they'd get picked up by a rescue helicopter.

Before going to bed Lopez wrote to Rosie and Tom. He didn't even hint at what he was going to do, but he told them that he loved them. He knew that by the time they received the letter he would already have been reported as dead or missing in action. He hoped that the letter would somehow explain something beyond its words. He picked up Tom's last letter to him and read it yet again.

Rideout's Landing Home for Old Crocks
May 4th, 1968

Dear Francis,

Your letters always make us laugh, especially your last one about the priest coming for the Easter blessing of the water buffalo. But surely you don't spend *every* day swimming in crystal clear rivers, or lying in a hammock reading your way through all twelve volumes of *A La Recherche du Temps Perdu*, being pelted with lotus blossoms by nubile dusky maidens? Methinks – as Chaucer used to say – you are fibbing, young man.

You asked about my involvement in the '54 Geneva Accords. Well, I advised Ike to accept them, though at the time – being a Roosevelt era antique – it was not easy for me to see the President. As you know, the accords called for Vietnam's general elections to take place in July 56. It was, however, obvious that Ho Chi Minh would have carried the day with an overwhelming mandate (80 percent) in favor of reunification under the Communists. So what did we do? We used our UN veto to prevent the elections from taking place. Allan Dulles, the whole NSC, the CIA, the JCS, all supported the veto – mine was the only dissenting voice.

Ike agreed to see me 'for a few minutes'. In the event, he gave me half an hour. We talked about family and friends, and I remember he asked about the pigs. I had to cut in. I said, 'Mr President, about the elections in Vietnam –' The President leaned forward, touching my knee, and he said, 'I don't like doing this either, Tom. And I don't like Ho Chi Minh quoting the American Declaration of Independence back in our faces.'

Now, I'd been a servant of the state for forty years even back then, and I have always believed that America's national interest comes first, before morality, before democracy in other countries, even before human lives. 'But this time, Mr President,' I said, 'I believe our national interest is on the side of the angels. Ho Chi Minh is not a Soviet style imperialist; he's a Vietnamese nationalist.' For the first time, Ike was really listening. I explained that Vietnam's natural enemy was not the USA or the West, but China. Maoist or Taoist, China is always the great threat.

Ike chewed on his reading glasses and stared out of the window, and finally he said, 'There's another reason – a reason right here in the USA – why we have to veto those elections.' He meant McCarthy.

I said, 'Ike, he's dead.' He might be dead but, Ike said, he was buried in a shallow grave, and could rise again if we were to 'let Vietnam go Communist.' And that was not a chance the President was prepared to take with America's constitution and democracy.

That was my last visit to the Oval Office. But I thought then of my first, twenty years earlier. At that time – back in the Thirties – I was looking after Ianthe's great-uncle Sir Ronald Davison, who was briefing Roosevelt on dealing with mass unemployment and poverty. I remember FDR saying, 'Congress is right behind me, but the problem is a reactionary cabal in the Supreme Court.'

'Lloyd George,' Ronald said, 'had the same problem with the House of Lords, so he simply created more peers. Pity you can't do that with your judges.'

FDR just threw back his head and laughed. 'Oh, can't I? Just you watch.'

FDR was a rogue, but a rogue with vision; he understood that 2,000 million brown and black people resented being ruled by a handful of white ones. I'm not sure we understand that even today, especially if it means 'letting' a country go Communist. Well, my generation created this mess, and now it's up to yours to clean it up.

Francis, you must never think that you are anything less than our dearest, most precious son. We loved Arthur and Peter, and Ianthe, and losing them has broken our hearts so that they will never mend. But you and you alone are our shining hope, not because they are dead, but because you are you.

Rosie sends you her love, as I do.

Tom

PS. The raccoon had cubs last week.

Lopez wiped his tears and folded the letter into his breast pocket; he didn't want to ever lose it. He wanted them to understand; he really did.

He checked the explosives box for the hundredth time. It was lying under his bunk, still looking like a cache of whiskey. If anyone snooped, they'd just think he'd developed an even more serious drink problem.

For some reason Boca had turned friendly and talkative. Lopez wondered if he had finally wised up to the fact that the 'unauthorized' evacuation of the Phu Gia civilians indicted him too. Or whether he had begun to discover a conscience, or – more likely – if he realized how much of a danger Lopez was to him, and that it might be best to humor him. One evening they had a long chat on top of the command bunker during Boca's duty watch. Lopez remembered the saying about using a long spoon if you sup with the devil. He wondered if Boca was also using a long spoon.

'You finish your tour next month, isn't that right?'

Lopez nodded. 'That's right.'

'You got any plans, Lopez, 'bout what you're going to do next?'

'Oh, I don't know. Might extend for six months or a year, but I'm thinking of a staff job in Da Nang. Or the Mobile Strike Force. Gets a bit boring out here when nothing's happening. What about you?'

'I'm gonna apply for a transfer to the hundred-and-first, or even a leg infantry division. Special Forces is just too small a unit. It's no good for your career to spend too much time in places like this. And, you know, there's a lot of top brass who'd like to get rid of SF altogether – too many snake-eating weirdos.'

Lopez asked about his family. He knew there were a son and a daughter, both still very young. Boca kept photos of the wife and kids on his desk – Mrs Boca was surprisingly good looking. 'Do you want your boy to become a soldier?'

'Hell, no. We just break things and blow them up. I want my kid to build things instead.'

Lopez was mildly abashed. 'What would you like him to do?'

'Well, he's only young, but he already seems good at putting things together – like Meccano and Lego. I'd like to see him become an architect or engineer.'

'And the girl?'

'Bossy little chatterbox – she'll run her brother's business.'

For a while Lopez searched his soul for even a shred of compassion for Boca. He wanted to find something, the merest speck of human kinship, that would soften him and make him uneasy about killing Boca the husband and father. Lopez tried, but he couldn't find anything to make him relent, nothing. Boca's kids were going to grow up and be just fine, because Boca only napalmed little dark-haired kids in rice paddies. Boca was going to die.

Lopez knew that it was going to be his last patrol before his defection, but he still had to do it. His job was to check out the abandoned paddy fields and hamlets opposite Phu Gia. He wondered if Dieu had felt the same way about leading a double life. He also wondered if he was over-playing his false persona. Lopez was checking equipment and eagerly getting the CIDG organized for the patrol when Boca came over. 'What's gotten into you, Lopez? Why're you so gung-ho all of a sudden?'

The river plain was flat until they got to the square imposing bulk of Hill 110 which blocked off the rest of the river valley.

They swept through the hamlets and fields until they were in the shadow of Hill 110's sinister mass. They found nothing – not a bunker, an empty cartridge case or even a boot print – absolutely nothing. After the paddy ended, the land turned into grassy hillocks rising towards 110. They had to turn back, because to go further meant trouble.

Nothing happened until they reached a place where wild bamboo thicket and scrub had started to take over the abandoned paddy. Lopez found it a sad desolate place, the ruins of where people had once made their lives and grown their food. He was in a mood of twilight nothingness when they started receiving sniper fire from their rear. The CIDG started to run toward the cover of the bamboo. Lopez winced, but it was too late to stop them. He knew that if the enemy had put a machine-gun and a few riflemen in that bamboo thicket they would have been trapped and slaughtered in a classic crossfire. But they were lucky: there was no one there.

Lopez followed the CIDG, ducking and weaving like an extra in a B-movie, and, once inside the thicket, hunkered down with the rest of them behind an old paddy dyke. The sniper was a good distance away – about seven hundred meters – and was probably firing from the grassy hillocks below 110. It wasn't a big problem. Lopez got on the radio to call up some fire support. If the mortar shells didn't kill the sniper, they should at least chase him away. While Lopez was giving the target grid coordinates, one of the CIDG slumped and went all floppy. He must have put his head up above the dyke to take a look. Lopez couldn't even remember hearing the shot that killed him.

They were back in the camp a few hours later. Lopez showered and drank several cold beers – it was best to put it all away, just to forget that it happened and think about other things. It was part of the survival rhythm. Lopez hadn't recognized the rhythm at first, but after a few months he had learned to beat the cadence without even thinking. Castro hadn't been there long enough to learn it. He'd been on the same patrol and was brooding – it was the first time he had seen death in the field. For some reason, he felt he needed to apologize to Lopez. 'I feel terribly guilty, sir.'

'Why should you?'

'I'm supposed to be a medic, but I was useless. I wasn't able to do anything.'

'There was nothing you could do. That guy was dead meat as soon as the round hit him. Clean kill. Look, it was my fault more than anyone's for taking the patrol too near 110. Do I look guilty?' The medic didn't say anything. 'In any case, chico...' – it was the first time Lopez had ever called anyone that – 'in any case, picking that guy off from that distance, out of that thicket, was five per cent skill and ninety-five per cent luck. Listen, you have to think that way about it, otherwise you'll crack up.' Lopez left it at that. He suspected that Fernando Castro probably thought that he was a cold unfeeling monster, just like the rest of them. Maybe he was right. Lopez finished his beer and went to have a look at the dead soldier.

They had laid him out on a table in the LLDB teamhouse, the same table on which Lopez laid out the piles of banknotes for the monthly pay parade. He was a very handsome soldier, about twenty years old, with the spare athletic body of the healthier sort of peasant. There was no sign of any wound at all. A lock of hair hid the bullet hole and there was no exit wound. Lopez brushed aside the dead soldier's hair, and shooed away a fly that had been drawn to the congealed dot of blood.

It was such a tiny hole; otherwise, the young soldier was still perfect, unblemished. Lopez thought, fancifully, that when he got to wherever Vietnamese go when they die – and he realized that if the dead soldier wasn't a Catholic he didn't know where that was – the angels, or whatever, wouldn't know what to make of him. Most of the soldiers they sent there would arrive in quite a state, often with large chunks missing. Maybe, he thought, they'd think there'd been some mistake, and that the soldier didn't belong in the underworld. Maybe they'd even chase him all the way back again, to life. Lopez prayed this was true and willed with all his might to see that broad young chest fill with breath and heave again – but it didn't and he started to cry. He couldn't stand much more. He couldn't hide from the reality of what was going to happen and who was going to die. It wasn't just bastards like Boca who were going to die, but young Vietnamese soldiers too whose only crime was being conscripted into the wrong army.

For a while Lopez thought about ditching the explosives and dropping the whole thing, but then images he could no longer confine to nightmares invaded his brain. Travis, Bobby, Xuan Huong, the little girl who had so innocently played with the live grenade, Kim's face in the shadows as he told Lopez about his last glimpse of his wife and baby – those he couldn't ditch. Just because his decision meant blood – even innocent blood – didn't absolve him of his duty to carry it out.

The camp nurse arrived with a bucket of soapy water to wash the body, and Lopez swallowed his tears. He didn't want her, or anyone, to see him like that. The nurse was an attractive woman with full breasts that darted about like carp beneath her loose cotton blouse. She smiled at Lopez. He knew that she gave everyone the eye and drove her husband – a CIDG company commander – crazy. He'd been in two fights on her account since Tet. Lopez left her to her duty. He turned in the doorway and looked back. The nurse had undone his trousers, but the handsome soldier was still dead.

Moc the coffin-maker was already at work. His coffins –

finished in a watery matte red – were only for Vietnamese corpses; dead Americans were zipped into plastic bags. Moc no longer had to design the coffins from start to finish, he merely had to nail them together. Before Lopez arrived, when there weren't so many deaths, he used to make beautiful coffins out of local hard wood and finish them by carving the lids with the Chinese symbol for happiness and long life. Back then Moc had to work all day for two days. Otherwise, the coffins wouldn't be ready before the bodies began to stink too badly. The previous May, after the first batch of bad casualties, the American supply section at China Beach tried to end the coffin shortage by sending a consignment of twenty pine ones. The Vietnamese reacted badly. They refused to go on patrol and began to make threatening noises about the safety of the team. Americans, however, are an ingenious people and solved the problem in a way that satisfied everyone. The next consignment of coffins arrived in prefabricated flat packs that merely required assembling. The Vietnamese were happy to think that the packages were nothing more than stacked timber; the Americans were happy because the disassembled coffins took up a lot less space. And Moc the coffin-maker was happiest of all because he got paid the same rate for a job that took a tenth of the time.

There were times when Lopez felt a great sense of release. It was the most exciting thing he had ever done; sometimes there was nothing but exhilaration fueled by rushing adrenalin. Late the previous evening he had disabled the emergency radio in the 'endgame' bunker, the bunker where the American team were supposed to hole up for a last-ditch stand. The radio was connected to a secret underground antenna reinforced by armored cable that would continue to transmit if the other antennas had been knocked out. Lopez had felt so charged when he cut the coaxial cable connecting the radio to the antenna that he was afraid that his body itself would start transmitting. He had felt as he imagined an Aztec priest might feel, holding the execution blade in both hands and raising it high above his victims. That power was more potent even than the morphine.

But later the exhilaration dissipated and cold fear crept in. But he had gone too far to back out. Besides, it had to be done; it had become an inevitability. What had started as mere hate and moral outrage had become something else, something far bigger than his individual self. Lopez felt that he had surrendered himself to history. He wasn't just carrying out a personal vendetta, he was acting as an agent of positive historical change. In this he was beyond blame, beyond guilt – but not beyond uncertainty. He remembered a political science professor at Harvard – a German Jew – who used to argue that pragmatic self-interest caused far less human misery than ideology. Perhaps, thought Lopez, the tragedy of that man's personal experience was speaking too. What the professor had failed to admit was that 'pragmatic self-interest' was an ideology too, a powerful and insidious one that starved peasants and sold arms to tyrants.

Lopez slid the box out from under his bed. It was time to booby trap the mortars; the explosives were primed and ready to slide down the tubes.

Lopez finished his final job – rigging trip-wired explosives in the escape tunnel – twenty minutes before the attack began. He then crawled the rest of the way through the tunnel to an exit concealed by rocks and thick vegetation. The stars were out and the night, after the deathly dank of the tunnel, was fresh and clear. He felt that he was being reborn, that he was wearing his own skin for the first time. He could see the river, a faint silver thread, reflecting all the stars and constellations that had guided men and women since time began. He had to get to the river...

RUMORS ABOUT AN IMMINENT ATTACK had swept through the camp early that evening and more than half the CIDG deserted before the assault had even started. It began with a mortar barrage. While the remaining defenders huddled in their bunkers, the sappers cut their way through the barbed wire.

The attack was a great success. All the Americans were killed as well as twenty-eight Vietnamese defenders. Mendy was splattered over the 4.2 mortar pit when the tube exploded. The best resistance came from the weapons NCOs, who managed to remove the explosives from the 81mm, and then started dropping rounds into the camp itself by firing the mortar in a vertical position. They were killed when Kim lobbed two fragmentation grenades over the wire and into the mortar pit. Two other Americans were killed immediately and two buried alive when the secret escape tunnel exploded and collapsed. Boca, terrified into urinary and fecal incontinence by the tunnel blast, dug his way back into the bunker and cowered under his bed praying for help to arrive before the Communist sappers blasted their way in. He waited some time, soaked in his own piss and excrement, before a sapper managed to feel his way through the ruins of the bunker and hurl two satchel charges into the darkness. Boca squealed like a pig as he listened to the pre-death hisses of the time delay fuses.

The following day the 199th Light Infantry Brigade re-took Nui Hoa Den in a helicopter assault after massive bombing. The Communists had already withdrawn by the time the brigade arrived, but twenty-three Americans from the 199th were killed when a booby-trapped ammunition bunker blew up. Later that day Jackson, Castro and their patrol were found safe and sound, and airlifted back to Da Nang.

Epilog

Vietnam, May 1997

THE MINE IS A SMEAR on an otherwise idyllic landscape. The coal is strip-mined, scarring the rich green of the mountain with yellow concentric rings and leaving a cloud of gray dust over the immediate surroundings. The Vietnamese think it is ugly, but an ugliness worth paying for to break the economic cycle of rice-paddy dependency. An American bulldozer is gouging away at the base of the mountain. Vietnamese mechanics, ingeniously tooling ersatz replacement parts from scrap metal, have managed to keep it running ever since it was captured in 1975.

Kim was badly wounded in the 1972 offensive, but survived the rest of the war and afterwards retrained as a primary school teacher. He returned to the valley of the Son Thu Bon with Nhung, whose husband had deserted her because she couldn't have children, to run the school in Dai Binh. Nhung was surprised at first that Kim loved her and wanted to live with her. 'Surely,' she said, 'you must want to have children to replace the ones you lost.'

'No, I want to be alone with their spirits.'

Sometimes, when Kim cried out their names in the night, Nhung became angry, jealous of this other family that had preceded her and which she couldn't displace. Once she said, 'But Kim, they were only babies.'

'To lose an infant isn't to lose one child, it is to lose a hundred – the child that speaks his first word, the child that takes his first step, the child that learns to swim, to sing, to make friends, to fall in love, to write a poem and show it you. I have lost all of these children.'

One of the things that Kim liked best was getting his

children out of the classroom and into the countryside. At the end of the academic year he took them to the pig farm at Phu Gia. The bombing had destroyed the paddy dykes beyond repair, so a scheme was launched to breed Vietnamese pot-bellied pigs on the site of the old village. When the minefields had finally been cleared, the pigs were allowed to roam about on the low hill overlooking the river where Bobby Hatch had been fatally wounded. They were handsome pigs with blackberry-purple bodies.

As the boat carrying the schoolchildren churned past Nui Hoa Den, Kim called for the attention of his class. 'Look, the Tran brothers are going to go for a swim.' Two middle-aged men with lean sinewy bodies blackened by coal dust had began to undress on the river bank. When they slipped off their baggy trousers it became apparent that they were both amputees. One brother, who had been wounded the day of the Phu Gia evacuation, had lost his left leg just above the knee; the other had lost his right leg just below the knee during the 1972 offensive. They sat down and helped each other undo the crude prosthetic contraptions of wood, steel and leather straps that had replaced their limbs. 'You must watch them,' shouted Kim in his schoolteacher voice. 'They are an amazing example of what co-operation and brotherhood really mean.'

The children watched as Tran Van Loc and Tran Ngoc Troi linked arms and slid into the river. The brothers swam, stump against stump, one complete pair of legs beating the water in perfect harmony. They swirled through the water with all the swiftness and grace of otters. Their laughter rang out over the river as they left a trail of whirlpools and bubbles in their wake.

That evening, after dinner, Kim returned to the empty classroom and took out his writing materials so he could work on his poem. He took off his sandals and felt the tiles cool under his bare feet.

He remembered what the river had looked like and felt like that morning: the laughter and noise of the children, the river gleaming like silver reflecting the sun, the sky, heaven.

Then he saw a great throng of children coming to the river, and saw that his generation, who had suffered to the limit of human endurance, *were* the river. If only it could be true, if only for a fraction of a second...

>*I see them coming to the river*
>*From Nui Hoa, from Phu Gia, from My Lai,*
>*From Xuan Hoa, from Hue, Hanoi,*
>*From Haiphong, from the highlands too.*
>
>*The Rhadé, the Katu, the Jarai,*
>*And the Chams, the Chinese and the Khmer.*
>*When I close my eyes I see them,*
>*Children, coming to the river.*
>
>*From the Mekong Delta,*
>*From Pleiku, Da Lat and Da Nang,*
>*From Quang Tri, Quang Nam, Nam Dinh,*
>*They are all coming to the river.*
>
>*Ho Cuc's children, Kim's children, my own,*
>*They are leaping, splashing,*
>*Laughing in our arms, whole and happy.*
>*In crystals of water shine the rainbow arches of heaven.*
>
>*For one second, let us hear the laughter of their spirits.*
>*For one moment, let us have a miracle.*
>*Let us hold them, whole and well again,*
>*The war-killed children of Vietnam.*